PRELUDE TO FOUNDATION

Prelude to Foundation *(1988)*

Other Universes of Isaac Asimov *(1987)*

Norby Finds a Villain *(1987)* (with Janet Asimov)

Fantastic Voyage II: Destination Brain *(1987)*

Norby and the Queen's Necklace *(1986)* (with Janet Asimov)

Robot Dreams *(1986)*

Foundation and Earth *(1986)*

The Best Science Fiction of Isaac Asimov *(1986)*

The Best Mysteries of Isaac Asimov *(1986)*

The Alternate Asimovs *(1986)*

Norby and the Invaders *(1985)* (with Janet Asimov)

Robots and Empire *(1985)*

The Disappearing Man and Other Mysteries *(1985)*

Norby and the Lost Princess *(1985)* (with Janet Asimov)

Banquets of the Black Widowers *(1984)*

Norby's Other Secret *(1984)* (with Janet Asimov)

The Robots of Dawn *(1983)*

Norby, the Mixed-Up Robot *(1983)* (with Janet Asimov)

The Union Club Mysteries *(1983)*

The Winds of Change and Other Stories *(1983)*

Foundation's Edge *(1982)*

The Complete Robot *(1982)*

The Casebook of the Black Widowers *(1980)*

The Key Word and Other Mysteries *(1977)*

More Tales of the Black Widowers *(1976)*

The Bicentennial Man and Other Stories *(1976)*

Murder at the ABA *(1976)*

The Heavenly Host *(1975)*

Buy Jupiter and Other Stories *(1975)*

Tales of the Black Widowers *(1974)*

Have You Seen These? *(1974)*

The Best of Isaac Asimov *(1973)*

The Early Asimov *(1972)*

The Gods Themselves *(1972)*

Nightfall and Other Stories *(1969)*

Asimov's Mysteries *(1968)*

Through a Glass, Clearly *(1967)*

Fantastic Voyage *(1966)*

The Rest of the Robots *(1964)*

Nine Tomorrows *(1959)*

The Death Dealers (A Whiff of Death) *(1958)*

Lucky Starr and the Rings of Saturn *(1958)*

Earth Is Room Enough *(1957)*

Lucky Starr and the Moons of Jupiter *(1957)*

The Naked Sun *(1957)*

Lucky Starr and the Big Sun of Mercury *(1956)*

The End of Eternity *(1955)*

The Martian Way and Other Stories *(1955)*

Lucky Starr and the Oceans of Venus *(1954)*

The Caves of Steel *(1954)*

Lucky Starr and the Pirates of the Asteroids *(1953)*

Second Foundation *(1953)*

The Currents of Space *(1952)*

Foundation and Empire *(1952)*

David Starr: Space Ranger *(1952)*

Foundation *(1951)*

The Stars, Like Dust— *(1951)*

I, Robot *(1950)*

Pebble in the Sky *(1950)*

ISAAC ASIMOV
PRELUDE TO
FOUNDATION

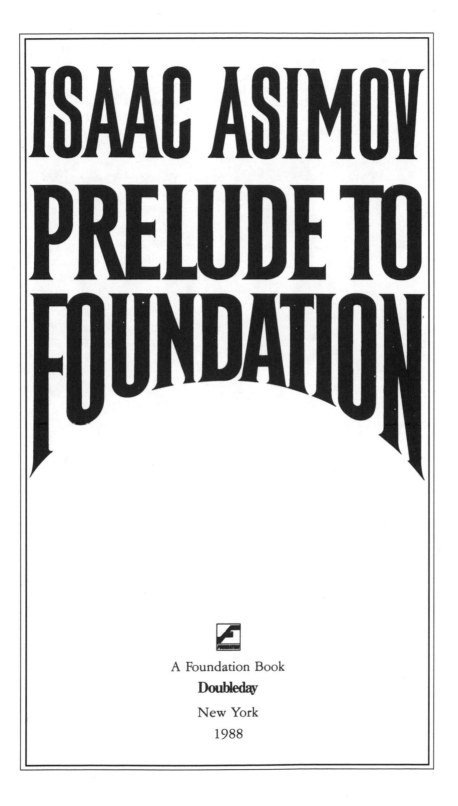

A Foundation Book

Doubleday

New York

1988

All characters in this book are fictional
and any resemblance to actual persons,
living or dead, is entirely coincidental.

DESIGNED BY PETER R. KRUZAN

Limited Edition frontispiece by Boris Vallejo

Library of Congress Cataloging-in-Publication Data
Asimov, Isaac, 1920–
Prelude to foundation/Isaac Asimov.
p. cm.
"A Foundation Book (New York, N.Y.)."
I. Title.
PS3551.S5P7 1988
813'.54—dc19   87-33086
CIP
ISBN 0-385-23313-2
0-385-24585-8 (Limited Edition)

To Jennifer "Green Pencil" Brehl,
the best and hardest-working editor in the world.

CONTENTS

AUTHOR'S NOTE

When I wrote "Foundation," which appeared in the May 1942 issue of *Astounding Science Fiction,* I had no idea that I had begun a series of stories that would eventually grow into six volumes and a total of 650,000 words (so far). Nor did I have any idea that it would be unified with my series of short stories and novels involving robots and my novels involving the Galactic Empire for a grand total (so far) of fourteen volumes and a total of about 1,450,000 words.

You will see, if you study the publication dates of these books, that there was a twenty-five-year hiatus between 1957 and 1982, during which I did not add to this series. This was not because I had stopped writing. Indeed, I wrote full-speed throughout the quarter century, but I wrote other things. That I returned to the series in 1982 was not my own notion but was the result of a combination of pressures from readers and publishers that eventually became overwhelming.

In any case, the situation has become sufficiently complicated for me to feel that the readers might welcome a kind of guide to the series, since they were not written in the order in which (perhaps) they should be read.

The fourteen books, all published by Doubleday, offer a kind of history of the future, which is, perhaps, not completely consistent, since I did not plan consistency to begin with. The chronological order of the books, in terms of future history (and *not* of publication date), is as follows:

1. *The Complete Robot* (1982). This is a collection of thirty-one robot short stories published between 1940 and 1976 and includes every story in my earlier collection *I, Robot* (1950). Only one robot short story has been written since this collection appeared. That is "Robot Dreams," which has not yet appeared in any Doubleday collection.
2. *The Caves of Steel* (1954). This is the first of my robot novels.
3. *The Naked Sun* (1957). The second robot novel.

4. *The Robots of Dawn* (1983). The third robot novel.

5. *Robots and Empire* (1985). The fourth robot novel.

6. *The Currents of Space* (1952). This is the first of my Empire novels.

7. *The Stars, Like Dust—* (1951). The second Empire novel.

8. *Pebble in the Sky* (1950). The third Empire novel.

9. *Prelude to Foundation* (1988). This is the first Foundation novel (although it is the latest written, so far).

10. *Foundation* (1951). The second Foundation novel. Actually, it is a collection of four stories, originally published between 1942 and 1944, plus an introductory section written for the book in 1949.

11. *Foundation and Empire* (1952). The third Foundation novel, made up of two stories, originally published in 1945.

12. *Second Foundation* (1953). The fourth Foundation novel, made up of two stories, originally published in 1948 and 1949.

13. *Foundation's Edge* (1982). The fifth Foundation novel.

14. *Foundation and Earth* (1983). The sixth Foundation novel.

Will I add additional books to the series? I might. There is room for a book between *Robots and Empire* (5) and *The Currents of Space* (6) and between *Prelude to Foundation* (9) and *Foundation* (10) and of course between others as well. And then I can follow *Foundation and Earth* (14) with additional volumes—as many as I like.

Naturally, there's got to be some limit, for I don't expect to live forever, but I do intend to hang on as long as possible.

PRELUDE TO FOUNDATION

MATHEMATICIAN

. . . . .

CLEON I— . . . The last Galactic Emperor of the Entun dynasty. He was born in the year 11,988 of the Galactic Era, the same year in which Hari Seldon was born. (It is thought that Seldon's birthdate, which some consider doubtful, may have been adjusted to match that of Cleon, whom Seldon, soon after his arrival on Trantor, is supposed to have encountered.)

Having succeeded to the Imperial throne in 12,010 at the age of twenty-two, Cleon I's reign represented a curious interval of quiet in those troubled times. This is undoubtedly due to the skills of his Chief of Staff, Eto Demerzel, who so carefully obscured himself from public record that little is known about him.

Cleon himself . . .

ENCYCLOPEDIA GALACTICA*

1.

Suppressing a small yawn, Cleon said, "Demerzel, have you by any chance ever heard of a man named Hari Seldon?"

Cleon had been Emperor for just over ten years and there were times at state occasions when, dressed in the necessary robes and regalia, he could manage to look stately. He did so, for instance, in the holograph of himself that stood in the niche in the wall behind him. It was placed so that it clearly dominated the other niches holding the holographs of several of his ancestors.

The holograph was not a totally honest one, for though Cleon's hair was light brown in hologram and reality alike, it was a bit thicker in the holograph. There was a certain asymmetry to his real face, for the left

---

* All quotations from the Encyclopedia Galactica here reproduced are taken from the 116th Edition, published 1,020 F.E. by the Encyclopedia Galactica Publishing Co., Terminus, with permission of the publishers.

side of his upper lip raised itself a bit higher than the right side, and this was somehow not evident in the holograph. And if he had stood up and placed himself beside the holograph, he would have been seen to be 2 centimeters under the 1.83-meter height that the image portrayed—and perhaps a bit stouter.

Of course, the holograph was the official coronation portrait and he had been younger then. He still looked young and rather handsome, too, and when he was not in the pitiless grip of official ceremony, there was a kind of vague good nature about his face.

Demerzel said, with the tone of respect that he carefully cultivated, "Hari Seldon? It is an unfamiliar name to me, Sire. Ought I to know of him?"

"The Minister of Science mentioned him to me last night. I thought you might."

Demerzel frowned slightly, but only very slightly, for one does not frown in the Imperial presence. "The Minister of Science, Sire, should have spoken of this man to *me* as Chief of Staff. If you are to be bombarded from every side—"

Cleon raised his hand and Demerzel stopped at once. "Please, Demerzel, one can't stand on formality at all times. When I passed the Minister at last night's reception and exchanged a few words with him, he bubbled over. I could not refuse to listen and I was glad I had, for it was interesting."

"In what way interesting, Sire?"

"Well, these are not the old days when science and mathematics were all the rage. That sort of thing seems to have died down somehow, perhaps because all the discoveries have been made, don't you think? Apparently, however, interesting things can still happen. At least I was told it was interesting."

"By the Minister of Science, Sire?"

"Yes. He said that this Hari Seldon had attended a convention of mathematicians held here in Trantor—they do this every ten years, for some reason—and he said that he had proved that one could foretell the future mathematically."

Demerzel permitted himself a small smile. "Either the Minister of Science, a man of little acumen, is mistaken or the mathematician is. Surely, the matter of foretelling the future is a children's dream of magic."

"Is it, Demerzel? People believe in such things."

"People believe in many things, Sire."

"But they believe in *such* things. Therefore, it doesn't matter whether the forecast of the future is true or not. If a mathematician should predict a long and happy reign for me, a time of peace and prosperity for the Empire— Eh, would that not be well?"

"It would be pleasant to hear, certainly, but what would it accomplish, Sire?"

"But surely if people believe this, they would act on that belief. Many a prophecy, by the mere force of its being believed, is transmuted to fact. These are 'self-fulfilling prophecies.' Indeed, now that I think of it, it was you who once explained this to me."

Demerzel said, "I believe I did, Sire." His eyes were watching the Emperor carefully, as though to see how far he might go on his own. "Still, if that be so, one could have any person make the prophecy."

"Not all persons would be equally believed, Demerzel. A mathematician, however, who could back his prophecy with mathematical formulas and terminology, might be understood by no one and yet believed by everyone."

Demerzel said, "As usual, Sire, you make good sense. We live in troubled times and it would be worthwhile to calm them in a way that would require neither money nor military effort—which, in recent history, have done little good and much harm."

"Exactly, Demerzel," said the Emperor with excitement. "Reel in this Hari Seldon. You tell me you have your strings stretching to every part of this turbulent world, even where my forces dare not go. Pull on one of those strings, then, and bring in this mathematician. Let me see him."

"I will do so, Sire," said Demerzel, who had already located Seldon and who made a mental note to commend the Minister of Science for a job well done.

2.

Hari Seldon did not make an impressive appearance at this time. Like the Emperor Cleon I, he was thirty-two years old, but he was only 1.73 meters tall. His face was smooth and cheerful, his hair dark brown, almost black, and his clothing had the unmistakable touch of provinciality about it.

To anyone in later times who knew of Hari Seldon only as a legendary demigod, it would seem almost sacrilegious for him not to have white hair, not to have an old lined face, a quiet smile radiating wisdom, not to be seated in a wheelchair. Even then, in advanced old age, his eyes had been cheerful, however. There was that.

And his eyes were particularly cheerful now, for his paper had been given at the Decennial Convention. It had even aroused some interest in a distant sort of way and old Osterfith had nodded his head at him and had said, "Ingenious, young man. Most ingenious." Which, coming from Osterfith, was satisfactory. Most satisfactory.

But now there was a new—and quite unexpected—development and Seldon wasn't sure whether it should increase his cheer and intensify his satisfaction or not.

He stared at the tall young man in uniform—the Spaceship-and-Sun neatly placed on the left side of his tunic.

"Lieutenant Alban Wellis," said the officer of the Emperor's Guard before putting away his identification. "Will you come with me now, sir?"

Wellis was armed, of course. There were two other Guardsmen waiting outside his door. Seldon knew he had no choice, for all the other's careful politeness, but there was no reason he could not seek information. He said, "To see the Emperor?"

"To be brought to the Palace, sir. That's the extent of my instructions."

"But why?"

"I was not told why, sir. And I have my strict instructions that you must come with me—one way or another."

"But this seems as though I am being arrested. I have done nothing to warrant that."

"Say, rather, that it seems you are being given an escort of honor—if you delay me no further."

Seldon delayed no further. He pressed his lips together, as though to block off further questions, nodded his head, and stepped forward. Even if he was going to meet the Emperor and to receive Imperial commendation, he found no joy in it. He was for the Empire—that is, for the worlds of humanity in peace and union—but he was not for the Emperor.

The lieutenant walked ahead, the other two behind. Seldon smiled at those he passed and managed to look unconcerned. Outside the hotel they climbed into an official ground-car. (Seldon ran his hand over the upholstery; he had never been in anything so ornate.)

They were in one of the wealthiest sections of Trantor. The dome was high enough here to give a sensation of being in the open and one could swear—even one such as Hari Seldon, who had been born and brought up on an open world—that they were in sunlight. You could see no sun and no shadows, but the air was light and fragrant.

And then it passed and the dome curved down and the walls narrowed in and soon they were moving along an enclosed tunnel, marked periodically with the Spaceship-and-Sun and so clearly reserved (Seldon thought) for official vehicles.

A door opened and the ground-car sped through. When the door closed behind them, they were in the open—the true, the real open. There were 250 square kilometers of the only stretch of open land on Trantor and on it stood the Imperial Palace. Seldon would have liked a chance to wander through that open land—not because of the Palace, but because it also contained the Galactic University and, most intriguing of all, the Galactic Library.

And yet, in passing from the enclosed world of Trantor into the open patch of wood and parkland, he had passed into a world in which clouds dimmed the sky and a chill wind ruffled his shirt. He pressed the contact that closed the ground-car's window.

It was a dismal day outside.

3.

Seldon was not at all sure he would meet the Emperor. At best, he would meet some official in the fourth or fifth echelon who would claim to speak for the Emperor.

How many people ever did see the Emperor? In person, rather than on holovision? How many people saw the real, tangible Emperor, an Emperor who never left the Imperial grounds that he, Seldon, was now rolling over.

The number was vanishingly small. Twenty-five million inhabited worlds, each with its cargo of a billion human beings or more—and among all those quadrillions of human beings, how many had, or would ever, lay eyes on the living Emperor. A thousand?

And did anyone care? The Emperor was no more than a symbol of Empire, like the Spaceship-and-Sun but far less pervasive, far less real. It was his soldiers and his officials, crawling everywhere, that now represented an Empire that had become a dead weight upon its people—not the Emperor.

So it was that when Seldon was ushered into a moderately sized, lavishly furnished room and found a young-looking man sitting on the edge of a table in a windowed alcove, one foot on the ground and one swinging over the edge, he found himself wondering that any official should be looking at him in so blandly good-natured a way. He had already experienced the fact, over and over, that government officials—and particularly those in the Imperial service—looked grave at all times, as though bearing the weight of the entire Galaxy on their shoulders. And it seemed the lower in importance they were, the graver and more threatening their expression.

This, then, might be an official so high in the scale, with the sun of power so bright upon him, that he felt no need of countering it with clouds of frowning.

Seldon wasn't sure how impressed he ought to be, but he felt that it would be best to remain silent and let the other speak first.

The official said, "You are Hari Seldon, I believe. The mathematician."

Seldon responded with a minimal "Yes, sir," and waited again.

The young man waved an arm. "It should be 'Sire,' but I hate ceremony. It's all I get and I weary of it. We are alone, so I will pamper myself and eschew ceremony. Sit down, professor."

Halfway through the speech, Seldon realized that he was speaking to the Emperor Cleon, First of that Name, and he felt the wind go out of him. There was a faint resemblance (now that he looked) to the official holograph that appeared constantly in the news, but in that holograph, Cleon was always dressed imposingly, seemed taller, nobler, frozen-faced.

And here he was, the original of the holograph, and somehow he appeared to be quite ordinary.

Seldon did not budge.

The Emperor frowned slightly and, with the habit of command present even in the attempt to abolish it, at least temporarily, said peremptorily, "I said, 'Sit down,' man. That chair. Quickly."

Seldon sat down, quite speechless. He could not even bring himself to say, "Yes, Sire."

Cleon smiled. "That's better. Now we can talk like two fellow human beings, which, after all, is what we are once ceremony is removed. Eh, my man?"

Seldon said cautiously, "If Your Imperial Majesty is content to say so, then it is so."

"Oh, come, why are you so cautious? I want to talk to you on equal terms. It is my pleasure to do so. Humor me."

"Yes, Sire."

"A simple 'Yes,' man. Is there no way I can reach you?"

Cleon stared at Seldon and Seldon thought it was a lively and interested stare.

Finally the Emperor said, "You don't *look* like a mathematician."

At last, Seldon found himself able to smile. "I don't know what a mathematician is suppose to look like, Your Imp—"

Cleon raised a cautioning hand and Seldon choked off the honorific.

Cleon said, "White-haired, I suppose. Bearded, perhaps. Old, certainly."

"Yet even mathematicians must be young to begin with."

"But they are then without reputation. By the time they obtrude themselves on the notice of the Galaxy, they are as I have described."

"I am without reputation, I'm afraid."

"Yet you spoke at this convention they held here."

"A great many of us did. Some were younger than myself. Few of us were granted any attention whatever."

"Your talk apparently attracted the attention of some of my officials. I am given to understand that you believe it possible to predict the future."

Seldon suddenly felt weary. It seemed as though this misinterpretation of his theory was constantly going to occur. Perhaps he should not have presented his paper.

He said, "Not quite, actually. What I have done is much more limited than that. In many systems, the situation is such that under some conditions chaotic events take place. That means that, given a particular starting point, it is impossible to predict outcomes. This is true even in some quite simple systems, but the more complex a system, the more likely it is to become chaotic. It has always been assumed that anything as complicated as human society would quickly become chaotic and, therefore, unpredictable. What I have done, however, is to show that, in studying human society, it is possible to choose a starting point and to make appropriate assumptions that will suppress the chaos. That will make it possible to predict the future, not in full detail, of course, but in broad sweeps; not with certainty, but with calculable probabilities."

The Emperor, who had listened carefully, said, "But doesn't that mean that you have shown how to predict the future?"

"Again, not quite. I have showed that it is theoretically possible, but no more. To do more, we would actually have to choose a correct starting point, make correct assumptions, and then find ways of carrying through calculations in a finite time. Nothing in my mathematical argument tells us how to do any of this. And even if we could do it all, we would, at best, only assess probabilities. That is not the same as predicting the future; it is merely a guess at what is likely to happen. Every successful politician, businessman, or human being of any calling must make these estimates of the future and do it fairly well or he or she would not be successful."

"They do it without mathematics."

"True. They do it by intuition."

"With the proper mathematics, anyone would be able to assess the probabilities. It wouldn't take the rare human being who is successful because of a remarkable intuitive sense."

"True again, but I have merely shown that mathematical analysis is possible; I have not shown it to be practical."

"How can something be possible, yet not practical?"

"It is theoretically possible for me to visit each world of the Galaxy and greet each person on each world. However, it would take far longer to do this than I have years to live and, even if I was immortal, the rate at which new human beings are being born is greater than the rate at which I could interview the old and, even more to the point, old human beings would die in great numbers before I could ever get to them."

"And is this sort of thing true of your mathematics of the future?"

Seldon hesitated, then went on. "It might be that the mathematics would take too long to work out, even if one had a computer the size of the Universe working at hyperspatial velocities. By the time any answer had been received, enough years would have elapsed to alter the situation so grossly as to make the answer meaningless."

"Why cannot the process be simplified?" Cleon asked sharply.

"Your Imperial Majesty"—Seldon felt the Emperor growing more formal as the answers grew less to his liking and responded with greater formality of his own—"consider the manner in which scientists have dealt with subatomic particles. There are enormous numbers of these, each moving or vibrating in random and unpredictable manner, but this chaos turns out to have an underlying order, so that we can work out a quantum mechanics that answers all the questions we know how to ask. In studying society, we place human beings in the place of subatomic particles, but now there is the added factor of the human mind. Particles move mindlessly; human beings do not. To take into account the various attitudes and impulses of mind adds so much complexity that there lacks time to take care of all of it."

"Could not mind, as well as mindless motion, have an underlying order?"

"Perhaps. My mathematical analysis implies that order must underlie everything, however disorderly it may appear to be, but it does not give any hint as to how this underlying order may be found. Consider— Twenty-five million worlds, each with its overall characteristics and culture, each being significantly different from all the rest, each containing a billion or more human beings who each have an individual mind, and all the worlds interacting in innumerable ways and combinations! However theoretically possible a psychohistorical analysis may be, it is not likely that it can be done in any practical sense."

"What do you mean 'psychohistorical'?"

"I refer to the theoretical assessment of probabilities concerning the future as 'psychohistory.' "

The Emperor rose to his feet suddenly, strode to the other end of the room, turned, strode back, and stopped before the still-sitting Seldon.

"Stand up!" he commanded.

Seldon rose and looked up at the somewhat taller Emperor. He strove to keep his gaze steady.

Cleon finally said, "This psychohistory of yours . . . if it could be made practical, it would be of great use, would it not?"

"Of enormous use, obviously. To know what the future holds, in even the most general and probabilistic way, would serve as a new and marvelous guide for our actions, one that humanity has never before had. But, of course—" He paused.

"Well?" said Cleon impatiently.

"Well, it would seem that, except for a few decision-makers, the results of psychohistorical analysis would have to remain unknown to the public."

"Unknown!" exclaimed Cleon with surprise.

"It's clear. Let me try to explain. If a psychohistorical analysis is made and the results are then given to the public, the various emotions and reactions of humanity would at once be distorted. The psychohistorical analysis, based on emotions and reactions that take place *without* knowledge of the future, become meaningless. Do you understand?"

The Emperor's eyes brightened and he laughed aloud. "Wonderful!"

He clapped his hand on Seldon's shoulder and Seldon staggered slightly under the blow.

"Don't you see, man?" said Cleon. "Don't you see? There's your use. You don't need to predict the future. Just choose a future—a good future, a useful future—and make the kind of prediction that will alter human emotions and reactions in such a way that the future you predicted will be brought about. Better to make a good future than predict a bad one."

Seldon frowned. "I see what you mean, Sire, but that is equally impossible."

"Impossible?"

"Well, at any rate, impractical. Don't you see? If you can't start with human emotions and reactions and predict the future they will bring about, you can't do the reverse either. You can't start with a future and predict the human emotions and reactions that will bring it about."

Cleon looked frustrated. His lips tightened. "And your paper, then? . . . Is that what you call it, a paper? . . . Of what use is it?"

"It was merely a mathematical demonstration. It made a point of interest to mathematicians, but there was no thought in my mind of its being useful in any way."

"I find that disgusting," said Cleon angrily.

Seldon shrugged slightly. More than ever, he knew he should never have given the paper. What would become of him if the Emperor took it into his head that he had been made to play the fool?

And indeed, Cleon did not look as though he was very far from believing that.

"Nevertheless," he said, "what if you were to make predictions of the future, mathematically justified or not; predictions that government officials, human beings whose expertise it is to know what the public is likely to do, will judge to be the kind that will bring about useful reactions?"

"Why would you need me to do that? The government officials could make those predictions themselves and spare the middleman."

"The government officials could not do so as effectively. Government officials *do* make statements of the sort now and then. They are not necessarily believed."

"Why would I be?"

"You are a mathematician. You would have *calculated* the future, not . . . not intuited it—if that is a word."

"But I would not have done so."

"Who would know that?" Cleon watched him out of narrowed eyes.

There was a pause. Seldon felt trapped. If given a direct order by the Emperor, would it be safe to refuse? If he refused, he might be imprisoned or executed. Not without trial, of course, but it is only with great difficulty that a trial can be made to go against the wishes of a heavy-handed officialdom, particularly one under the command of the Emperor of the vast Galactic Empire.

He said finally, "It wouldn't work."

"Why not?"

"If I were asked to predict vague generalities that could not possibly come to pass until long after this generation and, perhaps, the next were dead, we might get away with it, but, on the other hand, the public would pay little attention. They would not care about a glowing eventuality a century or two in the future.

"To attain results," Seldon went on, "I would have to predict matters of sharper consequence, more immediate eventualities. Only to these would the public respond. Sooner or later, though—and probably sooner —one of the eventualities would *not* come to pass and my usefulness would be ended at once. With that, your popularity might be gone, too, and, worst of all, there would be no further support for the development of psychohistory so that there would be no chance for any good to come of it if future improvements in mathematical insights help to make it move closer to the realm of practicality."

Cleon threw himself into a chair and frowned at Seldon. "Is that all you mathematicians can do? Insist on impossibilities?"

Seldon said with desperate softness, "It is you, Sire, who insist on impossibilities."

"Let me test you, man. Suppose I asked you to use your mathematics to tell me whether I would some day be assassinated? What would you say?"

"My mathematical system would not give an answer to so specific a question, even if psychohistory worked at its best. All the quantum mechanics in the world cannot make it possible to predict the behavior of one lone electron, only the average behavior of many."

"You know your mathematics better than I do. Make an educated guess based on it. Will I someday be assassinated?"

Seldon said softly, "You lay a trap for me, Sire. Either tell me what answer you wish and I will give it to you or else give me free right to make what answer I wish without punishment."

"Speak as you will."

"Your word of honor?"

"Do you want it in writing?" Cleon was sarcastic.

"Your spoken word of honor will be sufficient," said Seldon, his heart sinking, for he was not certain it would be.

"You have my word of honor."

"Then I can tell you that in the past four centuries nearly half the Emperors have been assassinated, from which I conclude that the chances of your assassination are roughly one in two."

"Any fool can give that answer," said Cleon with contempt. "It takes no mathematician."

"Yet I have told you several times that my mathematics is useless for practical problems."

"Can't you even suppose that I learn the lessons that have been given me by my unfortunate predecessors?"

Seldon took a deep breath and plunged in. "No, Sire. All history shows that we do not learn from the lessons of the past. For instance, you have allowed me here in a private audience. What if it were in my mind to assassinate you? —Which it isn't, Sire," he added hastily.

Cleon smiled without humor. "My man, you don't take into account our thoroughness—or advances in technology. We have studied your history, your complete record. When you arrived, you were scanned. Your expression and voiceprints were analyzed. We knew your emotional state in detail; we practically knew your thoughts. Had there been the slightest doubt of your harmlessness, you would not have been allowed near me. In fact, you would not now be alive."

A wave of nausea swept through Seldon, but he continued. "Outsiders have always found it difficult to get at Emperors, even with technology less advanced. However, almost every assassination has been a palace coup. It is those nearest the Emperor who are the greatest danger to him. Against that danger, the careful screening of outsiders is irrelevant. And as for your own officials, your own Guardsmen, your own intimates, you cannot treat them as you treat me."

Cleon said, "I know that, too, and at least as well as you do. The answer is that I treat those about me fairly and I give them no cause for resentment."

"A foolish—" began Seldon, who then stopped in confusion.

"Go on," said Cleon angrily. "I have given you permission to speak freely. How am I foolish?"

"The word slipped out, Sire. I meant 'irrelevant.' Your treatment of your intimates is irrelevant. You must be suspicious; it would be inhuman not to be. A careless word, such as the one I used, a careless gesture, a doubtful expression and you must withdraw a bit with narrowed eyes. And any touch of suspicion sets in motion a vicious cycle. The intimate will sense and resent the suspicion and will develop a changed behavior, try as he might to avoid it. You sense that and grow more suspicious and, in the end, either he is executed or you are assassinated. It is a process that has proved unavoidable for the Emperors of the past four centuries and it is but one sign of the increasing difficulty of conducting the affairs of the Empire."

"Then nothing I can do will avoid assassination."

"No, Sire," said Seldon, "but, on the other hand, you may prove fortunate."

Cleon's fingers were drumming on the arm of his chair. He said harshly, "You are useless, man, and so is your psychohistory. Leave me." And with those words, the Emperor looked away, suddenly seeming much older than his thirty-two years.

"I have said my mathematics would be useless to you, Sire. My profound apologies."

Seldon tried to bow but at some signal he did not see, two guards entered and took him away. Cleon's voice came after him from the royal chamber. "Return that man to the place from which he was brought earlier."

4.

Eto Demerzel emerged and glanced at the Emperor with a hint of proper deference. He said, "Sire, you have almost lost your temper."

Cleon looked up and, with an obvious effort, managed to smile. "Well, so I did. The man was very disappointing."

"And yet he promised no more than he offered."

"He offered nothing."

"And promised nothing, Sire."

"It was disappointing."

Demerzel said, "More than disappointing, perhaps. The man is a loose cannon, Sire."

"A loose *what*, Demerzel? You are always so full of strange expressions. What is a cannon?"

Demerzel said gravely, "It is simply an expression I heard in my youth, Sire. The Empire is full of strange expressions and some are unknown on Trantor, as those of Trantor are sometimes unknown elsewhere."

"Do you come to teach me the Empire is large? What do you mean by saying that the man is a loose cannon?"

"Only that he can do much harm without necessarily intending it. He does not know his own strength. Or importance."

"You deduce that, do you, Demerzel?"

"Yes, Sire. He is a provincial. He does not know Trantor or its ways. He has never been on our planet before and he cannot behave like a man of breeding, like a courtier. Yet he stood up to you."

"And why not? I gave him permission to speak. I left off ceremony. I treated him as an equal."

"Not entirely, Sire. You don't have it within you to treat others as equals. You have the habit of command. And even if you tried to put a person at his ease, there would be few who could manage it. Most would be speechless or, worse, subservient and sycophantic. This man stood up to you."

"Well, you may admire that, Demerzel, but I didn't like him." Cleon looked thoughtfully discontented. "Did you notice that he made no effort to explain his mathematics to me? It was as though he knew I would not understand a word of it."

"Nor would you have, Sire. You are not a mathematician, nor a scientist of any kind, nor an artist. There are many fields of knowledge in which others know more than you. It is their task to use their knowledge to serve you. You are the Emperor, which is worth all their specializations put together."

"Is it? I would not mind being made to feel ignorant by an old man who had accumulated knowledge over many years. But this man, Seldon, is just my age. How does he know so much?"

"He has not had to learn the habit of command, the art of reaching a decision that will affect the lives of others."

"Sometimes, Demerzel, I wonder if you are laughing at me."

"Sire?" said Demerzel reproachfully.

"But never mind. Back to that loose cannon of yours. Why should you consider him dangerous? He seems a naïve provincial to me."

"He is. But he has this mathematical development of his."

"He says it is useless."

"You thought it might be useful. I thought so, after you had explained it to me. Others might. The mathematician may come to think so himself, now that his mind has been focused on it. And who knows, he may yet work out some way of making use of it. If he does, then to foretell the future, however mistily, is to be in a position of great power. Even if he does not wish power for himself, a kind of self-denial that always seems to me to be unlikely, he might be used by others."

"I tried to use him. He would not."

"He had not given it thought. Perhaps now he will. And if he was not interested in being used by you, might he not be persuaded by—let us say—the Mayor of Wye?"

"Why should he be willing to help Wye and not us?"

"As he explained, it is hard to predict the emotions and behavior of individuals."

Cleon scowled and sat in thought. "Do you really think he might develop this psychohistory of his to the point where it is truly useful? He is so certain he cannot."

"He may, with time, decide he was wrong in denying the possibility."

Cleon said, "Then I suppose I ought to have kept him."

Demerzel said, "No, Sire. Your instinct was correct when you let him go. Imprisonment, however disguised, would cause resentment and despair, which would not help him either to develop his ideas further or make him eager to help us. Better to let him go as you have done, but to keep him forever on an invisible leash. In this way, we can see that he is not used by an enemy of yourself, Sire, and we can see that when the time comes and he has fully developed his science, we can pull on our leash and bring him in. Then we could be . . . more persuasive."

"But what if he *is* picked up by an enemy of mine or, better, of the Empire, for I am the Empire after all, or if, of his own accord, he wishes to serve an enemy— I don't consider that out of the question, you see."

"Nor should you. I will see to it that this doesn't happen, but if, against all striving, it *does* happen, it would be better if no one has him than if the wrong person does."

Cleon looked uneasy. "I'll leave that all in your hands, Demerzel, but I hope we're not too hasty. He could be, after all, nothing but the purveyor of a theoretical science that does not and cannot work."

"Quite possibly, Sire, but it would be safer to assume the man is—or might be—important. We lose only a little time and nothing more if we find that we have concerned ourselves with a nonentity. We may lose a Galaxy if we find we have ignored someone of great importance."

"Very well, then," said Cleon, "but I trust I won't have to know the details—if they prove unpleasant."

Demerzel said, "Let us hope that will not be the case."

5.

Seldon had had an evening, a night, and part of a morning to get over his meeting with the Emperor. At least, the changing quality of light within the walkways, moving corridors, squares, and parks of the Imperial Sector of Trantor made it seem that an evening, a night, and part of a morning had passed.

He sat now in a small park on a small plastic seat that molded itself neatly to his body and he was comfortable. Judging from the light, it seemed to be midmorning and the air was just cool enough to seem fresh without possessing even the smallest bite.

Was it like this all the time? He thought of the gray day outside when he went to see the Emperor. And he thought of all the gray days and cold days and hot days and rainy days and snowy days on Helicon, his home, and he wondered if one could miss them. Was it possible to sit in a park on Trantor, having ideal weather day after day, so that it felt as though you were surrounded by nothing at all—and coming to miss a howling wind or a biting cold or a breathless humidity?

Perhaps. But not on the first day or the second or the seventh. He would have only this one day and he would leave tomorrow. He meant to enjoy it while he could. He might, after all, never return to Trantor.

Still, he continued to feel uneasy at having spoken as independently as he had to a man who could, at will, order one's imprisonment or execution—or, at the very least, the economic and social death of loss of position and status.

Before going to bed, Seldon had looked up Cleon I in the encyclopedic portion of his hotel room computer. The Emperor had been highly praised as, no doubt, had all Emperors in their own lifetime, regardless of their deeds. Seldon had dismissed that, but he was interested in the fact that Cleon had been born in the Palace and had never left its grounds. He had never been in Trantor itself, in any part of the multi-domed world. It was a matter of security, perhaps, but what it meant was that the Emperor was in prison, whether he admitted the matter to himself or not. It might be the most luxurious prison in the Galaxy, but it was a prison just the same.

And though the Emperor had seemed mild-mannered and had shown no sign of being a bloody-minded autocrat as so many of his predecessors had been, it was not good to have attracted his attention. Seldon welcomed the thought of leaving tomorrow for Helicon, even though it would be winter (and a rather nasty one, so far) back home.

He looked up at the bright diffuse light. Although it could never rain in here, the atmosphere was far from dry. A fountain played not far from him; the plants were green and had probably never felt drought. Occasionally, the shrubbery rustled as though a small animal or two was hidden there. He heard the hum of bees.

Really, though Trantor was spoken of throughout the Galaxy as an artificial world of metal and ceramic, in this small patch it felt positively rustic.

There were a few other persons taking advantage of the park all wearing light hats, some quite small. There was one rather pretty young woman not far away, but she was bent over a viewer and he could not see her face clearly. A man walked past, looked at him briefly and incuriously, then sat down in a seat facing him and buried himself in a sheaf of teleprints, crossing one leg, in its tight pink trouser leg, over the other.

There was a tendency to pastel shades among the men, oddly enough, while the women mostly wore white. Being a clean environment, it made sense to wear light colors. He looked down in amusement at his own Heliconian costume, which was predominantly dull brown. If he were to stay on Trantor—as he was not—he would need to purchase suitable clothing or he would become an object of curiosity or laughter or repulsion. The man with the teleprints had, for instance, looked up at him more curiously this time—no doubt intrigued by his Outworldish clothing.

Seldon was relieved that he did not smile. He could be philosophical over being a figure of fun, but, surely, he could not be expected to enjoy it.

Seldon watched the man rather unobtrusively, for he seemed to be engaged in some sort of internal debate. At the moment he looked as if he was about to speak, then seemed to think better of it, then seemed to wish to speak again. Seldon wondered what the outcome would be.

He studied the man. He was tall, with broad shoulders and no sign of a paunch, darkish hair with a glint of blond, smooth-shaven, a grave expression, an air of strength though there were no bulging muscles, a face that was a touch rugged—pleasant, but with nothing "pretty" about it.

By the time the man had lost the internal fight with himself (or won, perhaps) and leaned toward him, Seldon had decided he liked him.

The man said, "Pardon me, weren't you at the Decennial Convention? Mathematics?"

"Yes, I was," said Seldon agreeably.

"Ah, I thought I saw you there. It was—excuse me—that moment of recognition that led me to sit here. If I am intruding on your privacy—"

"Not at all. I'm just enjoying an idle moment."

"Let's see how close I can get. You're Professor Seldom."

"Seldon. Hari Seldon. Quite close. And you?"

"Chetter Hummin." The man seemed slightly embarrassed. "Rather a homespun name, I'm afraid."

"I've never come across any Chetters before," said Seldon. "Or Hummins. So that makes you somewhat unique, I should think. It might be viewed as being better than being mixed up with all the countless Haris there are. Or Seldons, for that matter."

Seldon moved his chair closer to Hummin, scraping it against the slightly elastic ceramoid tiles.

"Talk about homespun," he said, "What about this Outworldish clothing I'm wearing? It never occurred to me that I ought to get Trantorian garb."

"You could buy some," said Hummin, eyeing Seldon with suppressed disapproval.

"I'll be leaving tomorrow and, besides, I couldn't afford it. Mathematicians deal with large numbers sometimes, but never in their income. —I presume you're a mathematician, Hummin."

"No. Zero talent there."

"Oh." Seldon was disappointed. "You said you saw me at the Decennial Convention."

"I was there as an onlooker. I'm a journalist." He waved his teleprints, seemed suddenly aware that he was holding them and shoved them into his jacket pouch. "I supply the material for the news holocasts." Then, thoughtfully, "Actually, I'm rather tired of it."

"The job?"

Hummin nodded. "I'm sick of gathering together all the nonsense from every world. I hate the downward spiral."

He glanced speculatively at Seldon. "Sometimes something interesting turns up, though. I've heard you were seen in the company of an Imperial Guard and making for the Palace gate. You weren't by any chance seen by the Emperor, were you?"

The smile vanished from Seldon's face. He said slowly, "If I was, it would scarcely be something I could talk about for publication."

"No no, not for publication. If you don't know this, Seldon, let me be the first to tell you— The first rule of the news game is that *nothing* is ever said about the Emperor or his personal entourage except what is officially given out. It's a mistake, of course, because rumors fly that are much worse than the truth, but that's the way it is."

"But if you can't report it, friend, why do you ask?"

"Private curiosity. Believe me, in my job I know a great deal more than ever gets on the air. —Let me guess. I didn't follow your paper, but

I gathered that you were talking about the possibility of predicting the future."

Seldon shook his head and muttered, "It was a mistake."

"Pardon me?"

"Nothing."

"Well, prediction—accurate prediction—would interest the Emperor, or any man in government, so I'm guessing that Cleon, First of that Name, asked you about it and wouldn't you please give him a few predictions."

Seldon said stiffly, "I don't intend to discuss the matter."

Hummin shrugged slightly. "Eto Demerzel was there, I suppose."

"Who?"

"You've never heard of Eto Demerzel?"

"Never."

"Cleon's alter ego—Cleon's brain—Cleon's evil spirit. He's been called all those things—if we confine ourselves to the nonvituperative. He must have been there."

Seldon looked confused and Hummin said, "Well, you may not have seen him, but he was there. And if he thinks you can predict the future—"

"I can't predict the future," said Seldon, shaking his head vigorously. "If you listened to my paper, you'll know that I only spoke of a theoretical possibility."

"Just the same, if he *thinks* you can predict the future, he will not let you go."

"He must have. Here I am."

"That means nothing. He knows where you are and he'll continue to know. And when he wants you, he'll get you, wherever you are. And if he decides you're useful, he'll squeeze the use out of you. And if he decides you're dangerous, he'll squeeze the life out of you."

Seldon stared. "What are you trying to do. Frighten me?"

"I'm trying to warn you."

"I don't believe what you're saying."

"Don't you? A while ago you said something was a mistake. Were you thinking that presenting the paper was a mistake and that it was getting you into the kind of trouble you don't want to be in?"

Seldon bit his lower lip uneasily. That was a guess that came entirely too close to the truth—and it was at this moment that Seldon felt the presence of intruders.

They did not cast a shadow, for the light was too soft and widespread. It was a simply a movement that caught the corner of his eye—and then it stopped.

FLIGHT

. . . . .

TRANTOR— . . . The capital of the First Galactic Empire . . . Under Cleon I, it had its "twilight glow." To all appearances, it was then at its peak. Its land surface of 200 million square kilometers was entirely domed (except for the Imperial Palace area) and underlaid with an endless city that extended beneath the continental shelves. The population was 40 billion and although the signs were plentiful (and clearly visible in hindsight) that there were gathering problems, those who lived on Trantor undoubtedly found it still the Eternal World of legend and did not expect it would ever . . .

ENCYCLOPEDIA GALACTICA

6.

Seldon looked up. A young man was standing before him, looking down at him with an expression of amused contempt. Next to him was another young man—a bit younger, perhaps. Both were large and appeared to be strong.

They were dressed in an extreme of Trantorian fashion, Seldon judged —boldly clashing colors, broad fringed belts, round hats with wide brims all about and the two ends of a bright pink ribbon extending from the brim to the back of the neck.

In Seldon's eyes, it was amusing and he smiled.

The young man before him snapped, "What're you grinning at, misfit?"

Seldon ignored the manner of address and said gently, "Please pardon my smile. I was merely enjoying your costume."

"My costume? So? And what are you wearing? What's that awful offal you call clothes?" His hand went out and his finger flicked at the lapel of Seldon's jacket—disgracefully heavy and dull, Seldon himself thought, in comparison to the other's lighthearted colors.

Seldon said, "I'm afraid it's my Outworlder clothes. They're all I have."

He couldn't help notice that the few others who were sitting in the small park were rising to their feet and walking off. It was as though they were expecting trouble and had no desire to remain in the vicinity. Seldon wondered if his new friend, Hummin, was leaving too, but he felt it injudicious to take his eyes away from the young man who was confronting him. He teetered back on his chair slightly.

The young man said, "You an Outworlder?"

"That's right. Hence my clothes."

"Hence? What kind of word's that? Outworld word?"

"What I meant was, that was why my clothes seem peculiar to you. I'm a visitor here."

"From what planet?"

"Helicon."

The young man's eyebrows drew together. "Never heard of it."

"It's not a large planet."

"Why don't you go back there?"

"I intend to. I'm leaving tomorrow."

"Sooner! Now!"

The young man looked at his partner. Seldon followed the look and caught a glimpse of Hummin. He had *not* left, but the park was now empty except for himself, Hummin, and the two young men.

Seldon said, "I'd thought I'd spend today sight-seeing."

"No. You don't want to do that. You go home now."

Seldon smiled. "Sorry. I won't."

The young man said to his partner. "You like his clothes, Marbie?"

Marbie spoke for the first time. "No. Disgusting. Turns the stomach."

"Can't let him go around turning stomachs, Marbie. Not good for people's health."

"No, not by no means, Alem," said Marbie.

Alem grinned. "Well now. You heard what Marbie said."

And now Hummin spoke. He said, "Look, you two, Alem, Marbie, whatever your names are. You've had your fun. Why don't you go away?"

Alem, who had been leaning slightly toward Seldon, straightened and turned. "Who are you?"

"That's not your business," snapped Hummin.

2 8

"You're Trantorian?" asked Alem.

"Also not your business."

Alem frowned and said, "You're dressed Trantorian. We're not interested in you, so don't go looking for problems."

"I intend to stay. That means there are two of us. Two against two doesn't sound like your kind of fight. Why don't you go away and get some friends so you can handle two people?"

Seldon said, "I really think you ought to get away if you can, Hummin. It's kind of you to try to protect me, but I don't want you harmed."

"These are not dangerous people, Seldon. Just half-credit lackeys."

"Lackeys!" The word seemed to infuriate Alem, so that Seldon thought it must have a more insulting meaning on Trantor than it had on Helicon.

"Here, Marbie," said Alem with a growl. "You take care of that other motherlackey and I'll rip the clothes off this Seldon. He's the one we want. Now—"

His hands came down sharply to seize Seldon's lapels and jerk him upright. Seldon pushed away, instinctively it would seem, and his chair tipped backward. He seized the hands stretched toward him, his foot went up, and his chair went down.

Somehow Alem streaked overhead, turning as he did so, and came down hard on his neck and back behind Seldon.

Seldon twisted as his chair went down and was quickly on his feet, staring down at Alem, then looking sharply to one side for Marbie.

Alem lay unmoving, his face twisted in agony. He had two badly sprained thumbs, excruciating pain in his groin, and a backbone that had been badly jarred.

Hummin's left arm had grabbed Marbie's neck from behind and his right arm had pulled the other's right arm backward at a vicious angle. Marbie's face was red as he labored uselessly for breath. A knife, glittering with a small laser inset, lay on the ground beside them.

Hummin eased his grip slightly and said, with an air of honest concern, "You've hurt that one badly."

Seldon said, "I'm afraid so. If he had fallen a little differently, he would have snapped his neck."

Hummin said, "What kind of a mathematician are you?"

"A Heliconian one." He stooped to pick up the knife and, after examining it, said, "Disgusting—and deadly."

Hummin said, "An ordinary blade would do the job without requiring a power source. —But let's let these two go. I doubt they want to continue any further."

He released Marbie, who rubbed first his shoulder then his neck. Gasping for air, he turned hate-filled eyes on the two men.

Hummin said sharply, "You two had better get out of here. Otherwise we'll have to give evidence against you for assault and attempted murder. This knife can surely be traced to you."

Seldon and Hummin watched while Marbie dragged Alem to his feet and then helped him stagger away, still bent in pain. They looked back once or twice, but Seldon and Hummin watched impassively.

Seldon held out his hand. "How do I thank you for coming to the aid of a stranger against two attackers? I doubt I would have been able to handle them both on my own."

Hummin raised his hand in a deprecatory manner. "I wasn't afraid of them. They're just street-brawling lackeys. All I had to do was get my hands on them—and yours, too, of course."

"That's a pretty deadly grip you have," Seldon mused.

Hummin shrugged. "You too." Then, without changing his tone of voice, he said, "Come on, we'd better get out of here. We're wasting time."

Seldon said, "Why do we have to get away? Are you afraid those two will come back?"

"Not in their lifetime. But some of those brave people who cleared out of the park so quickly in their eagerness to spare themselves a disagreeable sight may have alerted the police."

"Fine. We have the hoodlums' names. And we can describe them fairly well."

"Describe them? Why would the police want them?"

"They committed an assault—"

"Don't be foolish. We don't have a scratch. They're virtually hospital bait, especially Alem. *We're* the ones who will be charged."

"But that's impossible. Those people witnessed the fact that—"

"No people will be called. —Seldon, get this into your head. Those two came to find you—specifically *you*. They were told you were wearing Heliconian clothes and you must have been described precisely. Perhaps they were even shown a holograph. I suspect they were sent by the people who happen to control the police, so let's not wait any longer."

3 0

Hummin hurried off, his hand gripping Seldon's upper arm. Seldon found the grip impossible to shake and, feeling like a child in the hands of an impetuous nurse, followed.

They plunged into an arcade and, before Seldon's eyes grew accustomed to the dimmer light, they heard the burring sound of a ground-car's brakes.

"There they are," muttered Hummin. "Faster, Seldon." They hopped onto a moving corridor and lost themselves in the crowd.

7.

Seldon had tried to persuade Hummin to take him to his hotel room, but Hummin would have none of that.

"Are you mad?" he half-whispered. "They'll be waiting for you there."

"But all my belongings are waiting for me there too."

"They'll just have to wait."

And now they were in a small room in a pleasant apartment structure that might be anywhere for all that Seldon could tell. He looked about the one-room unit. Most of it was taken up by a desk and chair, a bed, and a computer outlet. There were no dining facilities or washstand of any kind, though Hummin had directed him to a communal washroom down the hall. Someone had entered before Seldon was quite through. He had cast one brief and curious look at Seldon's clothes, rather than at Seldon himself, and had then looked away.

Seldon mentioned this to Hummin, who shook his head and said, "We'll have to get rid of your clothes. Too bad Helicon is so far out of fashion—"

Seldon said impatiently, "How much of this might just be your imagination, Hummin? You've got me half-convinced and yet it may be merely a kind of . . . of—"

"Are you groping for the word 'paranoia'?"

"All right, I am. This may be some strange paranoid notion of yours."

Hummin said, "Think about it, will you? I can't argue it out mathematically, but you've seen the Emperor. Don't deny it. He wanted something from you and you didn't give it to him. Don't deny that either. I suspect that details of the future are what he wants and you refused.

3 1

Perhaps Demerzel thinks you're only pretending not to have the details —that you're holding out for a higher price or that someone else is bidding for it too. Who knows? I told you that if Demerzel wants you, he'll get you wherever you are. I told you that before those two splitheads ever appeared on the scene. I'm a journalist *and* a Trantorian. I know how these things go. At one point, Alem said, 'He's the one we want.' Do you remember that?"

"As it happens," said Seldon. "I do."

"To him I was only the 'other motherlackey' to be kept off, while he went about the real job of assaulting you."

Hummin sat down in the chair and pointed to the bed. "Stretch out, Seldon. Make yourself comfortable. Whoever sent those two—it must have been Demerzel, in my opinion—can send others, so we'll have to get rid of those clothes of yours. I think any other Heliconian in this sector caught in his own world's garb is going to have trouble until he can prove he isn't you."

"Oh come on."

"I mean it. You'll have to take off the clothes and we'll have to atomize them—if we can get close enough to a disposal unit without being seen. And before we can do that I'll have to get you a Trantorian outfit. You're smaller than I am and I'll take that into account. It won't matter if it doesn't fit exactly—"

Seldon shook his head. "I don't have the credits to pay for it. Not on me. What credits I have—and they aren't much—are in my hotel safe."

"We'll worry about that another time. You'll have to stay here for an hour or two while I go out in search of the necessary clothing."

Seldon spread his hands and sighed resignedly. "All right. If it's that important, I'll stay."

"You won't try to get back to your hotel? Word of honor?"

"My word as a mathematician. But I'm really embarrassed by all the trouble you're taking for me. And expense too. After all, despite all this talk about Demerzel, they weren't really out to hurt me or carry me off. All I was threatened with was the removal of my clothes."

"Not all. They were also going to take you to the spaceport and put you on a hypership to Helicon."

"That was a silly threat—not to be taken seriously."

"Why not?"

"I'm going to Helicon. I told them so. I'm going tomorrow."

"And you still plan to go tomorrow?" asked Hummin.

"Certainly. Why not?"

"There are enormous reasons why not."

Seldon suddenly felt angry. "Come on, Hummin, I can't play this game any further. I'm finished here and I want to go home. My tickets are in the hotel room. Otherwise I'd try to exchange them for a trip today. I mean it."

"You can't go back to Helicon."

Seldon flushed. "Why not? Are they waiting for me there too?"

Hummin nodded. "Don't fire up, Seldon. They *would* be waiting for you there too. Listen to me. If you go to Helicon, you are as good as in Demerzel's hands. Helicon is good, safe Imperial territory. Has Helicon ever rebelled, ever fallen into step behind the banner of an anti-Emperor?"

"No, it hasn't—and for good reason. It's surrounded by larger worlds. It depends on the Imperial peace for security."

"Exactly! Imperial forces on Helicon can therefore count on the full cooperation of the local government. You would be under constant surveillance at all times. Any time Demerzel wants you, he will be able to have you. And, except for the fact that I am now warning you, you would have no knowledge of this and you would be working in the open, filled with a false security."

"That's ridiculous. If he wanted me in Helicon, why didn't he simply leave me to myself? I was going there tomorrow. Why would he send those two hoodlums simply to hasten the matter by a few hours and risk putting me on my guard?"

"Why should he think you would be put on your guard? He didn't know I'd be with you, immersing you in what you call my paranoia."

"Even without the question of warning me, why all the fuss to hurry me by a few hours?"

"Perhaps because he was afraid you would change your mind."

"And go where, if not home? If he could pick me up on Helicon, he could pick me up anywhere. He could pick me up on . . . on Anacreon, a good ten thousand parsecs away—if it should fall into my head to go there. What's distance to hyperspatial ships? Even if I find a world that's not quite as subservient to the Imperial forces as Helicon is, what world is in actual rebellion? The Empire is at peace. Even if some worlds are still resentful of injustices in the past, none are going to defy the Imperial armed forces to protect me. Moreover, anywhere but on Helicon I won't be a local citizen and there won't even be that matter of principle to help keep the Empire at bay."

Hummin listened patiently, nodding slightly, but looking as grave and as imperturbable as ever. He said, "You're right, as far as you go, but there's one world that is not really under the Emperor's control. That, I think, is what must be disturbing Demerzel."

Seldon thought a while, reviewing recent history and finding himself unable to choose a world on which the Imperial forces might be helpless. He said at last, "What world is that?"

Hummin said, "You're on it, which is what makes the matter so dangerous in Demerzel's eyes, I imagine. It is not so much that he is anxious to have you go to Helicon, as that he is anxious to have you leave Trantor before it occurs to you, for any reason—even if only tourist's mania—to stay."

The two men sat in silence until Seldon finally said sardonically, "Trantor! The capital of the Empire, with the home base of the fleet on a space station in orbit about it, with the best units of the army quartered here. If you believe that it is *Trantor* that is the safe world, you're progressing from paranoia to outright fantasy."

"No! You're an Outworlder, Seldon. You don't know what Trantor is like. It's forty billion people and there are few other worlds with even a tenth of its population. It is of unimaginable technological and cultural complexity. Where we are now is the Imperial Sector—with the highest standard of living in the Galaxy and populated entirely by Imperial functionaries. Elsewhere on the planet, however, are over eight hundred other sectors, some of them with subcultures totally different from what we have here and most of them untouchable by Imperial forces."

"Why untouchable?"

"The Empire cannot seriously exert force against Trantor. To do so would be bound to shake some facet or other of the technology on which the whole planet depends. The technology is so interrelated that to snap one of the interconnections is to cripple the whole. Believe me, Seldon, we on Trantor observe what happens when there is an earthquake that manages to escape being damped out, a volcanic eruption that is not vented in time, a storm that is not defused, or just some human error that escapes notice. The planet totters and every effort must be made to restore the balance at once."

"I have never heard of such a thing."

A small smile flickered its way across Hummin's face. "Of course not. Do you want the Empire to advertise the weakness at its core? However, as a journalist, I know what happens even when the Outworlds don't, even when much of Trantor itself doesn't, even when the Imperial pressure is interested in concealing events. Believe me! The Emperor knows —and Eto Demerzel knows—even if you don't, that to disturb Trantor may destroy the Empire."

"Then are you suggesting I stay on Trantor for that reason?"

"Yes. I can take you to a place on Trantor where you will be absolutely safe from Demerzel. You won't have to change your name and you will be able to operate entirely in the open and he won't be able to touch you. That's why he wanted to force you off Trantor at once and if it hadn't been for the quirk of fate that brought us together and for your surprising ability to defend yourself, he would have succeeded in doing so."

"But how long will I have to remain on Trantor?"

"For as long as your safety requires it, Seldon. For the rest of your life, perhaps."

8.

Hari Seldon looked at the holograph of himself cast by Hummin's projector. It was more dramatic and useful than a mirror would have been. In fact, it seemed as though there were two of him in the room.

Seldon studied the sleeve of his new tunic. His Heliconian attitudes made him wish the colors were less vibrant, but he was thankful that, as it was, Hummin had chosen softer colors than were customary here on this world. (Seldon thought of the clothing worn by their two assailants and shuddered inwardly.)

He said, "And I suppose I must wear this hat."

"In the Imperial Sector, yes. To go bareheaded here is a sign of low breeding. Elsewhere, the rules are different."

Seldon sighed. The round hat was made of soft material and molded itself to his head when he put it on. The brim was evenly wide all around, but it was narrower than on the hats his attackers had worn. Seldon consoled himself by noticing that when he wore the hat the brim curved rather gracefully.

"It doesn't have a strap under the chin."

"Of course not. That's advanced fashion for young lanks."

"For young what?"

"A lank is someone who wears things for their shock value. I'm sure you have such people on Helicon."

Seldon snorted. "There are those who wear their hair shoulder-length on one side and shave the other." He laughed at the memory.

Hummin's mouth twisted slightly. "I imagine it looks uncommonly ugly."

"Worse. There are lefties and righties, apparently, and each finds the other version highly offensive. The two groups often engage in street brawls."

"Then I think you can stand the hat, especially without the strap."

Seldon said, "I'll get used to it."

"It will attract some attention. It's subdued for one thing and makes you look as if you're in mourning. And it doesn't *quite* fit. Then, too, you wear it with obvious discomfort. However, we won't be in the Imperial Sector long. —Seen enough?" And the holograph flickered out.

Seldon said, "How much did this cost you?"

"What's the difference?"

"It bothers me to be in your debt."

"Don't worry about it. This is my choice. But we've been here long enough. I will have been described, I'm quite certain. They'll track me down and they'll come here."

"In that case," said Seldon, "the credits you're spending are a minor matter. You're putting yourself into personal danger on my account. Personal danger!"

"I know that. But it's my free choice and I can take care of myself."

"But why—"

"We'll discuss the philosophy of it later. —I've atomized your clothes, by the way, and I don't think I was seen. There was an energy surge, of course, and that would be recorded. Someone might guess what happened from that—it's hard to obscure *any* action when probing eyes and mind are sharp enough. However, let us hope we'll be safely away before they put it all together."

9.

They traveled along walkways where the light was soft and yellow. Hummin's eyes moved this way and that, watchful, and he kept their pace at crowd speed, neither passing nor being passed.

He kept up a mild but steady conversation on indifferent topics.

Seldon, edgy and unable to do the same, said, "There seems to be a great deal of walking here. There are endless lines in both directions and along the crossovers."

"Why not?" said Hummin. "Walking is still the best form of short-distance transportation. It's the most convenient, the cheapest, and the most healthful. Countless years of technological advance have not changed that. —Are you acrophobic, Seldon?"

Seldon looked over the railing on his right into a deep declivity that separated the two walking lanes—each in an opposite direction between the regularly spaced crossovers. He shuddered slightly. "If you mean fear of heights, not ordinarily. Still, looking down isn't pleasant. How far does it go down?"

"Forty or fifty levels at this point, I think. This sort of thing is common in the Imperial Sector and a few other highly developed regions. In most places, one walks at what might be considered ground level."

"I should imagine this would encourage suicide attempts."

"Not often. There are far easier methods. Besides, suicide is not a matter of social obloquy on Trantor. One can end one's life by various recognized methods in centers that exist for the purpose—if one is willing to go through some psychotherapy at first. There are occasional accidents, for that matter, but that's not why I was asking about acrophobia. We're heading for a taxi rental where they know me as a journalist. I've done favors for them occasionally and sometimes they do favors for me in return. They'll forget to record me and won't notice that I have a companion. Of course, I'll have to pay a premium and, again of course, if Demerzel's people lean on them hard enough, they'll have to tell the truth and put it down to slovenly accounting, but that may take considerable time."

"Where does the acrophobia come in?"

"Well, we can get there a lot faster if we use a gravitic lift. Not many people use it and I must tell you that I'm not overjoyed at the idea myself, but if you think you can handle it, we had better."

"What's a gravitic lift?"

"It's experimental. The time may come when it will be widespread over Trantor, provided it becomes psychologically acceptable—or can be made so to enough people. Then, maybe, it will spread to other worlds too. It's an elevator shaft without an elevator cab, so to speak. We just step into empty space and drop slowly—or rise slowly—under the influence of antigravity. It's about the only application of antigravity that's been established so far, largely because it's the simplest possible application."

"What happens if the power blinks out while we're in transit?"

"Exactly what you would think. We fall and—unless we're quite near the bottom to begin with—we die. I haven't heard of it happening yet and, believe me, if it *had* happened I would know. We might not be able to give out the news for security reasons—that's the excuse they always advance for hiding bad news—but *I* would know. It's just up ahead. If you can't manage it, we won't do it, but the corridors are slow and tedious and many find them nauseating after a while."

Hummin turned down a crossover and into a large recess where a line of men and women were waiting, one or two with children.

Seldon said in a low voice, "I heard nothing of this back home. Of course, our own news media are terribly local, but you'd think there'd be some mention that this sort of thing exists."

Hummin said. "It's strictly experimental and is confined to the Imperial Sector. It uses more energy than it's worth, so the government is not really anxious to push it right now by giving it publicity. The old Emperor, Stanel VI, the one before Cleon who amazed everyone by dying in his bed, insisted on having it installed in a few places. He wanted his name associated with antigravity, they say, because he was concerned with his place in history, as old men of no great attainments frequently are. As I said, the technique may spread, but, on the other hand, it is possible that nothing much more than the gravitic lift will ever come of it."

"What do they want to come of it?" asked Seldon.

"Antigrav spaceflight. That, however, will require many breakthroughs and most physicists, as far as I know, are firmly convinced it is out of the question. —But, then, most thought that even gravitic lifts were out of the question."

The line ahead was rapidly growing shorter and Seldon found himself standing with Hummin at the edge of the floor with an open gap before him. The air ahead faintly glittered. Automatically, he reached out his hand and felt a light shock. It didn't hurt, but he snatched his hand back quickly.

Hummin grunted. "An elementary precaution to prevent anyone walking over the edge before activating the controls." He punched some numbers on the control board and the glitter vanished.

Seldon peered over the edge, down the deep shaft.

"You might find it better—or easier," said Hummin, "if we link arms and if you close your eyes. It won't take more than a few seconds."

He gave Seldon no choice, actually. He took his arm and once again there was no hanging back in that firm grip. Hummin stepped into nothingness and Seldon (who heard himself, to his own embarrassment, emit a small squeak) shuffled off with a lurch.

He closed his eyes tightly and experienced no sense of falling, no feeling of air movement. A few seconds passed and he was pulled forward. He tripped slightly, caught his balance, and found himself on solid ground.

He opened his eyes, "Did we make it?"

Hummin said dryly, "We're not dead," then walked away, his grip forcing Seldon to follow.

"I mean, did we get to the right level?"

"Of course."

"What would have happened if we were dropping down and someone else was moving upward?"

"There are two separate lanes. In one lane everyone drops at the same speed; in the other everyone rises at the same speed. The shaft clears only when there are no people within ten meters of each other. There is no chance of a collision if all works well."

"I didn't feel a thing."

"Why should you? There was no acceleration. After the first tenth of a second, you were at constant speed and the air in your immediate vicinity was moving down with you at the same speed."

"Marvelous."

"Absolutely. But uneconomic. And there seems no great pressure to increase the efficiency of the procedure and make it worthwhile. Everywhere one hears the same refrain. 'We can't do it. It can't be done.' It applies to everything." Hummin shrugged in obvious anger and said, "But we're here at the taxi rental. Let's get on with it."

10.

Seldon tried to look inconspicuous at the air-taxi rental terminus, which he found difficult. To look ostentatiously inconspicuous—to slink about, to turn his face away from all who passed, to study one of the vehicles overintently—was surely the way to invite attention. The way to behave was merely to assume an innocent normality.

But what was normality? He felt uncomfortable in his clothes. There were no pockets, so he had no place to put his hands. The two pouches, which dangled from his belt on either side, distracted him by hitting against him as he moved, so that he was continually thinking someone had nudged him.

He tried looking at women as they passed. They had no pouches, at least none dangling, but they carried little boxlike affairs that they occasionally clipped to one hip or another by some device he could not make out. It was probably pseudomagnetic, he decided. Their clothes were not particularly revealing, he noted regretfully, and not one had any sign of décolletage, although some dresses seemed to be designed to emphasize the buttocks.

Meanwhile, Hummin had been very businesslike, having presented the necessary credits and returned with the superconductive ceramic tile that would activate a specific air-taxi.

Hummin said, "Get in, Seldon," gesturing to a small two-seated vehicle.

Seldon asked, "Did you have to sign your name, Hummin?"

"Of course not. They know me here and don't stand on ceremony."

"What do they think you're doing?"

"They didn't ask and I volunteered no information." He inserted the tile and Seldon felt a slight vibration as the air-taxi came to life.

"We're headed for D-7," said Hummin, making conversation.

Seldon didn't know what D-7 was, but he assumed it meant some route or other.

The air-taxi found its way past and around other ground-cars and finally moved onto a smooth upward-slanting track and gained speed. Then it lifted upward with a slight jolt.

Seldon, who had been automatically strapped in by a webbed restraint, felt himself pushed down into his seat and then up against the webbing.

He said, "That didn't feel like antigravity."

"It wasn't," said Hummin. "That was a small jet reaction. Just enough to take us up to the tubes."

What appeared before them now looked like a cliff patterned with cave openings, much like a checkerboard. Hummin maneuvered toward the D-7 opening, avoiding other air-taxis that were heading for other tunnels.

"You could crash easily," said Seldon, clearing his throat.

"So I probably would if everything depended on my senses and reactions, but the taxi is computerized and the computer can overrule me without trouble. The same is true for the other taxis. —Here we go."

They slid into D-7 as if they had been sucked in and the bright light of the open plaza outside mellowed, turning a warmer yellow hue.

Hummin released the controls and sat back. He drew a deep breath and said, "Well, that's one stage successfully carried through. We might have been stopped at the station. In here, we're fairly safe."

The ride was smooth and the walls of the tunnel slipped by rapidly. There was almost no sound, just a steady velvety whirr as the taxi sped along.

"How fast are we going?" asked Seldon.

Hummin cast an eye briefly at the controls. "Three hundred and fifty kilometers per hour."

"Magnetic propulsion?"

"Yes. You have it on Helicon, I imagine."

"Yes. One line. I've never been on it myself, though I've always meant to. I don't think it's anything like this."

"I'm sure it isn't. Trantor has many thousands of kilometers of these tunnels honeycombing the land subsurface and a number that snake under the shallower extensions of the ocean. It's the chief method of long-distance travel."

"How long will it take us?"

"To reach our immediate destination? A little over five hours."

"Five hours!" Seldon was dismayed.

"Don't be disturbed. We pass rest areas every twenty minutes or so where we can stop, pull out of the tunnel, stretch our feet, eat, or relieve ourselves. I'd like to do that as few times as possible, of course."

They continued on in silence for a while and then Seldon started when a blaze of light flared at their right for a few seconds and, in the flash, he thought he saw two air-taxis.

"That was a rest area," said Hummin in answer to the unspoken question.

Seldon said, "Am I really going to be safe wherever it is you are taking me?"

Hummin said, "Quite safe from any open movement on the part of the Imperial forces. Of course, when it comes to the individual operator— the spy, the agent, the hired assassin—one must always be careful. Naturally, I will supply you with a bodyguard."

Seldon felt uneasy. "The hired assassin? Are you serious? Would they really want to kill me?"

Hummin said, "I'm sure Demerzel doesn't. I suspect he wants to use you rather than kill you. Still, other enemies may turn up or there may be unfortunate concatenations of events. You can't go through life sleep-walking."

Seldon shook his head and turned his face away. To think, only forty-eight hours ago he had been just an insignificant, virtually unknown Outworld mathematician, content only to spend his remaining time on Trantor sight-seeing, gazing at the enormity of the great world with his provincial eye. And now, it was finally sinking in: He was a wanted man, hunted by Imperial forces. The enormity of the situation seized him and he shuddered.

"And what about *you* and what you're doing right now?"

Hummin said thoughtfully, "Well, they won't feel kindly toward me, I suppose. I might have my head laid open or my chest exploded by some mysterious and never-found assailant."

Hummin said it without a tremor in his voice or a change in his calm appearance, but Seldon winced.

Seldon said, "I rather thought you would assume that might be in store for you. You don't seem to be . . . bothered by it."

"I'm an old Trantorian. I know the planet as well as anybody can. I know many people and many of them are under obligation to me. I like to think that I am shrewd and not easy to outwit. In short, Seldon, I am quite confident that I can take care of myself."

"I'm glad you feel that way and I hope you're justified in thinking so, Hummin, but I can't get it through my head why you're taking this chance at all. What am I to you? Why should you take even the smallest risk for someone who is a stranger to you?"

Hummin checked the controls in a preoccupied manner and then he faced Seldon squarely, eyes steady and serious.

"I want to save you for the same reason that the Emperor wants to use you—for your predictive powers."

Seldon felt a deep pang of disappointment. This was not after all a question of being saved. He was merely the helpless and disputed prey of competing predators. He said angrily, "I will never live down that presentation at the Decennial Convention. I have ruined my life."

"No. Don't rush to conclusions, mathematician. The Emperor and his officers want you for one reason only, to make their own lives more secure. They are interested in your abilities only so far as they might be used to save the Emperor's rule, preserve that rule for his young son, maintain the positions, status, and power of his officials. I, on the other hand, want your powers for the good of the Galaxy."

"Is there a distinction?" spat Seldon acidly.

And Hummin replied with the stern beginning of a frown, "If you do not see the distinction, then that is to your shame. The human occupants of the Galaxy existed before this Emperor who now rules, before the dynasty he represents, before the Empire itself. Humanity is far older than the Empire. It may even be far older than the twenty-five million worlds of the Galaxy. There are legends of a time when humanity inhabited a single world."

"Legends!" said Seldon, shrugging his shoulders.

"Yes, legends, but I see no reason why that may not have been so in fact, twenty thousand years ago or more. I presume that humanity did not come into existence complete with knowledge of hyperspatial travel. Surely, there must have been a time when people could *not* travel at superluminal velocities and they must then have been imprisoned in a single planetary system. And if we look forward in time, the human beings of the worlds of the Galaxy will surely continue to exist after you and the Emperor are dead, after his whole line comes to an end, and after the institutions of the Empire itself unravel. In that case, it is not important to worry overmuch about individuals, about the Emperor and the young Prince Imperial. It is not important to worry even about the mechanics of Empire. What of the quadrillions of people that exist in the Galaxy? What of them?"

Seldon said, "Worlds and people would continue, I presume."

"Don't you feel any serious need of probing the possible conditions under which they would continue to exist.

"One would assume they would exist much as they do now."

"One would *assume*. But could one *know* by this art of prediction that you speak of?"

"Psychohistory is what I call it. In theory, one could."

"And you feel no pressure to turn that theory into practice."

"I would love to, Hummin, but the desire to do so doesn't automatically manufacture the ability to do so. I told the Emperor that psychohistory could not be turned into a practical technique and I am forced to tell you the same thing."

"And you have no intention of even trying to find the technique?"

"No, I don't, any more than I would feel I ought to try to tackle a pile of pebbles the size of Trantor, count them one by one, and arrange them in order of decreasing mass. I would *know* it was not something I could accomplish in a lifetime and I would not be fool enough to make a pretense of trying."

"Would you try if you knew the truth about humanity's situation?"

"That's an impossible question. What *is* the truth about humanity's situation? Do you claim to know it?"

"Yes, I do. And in five words." Hummin's eyes faced forward again, turning briefly toward the blank changelessness of the tunnel as it pushed toward them, expanding until it passed and then dwindling as it slipped away. He then spoke those five words grimly.

He said, "The Galactic Empire is dying."

UNIVERSITY

. . . . .

STREELING UNIVERSITY— . . . An institution of
higher learning in the Streeling Sector of ancient Trantor
. . . Despite all these claims to fame in the fields of the
humanities and sciences alike, it is not for those that the
University looms large in today's consciousness. It would
probably have come as a total surprise to the generations of
scholars at the University to know that in later times Streeling University would be most remembered because a certain Hari Seldon, during the period of The Flight, had
been in residence there for a short time.

ENCYCLOPEDIA GALACTICA

11.

Hari Seldon remained uncomfortably silent for a while after Hummin's
quiet statement. He shrank within himself in sudden recognition of his
own deficiencies.

He had invented a new science: psychohistory. He had extended the
laws of probability in a very subtle manner to take into account new
complexities and uncertainties and had ended up with elegant equations
in innumerable unknowns. —Possibly an infinite number; he couldn't
tell.

But it was a mathematical game and nothing more.

He had psychohistory—or at least the basis of psychohistory—but only
as a mathematical curiosity. Where was the historical knowledge that
could perhaps give some meaning to the empty equations?

He had none. He had never been interested in history. He knew the
outline of Heliconian history. Courses in that small fragment of the human story had, of course, been compulsory in the Heliconian schools.
But what was there beyond that? Surely what else he had picked up was
merely the bare skeletons that everyone gathered—half legend, the other
half surely distorted.

Still, how could one say that the Galactic Empire was dying? It had existed for ten thousand years as an accepted Empire and even before that, Trantor, as the capital of the dominating kingdom, had held what was a virtual empire for two thousand years. The Empire had survived the early centuries when whole sections of the Galaxy would now and then refuse to accept the end of their local independence. It had survived the vicissitudes that went with the occasional rebellions, the dynastic wars, some serious periods of breakdown. Most worlds had scarcely been troubled by such things and Trantor itself had grown steadily until it was the worldwide human habitation that now called itself the Eternal World.

To be sure, in the last four centuries, turmoil had increased somehow and there had been a rash of Imperial assassinations and takeovers. But even that was calming down and right now the Galaxy was as quiet as it had ever been. Under Cleon I and before him under his father, Stanel VI, the worlds were prosperous—and Cleon himself was not considered a tyrant. Even those who disliked the Imperium as an institution rarely had anything truly bad to say about Cleon, much as they might inveigh against Eto Demerzel.

Why, then, should Hummin say that the Galactic Empire was dying— and with such conviction?

Hummin was a journalist. He probably knew Galactic history in some detail and he had to understand the current situation in great detail. Was it this that supplied him with the knowledge that lay behind his statement? In that case, just what was the knowledge?

Several times Seldon was on the point of asking, of demanding an answer, but there was something in Hummin's solemn face that stopped him. And there was something in his own ingrained belief that the Galactic Empire was a given, an axiom, the foundation stone on which all argument rested that prevented him too. After all, if *that* was wrong, he didn't want to know.

No, he couldn't believe that he was wrong. The Galactic Empire could no more come to an end than the Universe itself could. Or, if the Universe did end, then—and only then—would the Empire end.

Seldon closed his eyes, attempting to sleep but, of course, he could not. Would he have to study the history of the Universe in order to advance his theory of psychohistory?

How could he? Twenty-five million worlds existed, each with its own endlessly complex history. How could he study all that? There were book-films in many volumes, he knew, that dealt with Galactic history. He had even skimmed one once for some now-forgotten reason and had found it too dull to view even halfway through.

The book-films had dealt with important worlds. With some, it dealt through all or almost all their history; with others, only as they gained importance for a time and only till they faded away. He remembered having looked up Helicon in the index and having found only one citation. He had punched the keys that would turn up that citation and found Helicon included in a listing of worlds which, on one occasion, had temporarily lined up behind a certain claimant to the Imperial throne who had failed to make good his claim. Helicon had escaped retribution on that occasion, probably because it was not even sufficiently important to be punished.

What good was such a history? Surely, psychohistory would have to take into account the actions and reactions and interactions of each world —*each* and *every* world. How could one study the history of twenty-five million worlds and consider all their possible interactions? It would surely be an impossible task and this was just one more reinforcement of the general conclusion that psychohistory was of theoretical interest but could never be put to any practical use.

Seldon felt a gentle push forward and decided that the air-taxi must be decelerating.

"What's up?" he asked.

"I think we've come far enough," said Hummin, "to risk a small stop-over for a bite to eat, a glass of something or other, and a visit to a washroom."

And, in the course of the next fifteen minutes, during which the air-taxi slowed steadily, they came to a lighted recess. The taxi swerved inward and found a parking spot among five or six other vehicles.

12.

Hummin's practiced eye seemed to take in the recess, the other taxis, the diner, the walkways, and the men and women all at a glance. Seldon, trying to look inconspicuous and again not knowing how, watched him, trying not to do so too intently.

When they sat down at a small table and punched in their orders, Seldon, attempting to sound indifferent, said, "Everything okay?"

"Seems so," said Hummin.

"How can you tell?"

Hummin let his dark eyes rest on Seldon for a moment. "Instinct," he said. "Years of news gathering. You look and know, 'No news here.'"

Seldon nodded and felt relieved. Hummin might have said it sardonically, but there must be a certain amount of truth to it.

His satisfaction did not last through the first bite of his sandwich. He looked up at Hummin with his mouth full and with a look of hurt surprise on his face.

Hummin said, "This is a wayside diner, my friend. Cheap, fast, and not very good. The food's homegrown and has an infusion of rather sharp yeast. Trantorian palates are used to it."

Seldon swallowed with difficulty. "But back in the hotel—"

"You were in the Imperial Sector, Seldon. Food is imported there and where microfood is used it is high-quality. It is also expensive."

Seldon wondered whether to take another bite. "You mean that as long as I stay on Trantor—"

Hummin made a hushing motion with his lips. "Don't give anyone the impression that you're used to better. There are places on Trantor where to be identified as an aristocrat is worse than being identified as an Outworlder. The food won't be so bad everywhere, I assure you. These wayside places have a reputation for low quality. If you can stomach that sandwich, you'll be able to eat anywhere on Trantor. And it won't hurt you. It's not decayed or bad or anything like that. It just has a harsh, strong taste and, honestly, you may grow accustomed to it. I've met Trantorians who spit out honest food and say it lacks that homegrown tang."

"Do they grow much food on Trantor?" asked Seldon. A quick side glance showed him there was no one seated in the immediate vicinity and he spoke quietly. "I've always heard it takes twenty surrounding worlds to supply the hundreds of freight ships required to feed Trantor every day."

"I know. And hundreds to carry off the load of wastes. And if you want to make the story really good, you say that the same freight ships carry food one way and waste the other. It's true that we import considerable quantities of food, but that's mostly luxury items. And we export considerable waste, carefully treated into inoffensiveness, as important organic fertilizer—every bit as important to other worlds as the food is to us. But that's only a small fraction of the whole."

"It is?"

"Yes. In addition to fish in the sea, there are gardens and truck farms everywhere. And fruit trees and poultry and rabbits and vast microorganism farms—usually called yeast farms, though the yeast makes up a minority of the growths. And our wastes are mostly used right here at home to maintain all that growth. In fact, in many ways Trantor is very much like an enormous and overgrown space settlement. Have you ever visited one of those?"

"Indeed I have."

"Space settlements are essentially enclosed cities, with everything artificially cycled, with artificial ventilation, artificial day and night, and so on. Trantor is different only in that even the largest space settlement has a population of only ten million and Trantor has four thousand times that. Of course, we have real gravity. *And* no space settlement can match us in our microfoods. We have yeast vats, fungal mats, and algae ponds vast beyond the imagination. And we are strong on artificial flavoring, added with no light hand. That's what gives the taste to what you're eating."

Seldon had gotten through most of his sandwich and found it not as offensive as the first bite had been. "And it won't affect me?"

"It does hit the intestinal flora and every once in a while it afflicts some poor Outworlder with diarrhea, but that's rare, and you harden even to that quickly. Still, drink your milkshake, which you probably won't like. It contains an antidiarrhetic that should keep you safe, even if you tend to be sensitive to such things."

Seldon said querulously, "Don't talk about it, Hummin. A person can be suggestible to such things."

"Finish the milkshake and forget the suggestibility."

They finished the rest of their meal in silence and soon were on their way again.

13.

They were now racing rapidly through the tunnel once more. Seldon decided to give voice to the question that had been nagging at him for the last hour or so.

"Why do you say the Galactic Empire is dying?"

Hummin turned to look at Seldon again. "As a journalist, I have statistics poured into me from all sides till they're squeezing out of my ears. And I'm allowed to publish very little of it. Trantor's population is decreasing. Twenty-five years ago, it stood at almost forty-five billion.

"Partly, this decrease is because of a decline in the birthrate. To be sure, Trantor never has had a high birthrate. If you'll look about you when you're traveling on Trantor, you won't encounter very many children, considering the enormous population. But just the same it's declining. Then too there is emigration. People are leaving Trantor in greater numbers than are arriving."

"Considering its large population," said Seldon, "that's not surprising."

"But it's unusual just the same because it hasn't happened before. Again, all over the Galaxy trade is stagnating. People think that because there are no rebellions at the moment and because things are quiet that all is well and that the difficulties of the past few centuries are over. However, political infighting, rebellions, and unrest are all signs of a certain vitality too. But now there's a general weariness. It's quiet, not because people are satisfied and prosperous, but because they're tired and have given up."

"Oh, I don't know," said Seldon dubiously.

"I do. And the antigrav phenomenon we've talked about is another case in point. We have a few gravitic lifts in operation, but new ones aren't being constructed. It's an unprofitable venture and there seems no interest in trying to make it profitable. The rate of technological advance has been slowing for centuries and is down to a crawl now. In some cases, it has stopped altogether. Isn't this something you've noticed? After all, you're a mathematician."

"I can't say I've given the matter any thought."

"No one does. It's accepted. Scientists are very good these days at saying that things are impossible, impractical, useless. They condemn any speculation at once. You, for instance— What do you think of psychohistory? It is theoretically interesting, but it is useless in any practical sense. Am I right?"

"Yes and no," said Seldon, annoyed. "It *is* useless in any practical sense, but not because my sense of adventure has decayed, I assure you. It really *is* useless."

"That, at least," said Hummin with a trace of sarcasm, "is your impression in this atmosphere of decay in which all the Empire lives."

"This atmosphere of decay," said Seldon angrily, "is *your* impression. Is it possible that you are wrong?"

Hummin stopped and for a moment appeared thoughtful. Then he said, "Yes, I might be wrong. I am speaking only from intuition, from guesses. What I need is a working technique of psychohistory."

Seldon shrugged and did not take the bait. He said, "I don't have such a technique to give you. —But suppose you're right. Suppose the Empire *is* running down and will eventually stop and fall apart. The human species will still exist."

"Under what conditions, man? For nearly twelve thousand years, Trantor, under strong rulers, has largely kept the peace. There've been interruptions to that—rebellions, localized civil wars, tragedy in plenty— but, on the whole and over large areas, there has been peace. Why is Helicon so pro-Imperium? Your world, I mean. Because it is small and would be devoured by its neighbors were it not that the Empire keeps it secure."

"Are you predicting universal war and anarchy if the Empire fails?"

"Of course. I'm not fond of the Emperor or of the Imperial institutions in general, but I don't have any substitute for it. I don't know what else will keep the peace and I'm not ready to let go until I have something else in hand."

Seldon said, "You talk as though you are in control of the Galaxy. *You* are not ready to let go? *You* must have something else in hand? Who are you to talk so?"

"I'm speaking generally, figuratively," said Hummin. "I'm not worried about Chetter Hummin personally. It might be said that the Empire will last my time; it might even show signs of improvement in my time. Declines don't follow a straight-line path. It may be a thousand years before the final crash and you might well imagine I would be dead then and, certainly, I will leave no descendants. As far as women are concerned, I have nothing but the occasional casual attachment and I have no

children and intend to have none. I have given no hostages to fortune. —
I looked you up after your talk, Seldon. You have no children either."

"I have parents and two brothers, but no children." He smiled rather
weakly. "I was very attached to a woman at one time, but it seemed to
her that I was attached more to my mathematics."

"Were you?"

"It didn't seem so to me, but it seemed so to her. So she left."

"And you have had no one since?"

"No. I remember the pain too clearly as yet."

"Well then, it might seem we could both wait out the matter and leave
it to other people, well after our time, to suffer. I might have been
willing to accept that earlier, but no longer. For now I *have* a tool; I *am* in
command."

"What's your tool?" asked Seldon, already knowing the answer.

"You!" said Hummin.

And because Seldon had known what Hummin would say, he wasted
no time in being shocked or astonished. He simply shook his head and
said, "You are quite wrong. I am no tool fit for use."

"Why not?"

Seldon sighed. "How often must I repeat it? Psychohistory is not a
practical study. The difficulty is fundamental. All the space and time of
the Universe would not suffice to work out the necessary problems."

"Are you certain of that?"

"Unfortunately, yes."

"There's no question of your working out the entire future of the
Galactic Empire, you know. You needn't trace out in detail the workings
of every human being or even of every world. There are merely certain
questions you must answer: Will the Galactic Empire crash and, if so,
when? What will be the condition of humanity afterward? Can anything
be done to prevent the crash or to ameliorate conditions afterward?
These are comparatively simple questions, it seems to me."

Seldon shook his head and smiled sadly. "The history of mathematics
is full of simple questions that had only the most complicated of answers
—or none at all."

"Is there nothing to be done? I can see that the Empire is falling, but I
can't prove it. All my conclusions are subjective and I cannot show that I
am not mistaken. Because the view is a seriously unsettling one, people
would prefer not to believe my subjective conclusion and nothing will be

done to prevent the Fall or even to cushion it. You could *prove* the coming Fall or, for that matter, disprove it."

"But that is exactly what I cannot do. I can't find you proof where none exists. I can't make a mathematical system practical when it isn't. I can't find you two even numbers that will yield an odd number as a sum, no matter how vitally you—or all the Galaxy—may need that odd number."

Hummin said, "Well then, you're part of the decay. You're ready to accept failure."

"What choice have I?"

"Can't you *try?* However useless the effort may seem to you to be, have you anything better to do with your life? Have you some worthier goal? Have you a purpose that will justify you in your own eyes to some greater extent?"

Seldon's eyes blinked rapidly. "Millions of worlds. Billions of cultures. Quadrillions of people. Decillions of interrelationships. —And you want me to reduce it to order."

"No, I want you to *try.* For the sake of those millions of worlds, billions of cultures, and quadrillions of people. Not for the Emperor. Not for Demerzel. For humanity."

"I will fail," said Seldon.

"Then we will be no worse off. Will you try?"

And against his will and not knowing why, Seldon heard himself say, "I will try." And the course of his life was set.

14.

The journey came to its end and the air-taxi moved into a much larger lot than the one at which they had eaten. (Seldon still remembered the taste of the sandwich and made a wry face.)

Hummin turned in his taxi and came back, placing his credit slip in a small pocket on the inner surface of his shirt. He said, "You're completely safe here from anything outright and open. This is the Streeling Sector."

"Streeling?"

"It's named for someone who first opened up the area to settlement, I imagine. Most of the sectors are named for someone or other, which means that most of the names are ugly and some are hard to pronounce. Just the same, if you try to have the inhabitants here change Streeling to Sweetsmell or something like that, you'll have a fight on your hands."

"Of course," said Seldon, sniffing loudly, "it isn't exactly Sweetsmell."

"Hardly anywhere in Trantor is, but you'll get used to it."

"I'm glad we're here," said Seldon. "Not that I like it, but I got quite tired sitting in the taxi. Getting around Trantor must be a horror. Back on Helicon, we can get from any one place to any other by air, in far less time than it took us to travel less than two thousand kilometers here."

"We have air-jets too."

"But in that case—"

"I could arrange an air-taxi ride more or less anonymously. It would have been much more difficult with an air-jet. And regardless of how safe it is here, I'd feel better if Demerzel didn't know exactly where you were. —As a matter of fact, we're not done yet. We're going to take the Expressway for the final stage."

Seldon knew the expression. "One of those open monorails moving on an electromagnetic field, right?"

"Right."

"We don't have them on Helicon. Actually, we don't need them there. I rode on an Expressway the first day I was on Trantor. It took me from the airport to the hotel. It was rather a novelty, but if I were to use it all the time, I imagine the noise and crowds would become overpowering."

Hummin looked amused. "Did you get lost?"

"No, the signs were useful. There was trouble getting on and off, but I was helped. Everyone could tell I was an Outworlder by my clothes, I now realize. They seemed eager to help, though; I guess because it was amusing to watching me hesitate and stumble."

"As an expert in Expressway travel by now, you will neither hesitate nor stumble." Hummin said it pleasantly enough, though there was a slight twitch to the corners of his mouth. "Come on, then."

They sauntered leisurely along the walkway, which was lit to the extent one might expect of an overcast day and that brightened now and then as though the sun occasionally broke through the clouds. Automatically, Seldon looked upward to see if that were indeed the case, but the "sky" above was blankly luminous.

Hummin saw this and said, "This change in brightness seems to suit the human psyche. There are days when the street seems to be in bright sunlight and days when it is rather darker than it is now."

"But no rain or snow?"

"Or hail or sleet. No. Nor high humidity nor bitter cold. Trantor has its points, Seldon, even now."

There were people walking in both directions and there were a considerable number of young people and also some children accompanying the adults, despite what Hummin had said about the birthrate. All seemed reasonably prosperous and reputable. The two sexes were equally represented and the clothing was distinctly more subdued than it had been in the Imperial Sector. His own costume, as chosen by Hummin, fit right in. Very few were wearing hats and Seldon thankfully removed his own and swung it at his side.

There was no deep abyss separating the two sides of the walkway and as Hummin had predicted in the Imperial Sector, they were walking at what seemed to be ground level. There were no vehicles either and Seldon pointed this out to Hummin.

Hummin said, "There are quite a number of them in the Imperial Sector because they're used by officials. Elsewhere, private vehicles are rare and those that are used have separate tunnels reserved for them. Their use is not really necessary, since we have Expressways and, for shorter distances, moving corridors. For still shorter distances, we have walkways and we can use our legs."

Seldon heard occasional muted sighs and creaks and saw, some distance off, the endless passing of Expressway cars.

"There it is," he said, pointing.

"I know, but let us move on to a boarding station. There are more cars there and it is easier to get on."

Once they were safely ensconced in an Expressway car, Seldon turned to Hummin and said, "What amazes me is how quiet the Expressways are. I realize that they are mass-propelled by an electromagnetic field, but it seems quiet even for that." He listened to the occasional metallic groan as the car they were on shifted against its neighbors.

"Yes, it's a marvelous network," said Hummin, "but you don't see it at its peak. When I was younger, it was quieter than it is now and there are those who say that there wasn't as much as a whisper fifty years ago— though I suppose we might make allowance for the idealization of nostalgia."

"Why isn't it that way now?"

"Because it isn't maintained properly. I told you about decay."

Seldon frowned. "Surely, people don't sit around and say, 'We're decaying. Let's let the Expressways fall apart.'"

"No, they don't. It's not a purposeful thing. Bad spots are patched, decrepit coaches refurbished, magnets replaced. However, it's done in more slapdash fashion, more carelessly, and at greater intervals. There just aren't enough credits available."

"Where have the credits gone?"

"Into other things. We've had centuries of unrest. The navy is much larger and many times more expensive than it once was. The armed forces are much better-paid, in order to keep them quiet. Unrest, revolts, and minor blazes of civil war all take their toll."

"But it's been quiet under Cleon. And we've had fifty years of peace."

"Yes, but soldiers who are well-paid would resent having that pay reduced just because there is peace. Admirals resist mothballing ships and having themselves reduced in rank simply because there is less for them to do. So the credits still go—unproductively—to the armed forces and vital areas of the social good are allowed to deteriorate. That's what I call decay. Don't you? Don't you think that eventually you would fit that sort of view into your psychohistorical notions?"

Seldon stirred uneasily. Then he said, "Where are we going, by the way?"

"Streeling University."

"Ah, that's why the sector's name was familiar. I've heard of the University."

"I'm not surprised. Trantor has nearly a hundred thousand institutions of higher learning and Streeling is one of the thousand or so at the top of the heap."

"Will I be staying there?"

"For a while. University campuses are unbreachable sanctuaries, by and large. You will be safe there."

"But will I be welcome there?"

"Why not? It's hard to find a good mathematician these days. They might be able to use you. And you might be able to use them too—and for more than just a hiding place."

"You mean, it will be a place where I can develop my notions."

"You have promised," said Hummin gravely.

"I have promised to *try,*" said Seldon and thought to himself that it was about like promising to try to make a rope out of sand.

15.

Conversation had run out after that and Seldon watched the structures of the Streeling Sector as they passed. Some were quite low, while some seemed to brush the "sky." Wide crosspassages broke the progression and frequent alleys could be seen.

At one point, it struck him that though the buildings rose upward they also swept downward and that perhaps they were deeper than they were high. As soon as the thought occurred to him, he was convinced it was true.

Occasionally, he saw patches of green in the background, farther back from the Expressway, and even small trees.

He watched for quite a while and then became aware that the light was growing dimmer. He squinted about and turned to Hummin, who guessed the question.

"The afternoon is waning," he said, "and night is coming on."

Seldon's eyebrows raised and the corners of his mouth turned downward. "That's impressive. I have a picture of the entire planet darkening and then, some hours from now, lighting up again."

Hummin smiled his small, careful smile. "Not quite, Seldon. The planet is never turned off altogether—or turned on either. The shadow of twilight sweeps across the planet gradually, followed half a day later by the slow brightening of dawn. In fact, the effect follows the actual day and night above the domes quite closely, so that in higher altitudes day and night change length with the seasons."

Seldon shook his head, "But why close in the planet and then mimic what would be in the open?"

"I presume because people like it better that way. Trantorians like the advantages of being enclosed, but they don't like to be reminded of it unduly, just the same. You know very little about Trantorian psychology, Seldon."

Seldon flushed slightly. He was only a Heliconian and he knew very little about the millions of worlds outside Helicon. His ignorance was not confined to Trantor. How, then, could he hope to come up with any practical applications for his theory of psychohistory?

How could any number of people—all together—know enough?

It reminded Seldon of a puzzle that had been presented to him when he was young: Can you have a relatively small piece of platinum, with handholds affixed, that could not be lifted by the bare, unaided strength of any number of people, no matter how many?

The answer was yes. A cubic meter of platinum weighs 22,420 kilograms under standard gravitational pull. If it is assumed that each person could heave 120 kilograms up from the ground, then 188 people would suffice to lift the platinum. —But you could not squeeze 188 people around the cubic meter so that each one could get a grip on it. You could perhaps not squeeze more than 9 people around it. And levers or other such devices were not allowed. It had to be "bare, unaided strength."

In the same way, it could be that there was no way of getting enough people to handle the total amount of knowledge required for psychohistory, even if the facts were stored in computers rather than in individual human brains. Only so many people could gather round the knowledge, so to speak, and communicate it.

Hummin said, "You seem to be in a brown study, Seldon."

"I'm considering my own ignorance."

"A useful task. Quadrillions could profitably join you. —But it's time to get off."

Seldon looked up. "How can you tell?"

"Just as you could tell when you were on the Expressway your first day on Trantor. I go by the signs."

Seldon caught one just as it went by: STREELING UNIVERSITY—3 MINUTES.

"We get off at the next boarding station. Watch your step."

Seldon followed Hummin off the coach, noting that the sky was deep purple now and that the walkways and corridors and buildings were all lighting up, suffused with a yellow glow.

It might have been the gathering of a Heliconian night. Had he been placed here blindfolded and had the blindfold been removed, he might have been convinced that he was in some particularly well-built-up inner region of one of Helicon's larger cities.

"How long do you suppose I will remain at Streeling University, Hummin?" he asked.

Hummin said in his usual calm fashion, "That would be hard to say, Seldon. Perhaps your whole life."

"What!"

"Perhaps not. But your life stopped being your own once you gave that paper on psychohistory. The Emperor and Demerzel recognized your importance at once. So did I. For all I know, so did many others. You see, that means you don't belong to yourself anymore."

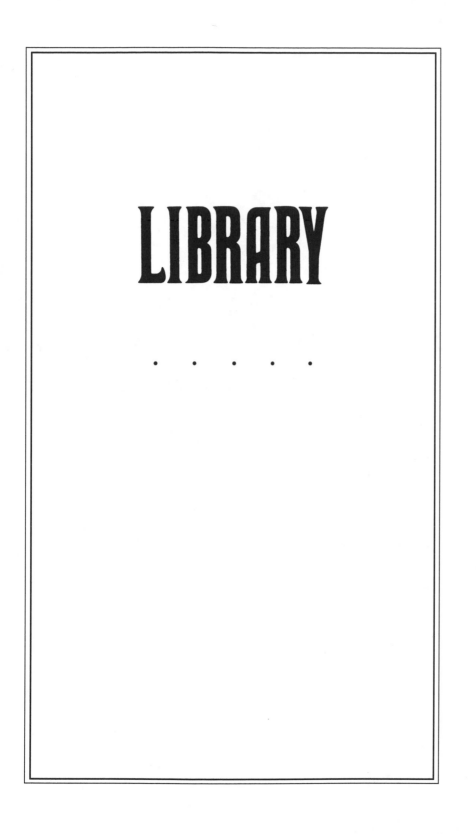

LIBRARY

. . . . .

VENABILI, DORS— . . . Historian, born in Cinna
. . . Her life might well have continued on its uneventful
course were it not for the fact that, after she had spent two
years on the faculty of Streeling University, she became
involved with the young Hari Seldon during The
Flight . . .

ENCYCLOPEDIA GALACTICA

16.

The room that Hari Seldon found himself in was larger than Hummin's
room in the Imperial Sector. It was a bedroom with one corner serving as
a washroom and with no sign of any cooking or dining facilities. There
was no window, though set in the ceiling was a grilled ventilator that
made a steady sighing noise.

Seldon looked about a bit ruefully.

Hummin interpreted that look with his usual assured manner and said,
"It's only for tonight, Seldon. Tomorrow morning someone will come to
install you at the University and you will be more comfortable."

"Pardon me, Hummin, but how do you know that?"

"I will make arrangements. I know one or two people here"—he
smiled briefly without humor—"and I have a favor or two I can ask
repayment for. Now let's go into some details."

He gazed steadily at Seldon and said, "Whatever you have left in your
hotel room is lost. Does that include anything irreplaceable?"

"Nothing really irreplaceable. I have some personal items I value for
their association with my past life, but if they are gone, they are gone.
There are, of course, some notes on my paper. Some calculations. The
paper itself."

"Which is now public knowledge until such time as it is removed from
circulation as dangerous—which it probably will be. Still, I'll be able to

6 5

get my hands on a copy, I'm sure. In any case, you can reconstruct it, can't you?"

"I can. That's why I said there was nothing really irreplaceable. Also, I've lost nearly a thousand credits, some books, clothing, my tickets back to Helicon, things like that."

"All replaceable. —Now I will arrange for you to have a credit tile in my name, charged to me. That will take care of ordinary expenses."

"That's unusually generous of you. I can't accept it."

"It's not generous at all, since I'm hoping to save the Empire in that fashion. You *must* accept it."

"But how much can you afford, Hummin? I'll be using it, at best, with an uneasy conscience."

"Whatever you need for survival or reasonable comfort I can afford, Seldon. Naturally, I wouldn't want you to try to buy the University gymnasium or hand out a million credits in largess."

"You needn't worry, but with my name on record—"

"It might as well be. It is absolutely forbidden for the Imperial government to exercise any security control over the University or its members. There is complete freedom. Anything can be discussed here, anything can be said here."

"What about violent crime?"

"Then the University authorities themselves handle it, with reason and care—and there are virtually no crimes of violence. The students and faculty appreciate their freedom and understand its terms. Too much rowdiness, the beginning of riot and bloodshed, and the government may feel it has a right to break the unwritten agreement and send in the troops. No one wants that, not even the government, so a delicate balance is maintained. In other words, Demerzel himself can not have you plucked out of the University without a great deal more cause than anyone in the University has given the government in at least a century and a half. On the other hand, if you are lured off the grounds by a student-agent—"

"Are there student-agents?"

"How can I say? There may be. Any ordinary individual can be threatened or maneuvered or simply bought—and may remain thereafter in the service of Demerzel or of someone else, for that matter. So I must emphasize this: You are safe in any reasonable sense, but *no one* is absolutely safe. You will have to be careful. But though I give you that warning, I don't want you to cower through life. On the whole, you will be far more secure here than you would have been if you had returned to Helicon or gone to any world of the Galaxy outside Trantor."

"I hope so," said Seldon drearily.

"I know so," said Hummin, "Or I would not feel it wise to leave you."

"Leave me?" Seldon looked up sharply. "You can't do that. You know this world. I don't."

"You will be with others who know this world, who know this part of it, in fact, even better than I do. As for myself, I must go. I have been with you all this day and I dare not abandon my own life any longer. I must not attract too much attention to myself. Remember that I have my own insecurities, just as you have yours."

Seldon blushed. "You're right. I can't expect you to endanger yourself indefinitely on my behalf. I hope you are not already ruined."

Hummin said coolly, "Who can tell? We live in dangerous times. Just remember that if anyone can make the times safe—if not for ourselves, then for those who follow after us—it is you. Let that thought be your driving force, Seldon."

17.

Sleep eluded Seldon. He tossed and turned in the dark, thinking. He had have never felt quite so alone or quite so helpless as he did after Hummin had nodded, pressed his hand briefly, and left him behind. Now he was on a strange world—and in a strange part of that world. He was without the only person he could consider a friend (and that of less than a day's duration) and he had no idea of where he was going or what he would be doing, either tomorrow or at any time in the future.

None of that was conducive to sleep so, of course, at about the time he decided, hopelessly, that he would not sleep that night or, possibly, ever again, exhaustion overtook him . . .

When he woke up it was still dark—or not quite, for across the room he saw a red light flashing brightly and rapidly, accompanied by a harsh, intermittent buzz. Undoubtedly, it was that which had awakened him.

As he tried to remember where he was and to make some sort of sense out of the limited messages his senses were receiving, the flashing and buzzing ceased and he became aware of a peremptory rapping.

Presumably, the rapping was at the door, but he didn't remember where the door was. Presumably, also, there was a contact that would flood the room with light, but he didn't remember where that was either.

He sat up in bed and felt along the wall to his left rather desperately while calling out, "One moment, please."

He found the necessary contact and the room suddenly bloomed with a soft light.

He scrambled out of bed, blinking, still searching for the door, finding it, reaching out to open it, remembering caution at the last moment, and saying in a suddenly stern, no-nonsense voice, "Who's there?"

A rather gentle woman's voice said, "My name is Dors Venabili and I have come to see Dr. Hari Seldon."

Even as that was said, a woman was standing just in front of the door, without that door ever having been opened.

For a moment, Hari Seldon stared at her in surprise, then realized that he was wearing only a one-piece undergarment. He let out a strangled gasp and dashed for the bed and only then realized that he was staring at a holograph. It lacked the hard edge of reality and it became apparent the woman wasn't looking at him. She was merely showing herself for identification.

He paused, breathing hard, then said, raising his voice to be heard through the door, "If you'll wait, I'll be with you. Give me . . . maybe half an hour."

The woman—or the holograph, at any rate—said, "I'll wait," and disappeared.

There was no shower, so he sponged himself, making a rare mess on the tiled floor in the washroom corner. There was toothpaste but no toothbrush, so he used his finger. He had no choice but to put on the clothes he had been wearing the day before. He finally opened the door.

He realized, even as he did so, that she had not really identified herself. She had merely given a name and Hummin had not told him whom to expect, whether it was to be this Dors Somebody or anyone else. He had felt secure because the holograph was that of a personable young woman, but for all he knew there might be half a dozen hostile young men with her.

He peered out cautiously, saw only the woman, then opened the door sufficiently to allow her to enter. He immediately closed and locked the door behind her.

"Pardon me," he said, "What time is it?"

"Nine," she said, "The day has long since begun."

As far as official time was concerned, Trantor held to Galactic Standard, since only so could sense be made out of interstellar commerce and governmental dealings. Each world, however, also had a local time system and Seldon had not yet come to the point where he felt at home with casual Trantorian references to the hour.

"Midmorning?" he said.

"Of course."

"There are no windows in this room," he said defensively.

Dors walked to his bed, reached out, and touched a small dark spot on the wall. Red numbers appeared on the ceiling just over his pillow. They read: 0903.

She smiled without superiority. "I'm sorry," she said. "But I rather assumed Chetter Hummin would have told you I'd be coming for you at nine. The trouble with him is he's so used to *knowing,* he sometimes forgets that others occasionally *don't* know. —And I shouldn't have used radio-holographic identification. I imagine you don't have it on Helicon and I'm afraid I must have alarmed you."

Seldon felt himself relax. She seemed natural and friendly and the casual reference to Hummin reassured him. He said, "You're quite wrong about Helicon, Miss—"

"Please call me Dors."

"You're still wrong about Helicon, Dors. We *do* have radio-holography, but I've never been able to afford the equipment. Nor could anyone in my circle, so I haven't actually had the experience. But I understood what had happened soon enough."

He studied her. She was not very tall, average height for a woman, he judged. Her hair was a reddish-gold, though not very bright, and was arranged in short curls about her head. (He had seen a number of women in Trantor with their hair so arranged. It was apparently a local fashion that would have been laughed at in Helicon.) She was not amazingly beautiful, but was quite pleasant to look at, this being helped by full lips that seemed to have a slight humorous curl to them. She was slim, well-built, and looked quite young. (Too young, he thought uneasily, to be of use perhaps.)

"Do I pass inspection?" she asked. (She seemed to have Hummin's trick of guessing his thoughts, Seldon thought, or perhaps he himself lacked the trick of hiding them.)

He said, "I'm sorry. I seem to have been staring, but I've only been trying to evaluate you. I'm in a strange place. I know no one and have no friends."

"Please, Dr. Seldon, count me as a friend. Mr. Hummin has asked me to take care of you."

Seldon smiled ruefully. "You may be a little young for the job."

"You'll find I am not."

"Well, I'll try to be as little trouble as possible. Could you please repeat your name?"

"Dors Venabili." She spelled the last name and emphasized the stress on the second syllable. "As I said, please call me Dors and if you don't object too strenuously I will call you Hari. We're quite informal here at the University and there is an almost self-conscious effort to show no signs of status, either inherited or professional."

"Please, by all means, call me Hari."

"Good. I shall remain informal then. For instance, the instinct for formality, if there is such a thing, would cause me to ask permission to sit down. Informally, however, I shall just sit." She then sat down on the one chair in the room.

Seldon cleared his throat. "Clearly, I'm not at all in possession of my ordinary faculties. I should have asked you to sit." He sat down on the side of his crumpled bed and wished he had thought to straighten it out somewhat—but he had been caught by surprise.

She said pleasantly, "This is how it's going to work, Hari. First, we'll go to breakfast at one of the University cafés. Then I'll get you a room in one of the domiciles—a better room than this. You'll have a window. Hummin has instructed me to get you a credit tile in his name, but it will take me a day or two to extort one out of the University bureaucracy. Until that's done, I'll be responsible for your expenses and you can pay me back later. —And we can use you. Chetter Hummin told me you're a mathematician and for some reason there's a serious lack of good ones at the University."

"Did Hummin tell you that I was a good mathematician?"

"As a matter of fact, he did. He said you were a remarkable man."

"Well." Seldon looked down at his fingernails. "I would like to be considered so, but Hummin knew me for less than a day and, before that, he had heard me present a paper, the quality of which he has no way of judging. I think he was just being polite."

"I don't think so," said Dors. "He is a remarkable person himself and has had a great deal of experience with people. I'll go by his judgment. In any case, I imagine you'll have a chance to prove yourself. You can program computers, I suppose."

"Of course."

"I'm talking about teaching computers, you understand, and I'm asking if you can devise programs to teach various phases of contemporary mathematics."

"Yes, that's part of my profession. I'm assistant professor of mathematics at the University of Helicon."

She said, "Yes, I know. Hummin told me that. It means, of course, that everyone will know you are a non-Trantorian, but that will present no serious problems. We're mainly Trantorian here at the University, but there's a substantial minority of Outworlders from any number of different worlds and that's accepted. I won't say that you'll never hear a planetary slur but actually the Outworlders are more likely to use them than the Trantorians. I'm an Outworlder myself, by the way."

"Oh?" He hesitated and then decided it would be only polite to ask. "What world are you from?"

"I'm from Cinna. Have you ever heard of it?"

He'd be caught out if he was polite enough to lie, Seldon decided, so he said, "No."

"I'm not surprised. It's probably of even less account than Helicon is. —Anyway, to get back to the programming of mathematical teaching computers, I suppose that that can be done either proficiently or poorly."

"Absolutely."

"And you would do it proficiently."

"I would like to think so."

"There you are, then. The University will pay you for that, so let's go out and eat. Did you sleep well, by the way?"

"Surprisingly, I did."

"And are you hungry?"

"Yes, but—" He hesitated.

She said cheerfully, "But you're worried about the quality of the food, is that it? Well, don't be. Being an Outworlder myself, I can understand your feelings about the strong infusion of microfood into everything, but the University menus aren't bad. In the faculty dining room, at least. The students suffer a bit, but that serves to harden them."

She rose and turned to the door, but stopped when Seldon could not keep himself from saying, "Are you a member of the faculty?"

She turned and smiled at him impishly. "Don't I look old enough? I got my doctorate two years ago at Cinna and I've been here ever since. In two weeks, I'll be thirty."

"Sorry," said Seldon, smiling in his turn, "but you can't expect to look twenty-four and not raise doubts as to your academic status."

"Aren't you nice?" said Dors and Seldon felt a certain pleasure wash over him. After all, he thought, you can't exchange pleasantries with an attractive woman and feel entirely like a stranger.

18.

Dors was right. Breakfast was by no means bad. There was something that was unmistakably eggy and the meat was pleasantly smoked. The chocolate drink (Trantor was strong on chocolate and Seldon did not mind that) was probably synthetic, but it was tasty and the breakfast rolls were good.

He felt it only right to say as much. "This has been a very pleasant breakfast. Food. Surroundings. Everything."

"I'm delighted you think so," said Dors.

Seldon looked about. There were a bank of windows in one wall and while actual sunlight did not enter (he wondered if, after a while, he would learn to be satisfied with diffuse daylight and would cease to look for patches of sunlight in a room), the place was light enough. In fact, it was quite bright, for the local weather computer had apparently decided it was time for a sharp, clear day.

The tables were arranged for four apiece and most were occupied by the full number, but Dors and Seldon remained alone at theirs. Dors had called over some of the men and women and had introduced them. All had been polite, but none had joined them. Undoubtedly, Dors intended that to be so, but Seldon did not see how she managed to arrange it.

He said, "You haven't introduced me to any mathematicians, Dors."

"I haven't seen any that I know. Most mathematicians start the day early and have classes by eight. My own feeling is that any student so foolhardy as to take mathematics wants to get that part of the course over with as soon as possible."

"I take it you're not a mathematician yourself."

"Anything but," said Dors with a short laugh. *"Anything.* History is my field. I've already published some studies on the rise of Trantor—I mean the primitive kingdom, not this world. I suppose that will end up as my field of specialization—Royal Trantor."

"Wonderful," said Seldon.

"Wonderful?" Dors looked at him quizzically. "Are you interested in Royal Trantor too?"

"In a way, yes. That and other things like that. I've never really studied history and I should have."

"Should you? If you had studied history, you'd scarcely have had time to study mathematics and mathematicians are very much needed—especially at this University. We're full to here with historians," she said, raising her hand to her eyebrows, "and economists and political scientists, but we're short on science and mathematics. Chetter Hummin pointed that out to me once. He called it the decline of science and seemed to think it was a general phenomenon."

Seldon said, "Of course, when I say I should have studied history, I don't mean that I should have made it a life work. I meant I should have studied enough to help me in my mathematics. My field of specialization is the mathematical analysis of social structure."

"Sounds horrible."

"In a way, it is. It's very complicated and without my knowing a great deal more about how societies evolved it's hopeless. My picture is too static, you see."

"I can't see because I know nothing about it. Chetter told me you were developing something called psychohistory and that it was important. Have I got it right? Psychohistory?"

"That's right. I should have called it 'psychsociology,' but it seemed to me that was too ugly a word. Or perhaps I knew instinctively that a knowledge of history was necessary and then didn't pay sufficient attention to my thoughts."

"Psychohistory does sound better, but I don't know what it is."

"I scarcely do myself." He brooded a few minutes, looking at the woman on the other side of the table and feeling that she might make this exile of his seem a little less like an exile. He thought of the other woman he had known a few years ago, but blocked it off with a determined effort. If he ever found another companion, it would have to be one who understood scholarship and what it demanded of a person.

To get his mind onto a new track, he said, "Chetter Hummin told me that the University is in no way troubled by the government."

"He's right."

Seldon shook his head. "That seems rather unbelievably forbearing of the Imperial government. The educational institutions on Helicon are by no means so independent of governmental pressures."

"Nor on Cinna. Nor on any Outworld, except perhaps for one or two of the largest. Trantor is another matter."

"Yes, but why?"

"Because it's the center of the Empire. The universities here have enormous prestige. Professionals are turned out by any university anywhere, but the administrators of the Empire—the high officials, the countless millions of people who represent the tentacles of Empire reaching into every corner of the Galaxy—are educated right here on Trantor."

"I've never seen the statistics—" began Seldon.

"Take my word for it. It is important that the officials of the Empire have some common ground, some special feeling for the Empire. And they can't all be native Trantorians or else the Outworlds would grow restless. For that reason, Trantor must attract millions of Outworlders for education here. It doesn't matter where they come from or what their home accent or culture may be, as long as they pick up the Trantorian patina and identify themselves with a Trantorian educational background. That's what holds the Empire together. The Outworlds are also less restive when a noticeable portion of the administrators who represent the Imperial government are their own people by birth and upbringing."

Seldon felt embarrassed again. This was something he had never given any thought to. He wondered if anyone could be a truly great mathematician if mathematics was all he knew. He said, "Is this common knowledge?"

"I suppose it isn't," said Dors after some thought. "There's so *much* knowledge to be had that specialists cling to their specialties as a shield against having to know anything about anything else. They avoid being drowned."

"Yet *you* know it."

"But that's my specialty. I'm a historian who deals with the rise of Royal Trantor and this administrative technique was one of the ways in which Trantor spread its influence and managed the transition from Royal Trantor to Imperial Trantor."

Seldon said, almost as though muttering to himself, "How harmful overspecialization is. It cuts knowledge at a million points and leaves it bleeding."

Dors shrugged. "What can one do? —But you see, if Trantor is going to attract Outworlders to Trantorian universities, it has to give them something in return for uprooting themselves and going to a strange world with an incredibly artificial structure and unusual ways. I've been here two years and I'm still not used to it. I may never get used to it. But then, of course, I don't intend to be an administrator, so I'm not forcing myself to be a Trantorian.

"And what Trantor offers in exchange is not only the promise of a position with high status, considerable power, and money, of course, but also freedom. While students are having their education, they are free to denounce the government, demonstrate against it peacefully, work out their own theories and points of view. They enjoy that and many come here so that they can experience the sensation of liberty."

"I imagine," said Seldon, "that it helps relieve pressure as well. They work off all their resentments, enjoy all the smug self-satisfaction a young revolutionary would have, and by the time they take their place in the Imperial hierarchy, they are ready to settle down into conformity and obedience."

Dors nodded. "You may be right. In any case, the government, for all these reasons, carefully preserves the freedom of the universities. It's not a matter of their being forbearing at all—only clever."

"And if you're not going to be an administrator, Dors, what *are* you going to be?"

"A historian. I'll teach, put book-films of my own into the programming."

"Not much status, perhaps."

"Not much money, Hari, which is more important. As for status, that's the sort of push and pull I'd just as soon avoid. I've seen many people with status, but I'm still looking for a happy one. Status won't sit still under you; you have to continually fight to keep from sinking. Even

Emperors manage to come to bad ends most of the time. Someday I may just go back to Cinna and be a professor."

"And a Trantorian education will give you status."

Dors laughed. "I suppose so, but on Cinna who would care? It's a dull world, full of farms and with lots of cattle, both four-legged and two-legged."

"Won't you find it dull after Trantor?"

"Yes, that's what I'm counting on. And if it gets too dull, I can always wangle a grant to go here or there to do a little historical research. That's the advantage of my field."

"A mathematician, on the other hand," said Seldon with a trace of bitterness at something that had never before bothered him, "is expected to sit at his computer and think. And speaking of computers—" He hesitated. Breakfast was done and it seemed to him more than likely she had some duties of her own to attend to.

But she did not seem to be in any great hurry to leave. "Yes? Speaking of computers?"

"Would I be able to get permission to use the history library?"

Now it was she who hesitated. "I think that can be arranged. If you work on mathematics programming, you'll probably be viewed as a quasi-member of the faculty and I could ask for you to be given permission. Only—"

"Only?"

"I don't want to hurt your feelings, but you're a mathematician and you say you know nothing about history. Would you know how to make use of a history library?"

Seldon smiled. "I suppose you use computers very much like those in a mathematics library."

"We do, but the programming for each specialty has quirks of its own. You don't know the standard reference book-films, the quick methods of winnowing and skipping. You may be able to find a hyperbolic interval in the dark . . ."

"You mean hyperbolic integral," interrupted Seldon softly.

Dors ignored him. "But you probably won't know how to get the terms of the Treaty of Poldark in less than a day and a half."

"I suppose I could learn."

"If . . . if . . ." She looked a little troubled. "If you want to, I can make a suggestion. I give a week's course—one hour each day, no credit

—on library use. It's for undergraduates. Would you feel it beneath your dignity to sit in on such a course—with undergraduates, I mean? It starts in three weeks."

"You could give me private lessons." Seldon felt a little surprised at the suggestive tone that had entered his voice.

She did not miss it. "I dare say I could, but I think you'd be better off with more formal instruction. We'll be using the library, you understand, and at the end of the week you will be asked to locate information on particular items of historical interest. You will be competing with the other students all through and that will help you learn. Private tutoring will be far less efficient, I assure you. However, I understand the difficulty of competing with undergraduates. If you don't do as well as they, you may feel humiliated. You must remember, though, that they have already studied elementary history and you, perhaps, may not have."

"I haven't. No 'may' about it. But I won't be afraid to compete and I won't mind any humiliation that may come along—if I manage to learn the tricks of the historical reference trade."

It was clear to Seldon that he was beginning to like this young woman and that he was gladly seizing on the chance to be educated by her. He was also aware of the fact that he had reached a turning point in his mind.

He had promised Hummin to attempt to work out a practical psychohistory, but that had been a promise of the mind and not the emotions. Now he was determined to seize psychohistory by the throat—if he had to—in order to make it practical. That, perhaps, was the influence of Dors Venabili.

Or had Hummin counted on that? Hummin, Seldon decided, might well be a most formidable person.

19.

Cleon I had finished dinner, which, unfortunately, had been a formal state affair. It meant he had to spend time talking to various officials—not one of whom he knew or recognized—in set phrases designed to give each one his stroke and so activate his loyalty to the crown. It also meant that his food reached him but lukewarm and had cooled still further before he could eat it.

There had to be some way of avoiding that. Eat first, perhaps, on his own or with one or two close intimates with whom he could relax and then attend a formal dinner at which he could merely be served an imported pear. He loved pears. But would that offend the guests who would take the Emperor's refusal to eat with them as a studied insult.

His wife, of course, was useless in this respect, for her presence would but further exacerbate his unhappiness. He had married her because she was a member of a powerful dissident family who could be expected to mute their dissidence as a result of the union, though Cleon devoutly hoped that she, at least, would not do so. He was perfectly content to have her live her own life in her own quarters except for the necessary efforts to initiate an heir, for, to tell the truth, he didn't like her. And now that an heir had come, he could ignore her completely.

He chewed at one of a handful of nuts he had pocketed from the table on leaving and said, "Demerzel!"

"Sire?"

Demerzel always appeared at once when Cleon called. Whether he hovered constantly in earshot at the door or he drew close because the instinct of subservience somehow alerted him to a possible call in a few minutes, he *did* appear and that, Cleon thought idly, was the important thing. Of course, there were those times when Demerzel had to be away on Imperial business. Cleon always hated those absences. They made him uneasy.

"What happened to that mathematician? I forget his name."

Demerzel, who surely knew the man the Emperor had in mind, but who perhaps wanted to study how much the Emperor remembered, said, "What mathematician is it that you have in mind, Sire?"

Cleon waved an impatient hand. "The fortune-teller. The one who came to see me."

"The one we sent for?"

"Well, sent for, then. He *did* come to see me. You were going to take care of the matter, as I recall. Have you?"

Demerzel cleared his throat. "Sire, I have tried to."

"Ah! That means you have failed, doesn't it?" In a way, Cleon felt pleased. Demerzel was the only one of his Ministers who made no bones of failure. The others never admitted failure, and since failure was nevertheless common, it became difficult to correct. Perhaps Demerzel could afford to be more honest because he failed so rarely. If it weren't for Demerzel, Cleon thought sadly, he might never know what honesty sounded like. Perhaps no Emperor ever knew and perhaps that was one of the reasons that the Empire—

He pulled his thoughts away and, suddenly nettled at the other's silence and wanting an admission, since he had just admired Demerzel's honesty in his mind, said sharply, "Well, you *have* failed, haven't you?"

Demerzel did not flinch. "Sire, I have failed in part. I felt that to have him here on Trantor where things are—difficult—might present us with problems. It was easy to consider that he might be more conveniently placed on his home planet. He was planning to return to that home planet the next day, but there was always the chance of complications—of his deciding to remain on Trantor—so I arranged to have two young alley men place him on his plane that very day."

"Do you know alley men, Demerzel?" Cleon was amused.

"It is important, Sire, to be able to reach many kinds of people, for each type has its own variety of use—alley men not the least. As it happens, they did not succeed."

"And why was that?"

"Oddly enough, Seldon was able to fight them off."

"The mathematician could fight?"

"Apparently, mathematics and the martial arts are not necessarily mutually exclusive. I found out, not soon enough, that his world, Helicon, is noted for it—martial arts, not mathematics. The fact that I did not learn this earlier was indeed a failure, Sire, and I can only crave your pardon."

"But then, I suppose the mathematician left for his home planet the next day as he had planned."

"Unfortunately, the episode backfired. Taken aback by the event, he decided not to return to Helicon, but remained on Trantor. He may have been advised to this effect by a passerby who happened to be present on the occasion of the fight. That was another unlooked-for complication."

The Emperor Cleon frowned. "Then our mathematician—what *is* his name?"

"Seldon, Sire. Hari Seldon."

"Then this Seldon is out of reach."

"In a sense, Sire. We have traced his movements and he is now at Streeling University. While there, he is untouchable."

The Emperor scowled and reddened slightly. "I am annoyed at that word—'untouchable.' There should be nowhere in the Empire my hand cannot reach. Yet here, on my own world, you tell me someone can be untouchable. Insufferable!''

"Your hand can reach to the University, Sire. You can send in your army and pluck out this Seldon at any moment you desire. To do so, however, is . . . undesirable.''

"Why don't you say 'impractical,' Demerzel. You sound like the mathematician speaking of his fortune-telling. It is possible, but impractical. I am an Emperor who finds everything possible, but very little practical. Remember, Demerzel, if reaching Seldon is not practical, reaching you is entirely so.''

Eto Demerzel let this last comment pass. The "man behind the throne" knew his importance to the Emperor; he had heard such threats before. He waited in silence while the Emperor glowered. Drumming his fingers against the arm of his chair, Cleon asked, "Well then, what good is this mathematician to us if he is at Streeling University?''

"It may perhaps be possible, Sire, to snatch use out of adversity. At the University, he may decide to work on his psychohistory.''

"Even though he insists it's impractical?''

"He may be wrong and he may find out that he is wrong. And if he finds out that he is wrong, we would find some way of getting him out of the University. It is even possible he would join us voluntarily under those circumstances.''

The Emperor remained lost in thought for a while, then said, "And what if someone else plucks him out before we do?''

"Who would want to do that, Sire?'' asked Demerzel softly.

"The Mayor of Wye, for one,'' said Cleon, suddenly shouting. "He dreams still of taking over the Empire.''

"Old age has drawn his fangs, Sire.''

"Don't you believe it, Demerzel.''

"And we have no reason for supposing he has any interest in Seldon or even knows of him, Sire.''

"Come on, Demerzel. If we heard of the paper, so could Wye. If we see the possible importance of Seldon, so could Wye.''

"If that should happen,'' said Demerzel, "or even if there should be a reasonable chance of its happening, then we would be justified in taking strong measures.''

"How strong?''

Demerzel said cautiously, "It might be argued that rather than have

Seldon in Wye's hands, we might prefer to have him in no one's hands. To have him cease to exist, Sire."

"To have him killed, you mean," said Cleon.

"If you wish to put it that way, Sire," said Demerzel.

20.

Hari Seldon sat back in his chair in the alcove that had been assigned to him through Dors Venabili's intervention. He was dissatisfied.

As a matter of fact, although that was the expression he used in his mind, he knew that it was a gross underestimation of his feelings. He was not simply dissatisfied, he was furious—all the more so because he wasn't sure what it was he was furious about. Was it about the histories? The writers and compilers of histories? The worlds and people that made the histories?

Whatever the target of his fury, it didn't really matter. What counted was that his notes were useless, his new knowledge was useless, everything was useless.

He had been at the University now for almost six weeks. He had managed to find a computer outlet at the very start and with it had begun work—without instruction, but using the instincts he had developed over a number of years of mathematical labors. It had been slow and halting, but there was a certain pleasure in gradually determining the routes by which he could get his questions answered.

Then came the week of instruction with Dors, which had taught him several dozen shortcuts and had brought with it two sets of embarrassments. The first set included the sidelong glances he received from the undergraduates, who seemed contemptuously aware of his greater age and who were disposed to frown a bit at Dors's constant use of the honorific "Doctor" in addressing him.

"I don't want them to think," she said, "that you're some backward perpetual student taking remedial history."

"But surely you've established the point. Surely, a mere 'Seldon' is sufficient now."

"No," Dors said and smiled suddenly. "Besides, I like to call you 'Dr. Seldon.' I like the way you look uncomfortable each time."

"You have a peculiar sense of sadistic humor."

"Would you deprive me?"

For some reason, that made him laugh. Surely, the natural reaction would have been to deny sadism. Somehow he found it pleasant that she accepted the ball of conversation and fired it back. The thought led to a natural question. "Do you play tennis here at the University?"

"We have courts, but I don't play."

"Good. I'll teach you. And when I do, I'll call you Professor Venabili."

"That's what you call me in class anyway."

"You'll be surprised how ridiculous it will sound on the tennis court."

"I may get to like it."

"In that case, I will try to find what else you might get to like."

"I see you have a peculiar sense of salacious humor."

She had put that ball in that spot deliberately and he said, "Would you deprive me?"

She smiled and later did surprisingly well on the tennis court. "Are you sure you never played tennis?" he said, puffing, after one session.

"Positive," she said.

The other set of embarrassments was more private. He learned the necessary techniques of historical research and then burned—in private —at his earlier attempts to make use of the computer's memory. It was simply an entirely different mind-set from that used in mathematics. It was equally logical, he supposed, since it could be used, consistently and without error, to move in whatever direction he wanted to, but it was a substantially different brand of logic from that to which he was accustomed.

But with or without instructions, whether he stumbled or moved in swiftly, he simply didn't get any results.

His annoyance made itself felt on the tennis court. Dors quickly reached the stage where it was no longer necessary to lob easy balls at her to give her time to judge direction and distance. That made it easy to forget that she was just a beginner and he expressed his anger in his swing, firing the ball back at her as though it were a laser beam made solid.

She came trotting up to the net and said, "I can understand your wanting to kill me, since it must annoy you to watch me miss the shots so often. How is it, though, that you managed to miss my head by about three centimeters that time? I mean, you didn't even *nick* me. Can't you do better than that?"

Seldon, horrified, tried to explain, but only managed to sound incoherent.

She said, "Look. I'm not going to face any other returns of yours today, so why don't we shower and then get together for some tea and whatever and you can tell me just what you *were* trying to kill. If it wasn't my poor head and if you don't get the real victim off your chest, you'll be entirely too dangerous on the other side of the net for me to want to serve as a target."

Over tea he said, "Dors, I've scanned history after history; just scanned, browsed. I haven't had time for deep study yet. Even so, it's become obvious. All the book-films concentrate on the same few events."

"Crucial ones. History-making ones."

"That's just an excuse. They're copying each other. There are twenty-five million worlds out there and there's significant mention of perhaps twenty-five."

Dors said, "You're reading general Galactic histories only. Look up the special histories of some of the minor worlds. On every world, however small, the children are taught local histories before they ever find out there's a great big Galaxy outside. Don't you yourself know more about Helicon, right now, than you know about the rise of Trantor or of the Great Interstellar War?"

"That sort of knowledge is limited too," said Seldon gloomily. "I know Heliconian geography and the stories of its settlement and of the malfeasance and misfeasance of the planet Jennisek—that's our traditional enemy, though our teachers carefully told us that we ought to say 'traditional rival.' But I never learned anything about the contributions of Helicon to general Galactic history."

"Maybe there weren't any."

"Don't be silly. Of course there were. There may not have been great, huge space battles involving Helicon or crucial rebellions or peace treaties. There may not have been some Imperial competitor making his base on Helicon. But there *must* have been subtle influences. Surely, nothing can happen anywhere without affecting everywhere else. Yet there's nothing I can find to help me. —See here, Dors. In mathematics, *all* can be found in the computer; everything we know or have found out in twenty thousand years. In history, that's not so. Historians pick and choose and every one of them picks and chooses the same thing.''

"But, Hari," said Dors, "mathematics is an orderly thing of human invention. One thing follows from another. There are definitions and axioms, all of which are known. It is . . . it is . . . all one piece. History is different. It is the unconscious working out of the deeds and thoughts of quadrillions of human beings. Historians *must* pick and choose.''

"Exactly," said Seldon, "but I must know all of history if I am to work out the laws of psychohistory.''

"In that case, you won't ever formulate the laws of psychohistory.''

That was yesterday. Now Seldon sat in his chair in his alcove, having spent another day of utter failure, and he could hear Dors's voice saying, "In that case, you won't ever formulate the laws of psychohistory.''

It was what he had thought to begin with and if it hadn't been for Hummin's conviction to the contrary and his odd ability to fire Seldon with his own blaze of conviction, Seldon would have continued to think so.

And yet neither could he quite let go. Might there not be some way out?

He couldn't think of any.

UPPERSIDE

. . . . .

TRANTOR— . . . It is almost never pictured as a world seen from space. It has long since captured the general mind of humanity as a world of the interior and the image is that of the human hive that existed under the domes. Yet there was an exterior as well and there are holographs that still remain that were taken from space and show varying degrees of detail (see Figures 14 and 15). Note that the surface of the domes, the interface of the vast city and the overlying atmosphere, a surface referred to in its time as "Upperside," is . . .

ENCYCLOPEDIA GALACTICA

21.

Yet the following day found Hari Seldon back in the library. For one thing, there was his promise to Hummin. He had promised to try and he couldn't very well make it a halfhearted process. For another, he owed something to himself too. He resented having to admit failure. Not yet, at least. Not while he could plausibly tell himself he was following up leads.

So he stared at the list of reference book-films he had not yet checked through and tried to decide which of the unappetizing number had the slightest chance of being useful to him. He had about decided that the answer was "none of the above" and saw no way out but to look at samples of each when he was startled by a gentle tap against the alcove wall.

Seldon looked up and found the embarrassed face of Lisung Randa peering at him around the edge of the alcove opening. Seldon knew Randa, had been introduced to him by Dors, and had dined with him (and with others) on several occasions.

Randa, an instructor in psychology, was a little man, short and plump, with a round cheerful face and an almost perpetual smile. He had a sallow complexion and the narrowed eyes so characteristic of people on millions of worlds. Seldon knew that appearance well, for there were many of the great mathematicians who had borne it, and he had frequently seen their holograms. Yet on Helicon he had never seen one of these Easterners. (By tradition they were called that, though no one knew why; and the Easterners themselves were said to resent the term to some degree, but again no one knew why.)

"There's millions of us here on Trantor," Randa had said, smiling with no trace of self-consciousness, when Seldon, on first meeting him, had not been able to repress all trace of startled surprise. "You'll also find lot of Southerners—dark skins, tightly curled hair. Did you ever see one?"

"Not on Helicon," muttered Seldon.

"All Westerners on Helicon, eh? How dull! But it doesn't matter. Takes all kinds." (He left Seldon wondering at the fact that there were Easterners, Southerners, and Westerners, but no Northerners. He had tried finding an answer to why that might be in his reference searches and had not succeeded.)

And now Randa's good-natured face was looking at him with an almost ludicrous look of concern. He said, "Are you all right, Seldon?"

Seldon stared. "Yes, of course. Why shouldn't I be?"

"I'm just going by sounds, my friend. You were screaming."

"Screaming?" Seldon looked at him with offended disbelief.

"Not loud. Like this." Randa gritted his teeth and emitted a strangled high-pitched sound from the back of his throat. "If I'm wrong, I apologize for this unwarranted intrusion on you. Please forgive me."

Seldon hung his head. "You're forgiven, Lisung. I *do* make that sound sometimes, I'm told. I assure you it's unconscious. I'm never aware of it."

"Are you aware *why* you make it?"

"Yes. Frustration. *Frustration.*"

Randa beckoned Seldon closer and lowered his voice further. "We're disturbing people. Let's come out to the lounge before we're thrown out."

In the lounge, over a pair of mild drinks, Randa said, "May I ask you, as a matter of professional interest, *why* you are feeling frustration?"

Seldon shrugged. "Why does one usually feel frustration? I'm tackling something in which I am making no progress."

"But you're a mathematician, Hari. Why should anything in the history library frustrate you?"

"What were *you* doing here?"

"Passing through as part of a shortcut to where I was going when I heard you . . . moaning. Now you see"—and he smiled—"it's no longer a shortcut, but a serious delay—one that I welcome, however."

"I wish I were just passing through the history library, but I'm trying to solve a mathematical problem that requires some knowledge of history and I'm afraid I'm not handling it well."

Randa stared at Seldon with an unusually solemn expression on his face, then he said, "Pardon me, but I must run the risk of offending you now. I've been computing you."

"Computing *me!*" Seldon's eyes widened. He felt distinctly angry.

"I *have* offended you. But, you know, I had an uncle who was a mathematician. You might even have heard of him: Kiangtow Randa."

Seldon drew in his breath. "Are you a relative of *that* Randa?"

"Yes. He is my father's older brother and he was quite displeased with me for not following in his footsteps—he has no children of his own. I thought somehow that it might please him that I had met a mathematician and I wanted to boast of you—if I could—so I checked what information the mathematics library might have."

"I see. And that's what you were really doing there. Well—I'm sorry. I don't suppose you could do much boasting."

"You suppose wrong. I was impressed. I couldn't make heads or tails of the subject matter of your papers, but somehow the information seemed to be very favorable. And when I checked the news files, I found you were at the Decennial Convention earlier this year. So . . . what's 'psychohistory,' anyway? Obviously, the first two syllables stir my curiosity."

"I see you got that word out of it."

"Unless I'm totally misled, it seemed to me that you can work out the future course of history."

Seldon nodded wearily, "That, more or less, is what psychohistory is or, rather, what it is intended to be."

"But is it a serious study?" Randa was smiling. "You don't just throw sticks?"

"Throw sticks?"

"That's just a reference to a game played by children on my home planet of Hopara. The game is supposed to tell the future and if you're a smart kid, you can make a good thing out of it. Tell a mother that her child will grow up beautiful and marry a rich man and it's good for a piece of cake or a half-credit piece on the spot. She isn't going to wait and see if it comes true; you are rewarded just for saying it."

"I see. No, I don't throw sticks. Psychohistory is just an abstract study. Strictly abstract. It has no practical application at all, except—"

"Now we're getting to it. Exceptions are what are interesting."

"Except that I would like to work out such an application. Perhaps if I knew more about history—"

"Ah, that is why you are reading history?"

"Yes, but it does me no good," said Seldon sadly. "There is too much history and there is too little of it that is told."

"And that's what's frustrating you?"

Seldon nodded.

Randa said, "But, Hari, you've only been here a matter of weeks."

"True, but already I can see—"

"You can't see anything in a few weeks. You may have to spend your whole lifetime making one little advance. It may take many generations of work by many mathematicians to make a real inroad on the problem."

"I know that, Lisung, but that doesn't make me feel better. I want to make some visible progress myself."

"Well, driving yourself to distraction won't help either. If it will make you feel better, I can give you an example of a subject much less complex than human history that people have been working for I don't know how long without making much progress. I know because a group is working on it right here at the University and one of my good friends is involved. Talk about frustration! You don't know what frustration is!"

"What's the subject?" Seldon felt a small curiosity stirring within him.

"Meteorology."

"Meteorology!" Seldon felt revolted at the anticlimax.

"Don't make faces. Look. Every inhabited world has an atmosphere. Every world has its own atmospheric composition, its own temperature range, its own rotation and revolution rate, its own axial tipping, it's own land-water distribution. We've got twenty-five million different problems and no one has succeeded in finding a generalization."

"That's because atmospheric behavior easily enters a chaotic phase. Everyone knows that."

"So my friend Jenarr Leggen says. You've met him."

Seldon considered. "Tall fellow? Long nose? Doesn't speak much?"

"That's the one. —And Trantor itself is a bigger puzzle than almost any world. According to the records, it had a fairly normal weather pattern when it was first settled. Then, as the population grew and urbanization spread, more energy was used and more heat was discharged into the atmosphere. The ice cover contracted, the cloud layer thickened, and the weather got lousier. That encouraged the movement underground and set off a vicious cycle. The worse the weather got, the more eagerly the land was dug into and the domes built and the weather got still worse. Now the planet has become a world of almost incessant cloudiness and frequent rains—or snows when it's cold enough. The only thing is that no one can work it out properly. No one has worked out an analysis that can explain why the weather has deteriorated quite as it has or how one can reasonably predict the details of its day-to-day changes."

Seldon shrugged. "Is that sort of thing important?"

"To a meteorologist it is. Why can't they be as frustrated over their problems as you are over yours? Don't be a project chauvinist."

Seldon remembered the cloudiness and the dank chill on the way to the Emperor's Palace.

He said, "So what's being done about it?"

"Well, there's a big project on the matter here at the University and Jenarr Leggen is part of it. They feel that if they can understand the weather change on Trantor, they will learn a great deal about the basic laws of general meteorology. Leggen wants that as much as you want your laws of psychohistory. So he has set up an incredible array of instruments of all kinds Upperside . . . you know, above the domes. It hasn't helped them so far. And if there's so much work being done for many generations on the atmosphere, without results, how can you complain that you haven't gotten anything out of human history in a few weeks?"

Randa was right, Seldon thought, and he himself was being unreasonable and wrong. And yet . . . and yet . . . Hummin would say that this failure in the scientific attack on problems was another sign of the degeneration of the times. Perhaps he was right, also, except that he was speaking of a general degeneration and *average* effect. Seldon felt no degeneration of ability and mentality in himself.

He said with some interest then, "You mean that people climb up out of the domes and into the open air above?"

"Yes. Upperside. It's a funny thing, though. Most native Trantorians won't do it. They don't like to go Upperside. The idea gives them vertigo or something. Most of those working on the meteorology project are Outworlders."

Seldon looked out of the window and the lawns and small garden of the University campus, brilliantly lit without shadows or oppressive heat, and said thoughtfully, "I don't know that I can blame Trantorians for liking the comfort of being within, but I should think curiosity would drive *some* Upperside. It would drive me."

"Do you mean that you would like to see meteorology in action?"

"I think I would. How does one get Upperside?"

"Nothing to it. An elevator takes you up, a door opens, and there you are. I've been up there. It's . . . novel."

"It would get my mind off psychohistory for a while." Seldon sighed. "I'd welcome that."

"On the other hand," said Randa, "my uncle used to say, 'All knowledge is one,' and he may be right. You may learn something from meteorology that will help you with your psychohistory. Isn't that possible?"

Seldon smiled weakly. "A great many things are possible." And to himself he added: But not practical.

22.

Dors seemed amused. "Meteorology?"

Seldon said, "Yes. There's work scheduled for tomorrow and I'll go up with them."

"Are you tired of history?"

Seldon nodded his head somberly. "Yes, I am. I'll welcome the change. Besides, Randa says it's another problem that's too massive for mathematics to handle and it will do me good to see that my situation isn't unique."

"I hope you're not agoraphobic."

Seldon smiled. "No, I'm not, but I see why you ask. Randa says that Trantorians are frequently agoraphobic and won't go Upperside. I imagine they feel uncomfortable without a protective enclosure."

Dors nodded. "You can see where that would be natural, but there are also many Trantorians who are to be found among the planets of the Galaxy—tourists, administrators, soldiers. And agoraphobia isn't particularly rare in the Outworlds either."

"That may be, Dors, but I'm not agoraphobic. I am curious and I welcome the change, so I'll be joining them tomorrow."

Dors hesitated. "I should go up with you, but I have a heavy schedule tomorrow. —Still, if you're not agoraphobic, you'll have no trouble and you'll probably enjoy yourself. Oh, and stay close to the meteorologists. I've heard of people getting lost up there."

"I'll be careful. It's a long time since I've gotten truly lost anywhere."

23.

Jenarr Leggen had a dark look about him. It was not so much his complexion, which was fair enough. It was not even his eyebrows, which were thick and dark enough. It was, rather, that those eyebrows were hunched over deep-set eyes and a long and rather prominent nose. He had, as a result, a most unmerry look. His eyes did not smile and when he spoke, which wasn't often, he had a deep, strong voice, surprisingly resonant for his rather thin body.

He said, "You'll need warmer clothing than that, Seldon."

Seldon said, "Oh?" and looked about.

There were two men and two women who were making ready to go up with Leggen and Seldon and, as in Leggen's own case, their rather satiny Trantorian clothing was covered by thick sweaters that, not surprisingly, were brightly colored in bold designs. No two were even faintly alike, of course.

Seldon looked down at himself and said, "Sorry, I didn't know—but I don't have any suitable outer garment."

"I can give you one. I think there's a spare here somewhere. —Yes, here it is. A little threadbare, but it's better than nothing."

"Wearing sweaters like these can make you unpleasantly warm," said Seldon.

"Here they would," said Leggen. "Other conditions exist Upperside. Cold and windy. Too bad I don't have spare leggings and boots for you too. You'll want them later."

They were taking with them a cart of instruments, which they were testing one by one with what Seldon thought was unnecessary slowness.

"Your home planet cold?" asked Leggen.

Seldon said, "Parts of it, of course. The part of Helicon I come from is mild and often rainy."

"Too bad. You won't like the weather Upperside."

"I think I can manage to endure it for the time we'll be up there."

When they were ready, the group filed into an elevator that was marked: OFFICIAL USE ONLY.

"That's because it goes Upperside," said one of the young women, "and people aren't supposed to be up there without good reason."

Seldon had not met the young woman before, but he had heard her addressed as Clowzia. He didn't know if that was a first name, a last name, or a nickname.

The elevator seemed no different from others that Seldon had been on, either here on Trantor or at home in Helicon (barring, of course, the gravitic lift he and Hummin had used), but there was something about knowing that it was going to take him out of the confines of the planet and into emptiness above that made it feel like a spaceship.

Seldon smiled internally. A foolish fantasy.

The elevator quivered slightly, which remind Seldon of Hummin's forebodings of Galactic decay. Leggen, along with the other men and one of the women, seemed frozen and waiting, as though they had suspended thought as well as activity until they could get out, but Clowzia kept glancing at him as though she found him terribly impressive.

Seldon leaned close and whispered to her (he hesitated to disturb the others), "Are we going up very high?"

"High?" she repeated. She spoke in a normal voice, apparently not feeling that the others required silence. She seemed very young and it occurred to Seldon that she was probably an undergraduate. An apprentice, perhaps.

"We're taking a long time. Upperside must be many stories high in the air."

For a moment, she looked puzzled. Then, "Oh no. Not high at all. We started very deep. The University is at a low level. We use a great deal of energy and if we're quite deep, the energy costs are lower."

Leggen said, "All right. We're here. Let's get the equipment out."

The elevator stopped with a small shudder and the wide door slid open rapidly. The temperature dropped at once and Seldon thrust his hands into his pockets and was very glad he had a sweater on. A cold wind stirred his hair and it occurred to him that he would have found a hat useful and, even as he thought that, Leggen pulled something out of a fold in his sweater, snapped it open, and put it on his head. The others did the same.

Only Clowzia hesitated. She paused just before she put hers on, then offered it to Seldon.

Seldon shook his head. "I can't take your hat, Clowzia."

"Go ahead. I have long hair and it's pretty thick. Yours is short and a little . . . thin."

Seldon would have liked to deny that firmly and at another time he would have. Now, however, he took the hat and mumbled, "Thank you. If your head gets cold, I'll give it back."

Maybe she wasn't so young. It was her round face, almost a baby face. And now that she had called attention to her hair, he could see that it was a charming russet shade. He had never seen hair quite like that on Helicon.

Outside it was cloudy, as it had been the time he was taken across open country to the Palace. It was considerably colder than it had been then, but he assumed that was because they were six weeks farther into winter. The clouds were thicker than they had been on the earlier occasion and the day was distinctly darker and threatening—or was it just closer to night? Surely, they wouldn't come up to do important work without leaving themselves an ample period of daylight to do it in. Or did they expect to take very little time?

He would have liked to have asked, but it occurred to him that they might not like questions at this time. All of them seemed to be in states varying from excitement to anger.

Seldon inspected his surroundings.

He was standing on something that he thought might be dull metal from the sound it made when he surreptitiously thumped his foot down on it. It was not bare metal, however. When he walked, he left footprints. The surface was clearly covered by dust or fine sand or clay.

Well, why not? There could scarcely be anyone coming up here to dust the place. He bent down to pinch up some of the matter out of curiosity.

Clowzia had come up to him. She noticed what he was doing and said, with the air of a housewife caught at an embarrassing negligence, "We do sweep hereabouts for the sake of the instruments. It's much worse most places Upperside, but it really doesn't matter. It makes for insulation, you know."

Seldon grunted and continued to look about. There was no chance of understanding the instruments that looked as though they were growing out of the thin soil (if one could call it that). He hadn't the faintest idea of what they were or what they measured.

Leggen was walking toward him. He was picking up his feet and putting them down gingerly and it occurred to Seldon that he was doing so to avoid jarring the instruments. He made a mental note to walk that way himself.

"You! Seldon!"

Seldon didn't quite like the tone of voice. He replied coolly, "Yes, Dr. Leggen?"

"Well, Dr. Seldon, then." He said it impatiently. "That little fellow Randa told me you are a mathematician."

"That's right."

"A good one?"

"I'd like to think so, but it's a hard thing to guarantee."

"And you're interested in intractable problems?"

Seldon said feelingly, "I'm stuck with one."

"I'm stuck with another. You're free to look about. If you have any questions, our intern, Clowzia, will help out. You might be able to help us."

"I would be delighted to, but I know nothing about meteorology."

"That's all right, Seldon. I just want you to get a feel for this thing and then I'd like to discuss *my* mathematics, such as it is."

"I'm at your service."

Leggen turned away, his long scowling face looking grim. Then he turned back. "If you get cold—*too* cold—the elevator door is open. You just step in and touch the spot marked: UNIVERSITY BASE. It will take you down and the elevator will then return to us automatically. Clowzia will show you—if you forget."

"I won't forget."

This time he did leave and Seldon looked after him, feeling the cold wind knife through his sweater. Clowzia came back over to him, her face slightly reddened by that wind.

Seldon said, "Dr. Leggen seems annoyed. Or is that just his ordinary outlook on life?"

She giggled. "He does look annoyed most of the time, but right now he really is."

Seldon said very naturally, "Why?"

Clowzia looked over her shoulder, her long hair swirling. Then she said, "I'm not supposed to know, but I do just the same. Dr. Leggen had it all figured out that today, just at this time, there was going to be a break in the clouds and he'd been planning to make special measurements in sunlight. Only . . . well, look at the weather."

Seldon nodded.

"We have holovision receivers up here, so he knew it was cloudy—worse than usual—and I guess he was hoping there would be something wrong with the instruments so that it would be their fault and not that of his theory. So far, though, they haven't found anything out of the way."

"And that's why he looks so unhappy."

"Well, he never looks *happy.*"

Seldon looked about, squinting. Despite the clouds, the light was harsh. He became aware that the surface under his feet was not quite horizontal. He was standing on a shallow dome and as he looked outward there were other domes in all directions, with different widths and heights.

"Upperside seems to be irregular," he said.

"Mostly, I think. That's the way it worked out."

"Any reason for it?"

"Not really. The way I've heard it explained—I looked around and asked, just as you did, you know—was that originally the people on Trantor domed in places, shopping malls, sports arenas, things like that, then whole towns, so that there were lots of domes here and there, with different heights and different widths. When they all came together, it was all uneven, but by that time, people decided that's the way it ought to be."

"You mean that something quite accidental came to be viewed as a tradition?"

"I suppose so—if you want to put it that way."

(If something quite accidental can easily become viewed as a tradition and be made unbreakable or nearly so, thought Seldon, would that be a law of psychohistory? It sounded trivial, but how many other laws, equally trivial, might there be? A million? A billion? Were there a relatively few general laws from which these trivial ones could be derived as corollaries? How could he say? For a while, lost in thought, he almost forgot the biting wind.)

Clowzia was aware of that wind, however, for she shuddered and said, "It's very nasty. It's much better under the dome."

"Are you a Trantorian?" asked Seldon.

"That's right."

Seldon remembered Randa's dismissal of Trantorians as agoraphobic and said, "Do you mind being up here?"

"I hate it," said Clowzia, "but I want my degree and my specialty and status and Dr. Leggen says I can't get it without some field work. So here I am, hating it, especially when it's so cold. When it's this cold, by the way, you wouldn't dream that vegetation actually grows on these domes, would you?"

"It *does?*" He looked at Clowzia sharply, suspecting some sort of practical joke designed to make him look foolish. She looked totally innocent, but how much of that was real and how much was just her baby face?

"Oh sure. Even here, when it's warmer. You notice the soil here? We keep it swept away because of our work, as I said, but in other places it accumulates here and there and is especially deep in the low places where the domes meet. Plants grow in it."

"But where does the soil come from?"

"When the dome covered just part of the planet, the wind deposited soil on them, little by little. Then, when Trantor was all covered and the living levels were dug deeper and deeper, some of the material dug up, if suitable, would be spread over the top."

"Surely, it would break down the domes."

"Oh no. The domes are very strong and they're supported almost everywhere. The idea was, according to a book-film I viewed, that they were going to grow crops Upperside, but it turned out to be much more practical to do it inside the dome. Yeast and algae could be cultivated within the domes too, taking the pressure off the usual crops, so it was decided to let Upperside go wild. There are animals on Upperside too—butterflies, bees, mice, rabbits. Lots of them."

"Won't the plant roots damage the domes?"

"In thousands of years they haven't. The domes are treated so that they repel the roots. Most of the growth is grass, but there are trees too. You'd be able to see for yourself if this were the warm season or if we were farther south or if you were up in a spaceship." She looked at him with a sidewise flick of her eyes, "Did you see Trantor when you were coming down from space?"

"No, Clowzia, I must confess I didn't. The hypership was never well placed for viewing. Have *you* ever seen Trantor from space?"

She smiled weakly. "I've never been in space."

Seldon looked about. Gray everywhere.

"I can't make myself believe it," he said. "About vegetation Upperside, I mean."

"It's true, though. I've heard people say—Otherworlders, like yourself, who *did* see Trantor from space—that the planet looks green, like a lawn, because it's mostly grass and underbrush. There are trees too, actually. There's a copse not very far from here. I've seen it. They're evergreens and they're up to six meters high."

"Where?"

"You can't see it from here. It's on the other side of a dome. It's—"

The call came out thinly. (Seldon realized they had been walking while they had been talking and had moved away from the immediate vicinity of the others.) "Clowzia. Get back here. We need you."

Clowzia said, "Uh-oh. *Coming.* —Sorry, Dr. Seldon, I have to go." She ran off, managing to step lightly despite her lined boots.

Had she been playing with him? Had she been filling the gullible foreigner with a mess of lies for amusement's sake? Such things had been known to happen on every world and in every time. An air of transparent honesty was no guide either; in fact, successful tale-tellers would deliberately cultivate just such an air.

So could there really be six-meter trees Upperside? Without thinking much about it, he moved in the direction of the highest dome on the horizon. He swung his arms in an attempt to warm himself. And his feet *were* getting cold.

Clowzia hadn't pointed. She might have, to give him a hint of the direction of the trees, but she didn't. Why didn't she? To be sure, she had been called away.

The domes were broad rather than high, which was a good thing, since otherwise the going would have been considerably more difficult. On the other hand, the gentle grade meant trudging a distance before he could top a dome and look down the other side.

Eventually, he could see the other side of the dome he had climbed. He looked back to make sure he could still see the meteorologists and their instruments. They were a good way off, in a distant valley, but he could see them clearly enough. Good.

He saw no copse, no trees, but there was a depression that snaked about between two domes. Along each side of that crease, the soil was thicker and there were occasional green smears of what might be moss. If he followed the crease and if it got low enough and the soil was thick enough, there might be trees.

He looked back, trying to fix landmarks in his mind, but there were just the rise and fall of domes. It made him hesitate and Dors's warning against his being lost, which had seemed a rather unnecessary piece of advice then, made more sense now. Still, it seemed clear to him that the crease was a kind of road. If he followed it for some distance, he only had to turn about and follow it back to return to this spot.

He strode off purposefully, following the rounded crease downward. There was a soft rumbling noise above, but he didn't give it any thought. He had made up his mind that he wanted to see trees and that was all that occupied him at the moment.

The moss grew thicker and spread out like a carpet and here and there grassy tufts had sprung up. Despite the desolation Upperside, the moss was bright green and it occurred to Seldon that on a cloudy, overcast planet there was likely to be considerable rain.

The crease continued to curve and there, just above another dome, was a dark smudge against the gray sky and he knew he had found the trees.

Then, as though his mind, having been liberated by the sight of those trees, could turn to other things, Seldon took note of the rumble he had heard before and had, without thinking, dismissed as the sound of machinery. Now he considered that possibility: Was it, indeed, the sound of machinery?

Why not? He was standing on one of the myriad domes that covered hundreds of millions of square kilometers of the world-city. There must be machinery of all kinds hidden under those domes—ventilation motors, for one thing. Maybe it could be heard, where and when all the other sounds of the world-city were absent.

Except that it did not seem to come from the ground. He looked up at the dreary featureless sky. Nothing.

He continued to scan the sky, vertical creases appearing between his eyes and then, far off—

It was a small dark spot, showing up against the gray. And whatever it was it seemed to be moving about as though getting its bearings before it was obscured by the clouds again.

Then, without knowing why, he thought, They're after me.

And almost before he could work out a line of action, he had taken one. He ran desperately along the crease toward the trees and then, to reach them more quickly, he turned left and hurtled up and over a low dome, treading through brown and dying fernlike overgrowth, including thorny sprigs with bright red berries.

24.

Seldon panted, facing a tree, holding it closely, embracing it. He watched for the flying object to make its appearance again so that he could back about the tree and hide on the far side, like a squirrel.

The tree was cold, its bark was rough, it gave no comfort—but it offered cover. Of course, that might be insufficient, if he was being searched for with a heat-seeker, but, on the other hand, the cold trunk of a tree might blur even that.

Below him was hard-packed soil. Even in this moment of hiding, of attempting to see his pursuer while remaining unseen, he could not help wondering how thick the soil might be, how long it had taken to accumulate, how many domes in the warmer areas of Trantor carried forests on their back, and whether the trees were always confined to the creases between domes, leaving the higher regions to moss, grass, and underbrush.

He saw it again. It was not a hypership, nor even an ordinary air-jet. It was a jet-down. He could see the faint glow of the ion trails coming out at the vertices of a hexagon, neutralizing the gravitational pull and allowing the wings to keep it aloft like a large soaring bird. It was a vehicle that could hover and explore a planetary terrain.

It was only the clouds that had saved him. Even if they were using heat-seekers, that would only indicate there were people below. The jet-down would have to make a tentative dive below the banked ceiling before it could hope to know how many human beings there were and whether any of them might be the particular person the parties aboard were seeking.

The jet-down was closer now, but it couldn't hide from him either.

The rumble of the engine gave it away and they couldn't turn that off, not as long as they wished to continue their search. Seldon knew the jet-downs, for on Helicon or on any undomed world with skies that cleared now and then, they were common, with many in private hands.

Of what possible use would jet-downs be on Trantor, with all the human life of the world under domes, with low cloud ceilings all but perpetual—except for a few government vehicles designed for just this purpose, that of picking up a wanted person who had been lured above the domes?

Why not? Government forces could not enter the grounds of the University, but perhaps Seldon was no longer on the grounds. He was on top of the domes, which might be outside the jurisdiction of any local government. An Imperial vehicle might have every right to land on any part of the dome and question or remove any person found upon it. Hummin had not warned him of this, but perhaps he had merely not thought of doing so.

The jet-down was even closer now, nosing about like a blind beast sniffing out its prey. Would it occur to them to search this group of trees? Would they land and send out an armed soldier or two to beat through the copse?

And if so, what could he do? He was unarmed and all his quick-twist agility would be useless against the agonizing pain of a neuronic whip.

It was not attempting to land. Either they missed the significance of the trees—

Or—

A new thought suddenly hit him. What if this wasn't a pursuit vessel at all? What if it was part of the meteorological testing? Surely, meteorologists would want to test the upper reaches of the atmosphere.

Was he a fool to hide from it?

The sky was getting darker. The clouds were getting thicker or, much more likely, night was falling.

And it was getting colder and would get colder still. Was he going to stay out here freezing because a perfectly harmless jet-down had made an appearance and had activated a sense of paranoia that he had never felt before? He had a strong impulse to leave the copse and get back to the meteorological station.

After all, how would the man Hummin feared so much—Demerzel—

know that Seldon would, at this particular time, be Upperside and ready to be taken?

For a moment, that seemed conclusive and, shivering with the cold, he moved out from behind the tree.

And then he scurried back as the vessel reappeared even closer than before. He hadn't seen it do anything that would seem to be meteorological. It did nothing that might be considered sampling, measuring, or testing. *Would* he see such things if they took place? He did not know the precise sort of instruments the jet-down carried or how they worked. If they *were* doing meteorological work, he might not be able to tell. —Still, could he take the chance of coming into the open?

After all, what if Demerzel *did* know of his presence Upperside, simply because an agent of his, working in the University, knew about it and had reported the matter. Lisung Randa, that cheerful, smiling little Easterner, had suggested he go Upperside. He had suggested it quite forcefully and the subject had not arisen naturally out of the conversation; at least, not naturally enough. Was it possible that he was a government agent and had alerted Demerzel somehow?

Then there was Leggen, who had given him the sweater. The sweater was useful, but why hadn't Leggen told him he would need one earlier so he could get his own? Was there something special about the one he was wearing? It was uniformly purple, while all the others' indulged in the Trantorian fashion of bright patterns. Anyone looking down from a height would see a moving dull blotch in among others that were bright and know immediately whom they wanted.

And Clowzia? She was supposedly Upperside to learn meteorology and help the meteorologists. How was it possible that she could come to him, talk to him at ease, and quietly walk him away from the others and isolate him so that he could easily be picked up?

For that matter, what about Dors Venabili? She knew he was going Upperside. She did not stop it. She might have gone with him, but she was conveniently busy.

It was a conspiracy. Surely, it was a conspiracy.

He had convinced himself now and there was no further thought of getting out from the shelter of the trees. (His feet felt like lumps of ice and stamping them against the ground seemed to do no good.) Would the jet-down never leave?

And even as he thought that, the pitch of the engine's rumble heightened and the jet-down rose into the clouds and faded away.

Seldon listened eagerly, alert to the smallest sound, making sure it was finally gone. And then, even after he was sure it was gone, he wondered if that was just a device to flush him out of hiding. He remained where he was while the minutes slowly crawled on and night continued to fall.

And finally, when he felt that the true alternative to taking the chance of coming out in the open was that of freezing into insensibility, he stepped out and moved cautiously beyond the shelter of the trees.

It was dusky twilight, after all. They couldn't detect him except by a heat-seeker, but, if so, he would hear the jet-down return. He waited just beyond the trees, counting to himself, ready to hide in the copse again at the smallest sound—though what good that would do him once he was spotted, he couldn't imagine.

Seldon looked about. If he could find the meteorologists, they would surely have artificial light, but except for that, there would be nothing.

He could still just make out his surroundings, but in a matter of a quarter of an hour, half an hour at the outside, he would not. With no lights and a cloudy sky above, it would be dark—completely dark.

Desperate at the prospect of being enveloped in total darkness, Seldon realized that he would have to find his way back to the crease that had brought him there as quickly as possible and retrace his steps. Folding his arms tightly around himself for warmth, he set off in what he thought was the direction of the crease between the domes.

There might, of course, be more than one crease leading away from the copse, but he dimly made out some of the sprigs of berries he had seen coming in, which now looked almost black rather than bright red. He could not delay. He had to assume he was right. He moved up the crease as fast as he might, guided by failing sight and by the vegetation underfoot.

But he couldn't stay in the crease forever. He had come over what had seemed to him to be the tallest dome in sight and had found a crease that cut at right angles across his line of approach. By his reckoning, he should now turn right, then sharp left, and that would put him on the path toward the meteorologists' dome.

Seldon made the left turn and, lifting his head, he could just make out the curve of a dome against the fractionally lighter sky. That had to be it!

Or was that only wishful thinking?

He had no choice but to assume it wasn't. Keeping his eye on the peak so that he could move in a reasonably straight line, he headed for it as quickly as he could. As he got closer, he could make out the line of dome against sky with less and less certainty as it loomed larger and larger. Soon, if he was correct, he would be going up a gentle slope and when that slope became level he would be able to look down the other side and see the lights of the meteorologists.

In the inky dark, he could not tell what lay in his path. Wishing there were at least a few stars to shed some light, he wondered if this was how it felt to be blind. He waved his arms before him as if they were antennae.

It was growing colder by the minute and he paused occasionally to blow on his hands and hold them under his armpits. He wished earnestly he could do the same for his feet. By now, he thought, if it started to precipitate, it would be snow—or, worse yet, sleet.

On . . . on. There was nothing else to do.

Eventually, it seemed to him that he was moving downward. That was either wishful thinking or he had topped the dome.

He stopped. If he had topped the dome, he should be able to see the artificial light of the meteorological station. He would see the lights carried by the meteorologists themselves, sparkling or dancing like fireflies.

Seldon closed his eyes as though to accustom them to dark and then try again, but that was a foolish effort. It was no darker with his eyes closed than with them open and when he opened them it was no lighter than when he had had them closed.

Possibly Leggen and the others were gone, had taken their lights with them and had turned off any lights on the instruments. Or possibly Seldon had climbed the wrong dome. Or he had followed a curved path along the dome so that he was now facing in the wrong direction. Or he had followed the wrong crease and had moved away from the copse in the wrong direction altogether.

What should he do?

If he was facing the wrong direction, there was a chance that light would be visible right or left—and it wasn't. If he had followed the wrong crease, there was no possible way he could return to the copse and locate a different crease.

His only chance lay in the assumption that he was facing the right direction and that the meteorological station was more or less directly ahead of him, but that the meteorologists had gone and had left it in darkness.

Move forward, then. The chances of success might be small, but it was the only chance he had.

He estimated that it had taken him half an hour to move from the meteorological station to the top of the dome, having gone partway with Clowzia and sauntering with her rather than striding. He was moving at little better than a saunter now in the daunting darkness.

Seldon continued to slog forward. It would have been nice to know the time and he had a timeband, of course, but in the dark—

He stopped. He wore a Trantorian timeband, which gave Galactic Standard time (as all timebands did) and which also gave Trantorian local time. Timebands were usually visible in the dark, phosphorescing so that one could tell time in the quiet dark of a bedchamber. A Heliconian timeband certainly would; why not a Trantorian one?

He looked at his timeband with reluctant apprehension and touched the contact that would draw upon the power source for light. The timeband gleamed feebly and told him the time was 1847. For it to be nighttime already, Seldon knew that it must be the winter season. —How far past the solstice was it? What was the degree of axial tipping? How long was the year? How far from the equator was he at this moment? There was no hint of an answer to any of these things, but what counted was that the spark of light was visible.

He was not blind! Somehow the feeble glow of his timeband gave him renewed hope.

His spirits rose. He would move on in the direction he was going. He would move for half an hour. If he encountered nothing, he would move on five minutes more—no further—just five minutes. If he still encountered nothing, he would stop and think. That, however, would be thirty-five minutes from now. Till then, he would concentrate only on walking and on willing himself to feel warmer (He wiggled his toes, vigorously. He could still feel them.)

Seldon trudged onward and the half hour passed. He paused, then hesitantly, he moved on for five more minutes.

Now he had to decide. There was nothing. He might be nowhere, far removed from any opening into the dome. He might, on the other hand, be standing three meters to the left—or right—or short—of the meteorological station. He might be two arms' lengths from the opening into the dome, which would not, however, be open.

Now what?

Was there any point in shouting? He was enveloped by utter silence but for the whistling of the wind. If there were birds, beasts, or insects in among the vegetation on the domes, they were not here during this season or at this time of night or at this particular place. The wind continued to chill him.

Perhaps he should have been shouting all the way. The sound might have carried a good distance in the cold air. But would there have been anyone to hear him?

Would they hear him inside the dome? Were there instruments to detect sound or movement from above? Might there not be sentinels just inside?

That seemed ridiculous. They would have heard his footsteps, wouldn't they?

Still—

He called out. "Help! Help! Can someone hear me?"

His cry was strangled, half-embarrassed. It seemed silly shouting into vast black nothingness.

But then, he felt it was even sillier to hesitate in such a situation as this. Panic was welling up in him. He took in a deep, cold breath and screamed for as long as he could. Another breath and another scream, changing pitch. And another.

Seldon paused, breathless, turning his head every which way, even though there was nothing to see. He could not even detect an echo. There was nothing left to do but wait for the dawn. But how long was the night at this season of the year? And how cold would it get?

He felt a tiny cold touch sting his face. After a while, another.

It was sleeting invisibly in the pitch blackness. And there was no way to find shelter.

He thought: It would have been better if that jet-down had seen me and picked me up. I would be a prisoner at this moment, perhaps, but I'd be warm and comfortable, at least.

Or, if Hummin had never interfered, I might have been back in Helicon long ago. Under surveillance, but warm and comfortable. Right now that was all he wanted—to be warm and comfortable.

But at the moment he could only wait. He huddled down, knowing that however long the night, he dared not sleep. He slipped off his shoes and rubbed his icy feet. Quickly, he put his shoes back on.

He knew he would have to repeat this, as well as rubbing his hands and ears all night long to keep his circulation flowing. But most important to remember was that he *must not* let himself fall asleep. That would mean certain death.

And, having carefully thought all this out, his eyes closed and he nodded off to sleep with the sleet coming down.

RESCUE

. . . . .

LEGGEN, JENARR— . . . His contributions to meteorology, however, although considerable, pale before what has ever since been known as the Leggen Controversy. That his actions helped to place Hari Seldon in jeopardy is undisputable, but argument rages—and has always raged—as to whether those actions were the result of unintentional circumstance or part of a deliberate conspiracy. Passions have been raised on both sides and even the most elaborate studies have come to no definite conclusions. Nevertheless, the suspicions that were raised helped poison Leggen's career and private life in the years that followed . . .

ENCYCLOPEDIA GALACTICA

25.

It was not quite the end of daylight when Dors Venabili sought out Jenarr Leggen. He answered her rather anxious greeting with a grunt and a brief nod.

"Well," she said a trifle impatiently. "How was he?"

Leggen, who was entering data into his computer, said, "How was *who?*"

"My library student Hari. Dr. Hari Seldon. He went up with you. Was he any help to you?"

Leggen removed his hands from the keys of his computer and swivelled about. "That Heliconian fellow? He was of no use at all. Showed no interest whatever. He kept looking at the scenery when there was no scenery to look at. A real oddball. Why did you want to send him up?"

"It wasn't my idea. *He* wanted to. I can't understand it. He was very interested. —Where is he now?"

Leggen shrugged. "How would I know? Somewhere around."

"Where did he go after he came down with you? Did he say?"

"He didn't come down with us. I told you he wasn't interested."

1 1 1

"Then when did he come down?"

"I don't know. I wasn't watching him. I had an enormous amount of work to do. There must have been a windstorm and some sort of downpour about two days ago and neither was expected. Nothing our instruments showed offered a good explanation for it or for the fact that some sunshine we were expecting today *didn't* appear. Now I'm trying to make sense of it and you're *bothering* me."

"You mean you didn't see him go down?"

"Look. He wasn't on my mind. The idiot wasn't correctly dressed and I could see that inside of half an hour he wasn't going to be able to take the cold. I gave him a sweater, but that wasn't going to help much for his legs and feet. So I left the elevator open for him and I told him how to use it and explained that it would take him down and then return automatically. It was all very simple and I'm sure he did get cold and he did go down and the elevator did come back and then eventually we all went down."

"But you don't know exactly when he went down?"

"No, I don't. I told you. I was busy. He certainly wasn't up there when we left, though, and by that time twilight was coming on and it looked as though it might sleet. So he had to have gone down."

"Did anyone else see him go down?"

"I don't know. Clowzia may have. She was with him for a while. Why don't you ask her?"

Dors found Clowzia in her quarters, just emerging from a hot shower.

"It was cold up there," she said.

Dors said, "Were you with Hari Seldon Upperside?"

Clowzia said, eyebrows lifting, "Yes, for a while. He wanted to wander about and ask questions about the vegetation up there. He's a sharp fellow, Dors. Everything seemed to interest him, so I told him what I could till Leggen called me back. He was in one of his knock-your-head-off tempers. The weather wasn't working and he—"

Dors interrupted. "Then you didn't see Hari go down in the elevator?"

"I didn't see him at all after Leggen called me over. —But he *has* to be down here. He wasn't up there when we left."

"But I can't find him anywhere."

Clowzia looked perturbed. "Really?—But he's got to be *somewhere* down here."

"No, he *doesn't* have to be somewhere down here," said Dors, her anxiety growing. "What if he's still up there?"

"That's impossible. He wasn't. Naturally, we looked about for him before we left. Leggen had shown him how to go down. He wasn't properly dressed and it was rotten weather. Leggen told him if he got cold not to wait for us. He *was* getting cold. I know! So what else could he do *but* go down?"

"But no one *saw* him go down. —Did anything go wrong with him up there?"

"*Nothing.* Not while I was with him. He was perfectly fine—except that he had to be cold, of course."

Dors, by now quite unsettled, said, "Since no one saw him go down, he might still be up there. Shouldn't we go up and look?"

Clowzia said nervously, "I told you we looked around before we went down. It was still quite light and he was nowhere in sight."

"Let's look anyway."

"But *I* can't take you up there. I'm just an intern and I don't have the combination for the Upperside dome opening. You'll have to ask Dr. Leggen."

26.

Dors Venabili knew that Leggen would not willingly go Upperside now. He would have to be forced.

First, she checked the library and the dining areas again. Then she called Seldon's room. Finally, she went up there and signaled at the door. When Seldon did not respond, she had the floor manager open it. He wasn't there. She questioned some of those who, over the last few weeks, had come to know him. No one had seen him.

Well, then, she would *make* Leggen take her Upperside. By now, though, it was night. He would object strenuously and how long could she spend arguing if Hari Seldon was trapped up there on a freezing night with sleet turning to snow?

A thought occurred to her and she rushed to the small University computer, which kept track of the doings of the students, faculty, and service staff.

Her fingers flew over the keys and she soon had what she wanted.

There were three of them in another part of the campus. She signed out for a small glidecart to take her over and found the domicile she was looking for. Surely, *one* of them would be available—or findable.

Fortune was with her. The first door at which she signaled was answered by a query light. She punched in her identification number, which included her department affiliation. The door opened and a plump middle-aged man stared out at her. He had obviously been washing up before dinner. His dark blond hair was askew and he was not wearing any upper garment.

He said, "Sorry. You catch me at a disadvantage. What can I do for you, Dr. Venabili?"

She said a bit breathlessly, "You're Rogen Benastra, the Chief Seismologist, aren't you?"

"Yes."

"This is an emergency. I must see the seismological records for Upperside for the last few hours."

Benastra stared at her. "Why? Nothing's happened. I'd know if it had. The seismograph would inform us."

"I'm not talking about a meteoric impact."

"Neither am I. We don't need a seismograph for that. I'm talking about gravel, pinpoint fractures. Nothing today."

"Not that either. Please. Take me to the seismograph and read it for me. This is life or death."

"I have a dinner appointment—"

"I said life or death and I mean it."

Benastra said, "I don't see—" but he faded out under Dors's glare. He wiped his face, left quick word on his message relay, and struggled into a shirt.

They half-ran (under Dors's pitiless urging) to the small squat Seismology Building. Dors, who knew nothing about seismology, said, "Down? We're going down?"

"Below the inhabited levels. Of course. The seismograph has to be fixed to bedrock and be removed from the constant clamor and vibration of the city levels."

"But how can you tell what's happening Upperside from down here?"

"The seismograph is wired to a set of pressure transducers located within the thickness of the dome. The impact of a speck of grit will send the indicator skittering off the screen. We can detect the flattening effect on the dome of a high wind. We can—"

"Yes, yes," said Dors impatiently. She was not here for a lecture on the virtues and refinements of the instruments. "Can you detect human footsteps?"

"Human footsteps?" Benastra looked confused. "That's not likely Upperside."

"Of course it's likely. There were a group of meteorologists Upperside this afternoon."

"Oh. Well, footsteps would scarcely be noticeable."

"It would be noticeable if you looked hard enough and that's what I want you to do."

Benastra might have resented the firm note of command in her voice, but, if so, he said nothing. He touched a contact and the computer screen jumped to life.

At the extreme right center, there was a fat spot of light, from which a thin horizontal line stretched to the left limit of the screen. There was a tiny wriggle to it, a random nonrepetitive series of little hiccups and these moved steadily leftward. It was almost hypnotic in its effect on Dors.

Benastra said, "That's as quiet as it can possibly be. Anything you see is the result of changing air pressure above, raindrops maybe, the distant whirr of machinery. There's nothing up there."

"All right, but what about a few hours ago? Check on the records at fifteen hundred today, for instance. Surely, you have some recordings."

Benastra gave the computer its necessary instructions and for a second or two there was wild chaos on the screen. Then it settled down and again the horizontal line appeared.

"I'll sensitize it to maximum," muttered Benastra. There were now pronounced hiccups and as they staggered leftward they changed in pattern markedly.

"What's that?" said Dors. "Tell me."

"Since you say there were people up there, Venabili, I would guess they were footsteps—the shifting of weight, the impact of shoes. I don't know that I would have guessed it if I hadn't known about the people up there. It's what we call a benign vibration, not associated with anything we know to be dangerous."

"Can you tell how many people are present?"

"Certainly not by eye. You see, we're getting a resultant of all the impacts."

"You say 'not by eye.' Can the resultant be analyzed into its components by the computer?"

"I doubt it. These are minimal effects and you have to allow for the inevitable noise. The results would be untrustworthy."

"Well then. Move the time forward till the footstep indications stop. Can you make it fast-forward, so to speak?"

"If I do—the kind of fast-forward you're speaking of—then it will all just blur into a straight line with a slight haze above and below. What I can do is move it forward in fifteen-minute stages and study it quickly before moving on."

"Good. Do that!"

Both watched the screen until Benastra said, "There's nothing there now. See?"

There was again a line with nothing but tiny uneven hiccups of noise.

"When did the footsteps stop?"

"Two hours ago. A trifle more."

"And when they stopped were there fewer than there were earlier?"

Benastra looked mildly outraged. "I couldn't tell. I don't think the finest analysis could make a certain decision."

Dors pressed her lips together. Then she said, "Are you testing a transducer—is that what you called it—near the meteorological outlet?"

"Yes, that's where the instruments are and that's where the meteorologists would have been." Then, unbelievingly, "Do you want me to try others in the vicinity? One at a time?"

"No. Stay on this one. But keep on going forward at fifteen-minute intervals. One person may have been left behind and may have made his way back to the instruments."

Benastra shook his head and muttered something under his breath.

The screen shifted again and Dors said sharply, "What's that?" She was pointing.

"I don't know. Noise."

"No. It's periodic. Could it be a single person's footsteps?"

"Sure, but it could be a dozen other things too."

"It's coming along at about the time of footsteps, isn't it?" Then, after a while, she said, "Push it forward a little."

He did and when the screen settled down she said, "Aren't those unevennesses getting bigger?"

"Possibly. We can measure them."

"We don't have to. You can see they're getting bigger. The footsteps are approaching the transducer. Go forward again. See when they stop."

After a while Benastra said, "They stopped twenty or twenty-five minutes ago." Then cautiously, "Whatever they are."

"They're footsteps," said Dors with mountain-moving conviction. "There's a man up there and while you and I have been fooling around here, he's collapsed and he's going to freeze and die. Now don't say, 'Whatever they are!' Just call Meteorology and get me Jenarr Leggen. Life or death, I tell you. Say so!"

Benastra, lips quivering, had passed the stage where he could possibly resist anything this strange and passionate woman demanded.

It took no more than three minutes to get Leggen's hologram on the message platform. He had been pulled away from his dinner table. There was a napkin in his hand and a suspicious greasiness under his lower lip.

His long face was set in a fearful scowl. " 'Life or death?' What is this? Who are you?" Then his eye caught Dors, who had moved closer to Benastra so that her image would be seen on Jenarr's screen. He said, "*You* again. This is simple harassment."

Dors said, "It is not. I have consulted Rogen Benastra, who is Chief Seismologist at the University. After you and your party had left Upperside, the seismograph shows clear footsteps of one person still there. It's my student Hari Seldon, who went up there in your care and who is now, quite certainly, lying in a collapsed stupor and may not live long.

"You will, therefore, take me up there right now with whatever equipment may be necessary. If you do not do so *immediately,* I shall proceed to University security—to the President himself, if necessary. One way or another I'll get up there and if anything has happened to Hari because you delay one minute, I will see to it that you are hauled in for negligence, incompetence—whatever I can make stick—and will have you lose all status and be thrown out of academic life. And if he's dead, of course, that's manslaughter by negligence. Or worse, since I've now warned you he's dying."

Jenarr, furious, turned to Benastra. "Did you detect—"

But Dors cut in. "He told me what he detected and I've told you. I do not intend to allow you to bulldoze him into confusion. Are you coming? Now?''

"Has it occurred to you that you may be mistaken?" said Jenarr, thin-lipped. "Do you know what I can do to you if this is a mischievous false alarm? Loss of status works both ways."

"Murder doesn't," said Dors. "I'm ready to chance a trial for malicious mischief. Are you ready to chance a trial for murder?"

Jenarr reddened, perhaps more at the necessity of giving in than at the threat. "I'll come, but I'll have no mercy on you, young woman, if your student eventually turns out to have been safe within the dome these past three hours."

27.

The three went up the elevator in an inimical silence. Leggen had eaten only part of his dinner and had left his wife at the dining area without adequate explanation. Benastra had eaten no dinner at all and had possibly disappointed some woman companion, also without adequate explanation. Dors Venabili had not eaten either and she seemed the most tense and unhappy of the three. She carried a thermal blanket and two photonic founts.

When they reached the entrance to Upperside, Leggen, jaw muscles tightening, entered his identification number and the door opened. A cold wind rushed at them and Benastra grunted. None of the three was adequately dressed, but the two men had no intention of remaining up there long.

Dors said tightly, "It's snowing."

Leggen said, "It's wet snow. The temperature's just about at the freezing point. It's not a killing frost."

"It depends on how long one remains in it, doesn't it?" said Dors. "And being soaked in melting snow won't help."

Leggen grunted. "Well, where is he?" He stared resentfully out into utter blackness, made even worse by the light from the entrance behind him.

Dors said, "Here, Dr. Benastra, hold this blanket for me. And you, Dr. Leggen, close the door behind you without locking it."

"There's no automatic lock on it. Do you think we're foolish?"

"Perhaps not, but you can lock it from the inside and leave anyone outside unable to get into the dome."

"If someone's outside, point him out. Show him to me," said Leggen.

"He could be anywhere." Dors lifted her arms with a photonic fount circling each wrist.

"We can't look everywhere," mumbled Benastra miserably.

The founts blazed into light, spraying in every direction. The snowflakes glittered like a vast mob of fireflies, making it even more difficult to see.

"The footsteps were getting steadily louder," said Dors. "He had to be approaching the transducer. Where would it be located?"

"I haven't any idea," snapped Leggen. "That's outside my field and my responsibility."

"Dr. Benastra?"

Benastra's reply was hesitant. "I don't really know. To tell you the truth, I've never been up here before. It was installed before my time. The computer knows, but we never thought to ask it that. —I'm cold and I don't see what use I am up here."

"You'll have to stay up here for a while," said Dors firmly. "Follow me. I'm going to circle the entrance in an outward spiral."

"We can't see much through the snow," said Leggen.

"I know that. If it wasn't snowing, we'd have seen him by now. I'm sure of it. As it is, it may take a few minutes. We can stand that." She was by no means as confident as her words made it appear.

She began to walk, swinging her arms, playing the light over as large a field as she could, straining her eyes for a dark blotch against the snow.

And, as it happened, it was Benastra who first said, "What's that?" and pointed.

Dors overlapped the two founts, making a bright cone of light in the indicated direction. She ran toward it, as did the other two.

They had found him, huddled and wet, about ten meters from the door, five from the nearest meteorological device. Dors felt for his heartbeat, but it was not necessary for, responding to her touch, Seldon stirred and whimpered.

"Give me the blanket, Dr. Benastra," said Dors in a voice that was faint with relief. She flapped it open and spread it out in the snow. "Lift him onto it carefully and I'll wrap him. Then we'll carry him down."

In the elevator, vapors were rising from the wrapped Seldon as the blanket warmed to blood temperature.

Dors said, "Once we have him in his room, Dr. Leggen, you get a doctor—a good one—and see that he comes at once. If Dr. Seldon gets through this without harm, I won't say anything, but *only* if he does. Remember—"

"You needn't lecture me," said Leggen coldly. "I regret this and I will do what I can, but my only fault was in allowing this man to come Upperside in the first place."

The blanket stirred and a low, weak voice made itself heard.

Benastra started, for Seldon's head was cradled in the crook of his elbow. He said, "He's trying to say something."

Dors said, "I know. He said, 'What's going on?' "

She couldn't help but laugh just a little. It seemed such a normal thing to say.

28.

The doctor was delighted.

"I've never seen a case of exposure," he explained. "One doesn't get exposed on Trantor."

"That may be," said Dors coldly, "and I'm happy you have the chance to experience this novelty, but does it mean that you do not know how to treat Dr. Seldon?"

The doctor, an elderly man with a bald head and a small gray mustache, bristled. "Of course, I do. Exposure cases on the Outer Worlds are common enough—an everyday affair—and I've read a great deal about them."

Treatment consisted in part of an antiviral serum and the use of a microwave wrapping.

"This ought to take care of it," the doctor said. "On the Outer Worlds, they make use of much more elaborate equipment in hospitals, but we don't have that, of course, on Trantor. This is a treatment for mild cases and I'm sure it will do the job."

Dors thought later, as Seldon was recovering without particular injury, that it was perhaps because he was an Outworlder that he had survived so well. Dark, cold, even snow were not utterly strange to him. A

Trantorian probably would have died in a similar case, not so much from physical trauma as from psychic shock.

She was not sure of this, of course, since she herself was not a Trantorian either.

And, turning her mind away from these thoughts, she pulled up a chair near to Hari's bed and settled down to wait.

29.

On the second morning Seldon stirred awake and looked up at Dors, who sat at his bedside, viewing a book-film and taking notes.

In a voice that was almost normal, Seldon said, "Still here, Dors?"

She put down the book-film. "I can't leave you alone, can I? And I don't trust anyone else."

"It seems to me that every time I wake up, I see you. Have you been here all the time?"

"Sleeping or waking, yes."

"But your classes?"

"I have an assistant who has taken over for a while."

Dors leaned over and grasped Hari's hand. Noticing his embarrassment (he was, after all, in bed), she removed it.

"Hari, what happened? I was so frightened."

Seldon said, "I have a confession to make."

"What is it, Hari?"

"I thought perhaps you were part of a conspiracy—"

"A *conspiracy?*" she said vehemently.

"I mean, to maneuver me Upperside where I'd be outside University jurisdiction and therefore subject to being picked up by Imperial forces."

"But Upperside isn't outside University jurisdiction. Sector jurisdiction on Trantor is from the planetary center to the sky."

"Ah, I didn't know that. But you didn't come with me because you said you had a busy schedule and, when I was getting paranoid, I thought you were deliberately abandoning me. Please forgive me. Obviously, it was you who got me down from there. Did anyone else care?"

"They were busy men," said Dors carefully. "They thought you had come down earlier. I mean, it was a legitimate thought."

"Clowzia thought so too?"

121

"The young intern? Yes, she did."

"Well, it may still have been a conspiracy. Without you, I mean."

"No, Hari, it *is* my fault. I had absolutely no right to let you go Upperside alone. It was my job to protect you. I can't stop blaming myself for what happened, for you getting lost."

"Now, wait a minute," said Seldon, suddenly irritated. "I didn't get lost. What do you think I am?"

"I'd like to know what you call it. You were nowhere around when the others left and you didn't get back to the entrance—or to the neighborhood of the entrance anyway—till well after dark."

"But that's not what happened. I didn't get lost just because I wandered away and couldn't find my way back. I told you I was suspecting a conspiracy and I had cause to do so. I'm not totally paranoid."

"Well then, what *did* happen?"

Seldon told her. He had no trouble remembering it in full detail; he had lived with it in nightmare for most of the preceding day.

Dors listened with a frown. "But that's impossible. A jet-down? Are you sure?"

"Of course I'm sure. Do you think I was hallucinating?"

"But the Imperial forces could not have been searching for you. They could not have arrested you Upperside without creating the same ferocious rumpus they would have if they had sent in a police force to arrest you on campus."

"Then how do you explain it?"

"I'm not sure," said Dors, "but it's possible that the consequences of my failure to go Upperside with you might have been worse than they were and that Hummin will be seriously angry with me."

"Then let's not tell him," said Seldon. "It ended well."

"We must tell him," said Dors grimly. "This may not be the end."

30.

That evening Jenarr Leggen came to visit. It was after dinner and he looked from Dors to Seldon several times, as though wondering what to say. Neither offered to help him, but both waited patiently. He had not impressed either of them as being a master of small talk.

Finally he said to Seldon, "I've come to see how you are."

"Perfectly well," said Seldon, "except that I'm a little sleepy. Dr. Venabili tells me that the treatment will keep me tired for a few days, presumably so I'm sure of getting needed rest." He smiled. "Frankly, I don't mind."

Leggen breathed in deeply, let it out, hesitated, and then, almost as though he was forcing the words out of himself, said, "I won't keep you long. I perfectly understand you need to rest. I do want to say, though, that I am sorry it all happened. I should not have assumed—so casually—that you had gone down by yourself. Since you were a tyro, I should have felt more responsible for you. After all, I had agreed to let you come up. I hope you can find it in your heart to . . . forgive me. That's really all I wish to say."

Seldon yawned, putting his hand over his mouth. "Pardon me. —Since it seems to have turned out well, there need be no hard feelings. In some ways, it was not your fault. I should not have wandered away and, besides, what happened was—"

Dors interrupted. "Now, Hari, please, no conversation. Just relax. Now, I want to talk to Dr. Leggen just a bit before he goes. In the first place, Dr. Leggen, I quite understand you are concerned about how repercussions from this affair will affect you. I told you there would be no follow-up if Dr. Seldon recovered without ill effects. That seems to be taking place, so you may relax—for now. I would like to ask you about something else and I hope that this time I will have your free cooperation."

"I will try, Dr. Venabili," said Leggen stiffly.

"Did anything unusual happen during your stay Upperside?"

"You know it did. I lost Dr. Seldon, something for which I have just apologized."

"Obviously I'm not referring to that. Did anything else unusual happen?"

"No, nothing. Nothing at all."

Dors looked at Seldon and Seldon frowned. It seemed to him that Dors was trying to check on his story and get an independent account. Did she think he was imagining the search vessel? He would have liked to object heatedly, but she had raised a quieting hand at him, as though she was preventing that very eventuality. He subsided, partly because of this and partly because he really wanted to sleep. He hoped that Leggen would not stay long.

"Are you certain?" said Dors. "Were there no intrusions from out-side?"

"No, of course not. Oh—"

"Yes, Dr. Leggen?"

"There was a jet-down."

"Did that strike you as peculiar?"

"No, of course not."

"Why not?"

"This sounds very much as though I'm being cross-examined, Dr. Venabili. I don't much like it."

"I can appreciate that, Dr. Leggen, but these questions have something to do with Dr. Seldon's misadventure. It may be that this whole affair is more complicated than I had thought."

"In what way?" A new edge entered his voice. "Do you intend to raise new questions, requiring new apologies? In that case, I may find it necessary to withdraw."

"Not, perhaps, before you explain how it is you do not find a hovering jet-down a bit peculiar."

"Because, my dear woman, a number of meteorological stations on Trantor possess jet-downs for the direct study of clouds and the upper atmosphere. Our own meteorological station does not."

"Why not? It would be useful."

"Of course. But we're not competing and we're not keeping secrets. We will report on our findings; they will report on theirs. It makes sense, therefore, to have a scattering of differences and specializations. It would be foolish to duplicate efforts completely. The money and manpower we might spend on jet-downs can be spent on mesonic refractometers, while others will spend on the first and save on the latter. After all, there may be a great deal of competitiveness and ill feeling among the sectors, but science is one thing—the only thing—that holds us together. You know that, I presume," he added ironically.

"I do, but isn't it rather coincidental that someone should be sending a jet-down right to your station on the very day you were going to use the station?"

"No coincidence at all. We announced that we were going to make measurements on that day and, consequently, some other station thought, very properly, that they might make simultaneous nephelometric measurements—clouds, you know. The results, taken together, would make more sense and be more useful than either taken separately."

Seldon said suddenly in a rather blurred voice, "They were just measuring, then?" He yawned again.

"Yes," said Leggen. "What else could they possibly be doing?"

Dors blinked her eyes, as she sometimes did when she was trying to think rapidly. "That all makes sense. To which station did this particular jet-down belong?"

Leggen shook his head. "Dr. Venabili, how can you possibly expect me to tell?"

"I thought that each meteorological jet-down might possibly have its station's markings on it."

"Surely, but I wasn't looking up and studying it, you know. I had my own work to do and I let them do theirs. When they report, I'll know whose jet-down it was."

"What if they don't report?"

"Then I would suppose their instruments failed. That happens sometimes." His right fist was clenched. "Is that all, then?"

"Wait a moment. Where do you suppose the jet-down *might* have come from?"

"It might be any station with jet-downs. On a day's notice—and they got more than that—one of those vessels can reach us handily from anyplace on the planet."

"But who most likely?"

"Hard to say: Hestelonia, Wye, Ziggoreth, North Damiano. I'd say one of these four was the most likely, but it *might* be any of forty others at least."

"Just one more question, then. Just one. Dr. Leggen, when you announced that your group would be Upperside, did you by any chance say that a mathematician, Dr. Hari Seldon, would be with you?"

A look of apparently deep and honest surprise crossed Leggen's face, a look that quickly turned contemptuous. "Why should I list names? Of what interest would that be to anyone?"

"Very well," said Dors. "The truth of the matter, then, is that Dr. Seldon saw the jet-down and it disturbed him. I am not certain why and apparently his memory is a bit fuzzy on the matter. He more or less ran away from the jet-down, got himself lost, didn't think of trying to return —or didn't dare to—till it was well into twilight, and didn't quite make it back in the dark. You can't be blamed for that, so let's forget the whole incident on both sides. Agreed?"

"Agreed," said Leggen. "Good-bye!" He turned on his heel and left.

When he was gone, Dors rose, pulled off Seldon's slippers gently, straightened him in his bed, and covered him. He was sleeping, of course.

Then she sat down and thought. How much of what Leggen had said was true and what might possibly exist under the cover of his words? She did not know.

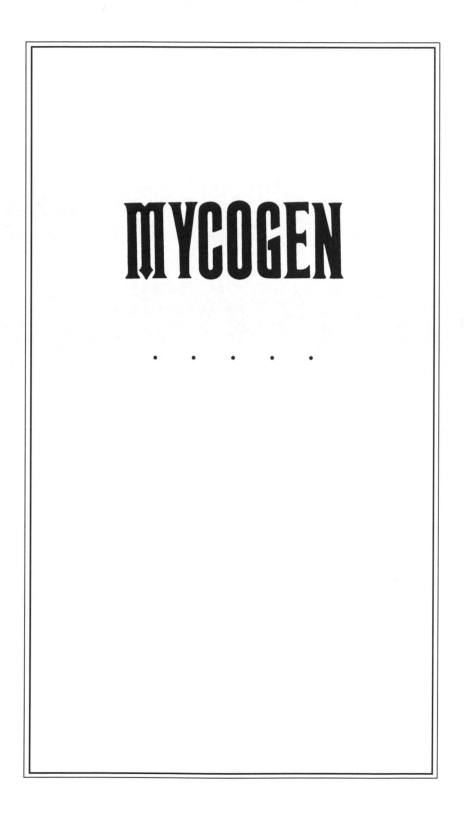

MYCOGEN

. . . . .

MYCOGEN— . . . A sector of ancient Trantor . . . Buried in the past of its own legends, Mycogen made little impact on the planet. Self-satisfied and self-separated to a degree . . .

ENCYCLOPEDIA GALACTICA

31.

When Seldon woke, he found a new face looking at him solemnly. For a moment he frowned owlishly and then he said, "Hummin?"

Hummin smiled very slightly. "You remember me, then?"

"It was only for a day, nearly two months ago, but I remember. You were not arrested, then, or in any way—"

"As you see, I am here, quite safe and whole, but"—and he glanced at Dors, who stood to one side—"it was not very easy for me to come here."

Seldon said, "I'm glad to see you. —Do you mind, by the way?" He jerked his thumb in the direction of the bathroom.

Hummin said, "Take your time. Have breakfast."

Hummin didn't join him at breakfast. Neither did Dors. Nor did they speak. Hummin scanned a book-film with an attitude of easy absorption. Dors inspected her nails critically and then, taking out a microcomputer, began making notes with a stylus.

Seldon watched them thoughtfully and did not try to start a conversation. The silence now might be in response to some Trantorian reserve customary at a sickbed. To be sure, he now felt perfectly normal, but perhaps they did not realize that.

It was only when he was done with his last morsel and with the final drop of milk (which he was obviously getting used to, for it no longer tasted odd) that Hummin spoke.

He said, "How are you, Seldon?"

129

"Perfectly well, Hummin. Sufficiently well, certainly, for me to be up and about."

"I'm glad to hear it," said Hummin dryly. "Dors Venabili was much to blame in allowing this to happen."

Seldon frowned. "No. I insisted on going Upperside."

"I'm sure, but she should, at all costs, have gone with you."

"I told her I didn't want her to go with me."

Dors said, "That's not so, Hari. Don't defend me with gallant lies."

Seldon said angrily, "But don't forget that Dors also came Upperside after me, against strong resistance, and undoubtedly saved my life. That's not bending the truth at all. Have you added that to your evaluation, Hummin?"

Dors interrupted again, obviously embarrassed. "Please, Hari. Chetter Hummin is perfectly correct in feeling that I should either have kept you from going Upperside or have gone up with you. As for my subsequent actions, he has praised them."

"Nevertheless," said Hummin, "that is past and we can let it go. Let us talk about what happened Upperside, Seldon."

Seldon looked about and said guardedly, "Is it safe to do so?"

Hummin smiled slightly. "Dors has placed this room in a Distortion Field. I can be pretty sure that no Imperial agent at the University—if there is one—has the expertise to penetrate it. You are a suspicious person, Seldon."

"Not by nature," said Seldon. "Listening to you in the park and afterward— You are a persuasive person, Hummin. By the time you were through, I was ready to fear that Eto Demerzel was lurking in every shadow."

"I sometimes think he might be," said Hummin gravely.

"If he was," said Seldon, "I wouldn't know it was he. What does he look like?"

"That scarcely matters. You wouldn't see him unless he wanted you to and by then it would all be over, I imagine—which is what we must prevent. Let's talk about that jet-down you saw."

Seldon said, "As I told you, Hummin, you filled me with fears of Demerzel. As soon as I saw the jet-down, I assumed he was after me, that I had foolishly stepped outside the protection of Streeling University by going Upperside, that I had been lured up there for the specific purpose of being picked up without difficulty."

Dors said, "On the other hand, Leggen—"

Seldon said quickly, "Was he here last night?"

"Yes, don't you remember?"

"Vaguely. I was dead tired. It's all a blur in my memory."

"Well, when he was here last night, Leggen said that the jet-down was merely a meteorological vessel from another station. Perfectly ordinary. Perfectly harmless."

"What?" Seldon was taken aback. "I don't believe that."

Hummin said, "Now the question is: *Why* don't you believe that? Was there anything about the jet-down that made you think it was dangerous? Something specific, that is, and not just a pervasive suspicion placed in your head by me."

Seldon thought back, biting his lower lip. He said, "Its *actions*. It seemed to push its forepart below the cloud deck, as though it were looking for something, then it would appear in another spot just the same way, then in another spot, and so on. It seemed to be searching Upperside methodically, section by section, and homing in on me."

Hummin said, "Perhaps you were personifying, Seldon. You may have been treating the jet-down as though it was a strange animal looking for you. It wasn't, of course. It was simply a jet-down and if it *was* a meteorological vessel, its actions were perfectly normal . . . and harmless."

Seldon said, "It didn't seem that way to me."

Hummin said, "I'm sure it didn't, but we don't actually know anything. Your conviction that you were in danger is simply an assumption. Leggen's decision that it was a meteorological vessel is also only an assumption."

Seldon said stubbornly, "I can't believe that it was an entirely innocent event."

"Well then," said Hummin, "suppose we assume the worst—that the vessel *was* looking for you. How would whoever sent that vessel know you would be there to seek?"

Dors interjected, "I asked Dr. Leggen if he had, in his report of the forthcoming meteorological work, included the information that Hari would be with the group. There was no reason he should in the ordinary course of events and he denied that he had, with considerable surprise at the question. I believed him."

Hummin said thoughtfully, "Don't believe him too readily. Wouldn't he deny it, in any case? Now ask yourself why he allowed Seldon to come along in the first place. We know he objected initially, but he did relent, without much fight. And that, to me, seems rather out of character for Leggen."

Dors frowned and said, "I suppose that does make it a bit more likely that he did arrange the entire affair. Perhaps he permitted Hari's company only in order to put him in the position of being taken. He might have received orders to that effect. We might further argue that he encouraged his young intern, Clowzia, to engage Hari's attention and draw him away from the group, isolating him. That would account for Leggen's odd lack of concern over Hari's absence when it came time to go below. He would insist that Hari had left earlier, something he would have laid the groundwork for, since he had carefully showed him how to go down by himself. It would also account for his reluctance to go back up in search of him, since he would not want to waste time looking for someone he assumed would not be found."

Hummin, who had listened carefully, said, "You make an interesting case against him, but let's not accept that too readily either. After all, he did come Upperside with you in the end."

"Because footsteps had been detected. The Chief Seismologist had borne witness to that."

"Well, did Leggen show shock and surprise when Seldon was found? I mean, beyond that of finding someone who had been brought into extreme peril through Leggen's own negligence. Did he act as though Seldon wasn't supposed to be there? Did he behave as though he were asking himself: How is it they didn't pick him up?"

Dors thought carefully, then said, "He was obviously shocked by the sight of Hari lying there, but I couldn't possibly tell if there was anything to his feelings beyond the very natural horror of the situation."

"No, I suppose you couldn't."

But now Seldon, who had been looking from one to the other as they spoke and who had been listening intently, said, "I don't think it was Leggen."

Hummin transferred his attention to Seldon. "Why do you say that?"

"For one thing, as you noted, he was clearly unwilling to have me come along. It took a whole day of argument and I think he agreed only because he had the impression that I was a clever mathematician who could help him out with meteorological theory. I was anxious to go up there and, if he had been under orders to see to it that I was taken Upperside, there would have been no need to be *so* reluctant about it."

"Is it reasonable to suppose he wanted you only for your mathematics? Did he discuss the mathematics with you? Did he make an attempt to explain his theory to you?"

"No," said Seldon, "he didn't. He did say something about going into it later on, though. The trouble was, he was totally involved with his instruments. I gathered he had expected sunshine that hadn't showed up and he was counting on his instruments having been at fault, but they were apparently working perfectly, which frustrated him. I think this was an unexpected development that both soured his temper and turned his attention away from me. As for Clowzia, the young woman who preoccupied me for a few minutes, I do not get the feeling, as I look back on it, that she deliberately led me away from the scene. The initiative was mine. I was curious about the vegetation on Upperside and it was I who drew her away, rather than vice versa. Far from Leggen encouraging her action, he called her back while I was still in sight and I moved farther away and out of sight entirely on my own."

"And yet," said Hummin, who seemed intent on objecting to every suggestion that was made, "if that ship was looking for you, those on board must have known you'd be there. How would they know—if not from Leggen?"

"The man I suspect," said Seldon, "is a young psychologist named Lisung Randa."

"Randa?" said Dors. "I can't believe that. I *know* him. He simply would not be working for the Emperor. He's anti-Imperialist to the core."

"He might pretend to be," said Seldon. "In fact, he would have to be openly, violently, and extremely anti-Imperialist if he was trying to mask the fact that he is an Imperial agent."

"But that's exactly what he's not like," said Dors. "He is *not* violent and extreme in anything. He's quiet and good-natured and his views are always expressed mildly, almost timidly. I'm convinced they're genuine."

"And yet, Dors," said Seldon earnestly, "it was he who first told me of the meteorological project, it was he who urged me to go Upperside, and it was he who persuaded Leggen to allow me to join him, rather exaggerating my mathematical prowess in the process. One must wonder why he was so anxious to get me up there, why he should labor so hard."

"For your good, perhaps. He was interested in you, Hari, and must have thought that meteorology might have been useful in psychohistory. Isn't that possible?"

Hummin said quietly, "Let's consider another point. There was a considerable lapse of time between the moment when Randa told you about the meteorology project and the moment you actually went Upperside. If Randa is innocent of anything underhanded, he would have no particular reason to keep quiet about it. If he is a friendly and gregarious person—"

"He is," said Dors.

"—then he might very likely tell a number of friends about it. In that case, we couldn't really tell who the informer might be. In fact, just to make another point, suppose Randa *is* anti-Imperialist. That would not necessarily mean he is not an agent. We would have to ask: Whom is he an agent for? On whose behalf does he work?"

Seldon was astonished. "Who else is there to work for but the Empire? Who else but Demerzel?"

Hummin raised his hand. "You are far from understanding the whole complexity of Trantorian politics, Seldon." He turned toward Dors. "Tell me again: Which were the four sectors that Dr. Leggen named as likely sources for a meteorological vessel?"

"Hestelonia, Wye, Ziggoreth, and North Damiano."

"And you did not ask the question in any leading way? You didn't ask if a particular sector might be the source?"

"No, definitely not. I simply asked if he could speculate as to the source of the jet-down."

"And you"—Hummin turned to Seldon—"may perhaps have seen some marking, some insigne, on the jet-down?"

Seldon wanted to retort heatedly that the vessel could hardly be seen through the clouds, that it emerged only briefly, that he himself was not looking for markings, but only for escape—but he held back. Surely, Hummin knew all that.

Instead, he said simply, "I'm afraid not."

Dors said, "If the jet-down was on a kidnapping mission, might not the insigne have been masked?"

"That is the rational assumption," said Hummin, "and it may well have been, but in this Galaxy rationality does not always triumph. However, since Seldon seems to have taken no note of any details concerning the vessel, we can only speculate. What I'm thinking is: Wye."

"Why?" echoed Seldon. "I presume they wanted to take me because whoever was on the ship wanted me for my knowledge of psychohistory."

"No no." Hummin lifted his right forefinger as if lecturing a young student. "*W-y-e.* It is the name of a sector on Trantor. A very special sector. It has been ruled by a line of Mayors for some three thousand years. It has been a continuous line, a single dynasty. There was a time, some five hundred years ago, when two Emperors and an Empress of the House of Wye sat on the Imperial throne. It was a comparatively short period and none of the Wye rulers were particularly distinguished or successful, but the Mayors of Wye have never forgotten this Imperial past.

"They have not been actively disloyal to the ruling houses that have succeeded them, but neither have they been known to volunteer much on behalf of those houses. During the occasional periods of civil war, they maintained a kind of neutrality, making moves that seemed best calculated to prolong the civil war and make it seem necessary to turn to Wye as a compromise solution. That never worked out, but they never stopped trying either.

"The present Mayor of Wye is particularly capable. He is old now, but his ambition hasn't cooled. If anything happens to Cleon—even a natural death—the Mayor will have a chance at the succession over Cleon's own too-young son. The Galactic public will always be a little more partial toward a claimant with an Imperial past.

"Therefore, if the Mayor of Wye has heard of you, you might serve as a useful scientific prophet on behalf of his house. There would be a traditional motive for Wye to try to arrange some convenient end for Cleon, use you to predict the inevitable succession of Wye and the coming of peace and prosperity for a thousand years after. Of course, once the Mayor of Wye is on the throne and has no further use for you, you might well follow Cleon to the grave."

Seldon broke the grim silence that followed by saying, "But we don't *know* that it is this Mayor of Wye who is after me."

"No, we don't. Or that anyone at all is after you, at the moment. The jet-down might, after all, have been an ordinary meteorological testing vessel as Leggen has suggested. Still, as the news concerning psychohistory and its potential spreads—and it surely must—more and more of the powerful and semipowerful on Trantor or, for that matter, elsewhere will want to make use of your services."

"What, then," said Dors, "shall we do?"

"That is the question, indeed." Hummin ruminated for a while, then said, "Perhaps it was a mistake to come here. For a professor, it is all too likely that the hiding place chosen would be a University. Streeling is one of many, but it is among the largest and most free, so it wouldn't be long before tendrils from here and there would begin feeling their soft, blind way toward this place. I think that as soon as possible—today, perhaps—Seldon should be moved to another and better hiding place. But—"

"But?" said Seldon.

"But I don't know where."

Seldon said, "Call up a gazeteer on the computer screen and choose a place at random."

"Certainly not," said Hummin. "If we do that, we are as likely to find a place that is less secure than average, as one that is more secure. No, this must be reasoned out. —Somehow."

32.

The three remained huddled in Seldon's quarters till past lunch. During that time, Hari and Dors spoke occasionally and quietly on indifferent subjects, but Hummin maintained an almost complete silence. He sat upright, ate little, and his grave countenance (which, Seldon thought, made him look older than his years) remained quiet and withdrawn.

Seldon imagined him to be reviewing the immense geography of Trantor in his mind, searching for a corner that would be ideal. Surely, it couldn't be easy.

Seldon's own Helicon was somewhat larger by a percent or two than Trantor was and had a smaller ocean. The Heliconian land surface was perhaps 10 percent larger than the Trantorian. But Helicon was sparsely populated, its surface only sprinkled with scattered cities; Trantor was *all* city. Where Helicon was divided into twenty administrative sectors; Trantor had over eight hundred and every one of those hundreds was itself a complex of subdivisions.

Finally Seldon said in some despair, "Perhaps it might be best, Hummin, to chose which candidate for my supposed abilities is most nearly benign, hand me over to that one, and count on him to defend me against the rest."

Hummin looked up and said in utmost seriousness, "That is not necessary. I know the candidate who is most nearly benign and he already has you."

Seldon smiled. "Do you place yourself on the same level with the Mayor of Wye and the Emperor of all the Galaxy?"

"In point of view of position, no. But as far as the desire to control you is concerned, I rival them. They, however, and anyone else I can think of want you in order to strengthen their own wealth and power, while I have no ambitions at all, except for the good of the Galaxy."

"I suspect," said Seldon dryly, "that each of your competitors—if asked—would insist that he too was thinking only of the good of the Galaxy."

"I am sure they would," said Hummin, "but so far, the only one of my competitors, as you call them, whom you have met is the Emperor and he was interested in having you advance fictionalized predictions that might stabilize his dynasty. I do not ask you for anything like that. I ask only that you perfect your psychohistorical technique so that mathematically valid predictions, even if only statistical in nature, can be made."

"True. So far, at least," said Seldon with a half-smile.

"Therefore, I might as well ask: How are you coming along with that task? Any progress?"

Seldon was uncertain whether to laugh or rage. After a pause, he did neither, but managed to speak calmly. "Progress? In less than two months? Hummin, this is something that might easily take me my whole life and the lives of the next dozen who follow me. —And even then end in failure."

"I'm not talking about anything as final as a solution or even as hopeful as the beginning of a solution. You've said flatly a number of times that a useful psychohistory is possible but impractical. All I am asking is whether there now seems any hope that it can be made practical."

"Frankly, no."

Dors said, "Please excuse me. I am not a mathematician, so I hope this is not a foolish question. How can you know something is both possible and impractical? I've heard you say that, in theory, you might personally meet and greet all the people in the Empire, but that it is not a practical feat because you couldn't live long enough to do it. But how can you tell that psychohistory is something of this sort?''

Seldon looked at Dors with some incredulity. "Do you want that *explained?*"

"Yes," she said, nodding her head vigorously so that her curled hair vibrated.

"As a matter of fact," said Hummin, "so would I."

"Without mathematics?" said Seldon with just a trace of a smile.

"Please," said Hummin.

"Well—" He retired into himself to choose a method of presentation. Then he said, "If you want to understand some aspect of the Universe, it helps if you simplify it as much as possible and include only those properties and characteristics that are essential to understanding. If you want to determine how an object drops, you don't concern yourself with whether it is new or old, is red or green, or has an odor or not. You eliminate those things and thus do not needlessly complicate matters. The simplification you can call a model or a simulation and you can present it either as an actual representation on a computer screen or as a mathematical relationship. If you consider the primitive theory of nonrelativistic gravitation—"

Dors said at once, "You promised there would be no mathematics. Don't try to slip it in by calling it 'primitive.' ''

"No no. I mean 'primitive' only in that it has been known as long as our records go back, that its discovery is shrouded in the mists of antiquity as is that of fire or the wheel. In any case, the equations for such gravitational theory contain within themselves a description of the motions of a planetary system, of a double star, of tides, and of many other things. Making use of such equations, we can even set up a pictorial simulation and have a planet circling a star or two stars circling each other on a two-dimensional screen or set up more complicated systems in a three-dimensional holograph. Such simplified simulations make it far easier to grasp a phenomenon than it would be if we had to study the phenomenon itself. In fact, without the gravitational equations, our knowledge of planetary motions and of celestial mechanics generally would be sparse indeed.

"Now, as you wish to know more and more about any phenomenon or as a phenomenon becomes more complex, you need more and more elaborate equations, more and more detailed programming, and you end with a computerized simulation that is harder and harder to grasp."

"Can't you form a simulation of the simulation?" asked Hummin. "You would go down another degree."

"In that case, you would have to eliminate some characteristic of the phenomenon which you want to include and your simulation becomes useless. The LPS—that is, 'the least possible simulation'—gains in complexity faster than the object being simulated does and eventually the simulation catches up with the phenomenon. Thus, it was established thousands of years ago that the Universe as a whole, in its *full* complexity, cannot be represented by any simulation smaller than itself.

"In other words, you can't get any picture of the Universe as a whole except by studying the entire Universe. It has been shown also that if one attempts to substitute simulations of a small part of the Universe, then another small part, then another small part, and so on, intending to put them all together to form a total picture of the Universe, one would find that there are an infinite number of such part simulations. It would therefore take an infinite time to understand the Universe in full and that is just another way of saying that it is impossible to gain all the knowledge there is."

"I understand you so far," said Dors, sounding a little surprised.

"Well then, we know that some comparatively simple things are easy to simulate and as things grow more and more complex they become harder to simulate until finally they become impossible to simulate. But at what level of complexity does simulation cease to be possible? Well, what I have shown, making use of a mathematical technique first invented in this past century and barely usable even if one employs a large and very fast computer, our Galactic society falls short of that mark. It *can* be represented by a simulation simpler than itself. And I went on to show that this would result in the ability to predict future events in a statistical fashion —that is, by stating the probability for alternate sets of events, rather than flatly predicting that one set *will* take place."

"In that case," said Hummin, "since you *can* profitably simulate Galactic society, it's only a matter of doing so. Why is it impractical?"

"All I have proved is that it will not take an infinite time to understand Galactic society, but if it takes a billion years it will still be impractical. That will be essentially the same as infinite time to us."

"Is that how long it would take? A billion years?"

"I haven't been able to work out how long it would take, but I strongly suspect that it will take at least a billion years, which is why I suggested that number."

"But you don't really know."

"I've been trying to work it out."

"Without success?"

"Without success."

"The University library does not help?" Hummin cast a look at Dors as he asked the question.

Seldon shook his head slowly. "Not at all."

"Dors can't help?"

Dors sighed. "I know nothing about the subject, Chetter. I can only suggest ways of looking. If Hari looks and doesn't find, I am helpless."

Hummin rose to his feet. "In that case, there is no great use in staying here at the University and I *must* think of somewhere else to place you."

Seldon reached out and touched his sleeve. "Still, I have an idea."

Hummin stared at him with a faint narrowing of eyes that might have belied surprise—or suspicion. "When did you get the idea? Just now?"

"No. It's been buzzing in my head for a few days before I went Upperside. That little experience eclipsed it for a while, but asking about the library reminded me of it."

Hummin seated himself again. "Tell me your idea—if it's not something that's totally marinated in mathematics."

"No mathematics at all. It's just that reading history in the library reminded me that Galactic society was less complicated in the past. Twelve thousand years ago, when the Empire was on the way to being established, the Galaxy contained only about ten million inhabited worlds. Twenty thousand years ago, the pre-Imperial kingdoms included only about ten thousand worlds altogether. Still deeper in the past, who knows how society shrinks down? Perhaps even to a single world as in the legends you yourself once mentioned, Hummin."

Hummin said, "And you think you might be able to work out psychohistory if you dealt with a much simpler Galactic society?"

"Yes, it seems to me that I might be able to do so."

"Then too," said Dors with sudden enthusiasm, "suppose you work out psychohistory for a smaller society of the past and suppose you can make predictions from a study of the pre-Imperial situation as to what might happen a thousand years after the formation of the Empire—you could then check the actual situation at that time and see how near the mark you were."

Hummin said coldly, "Considering that you would know in advance the situation of the year 1,000 of the Galactic Era, it would scarcely be a fair test. You would be unconsciously swayed by your prior knowledge and you would be bound to choose values for your equation in such a way as to give you what you would know to be the solution."

"I don't think so," said Dors. "We don't know the situation in 1,000 G.E. very well and we would have to dig. After all, that was eleven millennia ago."

Seldon's face turned into a picture of dismay. "What do you mean we don't know the situation in 1,000 G.E. very well? There were computers then, weren't there, Dors?"

"Of course."

"And memory storage units and recordings of ear and eye? We should have all the records of 1,000 G.E. as we have of the present year of 12,020 G.E."

"In theory, yes, but in actual practice— Well, you know, Hari, it's what you keep saying. It's possible to have full records of 1,000 G.E., but it's not practical to expect to have it."

"Yes, but what I keep saying, Dors, refers to mathematical demonstrations. I don't see the applications to historical records."

Dors said defensively, "Records don't last forever, Hari. Memory banks can be destroyed or defaced as a result of conflict or can simply deteriorate with time. Any memory bit, any record that is not referred to for a long time, eventually drowns in accumulated noise. They say that fully one third of the records in the Imperial Library are simply gibberish, but, of course, custom will not allow those records to be removed. Other libraries are less tradition-bound. In the Streeling University library, we discard worthless items every ten years.

"Naturally, records frequently referred to and frequently duplicated on various worlds and in various libraries—governmental and private— remain clear enough for thousands of years, so that many of the essential points of Galactic history remain known even if they took place in pre-Imperial times. However, the farther back you go, the less there is preserved."

"I can't believe that," said Seldon. "I should think that new copies would be made of any record in danger of withering. How could you let knowledge disappear?"

"Undesired knowledge is useless knowledge," said Dors. "Can you imagine all the time, effort, and energy expended in a continual refurbishing of unused data? And that wastage would grow steadily more extreme with time."

"Surely, you would have to allow for the fact that someone at some time might need the data being so carelessly disposed of."

"A particular item might be wanted once in a thousand years. To save it all just in case of such a need isn't cost-effective. Even in science. You spoke of the primitive equations of gravitation and say it is primitive because its discovery is lost in the mists of antiquity. Why should that be? Didn't you mathematicians and scientists save all data, all information, back and back to the misty primeval time when those equations were discovered?"

Seldon groaned and made no attempt to answer. He said, "Well, Hummin, so much for my idea. As we look back into the past and as society grows smaller, a useful psychohistory becomes more likely. But knowledge dwindles even more rapidly than size, so psychohistory becomes less likely—and the less outweighs the more."

"To be sure, there is the Mycogen Sector," said Dors, musing.

Hummin looked up quickly. "So there is and that would be the perfect place to put Seldon. I should have thought of it myself."

"Mycogen Sector," repeated Hari, looking from one to the other. "What and where is Mycogen Sector?"

"Hari, please, I'll tell you later. Right now, I have preparations to make. You'll leave tonight."

33.

Dors had urged Seldon to sleep a bit. They would be leaving halfway between lights out and lights on, under cover of "night," while the rest of the University slept. She insisted he could still use a little rest.

"And have you sleep on the floor again?" Seldon asked.

She shrugged. "The bed will only hold one and if we both try to crowd into it, neither of us will get much sleep."

He looked at her hungrily for a moment and said, "Then I'll sleep on the floor this time."

"No, you won't. I wasn't the one who lay in a coma in the sleet."

As it happened, neither slept. Though they darkened the room and though the perpetual hum of Trantor was only a drowsy sound in the relatively quiet confines of the University, Seldon found that he had to talk.

He said, "I've been so much trouble to you, Dors, here at the University. I've even been keeping you from your work. Still, I'm sorry I'll have to leave you."

Dors said, "You won't leave me. I'm coming with you. Hummin is arranging a leave of absence for me."

Seldon said, dismayed, "I can't ask you to do that."

"You're not. Hummin's asking it. I must guard you. After all, I failed in connection with Upperside and should make up for it."

"I told you. Please don't feel guilty about that. —Still, I must admit I would feel more comfortable with you at my side. If I could only be sure I wasn't interfering with your life . . ."

Dors said softly, "You're not, Hari. Please go to sleep."

Seldon lay silent for a while, then whispered, "Are you sure Hummin can really arrange everything, Dors?"

Dors said, "He's a remarkable man. He's got influence here at the University and everywhere else, I think. If he says he can arrange for an indefinite leave for me, I'm sure he can. He is a most *persuasive* man."

"I know," said Seldon. "Sometimes I wonder what he *really* wants of me."

"What he says," said Dors. "He's a man of strong and idealistic ideas and dreams."

"You sound as though you know him well, Dors."

"Oh yes, I know him well."

"Intimately?"

Dors made an odd noise. "I'm not sure what you're implying, Hari, but, assuming the most insolent interpretation— No, I don't know him intimately. What business would that be of yours anyway?"

"I'm sorry," said Seldon. "I just didn't want, inadvertently, to be invading someone else's—"

"Property? That's even more insulting. I think you had better go to sleep."

"I'm sorry again, Dors, but I *can't* sleep. Let me at least change the subject. You haven't explained what the Mycogen Sector is. Why will it be good for me to go there? What's it like?"

"It's a small sector with a population of only about two million—if I remember correctly. The thing is that the Mycogenians cling tightly to a set of traditions about early history and are supposed to have very ancient records not available to anyone else. It's just possible they would be of more use to you in your attempted examination of pre-Imperial times than orthodox historians might be. All our talk about early history brought the sector to mind."

"Have you ever seen their records?"

"No. I don't know anyone who has."

"Can you be sure that the records really exist, then?"

"Actually, I can't say. The assumption among non-Mycogenians is that they're a bunch of madcaps, but that may be quite unfair. They certainly *say* they have records, so perhaps they do. In any case, we would be out of sight there. The Mycogenians keep strictly to themselves. —And now please do go to sleep."

And somehow Seldon finally did.

34.

Hari Seldon and Dors Venabili left the University grounds at 0300. Seldon realized that Dors had to be the leader. She knew Trantor better than he did—two years better. She was obviously a close friend of Hummin (how close? the question kept nagging at him) and she understood his instructions.

Both she and Seldon were swathed in light swirling cloaks with tight-fitting hoods. The style had been a short-lived clothing fad at the University (and among young intellectuals, generally) some years back and though right now it might provoke laughter, it had the saving grace of covering them well and of making them unrecognizable—at least at a cursory glance.

Hummin had said, "There's a possibility that the event Upperside was completely innocent and that there are no agents after you, Seldon, but let's be prepared for the worst."

Seldon had asked anxiously, "Won't you come with us?"

"I would like to," said Hummin, "but I must limit my absence from work if I am not to become a target myself. You understand?"

Seldon sighed. He understood.

They entered an Expressway car and found a seat as far as possible from the few who had already boarded. (Seldon wondered why *anyone* should be on the Expressways at three in the morning—and then thought that it was lucky some were or he and Dors would be entirely too conspicuous.)

Seldon fell to watching the endless panorama that passed in review as the equally endless line of coaches moved along the endless monorail on an endless electromagnetic field.

The Expressway passed row upon row of dwelling units, few of them very tall, but some, for all he knew, very deep. Still, if tens of millions of square kilometers formed an urbanized total, even forty billion people would not require very tall structures or very closely packed ones. They did pass open areas, in most of which crops seemed to be growing—but some of which were clearly parklike. And there were numerous structures whose nature he couldn't guess. Factories? Office buildings? Who knew? One large featureless cylinder struck him as though it might be a water tank. After all, Trantor had to have a fresh water supply. Did they sluice rain from Upperside, filter and treat it, then store it? It seemed inevitable that they should.

Seldon did not have very long to study the view, however.

Dors muttered, "This is about where we should be getting off." She stood up and her strong fingers gripped his arm.

They were off the Expressway now, standing on solid flooring while Dors studied the directional signs.

The signs were unobtrusive and there were many of them. Seldon's heart sank. Most of them were in pictographs and initials, which were undoubtedly understandable to native Trantorians, but which were alien to him.

"This way," said Dors.

"Which way? How do you know?"

"See that? Two wings and an arrow."

"Two wings? Oh." He had thought of it as an upside-down "w," wide and shallow, but he could see where it might be the stylized wings of a bird.

"Why don't they use words?" he said sullenly.

"Because words vary from world to world. What an 'air-jet' is here could be a 'soar' on Cinna or a 'swoop' on other worlds. The two wings and an arrow are a Galactic symbol for an air vessel and the symbol is understood everywhere. —Don't you use them on Helicon?"

"Not much. Helicon is a fairly homogeneous world, culturally speaking, and we tend to cling to our private ways firmly because we're overshadowed by our neighbors."

"See?" said Dors. "There's where your psychohistory might come in. You could show that even with different dialects the use of set symbols, Galaxy-wide, is a unifying force."

"That won't help." He was following her through empty dim alley ways and part of his mind wondered what the crime rate might be on Trantor and whether this was a high-crime area. "You can have a billion rules, each covering a single phenomenon, and you can derive no generalizations from that. That's what one means when one says that a system might be interpreted only by a model as complex as itself. —Dors, are we heading for an air-jet?"

She stopped and turned to look at him with an amused frown. "If we're following the symbols for air-jets, do you suppose we're trying to reach a golf course? —Are you afraid of air-jets in the way so many Trantorians are?"

"No no. We fly freely on Helicon and I make use of air-jets frequently. It's just that when Hummin took me to the University, he avoided commercial air travel because he thought we would leave too clear a trail."

"That's because they knew where you were to begin with, Hari, and were after you already. Right now, it may be that they don't know where you are and we're using an obscure port and a *private* air-jet."

"And who'll be doing the flying?"

"A friend of Hummin's, I presume."

"Can he be trusted, do you suppose?"

"If he's a friend of Hummin's, he surely can."

"You certainly think highly of Hummin," said Seldon with a twinge of discontent.

"With reason," said Dors with no attempt at coyness. "He's the best."

Seldon's discontent did not dwindle.

"There's the air-jet," she said.

It was a small one with oddly shaped wings. Standing beside it was a small man, dressed in the usual glaring Trantorian colors.

146

Dors said, "We're psycho."

The pilot said, "And I'm history."

They followed him into the air-jet and Seldon said, "Whose idea were the passwords?"

"Hummin's," said Dors.

Seldon snorted. "Somehow I didn't think Hummin would have a sense of humor. He's so solemn."

Dors smiled.

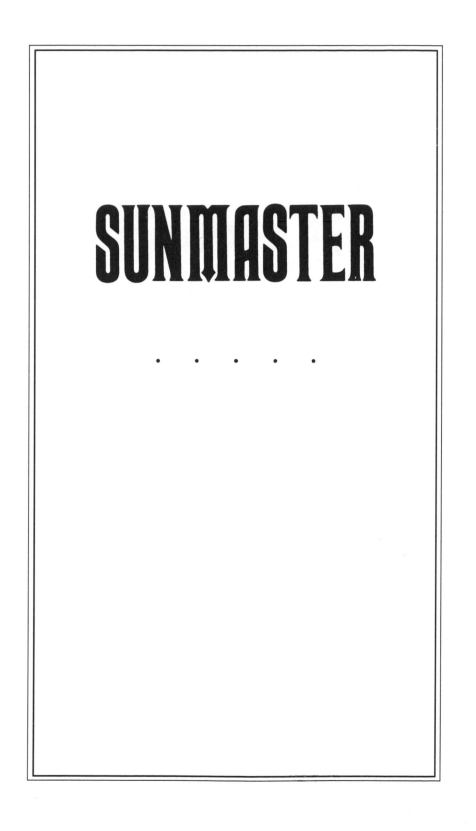

SUNMASTER

· · · · ·

SUNMASTER FOURTEEN— . . . A leader of the Mycogen Sector of ancient Trantor . . . As is true of all the leaders of this ingrown sector, little is known of him. That he plays any role at all in history is due entirely to his interrelationship with Hari Seldon in the course of The Flight . . .

ENCYCLOPEDIA GALACTICA

35.

There were just two seats behind the compact pilot compartment and when Seldon sat down on padding that gave slowly beneath him meshed fabric came forward to encircle his legs, waist, and chest and a hood came down over his forehead and ears. He felt imprisoned and when he turned to his left with difficulty—and only slightly—he could see that Dors was similarly enclosed.

The pilot took his own seat and checked the controls. Then he said, "I'm Endor Levanian, at your service. You're enmeshed because there will be a considerable acceleration at lift-off. Once we're in the open and flying, you'll be released. You needn't tell me your names. It's none of my business."

He turned in his seat and smiled at them out of a gnomelike face that wrinkled as his lips spread outward. "Any psychological difficulties, youngsters?"

Dors said lightly, "I'm an Outworlder and I'm used to flying."

"That is also true for myself," said Seldon with a bit of hauteur.

"Excellent, youngsters. Of course, this isn't your ordinary air-jet and you may not have done any night flying, but I'll count on you to bear up."

He was enmeshed too, but Seldon could see that his arms were entirely free.

A dull hum sounded inside the jet, growing in intensity and rising in pitch. Without actually becoming unpleasant, it threatened to do so and Seldon made a gesture as though to shake his head and get the sound out of his ears, but the attempt to do so merely seemed to stiffen the hold of the head-mesh.

The jet then sprang (it was the only verb Seldon could find to describe the event) into the air and he found himself pushed hard against the back and bottom of his seat.

Through the windshield in front of the pilot, Seldon saw, with a twinge of horror, the flat rise of a wall—and then a round opening appear in that wall. It was similar to the hole into which the air-taxi had plunged the day he and Hummin had left the Imperial Sector, but though this one was large enough for the body of the jet, it certainly did not leave room for the wings.

Seldon's head turned as far to the right as he could manage and did so just in time to see the wing on his side wither and collapse.

The jet plunged into the opening and was seized by the electromagnetic field and hurtled along a lighted tunnel. The acceleration was constant and there were occasional clicking noises that Seldon imagined might be the passing of individual magnets.

And then, in less than ten minutes, the jet was spewed out into the atmosphere, headlong into the sudden pervasive darkness of night.

The jet decelerated as it passed beyond the electromagnetic field and Seldon felt himself flung against the mesh and plastered there for a few breathless moments.

Then the pressure ceased and the mesh disappeared altogether.

"How are you, youngsters?" came the cheerful voice of the pilot.

"I'm not sure," said Seldon. He turned to Dors. "Are you all right?"

"Certainly," she answered. "I think Mr. Levanian was putting us through his paces to see if we were really Outworlders. Is that so, Mr. Levanian?"

"Some people like excitement," said Levanian. "Do you?"

"Within limits," said Dors.

Then Seldon added approvingly, "As any reasonable person would admit."

Seldon went on. "It might have seemed less humorous to you, sir, if you had ripped the wings off the jet."

"Impossible, sir. I told you this is not your ordinary air-jet. The wings are thoroughly computerized. They change their length, width, curvature, and overall shape to match the speed of the jet, the speed and direction of the wind, the temperature, and half a dozen other variables. The wings wouldn't tear off unless the jet itself was subjected to stresses that would splinter it."

There was a spatter against Seldon's window. He said, "It's raining."

"It often is," said the pilot.

Seldon peered out the window. On Helicon or on any other world, there would have been lights visible—the illuminated works of man. Only on Trantor would it be dark.

—Well, not entirely. At one point he saw the flash of a beacon light. Perhaps the higher reaches of Upperside had warning lights.

As usual, Dors took note of Seldon's uneasiness. Patting his hand, she said, "I'm sure the pilot knows what he's doing, Hari."

"I'll try to be sure of it, too, Dors, but I wish he'd share some of that knowledge with us," Seldon said in a voice loud enough to be overheard.

"I don't mind sharing," said the pilot. "To begin with, we're heading up and we'll be above the cloud deck in a few minutes. Then there won't be any rain and we'll even see the stars."

He had timed the remark beautifully, for a few stars began to glitter through the feathery cloud remnants and then all the rest sprang into brightness as the pilot flicked off the lights inside the cabin. Only the dim illumination of his own instrument panel remained to compete and outside the window the sky sparkled brightly.

Dors said, "That's the first time in over two years that I've seen the stars. Aren't they marvelous? They're so bright—and there are so many of them."

The pilot said, "Trantor is nearer the center of the Galaxy than most of the Outworlds."

Since Helicon was in a sparse corner of the Galaxy and its star field was dim and unimpressive, Seldon found himself speechless.

Dors said, "How quiet this flight has become."

"So it is," said Seldon. "What powers the jet, Mr. Levanian?"

"A microfusion motor and a thin stream of hot gas."

"I didn't know we had working microfusion air-jets. They talk about it, but—"

"There are a few small ones like this. So far they exist only on Trantor and are used entirely by high government officials."

Seldon said, "The fees for such travel must come high."

"Very high, sir."

"How much is Mr. Hummin being charged, then?"

"There's no charge for this flight. Mr. Hummin is a good friend of the company who owns these jets."

Seldon grunted. Then he asked, "Why aren't there more of these microfusion air-jets?"

"Too expensive for one thing, sir. Those that exist fulfill all the demand."

"You could create more demand with larger jets."

"Maybe so, but the company has never managed to make microfusion engines strong enough for large air-jets."

Seldon thought of Hummin's complaint that technological innovation had declined to a low level. "Decadent," he murmured.

"What?" said Dors.

"Nothing," said Seldon. "I was just thinking of something Hummin once said to me."

He looked out at the stars and said, "Are we moving westward, Mr. Levanian?"

"Yes, we are. How did you know?"

"Because I thought that we would see the dawn by now if we were heading east to meet it."

But dawn, pursuing the planet, finally caught up with them and sunlight—*real* sunlight—brightened the cabin walls. It didn't last long, however, for the jet curved downward and into the clouds. Blue and gold vanished and were replaced by dingy gray and both Seldon and Dors emitted disappointed cries at being deprived of even a few more moments of true sunlight.

When they sank beneath the clouds, Upperside was immediately below them and its surface—at least at this spot—was a rolling mixture of wooded grottos and intervening grassland. It was the sort of thing Clowzia had told Seldon existed on Upperside.

Again there was little time for observation, however. An opening appeared below them, rimmed by lettering that spelled MYCOGEN.

They plunged in.

36.

They landed at a jetport that seemed deserted to Seldon's wondering eyes. The pilot, having completed his task, shook hands with both Hari and Dors and took his jet up into the air with a rush, plunging it into an opening that appeared for his benefit.

There seemed, then, nothing to do but wait. There were benches that could seat perhaps a hundred people, but Seldon and Dors Venabili were the only two people around. The port was rectangular, surrounded by walls in which there must be many tunnels that could open to receive or deliver jets, but there were no jets present after their own had departed and none arrived while they waited.

There were no people arriving or any indications of habitation; the very life hum of Trantor was muted.

Seldon felt this aloneness to be oppressive. He turned to Dors and said, "What is it that we must do here? Have you any idea?"

Dors shook her head. "Hummin told me we would be met by Sunmaster Fourteen. I don't know anything beyond that."

"Sunmaster Fourteen? What would that be?"

"A human being, I presume. From the name I can't be certain whether it would be a man or a woman."

"An odd name."

"Oddity is in the mind of the receiver. I am sometimes taken to be a man by those who have never met me."

"What fools they must be," said Seldon, smiling.

"Not at all. Judging from my name, they *are* justified. I'm told it is a popular masculine name on various worlds."

"I've never encountered it before."

"That's because you aren't much of a Galactic traveler. The name 'Hari' is common enough everywhere, although I once knew a woman named 'Hare,' pronounced like your name but spelled with an 'e.' In Mycogen, as I recall, particular names are confined to families—and numbered."

"But Sunmaster seems so unrestrained a name."

"What's a little braggadocio? Back on Cinna, 'Dors' is from an old local expression meaning 'spring gift.' "

"Because you were born in the spring?"

"No. I first saw the light of day at the height of Cinna's summer, but the name struck my people as pleasant regardless of its traditional—and largely forgotten—meaning."

"In that case, perhaps Sunmaster—"

And a deep, severe voice said, "That is my name, tribesman."

Seldon, startled, looked to his left. An open ground-car had somehow drawn close. It was boxy and archaic, looking almost like a delivery wagon. In it, at the controls, was a tall old man who looked vigorous despite his age. With stately majesty, he got out of the ground-car.

He wore a long white gown with voluminous sleeves, pinched in at the wrists. Beneath the gown were soft sandals from which the big toe protruded, while his head, beautifully shaped, was completely hairless. He regarded the two calmly with his deep blue eyes.

He said, "I greet you, tribesman."

Seldon said with automatic politeness, "Greetings, sir." Then, honestly puzzled, he asked, "How did you get in?"

"Through the entrance, which closed behind me. You paid little heed."

"I suppose we didn't. But then we didn't know what to expect. Nor do we now."

"Tribesman Chetter Hummin informed the Brethren that there would be members from two of the tribes arriving. He asked that you be cared for."

"Then you know Hummin."

"We do. He has been of service to us. And because he, a worthy tribesman, has been of service to us, so must we be now to him. There are few who come to Mycogen and few who leave. I am to make you secure, give you houseroom, see that you are undisturbed. You will be safe here."

Dors bent her head. "We are grateful, Sunmaster Fourteen."

Sunmaster turned to look at her with an air of dispassionate contempt. "I am not unaware of the customs of the tribes," he said. "I know that among them a woman may well speak before being spoken to. I am therefore not offended. I would ask her to have a care among others of the Brethren who may be of lesser knowledge in the matter."

"Oh really?" said Dors, who was clearly offended, even if Sunmaster was not.

"In truth," agreed Sunmaster. "Nor is it needful to use my numerical identifier when I alone of my cohort am with you. 'Sunmaster' will be sufficient. —Now I will ask you to come with me so that we may leave this place which is of too tribal a nature to comfort me."

"Comfort is for all of us," said Seldon, perhaps a little more loudly than was necessary, "and we will not budge from this place unless we are assured that we will not be forcibly bent to your liking against our own natures. It is our custom that a woman may speak whenever she has something to say. If you have agreed to keep us secure, that security must be psychological as well as physical."

Sunmaster gazed at Seldon levelly and said, "You are bold, young tribesman. Your name?"

"I am Hari Seldon of Helicon. My companion is Dors Venabili of Cinna."

Sunmaster bowed slightly as Seldon pronounced his own name, did not move at the mention of Dors's name. He said, "I have sworn to Tribesman Hummin that we will keep you safe, so I will do what I can to protect your woman companion in this. If she wishes to exercise her impudence, I will do my best to see that she is held guiltless. —Yet in one respect you must conform."

And he pointed, with infinite scorn, first to Seldon's head and then to Dors's.

"What do you mean?" said Seldon.

"Your cephalic hair."

"What about it?"

"It must not be seen."

"Do you mean we're to shave our heads like you? Certainly not."

"My head is not shaven, Tribesman Seldon. I was depilated when I entered puberty, as are all the Brethren and their women."

"If we're talking about depilation, then more than ever the answer is no—never."

"Tribesman, we ask neither shaving nor depilation. We ask only that your hair be covered when you are among us."

"How?"

"I have brought skincaps that will mold themselves to your skulls, together with strips that will hide the superoptical patches—the eyebrows. You will wear them while with us. And of course, Tribesman Seldon, you will shave daily—or oftener if that becomes necessary."

"But why must we do this?"

"Because to us, hair on the head is repulsive and obscene."

"Surely, you and all your people know that it is customary for others, in all the worlds of the Galaxy, to retain their cephalic hair."

"We know. And those among us, like myself, who must deal with tribesmen now and then, must witness this hair. We manage, but it is unfair to ask the Brethren generally to suffer the sight."

Seldon said, "Very well, then, Sunmaster—but tell me. Since you are born with cephalic hair, as all of us are and as you all retain it visibly till puberty, why is it so necessary to remove it? Is it just a matter of custom or is there some rationale behind it?"

And the old Mycogenian said proudly, "By depilation, we demonstrate to the youngster that he or she has become an adult and through depilation adults will always remember who they are and never forget that all others are but tribesmen."

He waited for no response (and, in truth, Seldon could think of none) but brought out from some hidden compartment in his robe a handful of thin bits of plastic of varying color, stared keenly at the two faces before him, holding first one strip, then another, against each face.

"The colors must match reasonably," he said. "No one will be fooled into thinking you are not wearing a skincap, but it must not be repulsively obvious."

Finally, Sunmaster gave a particular strip to Seldon and showed him how it could be pulled out into a cap.

"Please put it on, Tribesman Seldon," he said. "You will find the process clumsy at first, but you will grow accustomed to it."

Seldon put it on, but the first two times it slipped off when he tried to pull it backward over his hair.

"Begin just above your eyebrows," said Sunmaster. His fingers seemed to twitch, as though eager to help.

Seldon said, suppressing a smile, "Would you do it for me?"

And Sunmaster drew back, saying, almost in agitation, "I couldn't. I would be touching your hair."

Seldon managed to hook it on and followed Sunmaster's advice, in pulling it here and there until all his hair was covered. The eyebrow patches fitted on easily. Dors, who had watched carefully, put hers on without trouble.

"How does it come off?" asked Seldon.

"You have but to find an end and it will peel off without trouble. You will find it easier both to put on and take off if you cut your hair shorter."

"I'd rather struggle a bit," said Seldon. Then, turning to Dors, he said in a low voice, "You're still pretty, Dors, but it does tend to remove some of the character from your face."

"The character is there underneath just the same," she answered. "And I dare say you'll grow accustomed to the hairless me."

In a still lower whisper, Seldon said, "I don't want to stay here long enough to get accustomed to this."

Sunmaster, who ignored, with visible haughtiness, the mumblings among mere tribesmen, said, "If you will enter my ground-car, I will now take you into Mycogen."

37.

"Frankly," whispered Dors, "I can scarcely believe I'm on Trantor."

"I take it, then, you've never seen anything like this before?" said Seldon.

"I've only been on Trantor for two years and I've spent much of my time at the University, so I'm not exactly a world traveler. Still, I've been here and there and I've heard of this and that, but I've never seen or heard of anything like this. The *sameness.*"

Sunmaster drove along methodically and without undue haste. There were other wagonlike vehicles in the roadway, all with hairless men at the controls, their bald pates gleaming in the light.

On either side there were three-story structures, unornamented, all lines meeting at right angles, everything gray in color.

"Dreary," mouthed Dors. "So dreary."

"Egalitarian," whispered Seldon. "I suspect no Brother can lay claim to precedence of any obvious kind over any other."

There were many pedestrians on the walkways as they passed. There were no signs of any moving corridors and no sound of any nearby Expressway.

Dors said, "I'm guessing the grays are women."

"It's hard to tell," said Seldon. "The gowns hide everything and one hairless head is like another."

"The grays are always in pairs or with a white. The whites can walk alone and Sunmaster is a white."

"You may be right." Seldon raised his voice. "Sunmaster, I am curious—"

"If you are, then ask what you wish, although I am by no means required to answer."

"We seem to be passing through a residential area. There are no signs of business establishments, industrial areas—"

"We are a farming community entirely. Where are you from that you do not know this?"

"You know I am an Outworlder," Seldon said stiffly. "I have been on Trantor for only two months."

"Even so."

"But if you are a farming community, Sunmaster, how is it that we have passed no farms either?"

"On lower levels," said Sunmaster briefly.

"Is Mycogen on this level entirely residential, then?"

"And on a few others. We are what you see. Every Brother and his family lives in equivalent quarters; every cohort in its own equivalent community; all have the same ground-cars and all Brothers drive their own. There are no servants and none are at ease through the labor of others. None may glory over another."

Seldon lifted his shielded eyebrows at Dors and said, "But some of the people wear white, while some wear gray."

"That is because some of the people are Brothers and some are Sisters."

"And we?"

"You are a tribesman and a guest. You and your"—he paused and then said—"companion will not be bound by all aspects of Mycogenian life. Nevertheless, you will wear a white gown and your companion will wear a gray one and you will live in special guest quarters like our own."

"Equality for all seems a pleasant ideal, but what happens as your numbers increase? Is the pie, then, cut into smaller pieces?"

"There is no increase in numbers. That would necessitate an increase in area, which the surrounding tribesmen would not allow, or a change for the worse in our way of life."

"But if—" began Seldon.

Sunmaster cut him off. "It is enough, Tribesman Seldon. As I warned you, I am not compelled to answer. Our task, which we have promised our friend Tribesman Hummin, is to keep you secure as long as you do not violate our way of life. That we will do, but there it ends. Curiosity is permitted, but it wears out our patience quickly if persisted in."

Something about his tone allowed no more to be said and Seldon chafed. Hummin, for all his help, had clearly mis-stressed the matter.

It was not security that Seldon sought. At least, not security alone. He needed information too and without that he could not—and would not—stay here.

38.

Seldon looked with some distress at their quarters. It had a small but individual kitchen and a small but individual bathroom. There were two narrow beds, two clothes closets, a table, and two chairs. In short there was everything that was necessary for two people who were willing to live under cramped conditions.

"We had an individual kitchen and bathroom at Cinna," said Dors with an air of resignation.

"Not I," said Seldon. "Helicon may be a small world, but I lived in a modern city. Community kitchens and bathrooms. —What a waste this is. You might expect it in a hotel, where one is compelled to make a temporary stay, but if the whole sector is like this, imagine the enormous number and duplications of kitchens and bathrooms."

"Part of the egalitarianism, I suppose," said Dors. "No fighting for favored stalls or for faster service. The same for everyone."

"No privacy either. Not that I mind terribly, Dors, but you might and I don't want to give the appearance of taking advantage. We ought to make it clear to them that we must have separate rooms—adjoining but separate."

Dors said, "I'm sure it won't work. Space is at a premium and I think they are amazed by their own generosity in giving us this much. We'll just make do, Hari. We're each old enough to manage. I'm not a blushing maiden and you'll never convince me that you're a callow youth."

"You wouldn't be here, were it not for me."

"What of it? It's an adventure."

"All right, then. Which bed will you take? Why don't you take the one nearer the bathroom?" He sat down on the other. "There's something else that bothers me. As long as we're here, we're tribespeople, you and

I, as is even Hummin. We're of the *other* tribes, not their own cohorts, and most things are none of our business. —But most things *are* my business. That's what I've come here for. I want to know some of the things they know."

"Or think they know," said Dors with a historian's skepticism. "I understand they have legends that are supposed to date back to primordial times, but I can't believe they can be taken seriously."

"We can't know that until we find out what those legends are. Are there no outside records of them?"

"Not that I know of. These people are terribly ingrown. They're almost psychotic in their inward clinging. That Hummin can break down their barriers somewhat and even get them to take us in is remarkable— *really* remarkable."

Seldon brooded. "There has to be an opening somewhere. Sunmaster was surprised—angry, in fact—that I didn't know Mycogen was an agricultural community. That seems to be something they don't want kept a secret."

"The point is, it *isn't* a secret. 'Mycogen' is supposed to be from archaic words meaning 'yeast producer.' At least, that's what I've been told. I'm not a paleolinguist. In any case, they culture all varieties of microfood—yeast, of course, along with algae, bacteria, multicellular fungi, and so on."

"That's not uncommon," said Seldon. "Most worlds have this microculture. We have some even on Helicon."

"Not like Mycogen. It's their specialty. They use methods as archaic as the name of their section—secret fertilizing formulas, secret environmental influences. Who knows what? All is secret."

"Ingrown."

"With a vengeance. What it amounts to is that they produce protein and subtle flavoring, so that *their* microfood isn't like any other in the world. They keep the volume comparatively low and the price is sky-high. I've never tasted any and I'm sure you haven't, but it sells in great quantities to the Imperial bureaucracy and to the upper classes on other worlds. Mycogen depends on such sales for its economic health, so they want everyone to know that they are the source of this valuable food. *That,* at least, is no secret."

"Mycogen must be rich, then."

"They're not poor, but I suspect that it's not wealth they're after. It's protection. The Imperial government protects them because, without them, there wouldn't be these microfoods that add the subtlest flavors, the tangiest spices, to every dish. That means that Mycogen can maintain its odd way of life and be haughty toward its neighbors, who probably find them insupportable."

Dors looked about. "They live an austere life. There's no holovision, I notice, and no book-films."

"I noticed one in the closet up on the shelf." Seldon reached for it, stared at the label, and then said in clear disgust, "A cookbook."

Dors held out her hand for it and manipulated the keys. It took a while, for the arrangement was not quite orthodox, but she finally managed to light the screen and inspect the pages. She said, "There are a few recipes, but for the most part this seems to consist of philsophical essays on gastronomy."

She shut it off and turned it round and about. "It seems to be a single unit. I don't see how one would eject the microcard and insert another. —A one-book scanner. Now *that's* a waste."

"Maybe they think this one book-film is all anyone needs." He reached toward the end table that was between the two beds and picked up another object. "This could be a speaker, except that there's no screen."

"Perhaps they consider the voice sufficient."

"How does it work, I wonder?" Seldon lifted it and looked at it from different sides. "Did you ever see anything like this?"

"In a museum once—if this is the same thing. Mycogen seems to keep itself deliberately archaic. I suppose they consider that another way of separating themselves from the so-called tribesmen that surround them in overwhelming numbers. Their archaism and odd customs make them indigestible, so to speak. There's a kind of perverse logic to all that."

Seldon, still playing with the device, said, "Whoops! It went on. Or something went on. But I don't hear anything."

Dors frowned and picked up a small felt-lined cylinder that remained behind on the end table. She put it to her ear. "There's a voice coming out of this," she said. "Here, try it." She handed it to him.

Seldon did so and said, "Ouch! It clips on." He listened and said, "Yes, it hurt my ear. You can hear me, I take it. —Yes, this is our room. —No, I don't know its number. Dors, have you any idea of the number?"

Dors said, "There's a number on the speaker. Maybe that will do."

"Maybe," said Seldon doubtfully. Then he said into the speaker, "The number on this device is 6LT-3648A. Will that do? —Well, where do I find out how to use this device properly and how to use the kitchen, for that matter? —What do you *mean*, 'It all works the usual way?' That doesn't do me any good. —See here, I'm a . . . a tribesman, an honored guest. I don't know the usual way. —Yes, I'm sorry about my accent and I'm glad you can recognize a tribesman when you hear one. —My name is Hari Seldon."

There was a pause and Seldon looked up at Dors with a long-suffering expression on his face. "He has to look me up. And I suppose he'll tell me he can't find me. —Oh, you have me? Good! In that case, can you give me the information? —Yes. —Yes. —Yes. —And how can I call someone outside Mycogen? —Oh, then what about contacting Sunmaster Fourteen, for instance? —Well, his assistant then, his aide, whatever? —Uh-huh. —Thank you."

He put the speaker down, unhooked the hearing device from his ear with a little difficulty, turned the whole thing off, and said, "They'll arrange to have someone show us anything we need to know, but he can't promise when that might be. You can't call outside Mycogen—not on this thing anyway—so we couldn't get Hummin if we needed him. And if I want Sunmaster Fourteen, I've got to go through a tremendous rigmarole. This may be an egalitarian society, but there seem to be exceptions that I bet no one will openly admit."

He looked at his watch. "In any case, Dors, I'm not going to view a cookbook and still less am I going to view learned essays. My watch is still telling University time, so I don't know if it's officially bedtime and at the moment I don't care. We've been awake most of the night and I would like to sleep."

"That's all right with me. I'm tired too."

"Thanks. And whenever a new day starts after we've caught up on our sleep, I'm going to ask for a tour of their microfood plantations."

Dors looked startled. "Are you *interested?*"

"Not really, but if that's the one thing they're proud of, they should be willing to talk about it and once I get them into a talking mood then, by exerting all my charm, I may get them to talk about their legends too. Personally, I think that's a clever strategy."

"I hope so," said Dors dubiously, "but I think that the Mycogenians will not be so easily trapped."

"We'll see," said Seldon grimly. "I mean to get those legends."

39.

The next morning found Hari using the calling device again. He was angry because, for one thing, he was hungry.

His attempt to reach Sunmaster Fourteen was deflected by someone who insisted that Sunmaster could not be disturbed.

"Why not?" Seldon had asked waspishly.

"Obviously, there is no need to answer that question," came back a cold voice.

"We were not brought here to be prisoners," said Seldon with equal coldness. "Nor to starve."

"I'm sure you have a kitchen and ample supplies of food."

"Yes, we do," said Seldon. "And I do not know how to use the kitchen devices, nor do I know how to prepare the food. Do you eat it raw, fry it, boil it, roast it . . . ?"

"I can't believe you are ignorant in such matters."

Dors, who had been pacing up and down during this colloquy, reached for the device and Seldon fended her off, whispering, "He'll break the connection if a woman tries to speak to him."

Then, into the device, he said more firmly than ever, "What you believe or don't believe doesn't matter to me in the least. You send someone here—someone who can do something about our situation—or when I reach Sunmaster Fourteen, as I will eventually, you will pay for this."

Nevertheless, it was two hours before someone arrived (by which time Seldon was in a state of savagery and Dors had grown rather desperate in her attempt to soothe him).

The newcomer was a young man whose bald pate was slightly freckled and who probably would have been a redhead otherwise.

He was bearing several pots and he seemed about to explain them when he suddenly looked uneasy and turned his back on Seldon in alarm. "Tribesman," he said, obviously agitated. "Your skincap is not well adjusted."

Seldon, whose impatience had reached the breaking point, said, "That doesn't bother me."

Dors, however, said, "Let me adjust it, Hari. It's just a bit too high here on the left side."

Seldon then growled, "You can turn now, young man. What is your name?"

"I am Graycloud Five," said the Mycogenian uncertainly as he turned and looked cautiously at Seldon. "I am a novitiate. I have brought a meal for you." He hesitated. "From my own kitchen, where my woman prepared it, tribesman."

He put the pots down on the table and Seldon raised one lid and sniffed the contents suspiciously. He looked up at Dors in surprise. "You know, it doesn't smell bad."

Dors nodded. "You're right. I can smell it too."

Graycloud said, "It's not as hot as it ought to be. It cooled off in transport. You must have crockery and cutlery in your kitchen."

Dors got what was needed, and after they had eaten, largely and a bit greedily, Seldon felt civilized once more.

Dors, who realized that the young man would feel unhappy at being alone with a woman and even unhappier if she spoke to him, found that, by default, it fell to her to carry the pots and dishes into the kitchen and wash them—once she deciphered the controls of the washing device.

Meanwhile, Seldon asked the local time and said, somewhat abashed, "You mean it's the middle of the night?"

"Indeed, tribesman," said Graycloud. "That's why it took a while to satisfy your need."

Seldon understood suddenly why Sunmaster could not be disturbed and thought of Graycloud's woman having to be awakened to prepare him a meal and felt his conscience gnaw at him. "I'm sorry," he said. "We are only tribespeople and we didn't know how to use the kitchen or how to prepare the food. In the morning, could you have someone arrive to instruct us properly?"

"The best I can do, tribesmen," said Graycloud placatingly, "is to have two Sisters sent in. I ask your pardon for inconveniencing you with feminine presence, but it is they who know these things."

Dors, who had emerged from the kitchen, said (before remembering her place in the masculine Mycogenian society), "That's fine, Graycloud. We'd love to meet the Sisters."

Graycloud looked at her uneasily and fleetingly, but said nothing.

Seldon, convinced that the young Mycogenian would, on principle, refuse to have heard what a woman said to him, repeated the remark. "That's fine, Graycloud. We'd love to meet the Sisters."

His expression cleared at once. "I will have them here as soon as it is day."

When Graycloud had left, Seldon said with some satisfaction, "The Sisters are likely to be exactly what we need."

"Indeed? And in what way, Hari?" asked Dors.

"Well, surely if we treat them as though they are human beings, they will be grateful enough to speak of their legends."

"If they know them," said Dors skeptically. "Somehow I have no faith that the Mycogenians bother to educate their women very well."

40.

The Sisters arrived some six hours later after Seldon and Dors had slept some more, hoping to readjust their biological clocks.

The Sisters entered the apartment shyly, almost on tiptoe. Their gowns (which, it turned out, were termed "kirtles" in the Mycogenian dialect) were soft velvety gray, each uniquely decorated by a subtle pattern of fine, darker gray webbing. The kirtles were not entirely unattractive, but they were certainly most efficient at covering up any human feature.

And, of course, their heads were bald and their faces were devoid of any ornamentation. They darted speculative glances at the touch of blue at the corners of Dors's eyes and at the slight red stain at the corners of her lips.

For a few moments, Seldon wondered how one could be certain that the Sisters were truly *Sisters.*

The answer came at once with the Sisters' politely formal greetings. Both twittered and chirped. Seldon, remembering the grave tones of Sunmaster and the nervous baritone of Graycloud, suspected that women, in default of obvious sexual identification, were forced to cultivate distinctive voices and social mannerisms.

"I'm Raindrop Forty-Three," twittered one, "and this is my younger sister."

"Raindrop Forty-Five," chirped the other. "We're very strong on 'Raindrops' in our cohort." She giggled.

"I am pleased to meet you both," said Dors gravely, "but now I must know how to address you. I can't just say 'Raindrop,' can I?"

"No," said Raindrop Forty-Three. "You must use the full name if we are both here."

Seldon said, "How about just Forty-Three and Forty-Five, ladies?"

They both stole a quick glance at him, but said not a word.

Dors said softly, "I'll deal with them, Hari."

Seldon stepped back. Presumably, they were single young women and, very likely, they were not supposed to speak to men. The older one seemed the graver of the two and was perhaps the more puritanical. It was hard to tell from a few words and a quick glance, but he had the feeling and was willing to go by that.

Dors said, "The thing is, Sisters, that we tribespeople don't know how to use the kitchen."

"You mean you can't cook?" Raindrop Forty-Three looked shocked and censorious. Raindrop Forty-Five smothered a laugh. (Seldon decided that his initial estimate of the two was correct.)

Dors said, "I once had a kitchen of my own, but it wasn't like this one and I don't know what the foods are or how to prepare them."

"It's really quite simple," said Raindrop Forty-Five. "We can show you."

"We'll make you a good nourishing lunch," said Raindrop Forty-Three. "We'll make it for . . . both of you." She hesitated before adding the final words. It clearly took an effort to acknowledge the existence of a man.

"If you don't mind," said Dors, "I would like to be in the kitchen with you and I would appreciate it if you'd explain everything exactly. After all, Sisters, I can't expect you to come here three times a day to cook for us."

"We will show you everything," said Raindrop Forty-Three, nodding her head stiffly. "It may be difficult for a tribeswoman to learn, however. You wouldn't have the . . . feeling for it."

"I shall try," said Dors with a pleasant smile.

They disappeared into the kitchen. Seldon stared after them and tried to work out the strategy he intended to use.

MICROFARM

. . . . .

MYCOGEN— . . . The microfarms of Mycogen are legendary, though they survive today only in such oft-used similes as "rich as the microfarms of Mycogen" or "tasty as Mycogenian yeast." Such encomiums tend to intensify with time, to be sure, but Hari Seldon visited those microfarms in the course of The Flight and there are references in his memoirs that would tend to support the popular opinion . . .

ENCYCLOPEDIA GALACTICA

41.

"That was *good!*" said Seldon explosively. "It was considerably better than the food Graycloud brought—"

Dors said reasonably, "You have to remember that Graycloud's woman had to prepare it on short notice in the middle of the night." She paused and said, "I *wish* they would say 'wife.' They make 'woman' sound like such an appanage, like 'my house' or 'my robe.' It is absolutely demeaning."

"I know. It's infuriating. But they might well make 'wife' sound like an appanage as well. It's the way they live and the Sisters don't seem to mind. You and I aren't going to change it by lecturing. —Anyway, did you see how the Sisters did it?"

"Yes, I did and they made everything seem very simple. I doubted I could remember everything they did, but they insisted I wouldn't have to. I could get away with mere heating. I gathered the bread had some sort of microderivative added to it in the baking that both raised the dough and lent it that crunchy consistency and warm flavor. Just a hint of pepper, didn't you think?"

"I couldn't tell, but whatever it was, I didn't get enough. And the soup. Did you recognize any of the vegetables?"

"No."

"And what was the sliced meat? Could you tell?"

"I don't think it was sliced meat, actually. We did have a lamb dish back on Cinna that it reminded me of."

"It was certainly not lamb."

"I *said* that I doubted it was meat at all. —I don't think anyone outside Mycogen eats like this either. Not even the Emperor, I'm sure. Whatever the Mycogenians sell is, I'm willing to bet, near the bottom of the line. They save the best for themselves. We had better not stay here too long, Hari. If we get used to eating like this, we'll *never* be able to acclimatize ourselves to the miserable stuff they have outside." She laughed.

Seldon laughed too. He took another sip at the fruit juice, which tasted far more tantalizing than any fruit juice he had ever sipped before, and said, "Listen, when Hummin took me to the University, we stopped at a roadside diner and had some food that was heavily yeasted. It tasted like — No, never mind what it tasted like, but I wouldn't have thought it conceivable, then, that microfood could taste like this. I wish the Sisters were still here. It would have been polite to thank them."

"I think they were quite aware of how we would feel. I remarked on the wonderful smell while everything was warming and they said, quite complacently, that it would taste even better."

"The older one said that, I imagine."

"Yes. The younger one giggled. —And they'll be back. They're going to bring me a kirtle, so that I can go out to see the shops with them. And they made it clear I would have to wash my face if I was to be seen in public. They will show me where to buy some good-quality kirtles of my own and where I can buy ready-made meals of all kinds. All I'll have to do is heat them up. They explained that decent Sisters wouldn't do that, but would start from scratch. In fact, some of the meal they prepared for us *was* simply heated and they apologized for that. They managed to imply, though, that tribespeople couldn't be expected to appreciate true artistry in cooking, so that simply heating prepared food would do for us. —They seem to take it for granted, by the way, that I will be doing all the shopping and cooking."

"As we say at home, 'When in Trantor, do as the Trantorians do.' "

"Yes, I was sure that would be your attitude in this case."

"I'm only human," said Seldon.

"The usual excuse," said Dors with a small smile.

172

Seldon leaned back with a satisfactory well-filled feeling and said, "You've been on Trantor for two years, Dors, so you might understand a few things that I don't. Is it your opinion that this odd social system the Mycogenians have is part of a supernaturalistic view they have?"

"Supernaturalistic?"

"Yes. Would you have heard that this was so?"

"What do you mean by 'supernaturalistic'?"

"The obvious. A belief in entities that are independent of natural law, that are not bound by the conservation of energy, for instance, or by the existence of a constant of action."

"I see. You're asking if Mycogen is a religious community."

It was Seldon's turn. "Religious?"

"Yes. It's an archaic term, but we historians use it—our study is riddled with archaic terms. 'Religious' is not precisely equivalent to 'supernaturalistic,' though it contains richly supernaturalistic elements. I can't answer your specific question, however, because I've never made any special investigation of Mycogen. Still, from what little I've seen of the place and from my knowledge of religions in history, I wouldn't be surprised if the Mycogenian society was religious in character."

"In that case, would it surprise you if Mycogenian legends were also religious in character?"

"No, it wouldn't."

"And therefore not based on historical matter?"

"That wouldn't necessarily follow. The core of the legends might still be authentically historic, allowing for distortion and supernaturalistic intermixture."

"Ah," said Seldon and seemed to retire into his thoughts.

Finally Dors broke the silence that followed and said, "It's not so uncommon, you know. There is a considerable religious element on many worlds. It's grown stronger in the last few centuries as the Empire has grown more turbulent. On my world of Cinna, at least a quarter of the population is tritheistic."

Seldon was again painfully and regretfully conscious of his ignorance of history. He said, "Were there times in past history when religion was more prominent than it is today?"

"Certainly. In addition, there are new varieties springing up constantly. The Mycogenian religion, whatever it might be, could be relatively new and may be restricted to Mycogen itself. I couldn't really tell without considerable study."

"But now we get to the point of it, Dors. Is it your opinion that women are more apt to be religious than men are?"

Dors Venabili raised her eyebrows. "I'm not sure if we can assume anything as simple as that." She thought a bit. "I suspect that those elements of a population that have a smaller stake in the material natural world are more apt to find solace in what you call supernaturalism—the poor, the disinherited, the downtrodden. Insofar as supernaturalism overlaps religion, they may also be more religious. There are obviously many exceptions in both directions. Many of the downtrodden may lack religion; many of the rich, powerful, and satisfied may possess it."

"But in Mycogen," said Seldon, "where the women seem to be treated as subhuman—would I be right in assuming they would be more religious than the men, more involved in the legends that the society has been preserving?"

"I wouldn't risk my life on it, Hari, but I'd be willing to risk a week's income on it."

"Good," said Seldon thoughtfully.

Dors smiled at him. "There's a bit of your psychohistory, Hari. Rule number 47,854: The downtrodden are more religious than the satisfied."

Seldon shook his head. "Don't joke about psychohistory, Dors. You know I'm not looking for tiny rules but for vast generalizations and for means of manipulation. I don't want comparative religiosity as the result of a hundred specific rules. I want something from which I can, after manipulation through some system of mathematicized logic, say, 'Aha, this group of people will tend to be more religious than that group, provided that the following criteria are met, and that, therefore, when humanity meets with these stimuli, it will react with these responses.'"

"How horrible," said Dors. "You are picturing human beings as simple mechanical devices. Press this button and you will get that twitch."

"No, because there will be many buttons pushing simultaneously to varying degrees and eliciting so many responses of different sorts that overall the predictions of the future will be statistical in nature, so that the individual human being will remain a free agent."

"How can you know this?"

"I can't," said Seldon. "At least, I don't *know* it. I *feel* it to be so. It is what I consider to be the way things *ought* to be. If I can find the axioms, the fundamental Laws of Humanics, so to speak, and the necessary mathematical treatment, then I will have my psychohistory. I have proved that, in theory, this is possible—"

"But impractical, right?"

"I keep saying so."

A small smile curved Dors's lips, "Is that what you are doing, Hari, looking for some sort of solution to this problem?"

"I don't know. I swear to you I don't know. But Chetter Hummin is so anxious to find a solution and, for some reason, I am anxious to please him. He is so persuasive a man."

"Yes, I know."

Seldon let that comment pass, although a small frown flitted across his face.

Seldon continued. "Hummin insists the Empire is decaying, that it will collapse, that psychohistory is the only hope for saving it—or cushioning it or ameliorating it—and that without it humanity will be destroyed or, at the very least, go through prolonged misery. He seems to place the responsibility for preventing that on *me*. Now, the Empire will certainly last my time, but if I'm to live at ease, I must lift that responsibility from my shoulders. I must convince myself—and even convince Hummin— that psychohistory is not a practical way out; that, despite theory, it cannot be developed. So I must follow up as many leads as I can and show that each one must fail."

"Leads? Like going back in history to a time when human society was smaller than it is now?"

"Much smaller. And far less complex."

"And showing that a solution is still impractical?"

"Yes."

"But who is going to describe the early world for you? If the Mycogenians have some coherent picture of the primordial Galaxy, Sunmaster certainly won't reveal it to a tribesman. No Mycogenian will. This is an ingrown society—how many times have we already said it?—and its members are suspicious of tribesmen to the point of paranoia. They'll tell us nothing."

"I will have to think of a way to persuade some Mycogenians to talk. Those Sisters, for instance."

"They won't even *hear* you, male that you are, any more than Sunmaster hears me. And even if they do talk to you, what would they know but a few catch phrases?"

"I must start somewhere."

Dors said, "Well, let me think. Hummin says I must protect you and I interpret that as meaning I must help you when I can. What do I know about religion? That's nowhere near my specialty, you know. I have always dealt with economic forces, rather than philosophic forces, but you can't split history into neat little nonoverlapping divisions. For instance, religions tend to accumulate wealth when successful and that eventually tends to distort the economic development of a society. — There, incidentally, is one of the numerous rules of human history that you'll have to derive from your basic Laws of Humanics or whatever you called them. But . . ."

And here, Dors's voice faded away as she lapsed into thought. Seldon watched her cautiously and Dors's eyes glazed as though she was looking deep within herself.

Finally she said, "This is not an invariable rule, but it seems to me that on many occasions, a religion has a book—or books—of significance; books that give their ritual, their view of history, their sacred poetry, and who knows what else. Usually, those books are open to all and are a means of proselytization. Sometimes they are secret."

"Do you think Mycogen has books of that sort?"

"To be truthful," said Dors thoughtfully, "I have never heard of any. I might have if they existed openly—which means they either don't exist or are kept secret. In either case, it seems to me you are not going to see them."

"At least it's a starting point," said Seldon grimly.

42.

The Sisters returned about two hours after Hari and Dors had finished lunch. They were smiling, both of them, and Raindrop Forty-Three, the graver one, held up a gray kirtle for Dors's inspection.

"It is very attractive," said Dors, smiling widely and nodding her head with a certain sincerity. "I like the clever embroidery here."

"It is nothing," twittered Raindrop Forty-Five. "It is one of my old things and it won't fit very well, for you are taller than I am. But it will do for a while and we will take you out to the very best kirtlery to get a few that will fit you and your tastes perfectly. You will see."

Raindrop Forty-Three, smiling a little nervously but saying nothing and keeping her eyes fixed on the ground, handed a white kirtle to Dors. It was folded neatly. Dors did not attempt to unfold it, but passed it on to Seldon. "From the color I should say it's yours, Hari."

"Presumably," said Seldon, "but give it back. She did not give it to me."

"Oh, Hari," mouthed Dors, shaking her head slightly.

"No," said Seldon firmly. "She did not give it to me. Give it back to her and I'll wait for her to give it to me."

Dors hesitated, then made a halfhearted attempt to pass the kirtle back to Raindrop Forty-Three.

The Sister put her hands behind her back and moved away, all life seeming to drain from her face. Raindrop Forty-Five stole a glance at Seldon, a very quick one, then took a quick step toward Raindrop Forty-Three and put her arms about her.

Dors said, "Come, Hari, I'm sure that Sisters are not permitted to talk to men who are not related to them. What's the use of making her miserable? She can't help it."

"I don't believe it," said Seldon harshly. "If there is such a rule, it applies only to Brothers. I doubt very much that she's ever met a tribesman before."

Dors said to Raindrop Forty-Three in a soft voice, "Have you ever met a tribesman before, Sister, or a tribeswoman?"

A long hesitation and then a slow negative shake of the head.

Seldon threw out his arms. "Well, there you are. If there is a rule of silence, it applies only to the Brothers. Would they have sent these young women—these Sisters—to deal with us if there was any rule against speaking to tribesmen?"

"It might be, Hari, that they were meant to speak only to me and I to you."

"Nonsense. I don't believe it and I won't believe it. I am not merely a tribesman, I am an honored guest in Mycogen, asked to be treated as such by Chetter Hummin and escorted here by Sunmaster Fourteen himself. I will not be treated as though I do not exist. I will be in communication with Sunmaster Fourteen and I will complain bitterly."

Raindrop Forty-Five began to sob and Raindrop Forty-Three, retaining her comparative impassivity, nevertheless flushed faintly.

Dors made as though to appeal to Seldon once again, but he stopped her with a brief and angry outward thrust of his right arm and then stared loweringly at Raindrop Forty-Three.

And finally she spoke and did not twitter. Rather, her voice trembled hoarsely, as though she had to force it to sound in the direction of a male being and was doing so against all her instincts and desires.

"You must not complain of us, tribesman. That would be unjust. You force me to break the custom of our people. What do you want of me?"

Seldon smiled disarmingly at once and held out his hand. "The garment you brought me. The kirtle."

Silently, she stretched out her arm and deposited the kirtle in his hand.

He bowed slightly and said in a soft warm voice, "Thank you, Sister." He then cast a very brief look in Dors's direction, as though to say: You see? But Dors looked away angrily.

The kirtle was featureless, Seldon saw as he unfolded it (embroidery and decorativeness were for women, apparently), but it came with a tasseled belt that probably had some particular way of being worn. No doubt he could work it out.

He said, "I'll step into the bathroom and put this thing on. It won't take but a minute, I suppose."

He stepped into the small chamber and found the door would not close behind him because Dors was forcing her way in as well. Only when the two of them were in the bathroom together did the door close.

"What were you doing?" Dors hissed angrily. "You were an absolute brute, Hari. Why did you treat the poor woman that way?"

Seldon said impatiently, "I had to make her talk to me. I'm counting on her for information. You know that. I'm sorry I had to be cruel, but how else could I have broken down her inhibitions?" And he motioned her out.

When he emerged, he found Dors in her kirtle too.

Dors, despite the bald head the skincap gave her and the inherent dowdiness of the kirtle, managed to look quite attractive. The stitching on the robe somehow suggested a figure without revealing it in the least. Her belt was wider than his own and was a slightly different shade of gray from her kirtle. What's more, it was held in front by two glittering blue stone snaps. (Women did manage to beautify themselves even under the greatest difficulty, Seldon thought.)

Looking over at Hari, Dors said, "You look quite the Mycogenian now. The two of us are fit to be taken to the stores by the Sisters."

"Yes," said Seldon, "but afterward I want Raindrop Forty-Three to take me on a tour of the microfarms."

Raindrop Forty-Three's eyes widened and she took a rapid step backward.

"I'd like to see them," said Seldon calmly.

Raindrop Forty-Three looked quickly at Dors. "Tribeswoman—"

Seldon said, "Perhaps you know nothing of the farms, Sister."

That seemed to touch a nerve. She lifted her chin haughtily as she still carefully addressed Dors. "I have worked on the microfarms. All Brothers and Sisters do at some point in their lives."

"Well then, take me on the tour," said Seldon, "and let's not go through the argument again. I am not a Brother to whom you are forbidden to speak and with whom you may have no dealings. I am a tribesman and an honored guest. I wear this skincap and this kirtle so as not to attract undue attention, but I am a scholar and while I am here I must learn. I cannot sit in this room and stare at the wall. I want to see the one thing you have that the rest of the Galaxy does not have . . . your microfarms. I should think you'd be *proud* to show them."

"We *are* proud," said Raindrop Forty-Three, finally facing Seldon as she spoke, "and I will show you and don't think you will learn any of our secrets if that is what you are after. I will show you the microfarms tomorrow morning. It will take time to arrange a tour."

Seldon said, "I will wait till tomorrow morning. But do you promise? Do I have your word of honor?"

Raindrop Forty-Three said with clear contempt, "I am a Sister and I will do as I say. I will keep my word, even to a tribesman."

Her voice grew icy at the last words, while her eyes widened and seemed to glitter. Seldon wondered what was passing through her mind and felt uneasy.

43.

Seldon passed a restless night. To begin with, Dors had announced that she must accompany him on the tour of the microfarm and he had objected strenuously.

"The whole purpose," he said, "is to make her talk freely, to present her with an unusual environment—alone with a male, even if a tribesman. Having broken custom so far, it will be easier to break it further. If you're along, she will talk to you and I will only get the leavings."

"And if something happens to you in my absence, as it did Upperside?"

"Nothing will happen. Please! If you want to help me, stay away. If not, I will have nothing further to do with you. I mean it, Dors. This is important to me. Much as I've grown fond of you, you cannot come ahead of this."

She agreed with enormous reluctance and said only, "Promise me you'll at least be nice to her, then."

And Seldon said, "Is it me you must protect or her? I assure you that I didn't treat her harshly for pleasure and I won't do so in the future."

The memory of this argument with Dors—their first—helped keep him awake a large part of the night; that, together with the nagging thought that the two Sisters might not arrive in the morning, despite Raindrop Forty-Three's promise.

They did arrive, however, not long after Seldon had completed a spare breakfast (he was determined not to grow fat through overindulgence) and had put on a kirtle that fitted him precisely. He had carefully organized the belt so that it hung perfectly.

Raindrop Forty-Three, still with a touch of ice in her eye, said, "If you are ready, Tribesman Seldon, my sister will remain with Tribeswoman Venabili." Her voice was neither twittery nor hoarse. It was as though she had steadied herself through the night, practicing, in her mind, how to speak to one who was a male but not a Brother.

Seldon wondered if *she* had lost sleep and said, "I am quite ready."

Together, half an hour later, Raindrop Forty-Three and Hari Seldon were descending level upon level. Though it was daytime by the clock, the light was dusky and dimmer than it had been elsewhere on Trantor.

There was no obvious reason for this. Surely, the artificial daylight that slowly progressed around the Trantorian sphere could include the

Mycogen Sector. The Mycogenians must want it that way, Seldon thought, clinging to some primitive habit. Slowly Seldon's eyes adjusted to the dim surroundings.

Seldon tried to meet the eyes of passersby, whether Brothers or Sisters, calmly. He assumed he and Raindrop Forty-Three would be taken as a Brother and his woman and that they would be given no notice as long as he did nothing to attract attention.

Unfortunately, it seemed as if Raindrop Forty-Three wanted to be noticed. She talked to him in few words and in low tones out of a clenched mouth. It was clear that the company of an unauthorized male, even though only she knew this fact, ravaged her self-confidence. Seldon was quite sure that if he asked her to relax, he would merely make her that much more uneasy. (Seldon wondered what she would do if she met someone who knew her. He felt more relaxed once they reached the lower levels, where human beings were fewer.)

The descent was not by elevators either, but by moving staired ramps that existed in pairs, one going up and one going down. Raindrop Forty-Three referred to them as "escalators." Seldon wasn't sure he had caught the word correctly, never having heard it before.

As they sank to lower and lower levels, Seldon's apprehension grew. Most worlds possessed microfarms and most worlds produced their own varieties of microproducts. Seldon, back on Helicon, had occasionally shopped for seasonings in the microfarms and was always aware of an unpleasant stomach-turning stench.

The people who worked at the microfarms didn't seem to mind. Even when casual visitors wrinkled their noses, they seemed to acclimate themselves to it. Seldon, however, was always peculiarly susceptible to the smell. He suffered and he expected to suffer now. He tried soothing himself with the thought that he was nobly sacrificing his comfort to his need for information, but that didn't keep his stomach from turning itself into knots in apprehension.

After he had lost track of the number of levels they had descended, with the air still seeming reasonably fresh, he asked, "When do we get to the microfarm levels?"

"We're there now."

Seldon breathed deeply. "It doesn't smell as though we are."

"Smell? What do you mean?" Raindrop Forty-Three was offended enough to speak quite loudly.

"There was always a putrid odor associated with microfarms, in my experience. You know, from the fertilizer that bacteria, yeast, fungi, and saprophytes generally need."

"In your experience?" Her voice lowered again. "Where was that?"

"On my home world."

The Sister twisted her face into wild repugnance. "And your people wallow in *gabelle?*"

Seldon had never heard the word before, but from the look and the intonation, he knew what it meant.

He said, "It doesn't smell like that, you understand, once it is ready for consumption."

"Ours doesn't smell like that at any time. Our biotechnicians have worked out perfect strains. The algae grow in the purest light and the most carefully balanced electrolyte solutions. The saprophytes are fed on beautifully combined organics. The formulas and recipes are something no tribespeople will ever know. —Come on, here we are. Sniff all you want. You'll find nothing offensive. That is one reason why our food is in demand throughout the Galaxy and why the Emperor, we are told, eats nothing else, though it is far too good for a tribesman if you ask me, even if he calls himself Emperor."

She said it with an anger that seemed directly aimed at Seldon. Then, as though afraid he might miss that, she added, "Or even if he calls himself an honored guest."

They stepped out into a narrow corridor, on each side of which were large thick glass tanks in which roiled cloudy green water full of swirling, growing algae, moving about through the force of the gas bubbles that streamed up through it. They would be rich in carbon dioxide, he decided.

Rich, rosy light shone down into the tanks, light that was much brighter than that in the corridors. He commented thoughtfully on that.

"Of course," she said. "These algae work best at the red end of the spectrum."

"I presume," said Seldon, "that everything is automated."

She shrugged, but did not respond.

"I don't see quantities of Brothers and Sisters in evidence," Seldon said, persisting.

"Nevertheless, there is work to be done and they do it, even if you don't see them at work. The details are not for you. Don't waste your time by asking about it.''

"Wait. Don't be angry with me. I don't expect to be told state secrets. Come on, dear." (The word slipped out.)

He took her arm as she seemed on the point of hurrying away. She remained in place, but he felt her shudder slightly and he released her in embarrassment.

He said, "It's just that it seems automated."

"Make what you wish of the seeming. Nevertheless, there is room here for human brains and human judgment. Every Brother and Sister has occasion to work here at some time. Some make a profession of it."

She was speaking more freely now but, to his continuing embarrassment, he noticed her left hand move stealthily toward her right arm and gently rub the spot where he had touched her, as though he had stung her.

"It goes on for kilometers and kilometers," she said, "but if we turn here there'll be a portion of the fungal section you can see."

They moved along. Seldon noted how clean everything was. The glass sparkled. The tiled floor seemed moist, though when he seized a moment to bend and touch it, it wasn't. Nor was it slippery—unless his sandals (with his big toe protruding in approved Mycogenian fashion) had non-slip soles.

Raindrop Forty-Three was right in one respect. Here and there a Brother or a Sister worked silently, studying gauges, adjusting controls, sometimes engaged in something as unskilled as polishing equipment— always absorbed in whatever they were doing.

Seldon was careful not to ask what they were doing, since he did not want to cause the Sister humiliation in having to answer that she did not know or anger in her having to remind him there were things he must not know.

They passed through a lightly swinging door and Seldon suddenly noticed the faintest touch of the odor he remembered. He looked at Raindrop Forty-Three, but she seemed unconscious of it and soon he too became used to it.

The character of the light changed suddenly. The rosiness was gone and the brightness too. All seemed to be in a twilight except where equipment was spotlighted and wherever there was a spotlight there seemed to be a Brother or a Sister. Some wore lighted headbands that gleamed with a pearly glow and, in the middle distance, Seldon could see, here and there, small sparks of light moving erratically.

As they walked, he cast a quick eye on her profile. It was all he could really judge by. At all other times, he could not cease being conscious of her bulging bald head, her bare eyes, her colorless face. They drowned her individuality and seemed to make her invisible. Here in profile, however, he could see something. Nose, chin, full lips, regularity, beauty. The dim light somehow smoothed out and softened the great upper desert.

He thought with surprise: She could be very beautiful if she grew her hair and arranged it nicely.

And then he thought that she *couldn't* grow her hair. She would be bald her whole life.

Why? Why did they have to do that to her? Sunmaster said it was so that a Mycogenian would know himself (or herself) for a Mycogenian all his (or her) life. Why was that so important that the curse of hairlessness had to be accepted as a badge or mark of identity?

And then, because he was used to arguing both sides in his mind, he thought: Custom is second nature. Be accustomed to a bald head, sufficiently accustomed, and hair on it would seem monstrous, would evoke nausea. He himself had shaved his face every morning, removing all the facial hair, uncomfortable at the merest stubble, and yet he did not think of his face as bald or as being in any way unnatural. Of course, he could grow his facial hair at any time he wished—but he didn't wish to do so.

He knew that there were worlds on which the men did not shave; in some, they did not even clip or shape the facial hair but let it grow wild. What would they say if they could see his own bald face, his own hairless chin, cheek, and lips?

And meanwhile, he walked with Raindrop Forty-Three—endlessly, it seemed—and every once in a while she guided him by the elbow and it seemed to him that she had grown accustomed to that, for she did not withdraw her hand hastily. Sometimes it remained for nearly a minute.

She said, "Here! Come here!"

"What is that?" asked Seldon.

They were standing before a small tray filled with little spheres, each about two centimeters in diameter. A Brother who was tending the area and who had just placed the tray where it was looked up in mild inquiry.

Raindrop Forty-Three said to Seldon in a low voice, "Ask for a few."

MICROFARM

Seldon realized she could not speak to a Brother until spoken to and said uncertainly, "May we have a few, B-brother?"

"Have a handful, Brother," said the other heartily.

Seldon plucked out one of the spheres and was on the point of handing it to Raindrop Forty-Three when he noticed that she had accepted the invitation as applying to herself and reached in for two handfuls.

The sphere felt glossy, smooth. Seldon said to Raindrop Forty-Three as they moved away from the vat and from the Brother who was in attendance, "Are these supposed to be eaten?" He lifted the sphere cautiously to his nose.

"They don't smell," she said sharply.

"What are they?"

"Dainties. Raw dainties. For the outside market they're flavored in different ways, but here in Mycogen we eat them unflavored—the only way."

She put one in her mouth and said, "I *never* have enough."

Seldon put his sphere into his mouth and felt it dissolve and disappear rapidly. His mouth, for a moment, ran liquid and then it slid, almost of its own accord, down his throat.

He stood for a moment, amazed. It was slightly sweet and, for that matter, had an even fainter bitter aftertaste, but the main sensation eluded him.

"May I have another?" he said.

"Have half a dozen," said Raindrop Forty-Three, holding out her hand. "They never have quite the same taste twice and have practically no calories. Just taste."

She was right. He tried to have the dainty linger in his mouth; he tried licking it carefully; tried biting off a piece. However, the most careful lick destroyed it. When a bit was crunched off a piece, the rest of it disappeared at once. And each taste was undefinable and not quite like the one before.

"The only trouble is," said the Sister happily, "that every once in a while you have a very unusual one and you never forget it, but you never have it again either. I had one when I was nine—" Her expression suddenly lost its excitement and she said, "It's a good thing. It teaches you the evanescence of things of the world."

185

It was a signal, Seldon thought. They had wandered about aimlessly long enough. She had grown used to him and was talking to him. And now the conversation had to come to its point. Now!

44.

Seldon said, "I come from a world which lies out in the open, Sister, as all worlds do but Trantor. Rain comes or doesn't come, the rivers trickle or are in flood, temperature is high or low. That means harvests are good or bad. Here, however, the environment is truly controlled. Harvests have no choice but to be good. How fortunate Mycogen is."

He waited. There were different possible answers and his course of action would depend on which answer came.

She was speaking quite freely now and seemed to have no inhibitions concerning his masculinity, so this long tour had served its purpose. Raindrop Forty-Three said, "The environment is not that easy to control. There are, occasionally, viral infections and there are sometimes unexpected and undesirable mutations. There are times when whole vast batches wither or are worthless."

"You astonish me. And what happens then?"

"There is usually no recourse but to destroy the spoiled batches, even those that are merely suspected of spoilage. Trays and tanks must be totally sterilized, sometimes disposed of altogether."

"It amounts to surgery, then," said Seldon. "You cut out the diseased tissue."

"Yes."

"And what do you do to prevent such things from happening?"

"What can we do? We test constantly for any mutations that may spring up, any new viruses that may appear, any accidental contamination or alteration of the environment. It rarely happens that we detect anything wrong, but if we do, we take drastic action. The result is that bad years are very few and even bad years affect only fractional bits here and there. The worst year we've ever had fell short of the average by only 12 percent—though that was enough to produce hardship. The trouble is that even the most careful forethought and the most cleverly designed computer programs can't always predict what is essentially unpredictable."

(Seldon felt an involuntary shudder go through him. It was as though she was speaking of psychohistory—but she was only speaking of the microfarm produce of a tiny fraction of humanity, while he himself was considering all the mighty Galactic Empire in every one of all its activities.)

Unavoidably disheartened, he said, "Surely, it's not all unpredictable. There are forces that guide and that care for us all."

The Sister stiffened. She turned around toward him, seeming to study him with her penetrating eyes.

But all she said was "What?"

Seldon felt uneasy. "It seems to me that in speaking of viruses and mutations, we're talking about the natural, about phenomena that are subject to natural law. That leaves out of account the supernatural, doesn't it? It leaves out that which is not subject to natural law and can, therefore, control natural law."

She continued to stare at him, as though he had suddenly begun speaking some distant, unknown dialect of Galactic Standard. Again she said, in half a whisper this time, "What?"

He continued, stumbling over unfamiliar words that half-embarrassed him. "You must appeal to some great essence, some great spirit, some . . . I don't know what to call it."

Raindrop Forty-Three said in a voice that rose into higher registers but remained low, "I thought so. I *thought* that was what you meant, but I couldn't believe it. You're accusing us of having *religion*. Why didn't you say so? Why didn't you use the word?"

She waited for an answer and Seldon, a little confused at the onslaught, said, "Because that's not a word I use. I call it 'supernaturalism.' "

"Call it what you will. It's religion and we don't have it. Religion is for the tribesmen, for the swarming sc—"

The Sister paused to swallow as though she had come near to choking and Seldon was certain the word she had choked over was "scum."

She was in control again. Speaking slowly and somewhat below her normal soprano, she said, "We are not a religious people. Our kingdom is of this Galaxy and always has been. If you have a religion—"

Seldon felt trapped. Somehow he had not counted on this. He raised a hand defensively. "Not really. I'm a mathematician and my kingdom is also of this Galaxy. It's just that I thought, from the rigidity of your customs, that *your* kingdom—"

"Don't think it, tribesman. If our customs are rigid, it is because we are mere millions surrounded by billions. Somehow we must mark ourselves off so that we precious few are not lost among your swarms and hordes. We must be marked off by our hairlessness, our clothing, our behavior, our way of life. We must know who we are and we must be sure that you tribesmen know who we are. We labor in our farms so that we can make ourselves valuable in your eyes and thus make certain that you leave us alone. That's all we ask of you . . . to leave us alone."

"I have no intention of harming you or any of your people. I seek only knowledge, here as everywhere."

"So you insult us by asking about our religion, as though we have ever called on a mysterious, insubstantial spirit to do for us what we cannot do for ourselves."

"There are many people, many worlds who believe in supernaturalism in one form or another . . . religion, if you like the word better. We may disagree with them in one way or another, but we are as likely to be wrong in our disbelief as they in their belief. In any case, there is no disgrace in such belief and my questions were not intended as insults."

But she was not reconciled. "Religion!" she said angrily. "We have no need of it."

Seldon's spirits, having sunk steadily in the course of this exchange, reached bottom. This whole thing, this expedition with Raindrop Forty-Three, had come to nothing.

But she went on to say, "We have something far better. We have *history.*"

And Seldon's feelings rebounded at once and he smiled.

BOOK

· · · · ·

HAND-ON-THIGH STORY— . . . An occasion cited by Hari Seldon as the first turning point in his search for a method to develop psychohistory. Unfortunately, his published writings give no indication as to what that "story" was and speculations concerning it (there have been many) are futile. It remains one of the many intriguing mysteries concerning Seldon's career.

ENCYCLOPEDIA GALACTICA

45.

Raindrop Forty-Three stared at Seldon, wild-eyed and breathing heavily.

"I can't stay here," she said.

Seldon looked about. "No one is bothering us. Even the Brother from whom we got the dainties said nothing about us. He seemed to take us as a perfectly normal pair."

"That's because there is nothing unusual about us—when the light is dim, when you keep your voice low so the tribesman accent is less noticeable, and when I seem calm. But now—" Her voice was growing hoarse.

"What of now?"

"I am nervous and tense. I am . . . in a perspiration."

"Who is to notice? Relax. Calm down."

"I can't relax here. I can't calm down while I may be noticed."

"Where are we to go, then?"

"There are little sheds for resting. I have worked here. I know about them."

She was walking rapidly now and Seldon followed. Up a small ramp, which he would not have noticed in the twilight without her, there was a line of doors, well spread apart.

"The one at the end," she muttered. "If it's free."

It was unoccupied. A small glowing rectangle said NOT IN USE and the door was ajar.

Raindrop Forty-Three looked about rapidly, motioned Seldon in, then stepped inside herself. She closed the door and, as she did so, a small ceiling light brightened the interior.

Seldon said, "Is there any way the sign on the door can indicate this shed is in use?"

"That happened automatically when the door closed and the light went on," said the Sister.

Seldon could feel air softly circulating with a small sighing sound, but where on Trantor was that ever-present sound and feel not apparent?

The room was not large, but it had a cot with a firm, efficient mattress, and what were obviously clean sheets. There was a chair and table, a small refrigerator, and something that looked like an enclosed hot plate, probably a tiny food-heater.

Raindrop Forty-Three sat down on the chair, sitting stiffly upright, visibly attempting to force herself into relaxation.

Seldon, uncertain as to what he ought to do, remained standing till she gestured—a bit impatiently—for him to sit on the cot. He did so.

Raindrop Forty-Three said softly, as though talking to herself, "If it is ever known that I have been here with a man—even if only a tribesman —I shall indeed be an outcast."

Seldon rose quickly. "Then let's not stay here."

"Sit down. I can't go out when I'm in this mood. You've been asking about religion. What *are* you after?"

It seemed to Seldon that she had changed completely. Gone was the passivity, the subservience. There was none of the shyness, the backwardness in the presence of a male. She was glaring at him through narrowed eyes.

"I told you. Knowledge. I'm a scholar. It is my profession and my desire to *know*. I want to understand people in particular, so I want to learn history. For many worlds, the ancient historical records—the *truly* ancient historical records—have decayed into myths and legends, often becoming part of a set of religious beliefs or of supernaturalism. But if Mycogen does not have a religion, then—"

"I said we have *history*."

Seldon said, "Twice you've said you have history. How old?"

"It goes back twenty thousand years."

"Truly? Let us speak frankly. Is it real history or is it something that has degenerated into legend?"

"It is real history, of course."

Seldon was on the point of asking how she could tell, but thought better of it. Was there really a chance that history might reach back twenty thousand years and be authentic? He was not a historian himself, so he would have to check with Dors.

But it seemed so likely to him that on every world the earliest histories were medleys of self-serving heroisms and minidramas that were meant as morality plays and were not to be taken literally. It was surely true of Helicon, yet you would find scarcely a Heliconian who would not swear by all the tales told and insist it was all true history. They would support, as such, even that perfectly ridiculous tale of the first exploration of Helicon and the encounters with large and dangerous flying reptiles— even though nothing like flying reptiles had been found to be native to any world explored and settled by human beings.

He said instead, "How does this history begin?"

There was a faraway look in the Sister's eyes, a look that did not focus on Seldon or on anything in the room. She said, "It begins with a world —*our* world. One world."

"*One* world?" (Seldon remembered that Hummin had spoken of legends of a single, original world of humanity.)

"One world. There were others later, but ours was the first. One world, with space, with open air, with room for everyone, with fertile fields, with friendly homes, with warm people. For thousands of years we lived there and then we had to leave and skulk in one place or another until some of us found a corner of Trantor where we learned to grow food that brought us a little freedom. And here in Mycogen, we now have our own ways—and our own dreams."

"And your histories give the full details concerning the original world? The one world?"

"Oh yes, it is all in a book and we all have it. Every one of us. We carry it at all times so that there is never a moment when any one of us cannot open it and read it and remember who we are and who we were and resolve that someday we will have our world back."

"Do you know where this world is and who lives on it now?"

Raindrop Forty-Three hesitated, then shook her head fiercely. "We do not, but someday we will find it."

"And you have this book in your possession now?"

"Of course."

"May I see that book?"

Now a slow smile crossed the face of the Sister. She said, "So that's what you want. I knew you wanted something when you asked to be guided through the microfarms by me alone." She seemed a little embarrassed. "I didn't think it was the *Book.*"

"It is all I want," said Seldon earnestly. "I really did not have my mind on anything else. If you brought me here because you thought—"

She did not allow him to finish. "But here we are. Do you or don't you want the Book?"

"Are you offering to let me see it?"

"On one condition."

Seldon paused, weighing the possibility of serious trouble if he had overcome the Sister's inhibitions to a greater extent than he had ever intended. "What condition?" he said.

Raindrop Forty-Three's tongue emerged lightly and licked quickly at her lips. Then she said with a distinct tremor in her voice, "That you remove your skincap."

46.

Hari Seldon stared blankly at Raindrop Forty-Three. There was a perceptible moment in which he did not know what she was talking about. He had forgotten he was wearing a skincap.

Then he put his hand to his head and, for the first time, consciously felt the skincap he was wearing. It was smooth, but he felt the tiny resilience of the hair beneath. Not much. His hair, after all, was fine and without much body.

He said, still feeling it, "Why?"

She said, "Because I want you to. Because that's the condition if you want to see the Book."

He said, "Well, if you really want me to." His hand probed for the edge, so that he could peel it off.

But she said, "No, let me do it. I'll do it." She was looking at him hungrily.

Seldon dropped his hands to his lap. "Go ahead, then."

The Sister rose quickly and sat down next to him on the cot. Slowly, carefully, she detached the skincap from his head just in front of his ear. Again she licked her lips and she was panting as she loosened the skincap about his forehead and turned it up. Then it came away and was gone and Seldon's hair, released, seemed to stir a bit in glad freedom.

He said, troubled, "Keeping my hair under the skincap has probably made my scalp sweat. If so, my hair will be rather damp."

He raised his hand, as though to check the matter, but she caught it and held it back. "I want to do that," she said. "It's part of the condition."

Her fingers, slowly and hesitantly, touched his hair and then withdrew. She touched it again and, very gently, stroked it.

"It's dry," she said. "It feels . . . good."

"Have you ever felt cephalic hair before?"

"Only on children sometimes. This . . . is different." She was stroking again.

"In what way?" Seldon, even amid his embarrassment, found it possible to be curious.

"I can't say. It's just . . . different."

After a while he said, "Have you had enough?"

"No. Don't rush me. Can you make it lie anyway you want it to?"

"Not really. It has a natural way of falling, but I need a comb for that and I don't have one with me."

"A comb?"

"An object with prongs . . . uh, like a fork . . . but the prongs are more numerous and somewhat softer."

"Can you use your fingers?" She was running hers through his hair.

He said, "After a fashion. It doesn't work very well."

"It's bristly behind."

"The hair is shorter there."

Raindrop Forty-Three seemed to recall something. "The eyebrows," she said. "Isn't that what they're called?" She stripped off the shields, then ran her fingers through the gentle arc of hair, against the grain.

"That's nice," she said, then laughed in a high-pitched way that was almost like her younger sister's giggle. "They're cute."

Seldon said a little impatiently, "Is there anything else that's part of the condition?"

In the rather dim light, Raindrop Forty-Three looked as though she might be considering an affirmative, but said nothing. Instead, she suddenly withdrew her hands and lifted them to her nose. Seldon wondered what she might be smelling.

"How odd," she said. "May I . . . may I do it again another time?"

Seldon said uneasily, "If you will let me have the Book long enough to study it, then perhaps."

Raindrop Forty-Three reached into her kirtle through a slit that Seldon had not noticed before and, from some hidden inner pocket, removed a book bound in some tough, flexible material. He took it, trying to control his excitement.

While Seldon readjusted his skincap to cover his hair, Raindrop Forty-Three raised her hands to her nose again and then, gently and quickly, licked one finger.

47.

"Felt your hair?" said Dors Venabili. She looked at Seldon's hair as though she was of a mind to feel it herself.

Seldon moved away slightly. "Please don't. The woman made it seem like a perversion."

"I suppose it was—from her standpoint. Did you derive no pleasure from it yourself?"

"Pleasure? It gave me gooseflesh. When she finally stopped, I was able to breathe again. I kept thinking: What other conditions will she make?"

Dors laughed. "Were you afraid that she would force sex upon you? Or hopeful?"

"I assure you I didn't dare think. I just wanted the Book."

They were in their room now and Dors turned on her field distorter to make sure they would not be overheard.

The Mycogenian night was about to begin. Seldon had removed his skincap and kirtle and had bathed, paying particular attention to his hair, which he had foamed and rinsed twice. He was now sitting on his cot, wearing a light nightgown that had been hanging in the closet.

Dors said, eyes dancing, "Did she know you have hair on your chest?"

"I was hoping earnestly she wouldn't think of that."

"Poor Hari. It was all perfectly natural, you know. I would probably have had similar trouble if I was alone with a Brother. Worse, I'm sure, since he would believe—Mycogenian society being what it is—that as a woman I would be bound to obey his orders without delay or demur."

"No, Dors. You may think it was perfectly natural, but you didn't experience it. The poor woman was in a high state of sexual excitement. She engaged all her senses . . . smelled her fingers, licked them. If she could have heard hair grow, she would have listened avidly."

"But that's what I mean by 'natural.' Anything you make forbidden gains sexual attractiveness. Would you be particularly interested in women's breasts if you lived in a society in which they were displayed at all times?"

"I think I might."

"Wouldn't you be *more* interested if they were always hidden, as in most societies they are? —Listen, let me tell you something that happened to me. I was at a lake resort back home on Cinna . . . I presume you have resorts on Helicon, beaches, that sort of thing?"

"Of course," said Seldon, slightly annoyed. "What do you think Helicon is, a world of rocks and mountains, with only well water to drink?"

"No offense, Hari. I just want to make sure you'll get the point of the story. On our beaches at Cinna, we're pretty lighthearted about what we wear . . . or don't wear."

"Nude beaches?"

"Not actually, though I suppose if someone removed all of his or her clothing it wouldn't be much remarked on. The custom is to wear a decent minimum, but I must admit that what we consider decent leaves very little to the imagination."

Seldon said, "We have somewhat higher standards of decency on Helicon."

"Yes, I could tell that by your careful treatment of me, but to each its own. In any case, I was sitting at the small beach by the lake and a young man approached to whom I had spoken earlier in the day. He was a decent fellow I found nothing particularly wrong with. He sat on the arm of my chair and placed his right hand on my left thigh, which was bare, of course, in order to steady himself.

"After we had spoken for a minute and a half or so, he said, impishly. 'Here I am. You know me hardly at all and yet it seems perfectly natural to me that I place my hand on your thigh. What's more, it seems perfectly natural to you, since you don't seem to mind that it remains there.'

"It was only then that I actually noticed that his hand was on my thigh.

Bare skin in public somehow loses some of its sexual quality. As I said, it's the hiding from view that is crucial.

"And the young man felt this too, for he went on to say, 'Yet if I were to meet you under more formal conditions and you were wearing a gown, you wouldn't dream of letting me lift your gown and place my hand on your thigh on the precise spot it now occupies.'

"I laughed and we continued to talk of this and that. Of course, the young man, now that my attention had been called to the position of his hand, felt it no longer appropriate to keep it there and removed it.

"That night I dressed for dinner with more than usual care and appeared in clothing that was considerably more formal than was required or than other women in the dining room were wearing. I found the young man in question. He was sitting at one of the tables. I approached, greeted him, and said, 'Here I am in a gown, but under it my left thigh is bare. I give you permission. Just lift the gown and place your hand on my left thigh where you had it earlier.'

"He tried. I'll give him credit for that, but everyone was staring. I wouldn't have stopped him and I'm sure no one else would have stopped him either, but he couldn't bring himself to do it. It was no more public then than it had been earlier and the same people were present in both cases. It was clear that I had taken the initiative and that I had no objections, but he could not bring himself to violate the proprieties. The conditions, which had been hand-on-thigh in the afternoon, were not hand-on-thigh in the evening and that meant more than anything logic could say."

Seldon said, "I would have put my hand on your thigh."

"Are you sure?"

"Positive."

"Even though your standards of decency on the beach are higher than ours are?"

"Yes."

Dors sat down on her own cot, then lay down with her hands behind her head. "So that you're not particularly disturbed that I'm wearing a nightgown with very little underneath it."

"I'm not particularly *shocked*. As for being disturbed, that depends on the definition of the word. I'm certainly aware of how you're dressed."

"Well, if we're going to be cooped up here for a period of time, we'll have to learn to ignore such things."

"Or take advantage of them," said Seldon, grinning. "And I like your hair. After seeing you bald all day, I like your hair."

"Well, don't touch it. I haven't washed it yet." She half-closed her eyes. "It's interesting. You've detached the informal and formal level of respectability. What you're saying is that Helicon is more respectable at the informal level than Cinna is and less respectable at the formal level. Is that right?"

"Actually, I'm just talking about the young man who placed his hand on your thigh and myself. How representative we are as Cinnians and Heliconians, respectively, I can't say. I can easily imagine some perfectly proper individuals on both worlds—and some madcaps too."

"We're talking about social pressures. I'm not exactly a Galactic traveler, but I've had to involve myself in a great deal of social history. On the planet of Derowd, there was a time when premarital sex was absolutely free. Multiple sex was allowed for the unmarried and public sex was frowned upon only when traffic was blocked. And yet, after marriage, monogamy was absolute and unbroken. The theory was that by working off all one's fantasies first, one could settle down to the serious business of life."

"Did it work?"

"About three hundred years ago that stopped, but some of my colleagues say it stopped through external pressure from other worlds who were losing too much tourist business to Derowd. There is such a thing as overall Galactic social pressure too."

"Or perhaps economic pressure, in this case."

"Perhaps. And being at the University, by the way, I get a chance to study social pressures, even without being a Galactic traveler. I meet people from scores of places inside and outside of Trantor and one of the pet amusements in the social science departments is the comparison of social pressures.

"Here in Mycogen, for instance, I have the impression that sex is strictly controlled and is permitted under only the most stringent rules, all the more tightly enforced because it is never discussed. In the Streeling Sector, sex is never discussed either, but it isn't condemned. In the Jennat Sector, where I spent a week once doing research, sex is discussed endlessly, but only for the purpose of condemning it. I don't suppose there are any two sectors in Trantor—or any two worlds outside Trantor —in which attitudes toward sex are completely duplicated."

Seldon said, "You know what you make it sound like? It would appear—"

Dors said, "I'll tell you how it appears. All this talk of sex makes one thing clear to me. I'm simply not going to let you out of my sight anymore."

"What?"

"Twice I let you go, the first time through my own misjudgment and the second because you bullied me into it. Both times it was clearly a mistake. You know what happened to you the first time."

Seldon said indignantly, "Yes, but nothing happened to me the second time."

"You nearly got into a lot of trouble. Suppose you had been caught indulging in sexual escapades with a Sister?"

"It wasn't a sexual—"

"You yourself said she was in a high state of sexual excitement."

"But—"

"It was wrong. Please get it through your head, Hari. From now on, you go nowhere without me."

"Look," said Seldon freezingly, "my object was to find out about Mycogenian history and as a result of the so-called sexual escapade with a Sister, I have a book—the Book."

"The Book! True, there's the Book. Let's see it."

Seldon produced it and Dors thoughtfully hefted it.

She said, "It might not do us any good, Hari. This doesn't look as though it will fit any projector I've ever encountered. That means you'll have to get a Mycogenian projector and they'll want to know why you want it. They'll then find out you have this Book and they'll take it away from you."

Seldon smiled. "If your assumptions were correct, Dors, your conclusions would be inescapable, but it happens that this is not the kind of book you think it is. It's not meant to be projected. The material is printed on various pages and the pages are turned. Raindrop Forty-Three explained that much to me."

"A *print*-book!" It was hard to tell whether Dors was shocked or amused. "That's from the Stone Age."

"It's certainly pre-Empire," said Seldon, "but not entirely so. Have you ever seen a print-book?"

"Considering that I'm a historian? Of course, Hari."

"Ah, but like this one?"

He handed over the Book and Dors, smiling, opened it—then turned to another page—then flipped the pages. "It's blank," she said.

"It *appears* to be blank. The Mycogenians are stubbornly primitivistic, but not entirely so. They will keep to the essence of the primitive, but have no objection to using modern technology to modify it for convenience's sake. Who knows?"

"Maybe so, Hari, but I don't understand what you're saying."

"The pages aren't blank, they're covered with microprint. Here, give it back. If I press this little nubbin on the inner edge of the cover—Look!"

The page to which the book lay open was suddenly covered with lines of print that rolled slowly upward.

Seldon said, "You can adjust the rate of upward movement to match your reading speed by slightly twisting the nubbin one way or the other. When the lines of print reach their upward limit—when you reach the bottom line, that is—they snap downward and turn off. You turn to the next page and continue."

"Where does the energy come from that does all this?"

"It has an enclosed microfusion battery that lasts the life of the book."

"Then when it runs down—"

"You discard the book, which you may be required to do even before it runs down, given wear and tear, and get another copy. You never replace the battery."

Dors took the Book a second time and looked at it from all sides. She said, "I must admit I never heard of a book like this."

"Nor I. The Galaxy, generally, has moved into visual technology so rapidly, it skipped over this possibility."

"This *is* visual."

"Yes, but not with the orthodox effects. This type of book has its advantages. It holds far more than an ordinary visual book does."

Dors said, "Where's the turn-on? —Ah, let me see if I can work it." She had opened to a page at random and set the lines of print marching upward. Then she said, "I'm afraid this won't do you any good, Hari. It's pre-Galactic. I don't mean the book. I mean the print . . . the language."

"Can *you* read it, Dors? As a historian—"

"As a historian, I'm used to dealing with archaic language—but within limits. This is far too ancient for me. I can make out a few words here and there, but not enough to be useful."

"Good," said Seldon. "If it's really ancient, it will be useful."

"Not if you can't read it."

"I can read it," said Seldon. "It's bilingual. You don't suppose that Raindrop Forty-Three can read the ancient script, do you?"

"If she's educated properly, why not?"

"Because I suspect that women in Mycogen are not educated past household duties. Some of the more learned men can read this, but everyone else would need a translation to Galactic." He pushed another nubbin. "And this supplies it."

The lines of print changed to Galactic Standard.

"Delightful," said Dors in admiration.

"We could learn from these Mycogenians, but we don't."

"We haven't known about it."

"I can't believe that. I know about it now. And you know about it. There must be outsiders coming into Mycogen now and then, for commercial or political reasons, or there wouldn't be skincaps so ready for use. So every once in a while someone must have caught a glimpse of this sort of print-book and seen how it works, but it's probably dismissed as something curious but not worth further study, simply because it's Mycogenian."

"But is it worth study?"

"Of course. Everything is. Or should be. Hummin would probably point to this lack of concern about these books as a sign of degeneration in the Empire."

He lifted the Book and said with a gush of excitement, "But *I* am curious and I will read this and it may push me in the direction of psychohistory."

"I hope so," said Dors, "but if you take my advice, you'll sleep first and approach it fresh in the morning. You won't learn much if you nod over it."

Seldon hesitated, then said, "How maternal you are!"

"I'm watching over you."

"But I have a mother alive on Helicon. I would rather you were my friend."

"As for that, I have been your friend since first I met you."

She smiled at him and Seldon hesitated as though he were not certain as to the appropriate rejoinder. Finally he said, "Then I'll take your advice—as a friend—and sleep before reading."

He made as though to put the Book on a small table between the two cots, hesitated, turned, and put it under his pillow.

Dors Venabili laughed softly. "I think you're afraid I will wake during the night and read parts of the Book before you have a chance to. Is that it?"

"Well," said Seldon, trying not to look ashamed, "that may be it. Even friendship only goes so far and this is *my* book and it's *my* psychohistory."

"I agree," said Dors, "and I promise you that we won't quarrel over that. By the way, you were about to say something earlier when I interrupted you. Remember?"

Seldon thought briefly. "No."

In the dark, he thought only of the Book. He gave no thought to the hand-on-thigh story. In fact, he had already quite forgotten it, consciously at least.

48.

Venabili woke up and could tell by her timeband that the night period was only half over. Not hearing Hari's snore, she could tell that his cot was empty. If he had not left the apartment, then he was in the bathroom.

She tapped lightly on the door and said softly, "Hari?"

He said, "Come in," in an abstracted way and she did.

The toilet lid was down and Seldon, seated upon it, held the Book open on his lap. He said, quite unnecessarily, "I'm reading."

"Yes, I see that. But why?"

"I couldn't sleep. I'm sorry."

"But why read in here?"

"If I had turned on the room light, I would have woken you up."

"Are you sure the Book can't be illuminated?"

"Pretty sure. When Raindrop Forty-Three described its workings, she never mentioned illumination. Besides, I suppose that would use up so much energy that the battery wouldn't last the life of the Book." He sounded dissatisfied.

Dors said, "You can step out, then. I want to use this place, as long as I'm here."

When she emerged, she found him sitting cross-legged on his cot, still reading, with the room well lighted.

She said, "You don't look happy. Does the Book disappoint you?"

He looked up at her, blinking. "Yes, it does. I've sampled it here and there. It's all I've had time to do. The thing is a virtual encyclopedia and the index is almost entirely a listing of people and places that are of little use for my purposes. It has nothing to do with the Galactic Empire or the pre-Imperial Kingdoms either. It deals almost entirely with a single world and, as nearly as I can make out from what I have read, it is an endless dissertation on internal politics."

"Perhaps you underestimate its age. It may deal with a period when there was indeed only one world . . . one inhabited world."

"Yes, I know," said Seldon a little impatiently. "That's actually what I want—provided I can be sure its history, not legend. I wonder. I don't want to believe it just because I *want* to believe it."

Dors said, "Well, this matter of a single-world origin is much in the air these days. Human beings are a single species spread all over the Galaxy, so they must have originated *somewhere*. At least that's the popular view at present. You can't have independent origins producing the same species on different worlds."

"But I've never seen the inevitability of that argument," said Seldon. "If human beings arose on a number of worlds as a number of different species, why couldn't they have interbred into some single intermediate species?"

"Because species can't interbreed. That's what makes them species."

Seldon thought about it a moment, then dismissed it with a shrug. "Well, I'll leave it to the biologists."

"They're precisely the ones who are keenest on the Earth hypothesis."

"Earth? Is that what they call the supposed world of origin?"

"That's a *popular* name for it, though there's no way of telling what it was called, assuming there was one. And no one has any clue to what its location might be."

"Earth!" said Seldon, curling his lips. "It sounds like a belch to me. In any case, if the book deals with the original world, I didn't come across it. How do you spell the word?"

She told him and he checked the Book quickly. "There you are. The name is not listed in the index, either by that spelling or any reasonable alternative."

"Really?"

"And they do mention other worlds in passing. Names aren't given and there seems no interest in those other worlds except insofar as they directly impinge on the local world they speak of . . . at least as far as I can see from what I've read. In one place, they talked about 'The Fifty.' I don't know what they meant. Fifty leaders? Fifty cities? It seemed to me to be fifty worlds."

"Did they give a name to their own world, this world that seems to preoccupy them entirely?" asked Dors. "If they don't call it Earth, what *do* they call it?"

"As you'd expect, they call it 'the world' or 'the planet.' Sometimes they call it 'the Oldest' or 'the World of the Dawn,' which has a poetic significance, I presume, that isn't clear to me. I suppose one ought to read the Book entirely through and some matters will then grow to make more sense." He looked down at the Book in his hand with some distaste. "It would take a very long time, though, and I'm not sure that I'd end up any the wiser."

Dors sighed. "I'm sorry, Hari. You sound so disappointed."

"That's because I *am* disappointed. It's my fault, though. I should not have allowed myself to expect too much. —At one point, come to think of it, they referred to their world as 'Aurora.' "

"Aurora?" said Dors, lifting her eyebrows.

"It sounds like a proper name. It doesn't make any sense otherwise, as far as I can see. Does it mean anything to you, Dors?"

"Aurora." Dors thought about it with a slight frown on her face. "I can't say I've ever heard of a planet with that name in the course of the history of the Galactic Empire or during the period of its growth, for that matter, but I won't pretend to know the name of every one of the twenty-five million worlds. We could look it up in the University library—if we ever get back to Streeling. There's no use trying to find a library here in Mycogen. Somehow I have a feeling that all their knowledge is in the Book. If anything isn't there, they aren't interested."

Seldon yawned and said, "I think you're right. In any case, there's no use reading any more and I doubt that I can keep my eyes open any longer. Is it all right if I put out the light?"

"I would welcome it, Hari. And let's sleep a little later in the morning."

Then, in the dark, Seldon said softly, "Of course, some of what they say is ridiculous. For instance, they refer to a life expectancy on their world of between three and four centuries."

"Centuries?"

"Yes, they count their ages by decades rather than by years. It gives you a queer feeling, because so much of what they say is perfectly matter-of-fact that when they come out with something that odd, you almost find yourself trapped into believing it."

"If you feel yourself beginning to believe that, then you should realize that many legends of primitive origins assume extended life spans for early leaders. If they're pictured as unbelievably heroic, you see, it seems natural that they have life spans to suit."

"Is that so?" said Seldon, yawning again.

"It is. And the cure for advanced gullibility is to go to sleep and consider matters again the next day."

And Seldon, pausing only long enough to think that an extended life span might well be a simple necessity for anyone trying to understand a Galaxy of people, slept.

49.

The next morning, feeling relaxed and refreshed and eager to begin his study of the Book again, Hari asked Dors, "How old would you say the Raindrop sisters are?"

"I don't know. Twenty . . . twenty-two?"

"Well, suppose they *do* live three or four centuries—"

"Hari. That's ridiculous."

"I'm saying *suppose.* In mathematics, we say 'suppose' all the time and see if we can end up with something patently untrue or self-contradictory. An extended life span would almost surely mean an extended period of development. They might seem in their early twenties and actually be in their sixties."

"You can try asking them how old they are."

"We can assume they'd lie."

"Look up their birth certificates."

Seldon smiled wryly. "I'll bet you anything you like—a roll in the hay, if you're willing—that they'll claim they don't keep records or that, if they do, they will insist those records are closed to tribespeople."

"No bet," said Dors. "And if that's true, then it's useless trying to suppose anything about their age."

"Oh no. Think of it this way. If the Mycogenians are living extended life spans that are four or five times that of ordinary human beings, they can't very well give birth to very many children without expanding their population tremendously. You remember that Sunmaster said something about *not* having the population expand and bit off his remarks angrily at that time."

Dors said, "What are you getting at?"

"When I was with Raindrop Forty-Three, I saw no children."

"On the microfarms?"

"Yes."

"Did you expect children there? I was with Raindrop Forty-Five in the shops and on the residential levels and I assure you I saw a number of children of all ages, including infants. Quite a few of them."

"Ah." Seldon looked chagrined. "Then that would mean they can't be enjoying extended life spans."

Dors said, "By your line of argument, I should say definitely not. Did you really think they did?"

"No, not really. But then you can't close your mind either and make assumptions without testing them one way or another."

"You can waste a lot of time that way too, if you stop to chew away at things that are ridiculous on the face of it."

"Some things that *seem* ridiculous on the face of it aren't. That's all. Which reminds me. You're the historian. In your work, have you ever come across objects or phenomena called 'robots'?"

"Ah! Now you're switching to another legend and a very popular one. There are any number of worlds that imagine the existence of machines in human form in prehistoric times. These are called 'robots.'

"The tales of robots probably originate from one master legend, for the general theme is the same. Robots were devised, then grew in numbers and abilities to the status of the almost superhuman. They threatened humanity and were destroyed. In every case, the destruction took place before the actual reliable historic records available to us today existed. The usual feeling is that the story is a symbolic picture of the risks and dangers of exploring the Galaxy, when human beings expanded outward from the world or worlds that were their original homes. There must always have been the fear of encountering other—and superior—intelligences."

"Perhaps they did at least once and that gave rise to the legend."

"Except that on no human-occupied world has there been any record or trace of any prehuman or nonhuman intelligence."

"But why 'robots'? Does the word have meaning?"

"Not that I know of, but it's the equivalent of the familiar 'automata.'"

"Automata! Well, why don't they say so?"

"Because people do use archaic terms for flavor when they tell an ancient legend. Why do you ask all this, by the way?"

"Because in this ancient Mycogenian book, they talk of robots. And very favorably, by the way. —Listen, Dors, aren't you going out with Raindrop Forty-Five again this afternoon?"

"Supposedly—if she shows up."

"Would you ask her some questions and try to get the answers out of her?"

"I can try. What are the questions?"

"I would like to find out, as tactfully as possible, if there is some structure in Mycogen that is particularly significant, that is tied in with the past, that has a sort of mythic value, that can—"

Dors interrupted, trying not to smile. "I think that what you are trying to ask is whether Mycogen has a temple."

And, inevitably, Seldon looked blank and said, "What's a temple?"

"Another archaic term of uncertain origin. It means all the things you asked about—significance, past, myth. Very well, I'll ask. It's the sort of thing, however, that they might find difficult to speak of. To tribespeople, certainly."

"Nevertheless, do try."

SACRATORIUM

· · · · ·

AURORA— . . . A mythical world, supposedly inhabited in primordial times, during the dawn of interstellar
travel. It is thought by some to be the perhaps equally
mythical "world of origin" of humanity and to be another
name for "Earth." The people of the Mycogen *(q.v.)* Sector
of ancient Trantor reportedly held themselves to be descended from the inhabitants of Aurora and made that tenet
central to their system of beliefs, concerning which almost
nothing else is known . . .

ENCYCLOPEDIA GALACTICA

50.

The two Raindrops arrived at midmorning. Raindrop Forty-Five seemed
as cheerful as ever, but Raindrop Forty-Three paused just inside the
door, looking drawn and circumspect. She kept her eyes down and did
not as much as glance at Seldon.

Seldon looked uncertain and gestured to Dors, who said in a cheerful
businesslike tone of voice, "One moment, Sisters. I must give instructions to my man or he won't know what to do with himself today."

They moved into the bathroom and Dors whispered, "Is something
wrong?"

"Yes. Raindrop Forty-Three is obviously shattered. Please tell her that
I will return the Book as soon as possible."

Dors favored Seldon with a long surprised look. "Hari," she said,
"you're a sweet, caring person, but you haven't the good sense of an
amoeba. If I as much as mention the Book to the poor woman, she'll be
certain that you told me all about what happened yesterday and then
she'll *really* be shattered. The only hope is to treat her exactly as I would
ordinarily."

Seldon nodded his head and said dispiritedly, "I suppose you're right."

Dors returned in time for dinner and found Seldon on his cot, still leafing through the Book, but with intensified impatience.

He looked up with a scowl and said, "If we're going to be staying here any length of time, we're going to need a communication device of some sort between us. I had no idea when you'd get back and I was a little concerned."

"Well, here I am," she said, removing her skincap gingerly and looking at it with more than a little distaste. "I'm really pleased at your concern. I rather thought you'd be so lost in the Book, you wouldn't even realize I was gone."

Seldon snorted.

Dors said, "As for communications devices, I doubt that they are easy to come by in Mycogen. It would mean easing communication with tribespeople outside and I suspect the leaders of Mycogen are bound and determined to cut down on any possible interaction with the great beyond."

"Yes," said Seldon, tossing the Book to one side, "I would expect that from what I see in the Book. Did you find out about the whatever you called it . . . the temple?"

"Yes," she said, removing her eyebrow patches. "It exists. There are a number of them over the area of the sector, but there's a central building that seems to be the important one. —Would you believe that one woman noticed my eyelashes and told me that I shouldn't let myself be seen in public? I have a feeling she intended to report me for indecent exposure."

"Never mind that," said Seldon impatiently. "Do you know where the central temple is located?"

"I have directions, but Raindrop Forty-Five warned me that women were not allowed inside except on special occasions, none of which are coming up soon. It's called the Sacratorium."

"The *what?*"

"The Sacratorium."

"What an ugly word. What does it mean?"

Dors shook her head. "It's new to me. And neither Raindrop knew what it meant either. To them, Sacratorium isn't what the building is called, it's what it *is*. Asking them why they called it that probably sounded like asking them why a wall is called a wall."

"Is there anything about it they *do* know?"

"Of course, Hari. They know what it's for. It's a place that's devoted to something other than the life here in Mycogen. It's devoted to another world, a former and better one."

"The world they once lived on, you mean?"

"Exactly. Raindrop Forty-Five all but said so, but not quite. She couldn't bring herself to say the word."

"Aurora?"

"That's the word, but I suspect that if you were to say it out loud to a group of Mycogenians, they would be shocked and horrified. Raindrop Forty-Five, when she said, 'The Sacratorium is dedicated to—', stopped at that point and carefully wrote out the letters one by one with her finger on the palm of her hand. And she blushed, as though she was doing something obscene."

"Strange," said Seldon. "If the Book is an accurate guide, Aurora is their dearest memory, their chief point of unification, the center about which everything in Mycogen revolves. Why should its mention be considered obscene? —Are you sure you didn't misinterpret what the Sister meant?"

"I'm positive. And perhaps it's no mystery. Too much talk about it would get to tribespeople. The best way of keeping it secret unto themselves is to make its very mention taboo."

"Taboo?"

"A specialized anthropological term. It's a reference to serious and effective social pressure forbidding some sort of action. The fact that women are not allowed in the Sacratorium probably has the force of a taboo. I'm sure that a Sister would be horrified if it was suggested that she invade its precincts."

"Are the directions you have good enough for me to get to the Sacratorium on my own?"

"In the first place, Hari, you're not going alone. I'm going with you. I thought we had discussed the matter and that I had made it clear that I cannot protect you at long distance—not from sleet storms and not from feral women. In the second place, it's impractical to think of walking there. Mycogen may be a small sector, as sectors go, but it simply isn't *that* small."

"An Expressway, then."

"There are no Expressways passing through Mycogenian territory. It would make contact between Mycogenians and tribespeople too easy. Still, there are public conveyances of the kind that are found on less-developed planets. In fact, that's what Mycogen is, a piece of an undeveloped planet, embedded like a splinter in the body of Trantor, which is otherwise a patchwork of developed societies. —And Hari, finish with the Book as soon as possible. It's apparent that Rainbow Forty-Three is in trouble as long as you have it and so will we be if they find out."

"Do you mean a tribesperson reading it is taboo?"

"I'm sure of it."

"Well, it would be no great loss to give it back. I should say that 95 percent of it is incredibly dull; endless in-fighting among political groups, endless justification of policies whose wisdom I cannot possibly judge, endless homilies on ethical matters which, even when enlightened, and they usually aren't, are couched with such infuriating self-righteousness as to almost enforce violation."

"You sound as though I would be doing you a great favor it I took the thing away from you."

"Except that there's always the other 5 percent that discusses the never-to-be-mentioned Aurora. I keep thinking that there may be something there and that it may be helpful to me. That's why I wanted to know about the Sacratorium.

"Do you hope to find support for the Book's concept of Aurora in the Sacratorium?"

"In a way. And I'm also terribly caught up in what the Book has to say about automata, or robots, to use their term. I find myself attracted to the concept."

"Surely, you don't take it seriously?"

"Almost. If you accept some passages of the Book literally, then there is an implication that some robots were in human shape."

"Naturally. If you're going to construct a simulacrum of a human being, you will make it *look* like a human being."

"Yes, simulacrum means 'likeness,' but a likeness can be crude indeed. An artist can draw a stick figure and you might know he is representing a human being and recognize it. A circle for the head, a stalk for the body, and four bent lines for arms and legs and you have it. But I mean robots that *really* look like a human being, in every detail."

"Ridiculous, Hari. Imagine the time it would take to fashion the metal of the body into perfect proportions, with the smooth curve of underlying muscles."

"Who said 'metal,' Dors? The impression I got is that such robots were organic or pseudo-organic, that they were covered with skin, that you could not easily draw a distinction between them and human beings in any way."

"Does the Book say *that?*"

"Not in so many words. The inference, however—"

"Is *your* inference, Hari. You can't take it seriously."

"Let me try. I find four things that I can deduce from what the Book says about robots—and I followed up every reference the index gave. First, as I say, they—or some of them—exactly resembled human beings; second, they had very extended life spans—if you want to call it that."

"Better say 'effectiveness,' " said Dors, "or you'll begin thinking of them as human altogether."

"Third," said Seldon, ignoring her, "that some—or, at any rate, at least one—continues to live on to this day."

"Hari, that's one of the most widespread legends we have. The ancient hero does not die but remains in suspended animation, ready to return to save his people at some time of great need. *Really,* Hari."

"Fourth," said Seldon, still not rising to the bait, "there are some lines that seem to indicate that the central temple—or the Sacratorium, if that's what it is, though I haven't found that word in the Book, actually—contains a robot." He paused, then said, "Do you see?"

Dors said, "No. What should I see?"

"If we combine the four points, perhaps a robot that looks exactly like a human being and that is still alive, having been alive for, say, the last twenty thousand years, is in the Sacratorium."

"Come on, Hari, you *can't* believe that."

"I don't actually believe it, but I can't entirely let go either. What if it's true? What if—it's only one chance out of a million, I admit—it's true? Don't you see how useful he could be to me? He could *remember* the Galaxy as it was long before any reliable historical records existed. He *might* help make psychohistory possible."

"Even if it was true, do you suppose the Mycogenians would let you see and interview the robot?"

"I don't intend to ask permission. I can at least go to the Sacratorium and see if there's something to interview first."

"Not now. Tomorrow at the earliest. And if you don't think better of it by morning, *we* go."

"You told me yourself they don't allow women—"

"They allow women to look at it from outside, I'm sure, and I suspect that is all we'll get to do."

And there she was adamant.

51.

Hari Seldon was perfectly willing to let Dors take the lead. She had been out in the main roadways of Mycogen and was more at home with them than he was.

Dors Venabili, brows knitted, was less delighted with the prospect. She said, "We can easily get lost, you know."

"Not with that booklet," said Seldon.

She looked up at him impatiently. "Fix your mind on Mycogen, Hari. What I should have is a computomap, something I can ask questions of. This Mycogenian version is just a piece of folded plastic. I can't tell this thing where I am. I can't tell it by word of mouth and I can't even tell it by pushing the necessary contacts. It can't tell me anything either way. It's a *print* thing."

"Then read what it says."

"That's what I'm trying to do, but it's written for people who are familiar with the system to begin with. We'll have to ask."

"No, Dors. That would be a last resort. I don't want to attract attention. I would rather we take our chances and try to find our own way, even if it means making one or two wrong turns."

Dors leafed through the booklet with great attention and then said grudgingly, "Well, it gives the Sacratorium important mention. I suppose that's only natural. I presume everyone in Mycogen would want to get there at one time or another." Then, after additional concentration, she said, "I'll tell you what. There's no way of taking a conveyance from here to there."

"What?"

"Don't get excited. Apparently, there's a way of getting from here to another conveyance that *will* take us there. We'll have to change from one to another."

Seldon relaxed. "Well, of course. You can't take an Expressway to half the places on Trantor without changing."

Dors cast an impatient glance at Seldon. "I know that too. It's just that I'm used to having these things *tell* me so. When they expect you to find out for yourself, the simplest things can escape you for a while."

"All right, dear. Don't snap. If you know the way now, lead. I will follow humbly."

And follow her he did, until they came to an intersection, where they stopped.

Three white-kirtled males and a pair of gray-kirtled females were at the same intersection. Seldon tried a universal and general smile in their direction, but they responded with a blank stare and looked away.

And then the conveyance came. It was an outmoded version of what Seldon, back on Helicon, would have called a gravi-bus. There were some twenty upholstered benches inside, each capable of holding four people. Each bench had its own doors on both sides of the bus. When it stopped, passengers emerged on either side. (For a moment, Seldon was concerned for those who got out on the traffic side of the gravi-bus, but then he noticed that every vehicle approaching from either direction stopped as it neared the bus. None passed it while it was not moving.)

Dors pushed Seldon impatiently and he moved on to a bench where two adjoining seats were available. Dors followed after. (The men always got on and got off first, he noticed.)

Dors muttered to him. "Stop studying humanity. Be aware of your surroundings."

"I'll try."

"For instance," she said and pointed to a smooth boxed-off area on the back of the bench directly before each of them. As soon as the convey-ance had begun to move, words lit up, naming the next stop and the notable structures or crossways that were nearby.

"Now, that will probably tell us when we're approaching the change-over we want. At least the sector isn't completely barbaric."

"Good," said Seldon. Then, after a while, leaning toward Dors, he whispered, "No one is looking at us. It seems that artificial boundaries are set up to preserve individual privacy in any crowded place. Have you noticed that?"

"I've always taken it for granted. If that's going to be a rule of your psychohistory, no one will be very impressed by it."

As Dors had guessed, the direction plaque in front of them eventually announced the approach to the changeover for the direct line to the Sacratorium.

They exited and again had to wait. Some buses ahead had already left this intersection, but another gravi-bus was already approaching. They were on a well-traveled route, which was not surprising; the Sacratorium was bound to be the center and heartbeat of the sector.

They got on the gravi-bus and Seldon whispered, "We're not paying."

"According to the map, public transportation is a free service."

Seldon thrust out his lower lip. "How civilized. I suppose that nothing is all of a piece, not backwardness, not barbarism, nothing."

But Dors nudged him and whispered, "Your rule is broken. We're being watched. The man on your right."

52.

Seldon's eyes shifted briefly. The man to his right was rather thin and seemed quite old. He had dark brown eyes and a swarthy complexion, and Seldon was sure that he would have had black hair if he had not been depilated.

He faced front again, thinking. This Brother was rather atypical. The few Brothers he had paid any attention to had been rather tall, light-skinned, and with blue or gray eyes. Of course, he had not seen enough of them to make a general rule.

Then there was a light touch on the right sleeve of his kirtle. Seldon turned hesitantly and found himself looking at a card on which was written lightly, CAREFUL, TRIBESMAN!

Seldon started and put a hand to his skincap automatically. The man next to him silently mouthed, "Hair."

Seldon's hand found it, a tiny exposure of bristles at his temple. He must have disturbed the skincap at some point or another. Quickly and as unobtrusively as possible, he tugged the skincap, then made sure that it was snug under the pretence of stroking his head.

He turned to his neighbor on his right, nodded slightly, and mouthed, "Thank you."

His neighbor smiled and said in a normal speaking voice, "Going to the Sacratorium?"

Seldon nodded. "Yes, I am."

"Easy guess. So am I. Shall we get off together?" His smile was friendly.

"I'm with my—my—"

"With your woman. Of course. All three together, then?"

Seldon was not sure how to react. A quick look in the other direction showed him that Dors's eyes were turned straight ahead. She was showing no interest in masculine conversation—an attitude appropriate for a Sister. However, Seldon felt a soft pat on his left knee, which he took (with perhaps little justification) to mean: "It's all right."

In any case, his natural sense of courtesy was on that side and he said, "Yes, certainly."

There was no further conversation until the direction plaque told them they were arriving at the Sacratorium and Seldon's Mycogenian friend was rising to get off.

The gravi-bus made a wide turn about the perimeter of a large area of the Sacratorium grounds and there was a general exodus when it came to a halt, the men sliding in front of the women to exit first. The women followed.

The Mycogenian's voice crackled a bit with age, but it was cheerful. He said, "It's a little early for lunch my . . . friends, but take my word for it that things will be crowded in not too long a time. Would you be willing to buy something simple now and eat it outside? I am very familiar with this area and I know a good place."

Seldon wondered if this was a device to maneuver innocent tribespeople into something or other disreputable or costly, yet decided to chance it.

"You're very kind," he said. "Since we are not at all familiar with the place, we will be glad to let you take the lead."

They bought lunch—sandwiches and a beverage that looked like milk —at an open-air stand. Since it was a beautiful day and they were visitors, the old Mycogenian said, they would go to the Sacratorium grounds and eat out of doors, the better to become acquainted with their surroundings.

During their walk, carrying their lunch, Seldon noted that, on a very small scale, the Sacratorium resembled the Imperial Palace and that the grounds around it resembled, on a minute scale, the Imperial grounds. He could scarcely believe that the Mycogenian people admired the Imperial institution or, indeed, did anything but hate and despise it, yet the cultural attraction was apparently not to be withstood.

"It's beautiful," said the Mycogenian with obvious pride.

"Quite," said Seldon. "How it glistens in the daylight."

"The grounds around it," he said, "are constructed in imitation of the government grounds on our Dawn World . . . in miniature, to be sure."

"Did you ever see the grounds of the Imperial Palace?" asked Seldon cautiously.

The Mycogenian caught the implication and seemed in no way put out by it. *"They* copied the Dawn World as best they could too."

Seldon doubted that in the extreme, but he said nothing.

They came to a semicircular seat of white stonite, sparkling in the light as the Sacratorium did.

"Good," said the Mycogenian, his dark eyes gleaming with pleasure. "No one's taken my place. I call it mine only because it's my favorite seat. It affords a beautiful view of the side wall of the Sacratorium past the trees. Please sit down. It's not cold, I assure you. And your companion. She is welcome to sit too. She is a tribeswoman, I know, and has different customs. She . . . she may speak if she wishes."

Dors gave him a hard look and sat down.

Seldon, recognizing the fact that they might remain with this old Mycogenian a while, thrust out his hand and said, "I am Hari and my female companion is Dors. We don't use numbers, I'm afraid."

"To each his . . . or her . . . own," said the other expansively. "I am Mycelium Seventy-Two. We are a large cohort."

"Mycelium?" said Seldon a bit hesitantly.

"You seem surprised," said Mycelium. "I take it, then, you've only met members of our Elder families. Names like Cloud and Sunshine and Starlight—all astronomical."

"I must admit—" began Seldon.

"Well, meet one of the lower classes. We take our names from the ground and from the micro-organisms we grow. Perfectly respectable."

"I'm quite certain," said Seldon, "and thank you again for helping me with my . . . problem in the gravi-bus."

"Listen," said Mycelium Seventy-Two, "I saved you a lot of trouble. If

220

a Sister had seen you before I did, she would undoubtedly have screamed and the nearest Brothers would have hustled you off the bus—maybe not even waiting for it to stop moving."

Dors leaned forward so as to see across Seldon. "How is it you did not act in this way yourself?"

"I? I have no animosity against tribespeople. I'm a scholar."

"A scholar?"

"First one in my cohort. I studied at the Sacratorium School and did very well. I'm learned in all the ancient arts and I have a license to enter the tribal library, where they keep book-films and books by tribespeople. I can view any book-film or read any book I wish to. We even have a computerized reference library and I can handle that too. That sort of thing broadens your mind. I don't mind a little hair showing. I've seen pictures of men with hair many a time. And women too." He glanced quickly at Dors.

They ate in silence for a while and then Seldon said, "I notice that every Brother who enters or leaves the Sacratorium is wearing a red sash."

"Oh yes," said Mycelium Seventy-Two. "Over the left shoulder and around the right side of the waist—usually very fancily embroidered."

"Why is that?"

"It's called an 'obiah.' It symbolizes the joy felt at entering the Sacratorium and the blood one would spill to preserve it."

"Blood?" said Dors, frowning.

"Just a symbol. I never actually heard of anyone spilling blood over the Sacratorium. For that matter, there isn't that much joy. It's mostly wailing and mourning and prostrating one's self over the Lost World." His voice dropped and became soft. "Very silly."

Dors said, "You're not a . . . a believer?"

"I'm a scholar," said Mycelium with obvious pride. His face wrinkled as he grinned and took on an even more pronounced appearance of age. Seldon found himself wondering how old the man was. Several centuries? —No, they'd disposed of that. It couldn't be and yet—

"How old are you?" Seldon asked suddenly, involuntarily.

Mycelium Seventy-Two showed no signs of taking offense at the question, nor did he display any hesitation at answering, "Sixty-seven."

Seldon had to know. "I was told that your people believe that in very early times everyone lived for several centuries."

Mycelium Seventy-Two looked at Seldon quizzically. "Now how did you find that out? Someone must have been talking out of turn . . . but it's true. There is that belief. Only the unsophisticated believe it, but the Elders encourage it because it shows our superiority. Actually, our life expectancy is higher than elsewhere because we eat more nutritionally, but living even one century is rare."

"I take it you don't consider Mycogenians superior," said Seldon.

Mycelium Seventy-Two said, "There's nothing wrong with Mycogenians. They're certainly not *inferior*. Still, I think that all men are equal. —Even women," he added, looking across at Dors.

"I don't suppose," said Seldon, "that many of your people would agree with that."

"Or many of *your* people," said Mycelium Seventy-Two with a faint resentment. "I believe it, though. A scholar has to. I've viewed and even read all the great literature of the tribespeople. I understand your culture. I've written articles on it. I can sit here just as comfortably with you as though you were . . . *us.*"

Dors said a little sharply, "You sound proud of understanding tribespeople's ways. Have you ever traveled outside Mycogen?"

Mycelium Seventy-Two seemed to move away a little. "No."

"Why not? You would get to know us better."

"I wouldn't feel right. I'd have to wear a wig. I'd be ashamed."

Dors said, "Why a wig? You could stay bald."

"No," said Mycelium Seventy-Two, "I wouldn't be that kind of fool. I'd be mistreated by all the hairy ones."

"Mistreated? Why?" said Dors. "We have a great many naturally bald people everywhere on Trantor and on every other world too."

"My father is quite bald," said Seldon with a sigh, "and I presume that in the decades to come I will be bald too. My hair isn't all that thick now."

"That's not bald," said Mycelium Seventy-Two. "You keep hair around the edges and over your eyes. I mean *bald*—no hair at all."

"Anywhere on your body?" said Dors, interested.

And now Mycelium Seventy-Two looked offended and said nothing.

Seldon, anxious to get the conversation back on track, said, "Tell me, Mycelium Seventy-Two, can tribespeople enter the Sacratorium as spectators?"

Mycelium Seventy-Two shook his head vigorously. "Never. It's for the Sons of the Dawn only."

Dors said, "Only the Sons?"

Mycelium Seventy-Two looked shocked for a moment, then said forgivingly, "Well, you're tribespeople. Daughters of the Dawn enter only on certain days and times. That's just the way it is. I don't say *I* approve. If it was up to me, I'd say, 'Go in. Enjoy if you can.' Sooner others than me, in fact."

"Don't you ever go in?"

"When I was young, my parents took me, but"—he shook his head—"it was just people staring at the Book and reading from it and sighing and weeping for the old days. It's very depressing. You can't talk to each other. You can't laugh. You can't even look at each other. Your mind has to be totally on the Lost World. Totally." He waved a hand in rejection. "Not for me. I'm a scholar and I want the whole world open to me."

"Good," said Seldon, seeing an opening. "We feel that way too. We are scholars also, Dors and myself."

"I know," said Mycelium Seventy-Two.

"You know? How do you know?"

"You'd have to be. The only tribespeople allowed in Mycogen are Imperial officials and diplomats, important traders, and scholars—and to me you have the look of scholars. That's what interested me in you. Scholars together." He smiled delightedly.

"So we are. I am a mathematician. Dors is a historian. And you?"

"I specialize in . . . culture. I've read all the great works of literature of the tribespeople: Lissauer, Mentone, Novigor—"

"And we have read the great works of your people. I've read the Book, for instance. —About the Lost World."

Mycelium Seventy-Two's eyes opened wide in surprise. His olive complexion seemed to fade a little. "You have? How? Where?"

"At our University we have copies that we can read if we have permission."

"Copies of *the* Book?"

"Yes."

"I wonder if the Elders know this?"

Seldon said, "And I've read about robots."

"Robots?"

"Yes. That is why I would like to be able to enter the Sacratorium. I would like to see the robot." (Dors kicked lightly at Seldon's ankle, but he ignored her.)

Mycelium Seventy-Two said uneasily, "I don't believe in such things. Scholarly people don't." But he looked about as though he was afraid of being overheard.

Seldon said, "I've read that a robot still exists in the Sacratorium."

Mycelium Seventy-Two said, "I don't want to talk about such nonsense."

Seldon persisted. "Where would it be if it *was* in the Sacratorium?"

"Even if one was there, I couldn't tell you. I haven't been in there since I was a child."

"Would you know if there was a special place, a hidden place?"

"There's the Elders' aerie. Only Elders go there, but there's nothing there."

"Have you ever been there?"

"No, of course not."

"Then how do you know?"

"I don't know that there's no pomegranate tree there. I don't know that there's no laser-organ there. I don't know that there's no item of a million different kinds there. Does my lack of knowledge of their absence show they are all present?"

For the moment, Seldon had nothing to say.

A ghost of a smile broke through Mycelium Seventy-Two's look of concern. He said, "That's scholars' reasoning. I'm not an easy man to tackle, you see. Just the same, I wouldn't advise you to try to get up into the Elders' aerie. I don't think you'd like what would happen if they found a tribesman inside. —Well. Best of the Dawn to you." And he rose suddenly—without warning—and hurried away.

Seldon looked after him, rather surprised. "What made him rush off like that?"

"I think," said Dors, "it's because someone is approaching."

And someone was. A tall man in an elaborate white kirtle, crossed by an even more elaborate and subtly glittering red sash, glided solemnly toward them. He had the unmistakable look of a man with authority and the even more unmistakable look of one who is not pleased.

53.

Hari Seldon rose as the new Mycogenian approached. He hadn't the slightest idea whether that was the appropriate polite behavior, but he had the distinct feeling it would do no harm. Dors Venabili rose with him and carefully kept her eyes lowered.

The other stood before them. He too was an old man, but more subtly aged than Mycelium Seventy-Two. Age seemed to lend distinction to his still-handsome face. His bald head was beautifully round and his eyes were a startling blue, contrasting sharply with the bright all-but-glowing red of his sash.

The newcomer said, "I see you are tribespeople." His voice was more high-pitched than Seldon had expected, but he spoke slowly, as though conscious of the weight of authority in every word he uttered.

"So we are," said Seldon politely but firmly. He saw no reason not to defer to the other's position, but he did not intend to abandon his own.

"Your names?"

"I am Hari Seldon of Helicon. My companion is Dors Venabili of Cinna. And yours, man of Mycogen?"

The eyes narrowed in displeasure, but he too could recognize an air of authority when he felt it.

"I am Skystrip Two," he said, lifting his head higher, "an Elder of the Sacratorium. And your position, tribesman?"

"*We,*" said Seldon, emphasizing the pronoun, "are scholars of Streeling University. I am a mathematician and my companion is a historian and we are here to study the ways of Mycogen."

"By whose authority?"

"By that of Sunmaster Fourteen, who greeted us on our arrival."

Skystrip Two fell silent for a moment and then a small smile appeared on his face and he took on an air that was almost benign. He said, "The High Elder. I know him well."

"And so you should," said Seldon blandly. "Is there anything else, Elder?"

"Yes." The Elder strove to regain the high ground. "Who was the man who was with you and who hurried away when I approached?"

Seldon shook his head, "We never saw him before, Elder, and know nothing about him. We encountered him purely by accident and asked about the Sacratorium."

"What did you ask him?"

"Two questions, Elder. We asked if that building was the Sacratorium and if tribespeople were allowed to enter it. He answered in the affirmative to the first question and in the negative to the second."

"Quite so. And what is your interest in the Sacratorium?"

"Sir, we are here to study the ways of Mycogen and is not the Sacratorium the heart and brain of Mycogen?"

"It is entirely ours and reserved for us."

"Even if an Elder—the High Elder—would arrange for permission in view of our scholarly function?"

"Have you indeed the High Elder's permission?"

Seldon hesitated the slightest moment while Dors's eyes lifted briefly to look at him sideways. He decided he could not carry off a lie of this magnitude. "No," he said, "not yet."

"Or ever," said the Elder. "You are here in Mycogen by authority, but even the highest authority cannot exert total control over the public. We value our Sacratorium and the populace can easily grow excited over the presence of a tribesperson anywhere in Mycogen but, most particularly, in the vicinity of the Sacratorium. It would take one excitable person to raise a cry of 'Invasion!' and a peaceful crowd such as this one would be turned into one that would be thirsting to tear you apart. I mean that quite literally. For your own good, even if the High Elder has shown you kindness, leave. Now!"

"But the Sacratorium—" said Seldon stubbornly, though Dors was pulling gently at his kirtle.

"What is there in the Sacratorium that can possibly interest you?" said the Elder. "You see it now. There is nothing for you to see in the interior."

"There is the robot," said Seldon.

The Elder stared at Seldon in shocked surprise and then, bending to bring his lips close to Seldon's ear, whispered harshly, "Leave now or I will raise the cry of 'Invasion!' myself. Nor, were it not for the High Elder, would I give you even this one chance to leave."

And Dors, with surprising strength, nearly pulled Seldon off his feet as she stepped hastily away, dragging him along until he caught his balance and stepped quickly after her.

54.

It was over breakfast the next morning, not sooner, that Dors took up the subject—and in a way that Seldon found most wounding.

She said, "Well, that was a pretty fiasco yesterday."

Seldon, who had honestly thought he had gotten away with it without comment, looked sullen. "What made it a fiasco?"

"Driven out is what we were. And for what? What did we gain?"

"Only the knowledge that there is a robot in there."

"Mycelium Seventy-Two said there wasn't."

"Of course he said that. He's a scholar—or thinks he is—and what he doesn't know about the Sacratorium would probably fill that library he goes to. You saw the Elder's reaction."

"I certainly did."

"He would not have reacted like that if there was no robot inside. He was horrified we knew."

"That's just your guess, Hari. And even if there was, we couldn't get in."

"We could certainly try. After breakfast, we go out and buy a sash for me, one of those obiahs. I put it on, keep my eyes devoutly downward, and walk right in."

"Skincap and all? They'll spot you in a microsecond."

"No, they won't. We'll go into the library where all the tribespeople data is kept. I'd like to see it anyway. From the library, which is a Sacratorium annex, I gather, there will probably be an entrance into the Sacratorium—"

"Where you will be picked up at once."

"Not at all. You heard what Mycelium Seventy-Two had to say. Everyone keeps his eyes down and meditates on their great Lost World, Aurora. No one looks at anyone else. It would probably be a grievous breach of discipline to do so. Then I'll find the Elders' aerie—"

"Just like that?"

"At one point, Mycelium Seventy-Two said he would advise me not to try to get up into the Elders' aerie. *Up*. It must be somewhere in that tower of the Sacratorium, the central tower."

Dors shook her head. "I don't recall the man's exact words and I don't think you do either. That's a terribly weak foundation to— Wait." She stopped suddenly and frowned.

"Well?" said Seldon.

"There is an archaic word 'aerie' that means 'a dwelling place on high.' "

"Ah! There you are. You see, we've learned some vital things as the result of what you call a fiasco. And if I can find a living robot that's twenty thousand years old and if it can tell me—"

"Suppose that such a thing exists, which passes belief, and that you find it, which is not very likely, how long do you think you will be able to talk to it before your presence is discovered?"

"I don't know, but if I can prove it exists and if I can find it, then I'll think of some way to talk to it. It's too late for me to back out now under any circumstances. Hummin should have left me alone when I thought there was no way of achieving psychohistory. Now that it seems there may be, I won't let anything stop me—short of being killed."

"The Mycogenians may oblige, Hari, and you can't run that risk."

"Yes, I can. I'm going to try."

"No, Hari. I must look after you and I can't let you."

"You must let me. Finding a way to work out psychohistory is more important than my safety. My safety is only important because I may work out psychohistory. Prevent me from doing so and your task loses its meaning. —Think about it."

Hari felt himself infused with a renewed sense of purpose. Psychohistory—*his* nebulous theory that he had, such a short while ago, despaired ever of proving—loomed larger, more real. Now he *had* to believe that it was possible; he could feel it in his gut. The pieces seemed to be falling together and although he couldn't see the whole pattern yet, he was sure the Sacratorium would yield another piece to the puzzle.

"Then I'll go in with you so I can pull you out, you idiot, when the time comes."

"Women can't enter."

"What makes me a woman? Only this gray kirtle. You can't see my breasts under it. I don't have a woman's style hairdo with the skincap on. I have the same washed, unmarked face a man has. The men here don't have stubble. All I need is a white kirtle and a sash and I can enter. Any Sister could do it if she wasn't held back by a taboo. I am not held back by one."

"You're held back by me. I won't let you. It's too dangerous."

"No more dangerous for me than for you."

"But I *must* take the risk."

"Then so must I. Why is your imperative greater than mine?"

"Because—" Seldon paused in thought.

"Just tell yourself this," said Dors, her voice hard as rock. "I won't let you go there without me. If you try, I will knock you unconscious and tie you up. If you don't like that, then give up any thought of going alone."

Seldon hesitated and muttered darkly. He gave up the argument, at least for now.

55.

The sky was almost cloudless, but it was a pale blue, as though wrapped in a high thin mist. That, thought Seldon, was a good touch, but suddenly he missed the sun itself. No one on Trantor saw the planet's sun unless he or she went Upperside and even then only when the natural cloud layer broke.

Did native Trantorians miss the sun? Did they give it any thought? When one of them visited another world where a natural sun was in view, did he or she stare, half-blinded, at it with awe?

Why, he wondered, did so many people spend their lives not trying to find answers to questions—not even thinking of questions to begin with? Was there anything more exciting in life than seeking answers?

His glance shifted to ground level. The wide roadway was lined with low buildings, most of them shops. Numerous individual ground-cars moved in both directions, each hugging the right side. They seemed like a collection of antiques, but they were electrically driven and quite soundless. Seldon wondered if "antique" was always a word to sneer at. Could it be that silence made up for slowness? Was there any particular hurry to life, after all?

There were a number of children on the walkways and Seldon's lips pressed together in annoyance. Clearly, an extended life span for the Mycogenians was impossible unless they were willing to indulge in infanticide. The children of both sexes (though it was hard to tell the boys from the girls) wore kirtles that came only a few inches below the knee, making the wild activity of childhood easier.

The children also still had hair, reduced to an inch in length at most, but even so the older ones among them had hoods attached to their kirtles and wore them raised, hiding the top of the head altogether. It was as though they were getting old enough to make the hair seem a trifle obscene—or old enough to be wishing to hide it, in longing for the day of rite of passage when they were depilated.

A thought occurred to Seldon. He said, "Dors, when you've been out shopping, who paid, you or the Raindrop women?"

"I did of course. The Raindrops never produced a credit tile. But why should they? What was being bought was for us, not for them."

"But you have a Trantorian credit tile—a tribeswoman credit tile."

"Of course, Hari, but there was no problem. The people of Mycogen may keep their own culture and ways of thought and habits of life as they wish. They can destroy their cephalic hair and wear kirtles. Nevertheless, they must use the world's credits. If they don't, that would choke off commerce and no sensible person would want to do that. The credits nerve, Hari." She held up her hand as though she was holding an invisible credit tile.

"And they accepted your credit tile?"

"Never a peep out of them. And never a word about my skincap. Credits sanitize everything."

"Well, that's good. So I can buy—"

"No, I'll do the buying. Credits may sanitize everything, but they more easily sanitize a tribeswoman. They're so used to paying women little or no attention that they automatically pay me the same. —And here's the clothing store I've been using."

"I'll wait out here. Get me a nice red sash—one that looks impressive."

"Don't pretend you've forgotten our decision. I'll get two. And another white kirtle also . . . to *my* measurements."

"Won't they think it odd that a woman would be buying a white kirtle?"

"Of course not. They'll assume I'm buying it for a male companion who happens to be my size. Actually, I don't think they'll bother with any assumptions at all as long as my credit tile is good."

Seldon waited, half-expecting someone to come up and greet him as a tribesman or denounce him as one—more likely—but no one did. Those who passed him did so without a glance and even those who glanced in his direction moved on seemingly untouched. He was especially nervous about the gray kirtles—the women—walking by in pairs or, even worse,

230

with a man. They were downtrodden, unnoticed, snubbed. How better to gain a brief notoriety than by shrieking at the sight of a tribesman? But even the women moved on.

They're not expecting to see a tribesman, Seldon thought, so they don't see one.

That, he decided, augured well for their forthcoming invasion of the Sacratorium. How much less would anyone expect to see tribespeople there and how much more effectively would they therefore fail to see them!

He was in fairly good humor when Dors emerged.

"You have everything?"

"Absolutely."

"Then let's go back to the room, so you can change."

The white kirtle did not fit her quite as well as the gray one did. Obviously, she could not have tried it on or even the densest shopkeeper would have been struck with alarm.

"How do I look, Hari?" she asked.

"Exactly like a boy," said Seldon. "Now let's try the sash . . . or obiah. I had better get used to calling it that."

Dors, without her skincap, was shaking out her hair gratefully. She said sharply, "Don't put it on now. We're not going to parade through Mycogen with the sash on. The last thing we want to do is call attention to ourselves."

"No no. I just want to see how it goes on."

"Well, not that one. This one is better quality and more elaborate."

"You're right, Dors. I've got to gather in what attention there is. I don't want them to detect you as a woman."

"I'm not thinking of that, Hari. I just want you to look pretty."

"A thousand thanks, but that's impossible, I suspect. Now, let's see, how does this work?"

Together, Hari and Dors practiced putting their obiahs on and taking them off, over and over again, until they could do it in one fluid motion. Dors taught Hari how to do it, as she had seen a man doing it the day before at the Sacratorium.

When Hari praised her for her acute observations, she blushed and said, "It's really nothing, Hari, just something I noticed."

Hari replied, "Then you're a genius for noticing."

Finally satisfied, they stood well apart, each surveying the other. Hari's obiah glittered, a bright red dragonlike design standing out against a paler field of similar hue. Dors's was a little less bold, had a simple thin line down the center, and was very light in color. "There," she said, "just enough to show good taste." She took it off.

"Now," said Seldon, "we fold it up and it goes into one of the inner pockets. I have my credit tile—Hummin's, really—and the key to this place in this one and here, on the other side, the Book."

"*The* Book? Should you be carrying it around?"

"I must. I'm guessing that anyone going to the Sacratorium ought to have a copy of the Book with him. They may intone passages or have readings. If necessary, we'll share the Book and maybe no one will notice. Ready?"

"I'll never be ready, but I'm going with you."

"It will be a tedious trip. Will you check my skincap and make sure no hair shows this time? And don't scratch your head."

"I won't. You look all right."

"So do you."

"You also look nervous."

And Seldon said wryly, "Guess why!"

Dors reached out impulsively and squeezed Hari's hand, then drew back as if surprised at herself. Looking down, she straightened her white kirtle. Hari, himself a trifle surprised and peculiarly pleased, cleared his throat and said, "Okay, let's go."

AERIE

. . . . .

ROBOT— . . . A term used in the ancient legends of several worlds for what are more usually called "automata." Robots are described as generally human in shape and made of metal, although some are supposed to have been pseudo-organic in nature. Hari Seldon, in the course of The Flight, is popularly supposed to have seen an actual robot, but that story is of dubious origin. Nowhere in Seldon's voluminous writings does he mention robots at all, although . . .

ENCYCLOPEDIA GALACTICA

56.

They were not noticed.

Hari Seldon and Dors Venabili repeated the trip of the day before and this time no one gave them a second look. Hardly anyone even gave them a first look. On several occasions, they had to tuck their knees to one side to allow someone sitting on an inner seat to get past them and out. When someone got in, they quickly realized they had to move over if there was an inner empty seat.

This time they quickly grew tired of the smell of kirtles that were not freshly laundered because they were not so easily diverted by what went on outside.

But eventually they were there.

"That's the library," said Seldon in a low voice.

"I suppose so," said Dors. "At least that's the building that Mycelium Seventy-Two pointed out yesterday."

They sauntered toward it leisurely.

"Take a deep breath," said Seldon. "This is the first hurdle."

The door ahead was open, the light within subdued. There were five broad stone steps leading upward. They stepped onto the lowermost one and waited several moments before they realized that their weight did not cause the steps to move upward. Dors grimaced very slightly and gestured Seldon upward.

Together they walked up the stairs, feeling embarrassed on behalf of Mycogen for its backwardness. Then, through a door, where, at a desk immediately inside was a man bent over the simplest and clumsiest computer Seldon had ever seen.

The man did not look up at them. No need, Seldon supposed. White kirtle, bald head—all Mycogenians looked so nearly the same that one's eyes slid off them and that was to the tribespeople's advantage at the moment.

The man, who still seemed to be studying something on the desk, said, "Scholars?"

"Scholars," said Seldon.

The man jerked his head toward a door. "Go in. Enjoy."

They moved inward and, as nearly as they could see, they were the only ones in this section of the library. Either the library was not a popular resort or the scholars were few or—most likely—both.

Seldon whispered, "I thought surely we would have to present some sort of license or permission form and I would have to plead having forgotten it."

"He probably welcomes our presence under any terms. Did you ever see a place like this? If a place, like a person, could be dead, we would be inside a corpse."

Most of the books in this section were print-books like *the* Book in Seldon's inner pocket. Dors drifted along the shelves, studying them. She said, "Old books, for the most part. Part classic. Part worthless."

"Outside books? Non-Mycogen, I mean?"

"Oh yes. If they have their own books, they must be kept in another section. This one is for outside research for poor little self-styled scholars like yesterday's. —This is the reference department and here's an Imperial Encyclopedia . . . must be fifty years old if a day . . . and a computer."

She reached for the keys and Seldon stopped her. "Wait. Something could go wrong and we'll be delayed."

He pointed to a discreet sign above a free-standing set of shelves that glowed with the letters TO THE SACR TORIUM. The second A in SACRATORIUM was dead, possibly recently or possibly because no one cared. (The Empire, thought Sheldon, *was* in decay. All parts of it. Mycogen too.)

He looked about. The poor library, so necessary to Mycogenian pride, perhaps so useful to the Elders who could use it to find crumbs to shore up their own beliefs and present them as being those of sophisticated tribespeople, seemed to be completely empty. No one had entered after them.

Seldon said, "Let's step in here, out of eyeshot of the man at the door, and put on our sashes."

And then, at the door, aware suddenly there would be no turning back if they passed this second hurdle, he said, "Dors, don't come in with me."

She frowned. "Why not?"

"It's not safe and I don't want you to be at risk."

"I am here to protect you," she said with soft firmness.

"What kind of protection can you be? I can protect myself, though you may not think it. And I'd be handicapped by having to protect you. Don't you see that?"

"You mustn't be concerned about me, Hari," said Dors. "Concern is *my* part." She tapped her sash where it crossed in the space between her obscured breasts.

"Because Hummin asked you to?"

"Because those are my orders."

She seized Seldon's arms just above his elbow and, as always, he was surprised by her firm grip. She said, "I'm against this, Hari, but if you feel you must go in, then I must go in too."

"All right, then. But if anything happens and you can wriggle out of it, run. Don't worry about me."

"You're wasting your breath, Hari. And you're insulting me."

Seldon touched the entrance panel and the portal slid open. Together, almost in unison, they walked through.

57.

A large room, all the larger because it was empty of anything resembling furniture. No chairs, no benches, no seats of any kind. No stage, no drapery, no decorations.

No lights, merely a uniform illumination of mild, unfocused light. The walls were not entirely blank. Periodically, arranged in spaced fashion at various heights and in no easy repetitive order, there were small, primitive, two-dimensional television screens, all of which were operating. From where Dors and Seldon stood, there was not even the illusion of a third dimension, not a breath of true holovision.

There were people present. Not many and nowhere together. They stood singly and, like the television monitors, in no easy repetitive order. All were white-kirtled, all sashed.

For the most part, there was silence. No one talked in the usual sense. Some moved their lips, murmuring softly. Those who walked did so stealthily, eyes downcast.

The atmosphere was absolutely funereal.

Seldon leaned toward Dors, who instantly put a finger to her lips, then pointed to one of the television monitors. The screen showed an idyllic garden bursting with blooms, the camera panning over it slowly.

They walked toward the monitor in a fashion that imitated the others —slow steps, putting each foot down softly.

When they were within half a meter of the screen, a soft insinuating voice made itself heard: "The garden of Antennin, as reproduced from ancient guidebooks and photographs, located in the outskirts of Eos. Note the—"

Dors said in a whisper Seldon had trouble catching over the sound of the set, "It turns on when someone is close and it will turn off if we step away. If we're close enough, we can talk under cover, but don't look at me and stop speaking if anyone approaches."

Seldon, his head bent, his hands clasped before him (he had noted that this was a preferred posture), said, "Any moment I expect someone to start wailing."

"Someone might. They're mourning their Lost World," said Dors.

"I hope they change the films every once in a while. It would be deadly to always see the same ones."

"They're all different," said Dors, her eyes sliding this way and that. "They may change periodically. I don't know."

"Wait!" said Seldon just a hair's breadth too loud. He lowered his voice and said, "Come this way."

Dors frowned, failing to make out the words, but Seldon gestured slightly with his head. Again the stealthy walk, but Seldon's footsteps increased in length as he felt the need for greater speed and Dors, catching up, pulled sharply—if very briefly—at his kirtle. He slowed.

"Robots here," he said under the cover of the sound as it came on.

The picture showed the corner of a dwelling place with a rolling lawn and a line of hedges in the foreground and three of what could only be described as robots. They were metallic, apparently, and vaguely human in shape.

The recording said, "This is a view, recently constructed, of the establishment of the famous Wendome estate of the third century. The robot you see near the center was, according to tradition, named Bendar and served twenty-two years, according to the ancient records, before being replaced."

Dors said, " 'Recently constructed,' so they must change views."

"Unless they've been saying 'recently constructed' for the last thousand years."

Another Mycogenian stepped into the sound pattern of the scene and said in a low voice, though not as low as the whisperings of Seldon and Dors, "Greetings, Brothers."

He did not look at Seldon and Dors as he spoke and after one involuntary and startled glance, Seldon kept his head averted. Dors had ignored it all.

Seldon hesitated. Mycelium Seventy-Two had said that there was no talking in the Sacratorium. Perhaps he had exaggerated. Then too he had not been in the Sacratorium since he was a child.

Desperately, Seldon decided he must speak. He said in a whisper, "And to you, Brother, greetings."

He had no idea whether that was the correct formula of reply or if there was a formula, but the Mycogenian seemed to find nothing amiss in it.

"To you in Aurora," he said.

"And to you," said Seldon and because it seemed to him that the other expected more, he added, "in Aurora," and there was an impalpable release of tension. Seldon felt his forehead growing moist.

The Mycogenian said, "Beautiful! I haven't seen this before."

"Skillfully done," said Seldon. Then, in a burst of daring, he added, "A loss never to be forgotten."

The other seemed startled, then said, "Indeed, indeed," and moved away.

Dors hissed, "Take no chances. Don't say what you don't have to."

"It seemed natural. Anyway, this *is* recent. But those are disappointing robots. They are what I would expect automata to be. I want to see the organic ones—the humanoids."

"If they existed," said Dors with some hesitation, "it seems to me they wouldn't be used for gardening jobs."

"True," said Seldon. "We must find the Elders' aerie."

"If *that* exists. It seems to me there is nothing in this hollow cave but a hollow cave."

"Let's look."

They paced along the wall, passing from screen to screen, trying to wait at each for irregular intervals until Dors clutched Seldon's arms. Between two screens were lines marking out a faint rectangle.

"A door," Dors said. Then she weakened the assertion by adding, "Do you think?"

Seldon looked about surreptitiously. It was in the highest degree convenient that, in keeping with the mourning atmosphere, every face, when not fixed on a television monitor, was bent in sad concentration on the floor.

Seldon said, "How do you suppose it would open?"

"An entrance patch."

"I can't make out any."

"It's just not marked out, but there's a slight discoloration there. Do you see it? How many palms? How many times?"

"I'll try. Keep an eye out and kick me if anyone looks in this direction."

He held his breath casually, touched the discolored spot to no avail, and then placed his palm full upon it and pressed.

The door opened silently—not a creak, not a scrape. Seldon stepped through as rapidly as he could and Dors followed him. The door closed behind them.

"The question is," said Dors, "did anyone see us?"

Seldon said, "Elders must go through this door frequently."

"Yes, but will anyone think we are Elders?"

Seldon waited, then said, "If we were observed and if anyone thought something was wrong, this door would have been flung open again within fifteen seconds of our entering."

"Possibly," said Dors dryly, "or possibly there is nothing to be seen or done on this side of the door and no one cares if we enter."

"That remains to be seen," muttered Seldon.

The rather narrow room they had entered was somewhat dark, but as they stepped farther into it, the light brightened.

There were chairs, wide and comfortable, small tables, several davenports, a deep and tall refrigerator, cupboards.

"If this is the Elders' aerie," said Seldon, "the Elders seem to do themselves comfortably, despite the austerity of the Sacratorium itself."

"As would be expected," said Dors. "Asceticism among a ruling class —except for public show—is very rare. Put that down in your notebook for psychohistorical aphorisms." She looked about. "And there is no robot."

Seldon said, "A aerie is a high position, remember, and this ceiling is not. There must be upper storeys and that must be the way." He pointed to a well-carpeted stairway.

He did not advance toward it, however, but looked about vaguely.

Dors guessed what he was seeking. She said, "Forget about elevators. There's a cult of primitivism in Mycogen. Surely, you haven't forgotten that, have you? There would be no elevators and, what's more, if we place our weight at the foot of the stairs, I am quite certain it will *not* begin moving upward. We're going to have to climb it. Several flights, perhaps."

"*Climb* it?"

"It must, in the nature of things, lead to the aerie—if it leads anywhere. Do you want to see the aerie or don't you?"

Together they stepped toward the staircase and began the climb.

They went up three flights and, as they did, the light level decreased perceptibly and in steady increments. Seldon took a deep breath and whispered, "I consider myself to be in pretty good shape, but I hate this."

"You're not used to this precise type of physical exertion." She showed no signs of physical distress whatever.

At the top of the third flight the stairs ended and before them was another door.

"And if it's locked?" said Seldon, more to himself than to Dors. "Do we try to break it down?"

But Dors said, "Why should it be locked when the lower door was not? If this is the Elders' aerie, I imagine there's a taboo on anyone but Elders coming here and a taboo is much stronger than any lock.''

"As far as those who accept the taboo are concerned," said Seldon, but he made no move toward the door.

"There's still time to turn back, since you hesitate," said Dors. "In fact, I would advise you to turn back."

"I only hesitate because I don't know what we'll find inside. If it's empty—"

And then he added in a rather louder voice, "Then it's empty," and he strode forward and pushed against the entry panel.

The door retracted with silent speed and Seldon took a step back at the surprising flood of light from within.

And there, facing him, eyes alive with light, arms half-upraised, one foot slightly advanced before the other, gleaming with a faintly yellow metallic shine, was a human figure. For a few moments, it seemed to be wearing a tight-fitting tunic, but on closer inspection it became apparent that the tunic was part of the structure of the object.

"It's the robot," said Seldon in awe, "but it's metallic."

"Worse than that," said Dors, who had stepped quickly to one side and then to the other. "Its eyes don't follow me. Its arms don't as much as tremble. It's not alive—if one can speak of robots as being alive."

And a man—unmistakably a man—stepped out from behind the robot and said, "Perhaps not. But I am alive."

And almost automatically, Dors stepped forward and took her place between Seldon and the man who had suddenly appeared.

58.

Seldon pushed Dors to one side, perhaps a shade more roughly than he intended. "I don't need protection. This is our old friend Sunmaster Fourteen."

The man who faced them, wearing a double sash that was perhaps his right as High Elder, said, "And you are Tribesman Seldon."

"Of course," said Seldon.

"And this, despite her masculine dress, is Tribeswoman Venabili."

Dors said nothing.

Sunmaster Fourteen said, "You are right, of course, tribesman. You are in no danger of physical harm from me. Please sit down. Both of you. Since you are not a Sister, tribeswoman, you need not retire. There is a seat for you which, if you value such a distinction, you will be the first woman ever to have used."

"I do not value such a distinction," said Dors, spacing her words for emphasis.

Sunmaster Fourteen nodded. "That is as you wish. I too will sit down, for I must ask you questions and I do not care to do it standing."

They were sitting now in a corner of the room. Seldon's eyes wandered to the metal robot.

Sunmaster Fourteen said, "It *is* a robot."

"I know," said Seldon briefly.

"I know you do," said Sunmaster Fourteen with similar curtness. "But now that we have settled that matter, why are you here?"

Seldon gazed steadily at Sunmaster Fourteen and said, "To see the robot."

"Do you know that no one but an Elder is allowed in the aerie?"

"I did not know that, but I suspected it."

"Do you know that no tribesperson is allowed in the Sacratorium?"

"I was told that."

"And you ignored the fact, is that it?"

"As I said, we wanted to see the robot."

"Do you know that no woman, even a Sister, is allowed in the Sacratorium except at certain stated—and rare—occasions?"

"I was told that."

"And do you know that no woman is at any time—or for any reason— allowed to dress in masculine garb? That holds, within the borders of Mycogen, for tribeswomen as well as for Sisters."

"I was not told that, but I am not surprised."

"Good. I want you to understand all this. Now, why did you want to see the robot?"

Seldon said with a shrug, "Curiosity. I had never seen a robot or even known that such a thing existed."

"And how did you come to know that it did exist and, specifically, that it existed here?"

Seldon was silent, then said, "I do not wish to answer that question."

"Is that why you were brought to Mycogen by Tribesman Hummin? To investigate robots?"

"No. Tribesman Hummin brought us here that we might be secure. However, we are scholars, Dr. Venabili and I. Knowledge is our province and to gain knowledge is our purpose. Mycogen is little understood outside its borders and we wish to know more about your ways and your methods of thought. It is a natural desire and, it seems to us, a harmless—even praiseworthy—one."

"Ah, but we do not wish the outer tribes and worlds to know about us. That is *our* natural desire and *we* are the judge of what is harmless to us and what harmful. So I ask you again, tribesman: How did you know that a robot existed in Mycogen and that it existed in this room?"

"General rumor," said Seldon at length.

"Do you insist on that?"

"General rumor. I insist on it."

Sunmaster Fourteen's keen blue eyes seemed to sharpen and he said without raising his voice, "Tribesman Seldon, we have long cooperated with Tribesman Hummin. For a tribesman, he has seemed a decent and trustworthy individual. For a *tribesman!* When he brought you two to us and commended you to our protection, we granted it. But Tribesman Hummin, whatever his virtues, is still a tribesman and we had misgivings. We were not at all sure what your—or his—real purpose might be."

"Our purpose was knowledge," said Seldon. "Academic knowledge. Tribeswoman Venabili is a historian and I too have an interest in history. Why should we not be interested in Mycogenian history?"

"For one thing, because we do not wish you to be. —In any case, two of our trusted Sisters were sent to you. They were to cooperate with you, try to find out what it was you wanted, and—what is the expression you tribesmen use?—play along with you. Yet not in such a way that you would be too aware as to what was happening." Sunmaster Fourteen smiled, but it was a grim smile.

"Raindrop Forty-Five," Sunmaster Fourteen went on, "went shopping with Tribeswoman Venabili, but there seemed nothing out of the way in what happened on those trips. Naturally, we had a full report. Raindrop Forty-Three showed you, Tribesman Seldon, our microfarms. You might have been suspicious of her willingness to accompany you alone, something that is utterly out of the question for us, but you reasoned that what applied to Brothers did not apply to tribesmen and you flattered yourself that that flimsy bit of reasoning won her over. She complied with your desire, though at considerable cost to her peace of mind. And, eventually, you asked for the Book. To have handed it over too easily might have roused your suspicion, so she pretended to a perverse desire only you could satisfy. Her self-sacrifice will not be forgotten. —I take it, tribesman, you still have the Book and I suspect you have it with you now. May I have it?"

Seldon sat in bitter silence.

Sunmaster Fourteen's wrinkled hand remained obtrusively outstretched and he said, "How much better it would be than to wrest it from you by force."

And Seldon handed it over. Sunmaster Fourteen leafed through its pages briefly, as though to reassure himself it was unharmed.

He said with a small sigh, "It will have to be carefully destroyed in the approved manner. Sad! —But once you had this Book, we were, of course, not surprised when you made your way out to the Sacratorium. You were watched at all times, for you cannot think that any Brother or Sister, not totally absorbed, would not recognize you for tribespeople at a glance. We know a skincap when we see one and there are less than seventy of them in Mycogen . . . almost all belonging to tribesmen on official business who remain entirely in secular governmental buildings during the time they are here. So you were not only seen but unmistakably identified, over and over.

"The elderly Brother who met you was careful to tell you about the library as well as about the Sacratorium, but he was also careful to tell you what you were forbidden to do, for we did not wish to entrap you. Skystrip Two also warned you . . . and quite forcibly. Nevertheless, you did not turn away.

"The shop at which you bought the white kirtle and the two sashes informed us at once and from that we knew well what you intended. The library was kept empty, the librarian was warned to keep his eyes to himself, the Sacratorium was kept under-utilized. The one Brother who inadvertently spoke to you almost gave it away, but hastened off when he realized with whom he was dealing. And then you came up here.

"You see, then, that it was your intention to come up here and that we in no way lured you here. You came as a result of your own action, your own desire, and what I want to ask you—yet once again—is: Why?"

It was Dors who answered this time, her voice firm, her eyes hard. "We will tell you yet once again, Mycogenian. We are scholars, who consider knowledge sacred and it is only knowledge that we seek. You did not lure us here, but you did not stop us either, as you might have done before ever we approached this building. You smoothed our way and made it easy for us and even that might be considered a lure. And what harm have we done? We have in no way disturbed the building, or this room, or you, or *that.*"

She pointed to the robot. "It is a dead lump of metal that you hide here and we now know that it is dead and that is all the knowledge we sought. We thought it would be more significant and we are disappointed, but now that we know it is merely what it is, we will leave—and, if you wish, we will leave Mycogen as well."

Sunmaster Fourteen listened with no trace of expression on his face, but when she was done, he addressed Seldon, saying, "This robot, as you see it, is a symbol, a symbol of all we have lost and of all we no longer have, of all that, through thousands of years, we have not forgotten and what we intend someday to return to. Because it is all that remains to us that is both material and authentic, it is dear to us—yet to your woman it is only 'a dead lump of metal.' Do you associate yourself with that judgment, Tribesman Seldon?"

Seldon said, "We are members of societies that do not tie ourselves to a past that is thousands of years old, making no contact at all with what has existed between that past and ourselves. We live in the present, which we recognize as the product of *all* the past and not of one long-gone moment of time that we hug to our chests. We realize, intellectually, what the robot may mean to you and we are willing to let it continue to mean that to you. But *we* can only see it with our own eyes, as you can only see it with yours. To *us,* it is a dead lump of metal."

"And now," said Dors, "we will leave."

"You will *not,*" said Sunmaster Fourteen. "By coming here, you have committed a crime. It is a crime only in *our* eyes, as you will hasten to point out"—his lips curved in a wintry smile—"but this is our territory and, within it, we make the definitions. And this crime, as we define it, is punishable by death."

"And you are going to shoot us down?" said Dors haughtily.

Sunmaster Fourteen's expression was one of contempt and he continued to speak only to Seldon. "What do you think we are, Tribesman Seldon? Our culture is as old as yours, as complex, as civilized, as humane. I am not armed. You will be tried and, since you are manifestly guilty, executed according to law, quickly and painlessly.

"If you were to try to leave now, I would not stop you, but there are many Brothers below, many more than there appeared to be when you entered the Sacratorium and, in their rage at your action, they may lay rough and forceful hands on you. It has happened in our history that tribespeople have even died so and it is not a pleasant death—certainly not a painless one."

"We were warned of this," said Dors, "by Skystrip Two. So much for your complex, civilized, and humane culture."

"People can be moved to violence at moments of emotion, Tribesman Seldon," said Sunmaster Fourteen calmly, "whatever their humanity in moments of calm. This is true in every culture, as your woman, who is said to be a historian, must surely know."

Seldon said, "Let us remain reasonable, Sunmaster Fourteen. You may be the law in Mycogen over local affairs, but you are not the law over us and you know it. We are both non-Mycogenian citizens of the Empire and it is the Emperor and his designated legal officers who must remain in charge of any capital offense."

Sunmaster Fourteen said, "That may be so in statutes and on papers and on holovision screens, but we are not talking theory now. The High Elder has long had the power to punish crimes of sacrilege without interference from the Imperial throne."

"*If* the criminals are your own people," said Seldon. "It would be quite different if they were outsiders."

"I doubt it in this case. Tribesman Hummin brought you here as fugitives and we are not so yeast-headed in Mycogen that we don't strongly suspect that you are fugitives from the Emperor's laws. Why should he object if we do his work for him?"

"Because," said Seldon, "he would. Even if we were fugitives from the Imperial authorities and even if he wanted us only to punish us, he would still want us. To allow you to kill, by whatever means and for whatever reason, non-Mycogenians without due *Imperial* process would be to defy his authority and no Emperor could allow such a precedent. No matter how eager he might be to see that the microfood trade not be interrupted, he would still feel it necessary to re-establish the Imperial prerogative. Do you wish, in your eagerness to kill us, to have a division of Imperial soldiery loot your farms and your dwellings, desecrate your Sacratorium, and take liberties with the Sisters? Consider."

Sunmaster Fourteen smiled once again, but displayed no softness. "Actually, I have considered and there *is* an alternative. After we condemn you, we could delay your execution to allow you to appeal to the Emperor for a review of your case. The Emperor might be grateful at this evidence of our ready submission to his authority and grateful too to lay his hands on you two—for some reason of his own—and Mycogen might profit. Is that what you want, then? To appeal to the Emperor in due course and to be delivered to him?"

Seldon and Dors looked at each other briefly and were silent.

Sunmaster Fourteen said, "I feel you would rather be delivered to the Emperor than die, but why do I get the impression that the preference is only by a slight margin?"

"Actually," said a new voice, "I think neither alternative is acceptable and that we must search for a third."

59.

It was Dors who identified the newcomer first, perhaps because it was she who expected him.

"Hummin," she said, "thank goodness you found us. I got in touch with you the moment I realized I was not going to deflect Hari from"— she held up her hands in a wide gesture—"this."

Hummin's smile was a small one that did not alter the natural gravity of his face. There was a subtle weariness about him.

"My dear," he said, "I was engaged in other things. I cannot always pull away at a moment's notice. And when I got here, I had, like you two, to supply myself with a kirtle and sash, to say nothing of a skincap, and make my way out here. Had I been here earlier, I might have stopped this, but I believe I'm not too late."

Sunmaster Fourteen had recovered from what had seemed to be a painful shock. He said in a voice that lacked its customary severe depth, "How did you get in here, Tribesman Hummin?"

"It was not easy, High Elder, but as Tribeswoman Venabili likes to say, I am a very persuasive person. Some of the citizens here remember who I was and what I have done for Mycogen in the past, that I am even an honorary Brother. Have you forgotten, Sunmaster Fourteen?"

The Elder replied, "I have not forgotten, but even the most favorable memory can not survive certain actions. A tribesman here and a tribes*woman.* There is no greater crime. All you have done is not great enough to balance that. My people are not unmindful. We will make it up to you some other way. But these two must die or be handed over to the Emperor."

"I am also here," said Hummin calmly. "Is that not a crime as well?"

"For you," said Sunmaster Fourteen, "for you *personally,* as a kind of honorary Brother, I can . . . overlook it . . . once. Not these two."

"Because you expect a reward from the Emperor? Some favor? Some concession? Have you already been in touch with him or with his Chief of Staff, Eto Demerzel, more likely?"

"That is not a subject for discussion."

"Which is itself an admission. Come on, I don't ask what the Emperor promised, but it cannot be much. He does not have much to give in these degenerate days. Let *me* make you an offer. Have these two told you they are scholars?"

"They have."

"And they are. They are not lying. The tribeswoman is a historian and the tribesman is a mathematician. The two together are trying to combine their talents to make a mathematics of history and they call the combined subject 'psychohistory.' "

Sunmaster Fourteen said, "I know nothing about this psychohistory, nor do I care to know. Neither it nor any other facet of your tribal learning interests me."

"Nevertheless," said Hummin, "I suggest that you listen to me."

It took Hummin some fifteen minutes, speaking concisely, to describe the possibility of organizing the natural laws of society (something he always mentioned with audible quotation marks in the tone of his voice) in such a way as to make it possible to anticipate the future with a substantial degree of probability.

And when he was done, Sunmaster Fourteen, who had listened expressionlessly, said, "A highly unlikely piece of speculation, I should say."

Seldon, with a rueful expression, seemed about to speak, undoubtedly to agree, but Hummin's hand, resting lightly on the other's knee, tightened unmistakably.

Hummin said, "Possibly, High Elder, but the Emperor doesn't think so. And by the Emperor, who is himself an amiable enough personage, I really mean Demerzel, concerning whose ambitions you need no instruction. They would like very much to have these two scholars, which is why

I've brought them here for safekeeping. I had little expectation that you would do Demerzel's work for him by delivering the scholars to him."

"They have committed a crime that—"

"Yes, we know, High Elder, but it is only a crime because you choose to call it so. No real harm has been done."

"It has been done to our belief, to our deepest felt—"

"But imagine what harm will be done if psychohistory falls into the hands of Demerzel. Yes, I grant that nothing may come of it, but suppose for a moment that something does and that the Imperial government has the use of it—can foretell what is to come—can take measures with that foreknowledge which no one else would have—can take measures, in fact, designed to bring about an alternate future more to the Imperial liking."

"Well?"

"Is there any doubt, High Elder, that the alternate future more to the Imperial liking would be one of tightened centralization? For centuries now, as you very well know, the Empire has been undergoing a steady decentralization. Many worlds now acknowledge only lip service to the Emperor and virtually rule themselves. Even here on Trantor, there is decentralization. Mycogen, as only one example, is free of Imperial interference for the most part. You rule as High Elder and there is no Imperial officer at your side overseeing your actions and decisions. How long do you think that will last with men like Demerzel adjusting the future to their liking?"

"Still the flimsiest of speculation," said Sunmaster Fourteen, "but a disturbing one, I admit."

"On the other hand, if these scholars can complete their task, an unlikely if, you might say, but an if—then they are sure to remember that you spared them when you might have chosen not to. And it would then be conceivable that they would learn to arrange a future, for instance, that would allow Mycogen to be given a world of its own, a world that could be terraformed into a close replica of the Lost World. And even if these two forget your kindness, I will be here to remind them."

"Well—" said Sunmaster Fourteen.

"Come on," said Hummin, "it is not hard to decide what must be going through your mind. Of all tribespeople, you must trust Demerzel the least. And though the chance of psychohistory might be small (if I was not being honest with you, I would not admit that) it is not zero; and if it will bring about a restoration of the Lost World, what can you want more than that? What would you not risk for even a tiny chance of that? Come now—I promise you and my promises are not lightly given. Release these two and choose a tiny chance of your heart's desire over no chance at all."

There was silence and then Sunmaster Fourteen sighed. "I don't know how it is, Tribesman Hummin, but on every occasion that we meet, you persuade me into something I do not really want to do."

"Have I ever misled you, High Elder?"

"You have never offered me so small a chance?"

"And so high a possible reward. The one balances the other."

And Sunmaster Fourteen nodded his head. "You are right. Take these two and take them out of Mycogen and never let me see them again unless there comes a time when— But surely it will not be in my lifetime."

"Perhaps not, High Elder. But your people have been waiting patiently for nearly twenty thousand years. Would you then object to waiting another—perhaps—two hundred?"

"I would not willingly wait one moment, but my people will wait as long as they must."

And standing up, he said, "I will clear the path. Take them and go!"

60.

They were finally back in a tunnel. Hummin and Seldon had traveled through one when they went from the Imperial Sector to Streeling University in the air-taxi. Now they were in another tunnel, going from Mycogen to . . . Seldon did not know where. He hesitated to ask. Hummin's face seemed as if it was carved out of granite and it didn't welcome conversation.

Hummin sat in the front of the four-seater, with no one to his right. Seldon and Dors shared the backseat.

Seldon chanced a smile at Dors, who looked glum. "It's nice to be in real clothes again, isn't it?"

"I will never," said Dors with enormous sincerity, "wear or look at anything that resembles a kirtle. And I will never, under any circumstances, wear a skincap. In fact, I'm going to feel odd if I ever see a normally bald man."

And it was Dors who finally asked the question that Seldon had been reluctant to advance. "Chetter," she said rather petulantly, "why won't you tell us where we're going?"

Hummin hitched himself into a sideways position and he looked back at Dors and Seldon gravely. "Somewhere," he said, "where it may be difficult for you to get into trouble—although I'm not sure such a place exists."

Dors was at once crestfallen. "Actually, Chetter, it's my fault. At Streeling, I let Hari go Upperside without accompanying him. In Mycogen, I at least accompanied him, but I suppose I ought not to have let him enter the Sacratorium at all."

"I was determined," said Seldon warmly. "It was in no way Dors's fault."

Hummin made no effort to apportion blame. He simply said, "I gather you wanted to see the robot. Was there a reason for that? Can you tell me?"

Seldon could feel himself redden. "I was wrong in that respect, Hummin. I did not see what I expected to see or what I hoped to see. If I had known the content of the aerie, I would never have bothered going there. Call it a complete fiasco."

"But then, Seldon, what was it you hoped to see? Please tell me. Take your time if you wish. This is a long trip and I am willing to listen."

"The thing is, Hummin, that I had the idea that there were humaniform robots, that they were long-lived, that at least one might still be alive, and that it might be in the aerie. There *was* a robot there, but it was metallic, it was dead, and it was merely a symbol. Had I but known—"

"Yes. Did we all but know, there would be no need for questions or for research of any kind. Where did you get your information about humaniform robots? Since no Mycogenian would have discussed that with you, I can think of only one source. The Mycogenian Book—a powered print-book in ancient Auroran and modern Galactic. Am I right?"

"Yes."

"And how did you get a copy?"

Seldon paused, then muttered, "It's somewhat embarrassing."

"I am not easily embarrassed, Seldon."

Seldon told him and Hummin allowed a very small smile to twitch across his face.

Hummin said, "Didn't it occur to you that what occurred had to be a charade? No Sister would do a thing like that—except under instruction and with a great deal of persuading."

Seldon frowned and said with asperity, "That was not at all obvious. People *are* perverted now and then. And it's easy for you to grin. I didn't have the information you had and neither did Dors. If you did not wish me to fall into traps, you might have warned me of those that existed."

"I agree. I withdraw my remark. In any case, you don't have the Book any longer, I'm sure."

"No. Sunmaster Fourteen took it from me."

"How much of it did you read?"

"Only a small fraction. I didn't have time. It's a huge book and I must tell you, Hummin, it is dreadfully dull."

"Yes, I know that, for I think I have read more of it than you have. It is not only dull, it is totally unreliable. It is a one-sided, official Mycogenian view of history that is more intent on presenting that view than a reasoned objectivity. It is even deliberately unclear in spots so that outsiders —even if they were to read the Book—would never know entirely what they read. What was it, for instance, that you thought you read about robots that interested you?"

"I've already told you. They speak of humaniform robots, robots that could not be distinguished from human beings in outward appearance."

"How many of these would exist?" asked Hummin.

"They don't say. —At least, I didn't come across a passage in which they gave numbers. There may have been only a handful, but *one* of them, the Book refers to as 'Renegade.' It seems to have an unpleasant significance, but I couldn't make out what."

"You didn't tell me anything about that," interposed Dors. "If you had, I would have told you that it's not a proper name. It's another archaic word and it means, roughly, what 'traitor' would mean in Galactic. The older word has a greater aura of fear about it. A traitor, somehow, sneaks to his treason, but a renegade flaunts it."

Hummin said, "I'll leave the fine points of archaic language to you, Dors, but, in any case, if the Renegade actually existed and if it was a humaniform robot, then, clearly, as a traitor and enemy, it would not be preserved and venerated in the Elders' aerie."

Seldon said, "I didn't know the meaning of 'Renegade,' but, as I said, I did get the impression that it was an enemy. I thought it might have been defeated and preserved as a reminder of the Mycogenian triumph."

"Was there any indication in the Book that the Renegade was defeated?"

"No, but I might have missed that portion—"

"Not likely. Any Mycogenian victory would be announced in the Book unmistakably and referred to over and over again."

"There was another point the Book made about the Renegade," said Seldon, hesitating, "but I can't be at all sure I understood it."

Hummin said, "As I told you . . . They are deliberately obscure at times."

"Nevertheless, they seemed to say that the Renegade could somehow tap human emotions . . . influence them—"

"Any politician can," said Hummin with a shrug. "It's called charisma —when it works."

Seldon sighed. "Well, I wanted to believe. That was it. I would have given a great deal to find an ancient humaniform robot that was still alive and that I could question."

"For what purpose?" asked Hummin.

"To learn the details of the primordial Galactic society when it still consisted of only a handful of worlds. From so small a Galaxy psychohistory could be deduced more easily."

Hummin said, "Are you sure you could trust what you heard? After many thousands of years, would you be willing to rely on the robot's early memories? How much distortion would have entered into them?"

"That's right," said Dors suddenly. "It would be like the computerized records I told you of, Hari. Slowly, those robot memories would be discarded, lost, erased, distorted. You can only go back so far and the farther you go back, the less reliable the information becomes—no matter what you do."

Hummin nodded. "I've heard it referred to as a kind of uncertainty principle in information."

"But wouldn't it be possible," said Seldon thoughtfully, "that *some* information, for special reasons, would be preserved? Parts of the Mycogenian Book may well refer to events of twenty thousand years ago and yet be very largely as it had been originally. The more valued and the more carefully preserved particular information is, the more long-lasting and accurate it may be."

"The key word is 'particular.' What the Book may care to preserve may not be what *you* wish to have preserved and what a robot may remember best may be what you wish him to remember least."

Seldon said in despair, "In whatever direction I turn to seek a way of working out psychohistory, matters so arrange themselves as to make it impossible. Why bother trying?"

"It might seem hopeless now," said Hummin unemotionally, "but given the necessary genius, a route to psychohistory may be found that none of us would at this moment expect. Give yourself more time. —But we're coming to a rest area. Let us pull off and have dinner."

Over the lamb patties on rather tasteless bread (most unpalatable after the fare at Mycogen), Seldon said, "You seem to assume, Hummin, that I am the possessor of 'the necessary genius.' I may not be, you know."

Hummin said, "That's true. You may not be. However, I know of no alternate candidate for the post, so I must cling to you."

And Seldon sighed and said, "Well, I'll try, but I'm out of any spark of hope. Possible but not practical, I said to begin with, and I'm more convinced of that now than I ever was before."

HEATSINK

. . . . .

AMARYL, YUGO— . . . A mathematician who, next to Hari Seldon himself, may be considered most responsible for working out the details of psychohistory. It was he who . . .

. . . Yet the conditions under which he began life are almost more dramatic than his mathematical accomplishments. Born into the hopeless poverty of the lower classes of Dahl, a sector of ancient Trantor, he might have passed his life in utter obscurity were it not for the fact that Seldon, quite by accident, encountered him in the course of . . .

ENCYCLOPEDIA GALACTICA

61.

The Emperor of all the Galaxy felt weary—physically weary. His lips ached from the gracious smile he had had to place on his face at careful intervals. His neck was stiff from having inclined his head this way and that in a feigned show of interest. His ears pained from having to listen. His whole body throbbed from having to rise and to sit and to turn and to hold out his hand and to nod.

It was merely a state function where one had to meet Mayors and Viceroys and Ministers and their wives or husbands from here and there in Trantor and (worse) from here and there in the Galaxy. There were nearly a thousand present, all in costumes that varied from the ornate to the downright outlandish, and he had had to listen to a babble of different accents made the worse by an effort to speak the Emperor's Galactic as spoken at the Galactic University. Worst of all, the Emperor had had to remember to avoid making commitments of substance, while freely applying the lotion of words without substance.

All had been recorded, sight and sound—very discreetly—and Eto Demerzel would go over it to see if Cleon, First of that Name, had behaved himself. That, of course, was only the way that the Emperor put it to himself. Demerzel would surely say that he was merely collecting data on any unintentional self-revelation on the part of the guests. And perhaps he was.

Fortunate Demerzel!

The Emperor could not leave the Palace and its extensive grounds, while Demerzel could range the Galaxy if he wished. The Emperor was always on display, always accessible, always forced to deal with visitors, from the important to the merely intrusive. Demerzel remained anonymous and never allowed himself to be seen inside the Palace grounds. He remained merely a fearsome name and an invisible (and therefore the more frightening) presence.

The Emperor was the Inside Man with all the trappings and emoluments of power. Demerzel was the Outside Man, with nothing evident, not even a formal title, but with his fingers and mind probing everywhere and asking for no reward for his tireless labors but one—the reality of power.

It amused the Emperor—in a macabre sort of way—to consider that, at any moment, without warning, with a manufactured excuse or with none at all, he could have Demerzel arrested, imprisoned, exiled, tortured, or executed. After all, in these annoying centuries of constant unrest, the Emperor might have difficulty in exerting his will over the various planets of the Empire, even over the various sectors of Trantor—with their rabble of local executives and legislatures that he was forced to deal with in a maze of interlocking decrees, protocols, commitments, treaties, and general interstellar legalities—but at least his powers remained absolute over the Palace and its grounds.

And yet Cleon knew that his dreams of power were useless. Demerzel had served his father and Cleon could not remember a time when he did not turn to Demerzel for everything. It was Demerzel who knew it all, devised it all, did it all. More than that, it was on Demerzel that anything that went wrong could be blamed. The Emperor himself remained above criticism and had nothing to fear—except, of course, palace coups and assassination by his nearest and dearest. It was to prevent this, above all, that he depended upon Demerzel.

Emperor Cleon felt a tiny shudder at the thought of trying to do without Demerzel. There had been Emperors who had ruled personally, who had had a series of Chiefs of Staff of no talent, who had had incompetents serving in the post and had kept them—and somehow they had gotten along for a time and after a fashion.

But Cleon could not. He needed Demerzel. In fact, now that the thought of assassination had come to him—and, in view of the modern history of the Empire, it was inevitable that it had come to him—he could see that getting rid of Demerzel was quite impossible. It couldn't be done. No matter how cleverly he, Cleon, would attempt to arrange it, Demerzel (he was sure) would anticipate the move somehow, would know it was on its way, and would arrange, with far superior cleverness, a palace coup. Cleon would be dead before Demerzel could possibly be taken away in chains and there would simply be another Emperor that Demerzel would serve—and dominate.

Or would Demerzel tire of the game and make himself Emperor?

Never! The habit of anonymity was too strong in him. If Demerzel exposed himself to the world, then his powers, his wisdom, his luck (whatever it was) would surely desert him. Cleon was convinced of that. He felt it to be beyond dispute.

So while he behaved himself, Cleon was safe. With no ambitions of his own, Demerzel would serve him faithfully.

And now here was Demerzel, dressed so severely and simply that it made Cleon uneasily conscious of the useless ornamentation of his robes of state, now thankfully removed with the aid of two valets. Naturally, it would not be until he was alone and in dishabille that Demerzel would glide into view.

"Demerzel," said the Emperor of all the Galaxy, "I am tired!"

"State functions are tiring, Sire," murmured Demerzel.

"Then must I have them every evening?"

"Not *every* evening, but they are essential. It gratifies others to see you and to be taken note of by you. It helps keep the Empire running smoothly."

"The Empire used to be kept running smoothly by power," said the Emperor somberly. "Now it must be kept running by a smile, a wave of the hand, a murmured word, and a medal or a plaque."

"If all that keeps the peace, Sire, there is much to be said for it. And your reign proceeds well."

"You know why—because I have you at my side. My only real gift is that I am aware of your importance." He looked at Demerzel slyly. "My son need not be my heir. He is not a talented boy. What if I make *you* my heir?"

Demerzel said freezingly, "Sire, that is unthinkable. I would not usurp the throne. I would not steal it from your rightful heir. Besides, if I have displeased you, punish me justly. Surely, nothing I have done or could possibly do deserves the punishment of being made Emperor."

Cleon laughed. "For that true assessment of the value of the Imperial throne, Demerzel, I abandon any thought of punishing you. Come now, let us talk about something. I would sleep, but I am not yet ready for the ceremonies with which they put me to bed. Let us talk."

"About what, Sire?"

"About anything. —About that mathematician and his psychohistory. I think about him every once in a while, you know. I thought of him at dinner tonight. I wondered: What if a psychohistorical analysis would predict a method for making it possible to be an Emperor without endless ceremony?"

"I somehow think, Sire, that even the cleverest psychohistorian could not manage that."

"Well, tell me the latest. Is he still hiding among those peculiar baldheads of Mycogen? You promised you would winkle him out of there."

"So I did, Sire, and I moved in that direction, but I regret that I must say that I failed."

"Failed?" The Emperor allowed himself to frown. "I don't like that."

"Nor I, Sire. I planned to have the mathematician be encouraged to commit some blasphemous act—such acts are easy to commit in Mycogen, especially for an outsider—one that would call for severe punishment. The mathematician would then be forced to appeal to the Emperor and, as a result, we would get him. I planned it at the cost of insignificant concessions on our part—important to Mycogen, totally unimportant to us—and I meant to play no direct role in the arrangement. It was to be handled subtly."

"I dare say," said Cleon, "but it failed. Did the Mayor of Mycogen—"

"He is called the High Elder, Sire."

"Do not quibble over titles. Did this High Elder refuse?"

"On the contrary, Sire, he agreed and the mathematician, Seldon, fell into the trap neatly."

"Well then?"

"He was allowed to leave unharmed."

"Why?" said Cleon indignantly.

"Of this I am not certain, Sire, but I suspect we were outbid."

"By whom? By the Mayor of Wye?"

"Possibly, Sire, but I doubt that. I have Wye under constant surveillance. If they had gained the mathematician, I would know it by now."

The Emperor was not merely frowning. He was clearly enraged. "Demerzel, this is bad. I am greatly displeased. A failure like this makes me wonder if you are perhaps not the man you once were. What measures shall we take against Mycogen for this clear defiance of the Emperor's wishes?"

Demerzel bowed low in recognition of the storm unleashed, but he said in steely tones, "It would be a mistake to move against Mycogen now, Sire. The disruption that would follow would play into the hands of Wye."

"But we must do *something.*"

"Perhaps not, Sire. It is not as bad as it may seem."

"How can it be not as bad as it seems?"

"You'll remember, Sire, that this mathematician was convinced that psychohistory was impractical."

"Of course I remember that, but that doesn't matter, does it? For our purposes?"

"Perhaps not. But if it were to become practical, it would serve our purposes to an infinitely great extent, Sire. And from what I have been able to find out, the mathematician is now attempting to make psychohistory practical. His blasphemous attempt in Mycogen was, I understand, part of an attempt at solving the problem of psychohistory. In that case, it may pay us, Sire, to leave him to himself. It will serve us better to pick him up when he is closer to his goal or has reached it."

"Not if Wye gets him first."

"That, I shall see to it, will not happen."

"In the same way that you succeeded in winkling the mathematician out of Mycogen just now?"

"I will not make a mistake the next time, Sire," said Demerzel coldly.

The Emperor said, "Demerzel, you had better not. I will not tolerate another mistake in this respect." And then he added pettishly, "I think I shall not sleep tonight after all."

62.

Jirad Tisalver of the Dahl Sector was short. The top of his head came up only to Hari Seldon's nose. He did not seem to take that to heart, however. He had handsome, even features, was given to smiling, and sported a thick black mustache and crisply curling black hair.

He lived, with his wife and a half-grown daughter, in an apartment of seven small rooms, kept meticulously clean, but almost bare of furnishings.

Tisalver said, "I apologize, Master Seldon and Mistress Venabili, that I cannot give you the luxury to which you must be accustomed, but Dahl is a poor sector and I am not even among the better-off among our people."

"The more reason," responded Seldon, "that we must apologize to you for placing the burden of our presence upon you."

"No burden, Master Seldon. Master Hummin has arranged to pay us generously for your use of our humble quarters and the credits would be welcome even if you were not—and you *are.*"

Seldon remembered Hummin's parting words when they finally arrived in Dahl.

"Seldon," he had said, "this is the third place I've arranged as sanctuary. The first two were notoriously beyond the reach of the Imperium, which might well have served to attract their attention; after all, they were logical places for you. This one is different. It is poor, unremarkable, and, as a matter of fact, unsafe in some ways. It is not a natural refuge for you, so that the Emperor and his Chief of Staff may not think to turn their eyes in this direction. Would you mind staying out of trouble this time, then?"

"I will try, Hummin," said Seldon, a little offended. "Please be aware that the trouble is not of my seeking. I am trying to learn what may well take me thirty lifetimes to learn if I am to have the slightest chance of organizing psychohistory."

"I understand," said Hummin. "Your efforts at learning brought you to Upperside in Streeling and to the Elders' aerie in Mycogen and to who can guess where in Dahl. As for you, Dr. Venabili, I know you've been trying to take care of Seldon, but you must try harder. Get it fixed in your head that he is the most important person on Trantor—or in the Galaxy, for that matter—and that he must be kept secure at any cost."

"I will continue to do my best," said Dors stiffly.

"And as for your host family, they have their peculiarities, but they are essentially good people with whom I have dealt before. Try not to get them in trouble either."

But Tisalver, at least, did not seem to anticipate trouble of any kind from his new tenants and his expressed pleasure at the company he now had—quite apart from the rent credits he would be getting—seemed quite sincere.

He had never been outside Dahl and his appetite for tales of distant places was enormous. His wife too, bowing and smiling, would listen and their daughter, with a finger in her mouth, would allow one eye to peep from behind the door.

It was usually after dinner, when the entire family assembled, that Seldon and Dors were expected to talk of the outside world. The food was plentiful enough, but it was bland and often tough. So soon after the tangy food of Mycogen, it was all but inedible. The "table" was a long shelf against one wall and they ate standing up.

Gentle questioning by Seldon elicited the fact that this was the usual situation among Dahlites as a whole and was not due to unusual poverty. Of course, Mistress Tisalver explained, there were those with high government jobs in Dahl who were prone to adopt all kinds of effete customs like chairs—she called them "body shelves"—but this was looked down upon by the solid middle class.

Much as they disapproved of unnecessary luxury, though, the Tisalvers loved hearing about it, listening with a virtual storm of tongue-clicking when told of mattresses lifted on legs, of ornate chests and wardrobes, and of a superfluity of tableware.

They listened also to a description of Mycogenian customs, while Jirad Tisalver stroked his own hair complacently and made it quite obvious that he would as soon think of emasculation as of depilation. Mistress Tisalver was furious at any mention of female subservience and flatly refused to believe that the Sisters accepted it tranquilly.

They seized most, however, on Seldon's casual reference to the Imperial grounds. When, upon questioning, it turned out that Seldon had actually seen and spoken to the Emperor, a blanket of awe enveloped the family. It took a while before they dared ask questions and Seldon found that he could not satisfy them. He had not, after all, seen much of the grounds and even less of the Palace interior.

That disappointed the Tisalvers and they were unremitting in their attempts to elicit more. And, having heard of Seldon's Imperial adventure, they found it hard to believe Dors's assertion that, for her part, she had never been anywhere in the Imperial grounds. Most of all, they rejected Seldon's casual comment that the Emperor had talked and behaved very much as any ordinary human being would. That seemed utterly impossible to the Tisalvers.

After three evenings of this, Seldon found himself tiring. He had, at first, welcomed the chance to do nothing for a while (during the day, at least) but view some of the history book-films that Dors recommended. The Tisalvers turned over their book-viewer to their guests during the day with good grace, though the little girl seemed unhappy and was sent over to a neighbor's apartment to use theirs for her homework.

"It doesn't help," Seldon said restlessly in the security of his room after he had piped in some music to discourage eavesdropping. "I can see your fascination with history, but it's all endless detail. It's a mountainous heap—no, a Galactic heap—of data in which I can't see the basic organization."

"I dare say," said Dors, "that there must have been a time when human beings saw no organization in the stars in the sky, but eventually they discovered the Galactic structure."

"And I'm sure that took generations, not weeks. There must have been a time when physics seemed a mass of unrelated observations before the central natural laws were discovered and *that* took generations. —And what of the Tisalvers?"

"What of them? I think they're being very nice."

"They're curious."

"Of course they are. Wouldn't you be if you were in their place?"

"But is it just curiosity? They seem to be ferociously interested in my meeting with the Emperor."

Dors seemed impatient. "Again . . . it's only natural. Wouldn't you be—if the situation was reversed?"

"It makes me nervous."

"Hummin brought us here."

"Yes, but he's not perfect. He brought me to the University and I was maneuvered Upperside. He brought us to Sunmaster Fourteen, who entrapped us. You know he did. Twice bitten, at least once shy. I'm tired of being questioned."

"Then turn the tables, Hari. Aren't you interested in Dahl?"

"Of course. What do *you* know about it to begin with?"

"Nothing. It's just one of more than eight hundred sectors and I've only been on Trantor a little over two years."

"Exactly. And there are twenty-five million other worlds and I've been on this problem only a little over two months. —I tell you. I want to go back to Helicon and take up a study of the mathematics of turbulence, which was my Ph.D. problem, and forget I ever saw—or thought I saw—that turbulence gave an insight into human society."

But that evening he said to Tisalver, "But you know, Master Tisalver, you've never told me what you do, the nature of your work."

"Me?" Tisalver placed his fingers on his chest, which was covered by the simple white T-shirt with nothing underneath, which seemed to be the standard male uniform in Dahl. "Nothing much. I work at the local holovision station in programming. It's very dull, but it's a living."

"And it's respectable," said Mistress Tisalver. "It means he doesn't have to work in the heatsinks."

"The heatsinks?" said Dors, lifting her light eyebrows and managing to look fascinated.

"Oh well," said Tisalver, "that's what Dahl is best known for. It isn't much, but forty billion people on Trantor need energy and we supply a lot of it. We don't get appreciated, but I'd like to see some of the fancy sectors do without it."

Seldon looked confused. "Doesn't Trantor get its energy from solar power stations in orbit?"

"Some," said Tisalver, "and some from nuclear fusion stations out on the islands and some from microfusion motors and some from wind stations Upperside, but *half*"—he raised a finger in emphasis and his face looked unusually grave—"half comes from the heatsinks. There are heatsinks in lots of places, but none—*none*—as rich as those in Dahl. Are you serious that you don't know about the heatsinks? You sit there and stare at me."

Dors said quickly, "We are Outworlders, you know." (She had almost said 'tribespeople,' but had caught herself in time.) "Especially Dr. Seldon. He's only been on Trantor a couple of months."

"Really?" said Mistress Tisalver. She was a trifle shorter than her husband, was plump without quite being fat, had her dark hair drawn tightly back into a bun, and possessed rather beautiful dark eyes. Like her husband, she appeared to be in her thirties.

(After a period in Mycogen, not actually long in duration but intense, it struck Dors as odd to have a woman enter the conversation at will. How quickly modes and manners establish themselves, she thought, and made a mental note to mention that to Seldon—one more item for his psychohistory.)

"Oh yes," she said. "Dr. Seldon is from Helicon."

Mistress Tisalver registered polite ignorance. "And where might that be?"

Dors said, "Why, it's—" She turned to Seldon. "Where is it, Hari?"

Seldon looked abashed. "To tell you the truth, I don't think I could locate it very easily on a Galactic model without looking up the co-ordinates. All I can say is that it's on the other side of the central black hole from Trantor and getting there by hypership is rather a chore."

Mistress Tisalver said, "I don't think Jirad and I will ever be on a hypership."

"Someday, Casilia," said Tisalver cheerfully, "maybe we will. But tell us about Helicon, Master Seldon."

Seldon shook his head. "To me that would be dull. It's just a world, like any other. Only Trantor is different from all the rest. There are no heatsinks on Helicon—or probably anywhere else—except Trantor. Tell me about them."

("Only Trantor is different from all the rest." The sentence repeated itself in Seldon's mind and for a moment he grasped at it, and for some reason Dor's hand-on-thigh story suddenly recurred to him, but Tisalver was speaking and it passed out of Seldon's mind as quickly as it had entered.)

Tisalver said, "If you really want to know about heatsinks, I can show you." He turned to his wife. "Casilia, would you mind if tomorrow evening I take Master Seldon to the heatsinks."

"And me," said Dors quickly.

"And Mistress Venabili?"

Mistress Tisalver frowned and said sharply, "I don't think it would be a good idea. Our visitors would find it dull."

"I don't think so, Mistress Tisalver," said Seldon ingratiatingly. "We would very much like to see the heatsinks. We would be delighted if you would join us too . . . and your little daughter—if she wants to come."

"To the heatsinks?" said Mistress Tisalver, stiffening. "It's no place at all for a decent woman."

Seldon felt embarrassed at his gaffe. "I meant no harm, Mistress Tisalver."

"No offense," said Tisalver. "Casilia thinks it's beneath us and so it is, but as long as I don't work there, it's no distress merely to visit and show it to guests. But it is uncomfortable and I would never get Casilia to dress properly."

They got up from their crouching positions. Dahlite "chairs" were merely molded plastic seats on small wheels and they cramped Seldon's knees terribly and seemed to wiggle at his least body movement. The Tisalvers, however, had mastered the art of sitting firmly and rose without trouble and without needing to use their arms for help as Seldon had to. Dors also got up without trouble and Seldon once again marveled at her natural grace.

Before they parted to their separate rooms for the night, Seldon said to Dors, "Are you sure you know nothing about heatsinks? Mistress Tisalver makes them seem unpleasant."

"They can't be *that* unpleasant or Tisalver wouldn't suggest taking us on tour. Let's be content to be surprised."

63.

Tisalver said, "You'll need proper clothing." Mistress Tisalver sniffed markedly in the background.

Cautiously, Seldon, thinking of kirtles with vague distress, said, "What do you mean by proper clothing?"

"Something light, such as I wear. A T-shirt, very short sleeves, loose slacks, loose underpants, foot socks, open sandals. I have it all for you."

"Good. It doesn't sound bad."

"As for Mistress Venabili, I have the same. I hope it fits."

The clothes Tisalver supplied each of them (which were his own) fit fine—if a bit snugly. When they were ready, they bade Mistress Tisalver good-bye and she, with a resigned if still disapproving air, watched them from the doorway as they set off.

It was early evening and there was an attractive twilight glow above. It was clear that Dahl's lights would soon be winking on. The temperature was mild and there were virtually no vehicles to be seen; everyone was walking. In the distance was the everpresent hum of an Expressway and the occasional glitter of its lights could be easily seen.

The Dahlites, Seldon noted, did not seem to be walking toward any particular destination. Rather, there seemed to be a promenade going on, a walking for pleasure. Perhaps, if Dahl was an impoverished sector, as Tisalver had implied, inexpensive entertainment was at a premium and what was as pleasant—and as inexpensive—as an evening stroll?

Seldon felt himself easing automatically into the gait of an aimless stroll himself and felt the warmth of friendliness all around him. People greeted each other as they passed and exchanged a few words. Black mustaches of different shape and thickness flashed everywhere and seemed a requisite for the Dahlite male, as ubiquitous as the bald heads of the Mycogenian Brothers.

It was an evening rite, a way of making sure that another day had passed safely and that one's friends were still well and happy. And, it soon became apparent, Dors caught every eye. In the twilight glow, the ruddiness of her hair had deepened, but it stood out against the sea of black-haired heads (except for the occasional gray) like a gold coin winking its way across a pile of coal.

"This is very pleasant," said Seldon.

"It is," said Tisalver. "Ordinarily, I'd be walking with my wife and she'd be in her element. There is no one for a kilometer around whom she doesn't know by name, occupation, and interrelationships. I can't do that. Right now, half the people who greet me . . . I couldn't tell you their names. But, in any case, we mustn't creep along too slowly. We must get to the elevator. It's a busy world on the lower levels."

They were on the elevator going down when Dors said, "I presume, Master Tisalver, that the heatsinks are places where the internal heat of Trantor is being used to produce steam that will turn turbines and produce electricity."

"Oh no. Highly efficient large-scale thermopiles produce electricity directly. Don't ask me the details, please. I'm just a holovision programmer. In fact, don't ask anyone the details down there. The whole thing is one big black box. It works, but no one knows how."

"What if something goes wrong?"

"It doesn't usually, but if it does, some expert comes over from somewhere. Someone who understands computers. The whole thing is highly computerized, of course."

The elevator came to a halt and they stepped out. A blast of heat struck them.

"It's hot," said Seldon quite unnecessarily.

"Yes, it is," said Tisalver. "That's what makes Dahl so valuable as an energy source. The magma layer is nearer the surface here than it is anywhere else in the world. So you have to work in the heat."

"How about air-conditioning?" said Dors.

"There is air-conditioning, but it's a matter of expense. We ventilate and dehumidify and cool, but if we go too far, then we're using up too much energy and the whole process becomes too expensive."

Tisalver stopped at a door at which he signaled. It opened to a blast of cooler air and he muttered, "We ought to be able to get someone to help show us around and he'll control the remarks that Mistress Venabili will otherwise be the victim of . . . at least from the men."

"Remarks won't embarrass me," said Dors.

"They will embarrass me," said Tisalver.

A young man walked out of the office and introduced himself as Hano Linder. He resembled Tisalver quite closely, but Seldon decided that until he got used to the almost universal shortness, swarthiness, black hair, and luxuriant mustaches, he would not be able to see individual differences easily.

Lindor said, "I'll be glad to show you around for what there is to see. It's not one of your spectaculars, you know." He addressed them all, but his eyes were fixed on Dors. He said, "It's not going to be comfortable. I suggest we remove our shirts."

"It's nice and cool in here," said Seldon.

"Of course, but that's because we're executives. Rank has its privileges. Out there we can't maintain air-conditioning at this level. That's why they get paid more than I do. In fact, those are the best-paying jobs in Dahl, which is the only reason we get people to work down here. Even so, it's getting harder to get heatsinkers all the time." He took a deep breath. "Okay, out into the soup."

He removed his own shirt and tucked it into his waistband. Tisalver did the same and Seldon followed suit.

Lindor glanced at Dors and said, "For your own comfort, Mistress, but it's not compulsory."

"That's all right," said Dors and removed her shirt.

Her brassiere was white, unpadded, and showed considerable cleavage.

"Mistress," said Lindor, "That's not—" He thought a moment, then shrugged and said, "All right. We'll get by."

At first, Seldon was aware only of computers and machinery, huge pipes, flickering lights, and flashing screens.

The overall light was comparatively dim, though individual sections of machinery were illuminated. Seldon looked up into the almost-darkness. He said, "Why isn't it better lit?"

"It's lit well enough . . . where it should be," said Lindor. His voice was well modulated and he spoke quickly, but a little harshly. "Overall illumination is kept low for psychological reasons. Too bright is translated, in the mind, into heat. Complaints go up when we turn up the lights, even when the temperature is made to go down."

Dors said, "It seems to be well computerized. I should think the operations could be turned over to computers altogether. This sort of environment is made for artificial intelligence."

"Perfectly right," said Lindor, "but neither can we take a chance on any failures. We need people on the spot if anything goes wrong. A misfunctioning computer can raise problems up to two thousand kilometers away."

"So can human error. Isn't that so?" said Seldon.

"Oh yes, but with both people and computers on the job, computer error can be more quickly tracked down and corrected by people and, conversely, human error can be more quickly corrected by computers. What it amounts to is that nothing serious can happen unless human error and computer error take place simultaneously. And that hardly ever happens."

"Hardly ever, but not never, eh?" said Seldon.

"Almost never, but not never. Computers aren't what they used to be and neither are people."

"That's the way it always seems," said Seldon, laughing slightly.

"No no. I'm not talking memory. I'm not talking good old days. I'm talking statistics."

At this, Seldon recalled Hummin talking of the degeneration of the times.

"See what I mean?" said Lindor, his voice dropping. "There's a bunch of people, at the C-3 level from the looks of them, drinking. Not one of them is at his or her post."

"What are they drinking?" asked Dors.

"Special fluids for replacing electrolyte loss. Fruit juice."

"You can't blame them, can you?" said Dors indignantly. "In this dry heat, you would have to drink."

"Do you know how long a skilled C-3 can spin out a drink? And there's nothing to be done about it either. If we give them five-minute breaks for drinks and stagger them so they don't all congregate in a group, you simply stir up a rebellion."

They were approaching the group now. There were men and women (Dahl seemed to be a more or less amphisexual society) and both sexes were shirtless. The women wore devices that might be called brassieres, but they were strictly functional. They served to lift the breasts in order to improve ventilation and limit perspiration, but covered nothing.

Dors said in an aside to Seldon, "That makes sense, Hari. I'm soaking wet there."

"Take off your brassiere, then," said Seldon. "I won't lift a finger to stop you."

"Somehow," said Dors, "I guessed you wouldn't." She left her brassiere where it was.

They were approaching the congregation of people—about a dozen of them.

Dors said, "If any of them make rude remarks, I shall survive."

"Thank you," said Lindor. "I cannot promise they won't. —But I'll have to introduce you. If they get the idea that you two are inspectors and in my company, they'll become unruly. Inspectors are supposed to poke around on their own without anyone from management overseeing them."

He held up his arms. "Heatsinkers, I have two introductions to make. We have visitors from outside—two Outworlders, two scholars. They've got worlds running short on energy and they've come here to see how we do it here in Dahl. They think they may learn something."

"They'll learn how to sweat!" shouted a heatsinker and there was raucous laughter.

"*She's* got a sweaty chest right now," shouted a woman, "covering up like that."

273

Dors shouted back, "I'd take it off, but mine can't compete with yours." The laughter turned good-natured.

But one young man stepped forward, staring at Seldon with intense deep-set eyes, his face set into a humorless mask. He said, "I know you. You're the mathematician."

He ran forward, inspecting Seldon's face with eager solemnity. Automatically, Dors stepped in front of Seldon and Lindor stepped in front of her, shouting, "Back, heatsinker. Mind your manners."

Seldon said, "Wait! Let him talk to me. Why is everyone piling in front of me?"

Lindor said in a low voice, "If any of them get close, you'll find they don't smell like hothouse flowers."

"I'll endure it," said Seldon brusquely. "Young man, what is it you want?"

"My name is Amaryl. Yugo Amaryl. I've seen you on holovision."

"You might have, but what about it?"

"I don't remember your name."

"You don't have to."

"You talked about something called psychohistory."

"You don't know how I wish I hadn't."

"What?"

"Nothing. What is it you want?"

"I want to talk to you. Just for a little while. Now."

Seldon looked at Lindor, who shook his head firmly. "Not while he's on his shift."

"When does your shift begin, Mr. Amaryl?" asked Seldon.

"Sixteen hundred."

"Can you see me tomorrow at fourteen hundred?"

"Sure. Where?"

Seldon turned to Tisalver. Would you permit me to see him in your place?"

Tisalver looked very unhappy. "It's not necessary. He's just a heat-sinker."

Seldon said, "He recognized my face. He knows something about me. He can't be *just* an anything. I'll see him in my room." And then, as Tisalver's face didn't soften, he added, *"My* room, for which rent is being paid. And you'll be at work, out of the apartment."

Tisalver said in a low voice, "It's not me, Master Seldon. It's my wife, Casilia. She won't stand for it."

"I'll talk to her," said Seldon grimly. "She'll have to."

64.

Casilia Tisalver opened her eyes wide. "A heatsinker? Not in *my* apartment."

"Why not? Besides, he'll be coming to *my* room," said Seldon. "At fourteen hundred."

"I won't have it," said Mistress Tisalver. "This is what comes of going down to the heatsinks. Jirad was a fool."

"Not at all, Mistress Tisalver. We went at my request and I was fascinated. I must see this young man, since that is necessary to my scholarly work."

"I'm sorry if it is, but I won't have it."

Dors Venabili raised her hand. "Hari, let me take care of this. Mistress Tisalver, if Dr. Seldon must see someone in his room this afternoon, the additional person naturally means additional rent. We understand that. For today, then, the rent on Dr. Seldon's room will be doubled."

Mistress Tisalver thought about it. "Well, that's decent of you, but it's not only the credits. There's the neighbors to think of. A sweaty, smelly heatsinker—"

"I doubt that he'll be sweaty and smelly at fourteen hundred, Mistress Tisalver, but let me go on. Since Dr. Seldon *must* see him, then if he can't see him here, he'll have to see him elsewhere, but we can't run here and there. That would be too inconvenient. Therefore, what we will have to do is to get a room elsewhere. It won't be easy and we don't want to do it, but we will have to. So we will pay the rent through today and leave and of course we will have to explain to Master Hummin why we have had to change the arrangements that he so kindly made for us."

"Wait." Mistress Tisalver's face became a study of calculation. "We wouldn't like to disoblige Master Hummin . . . or you two. How long would this creature have to stay?"

"He's coming at fourteen hundred. He must be at work at sixteen hundred. He will be here for less than two hours, perhaps considerably less. We will meet him outside, the two of us, and bring him to Dr.

Seldon's room. Any neighbors who see us will think he is an Outworlder friend of ours.''

Mistress Tisalver nodded her head. "Then let it be as you say. Double rent for Master Seldon's room for today and the heatsinker will visit just this one time."

"Just this one time," said Dors.

But later, when Seldon and Dors were sitting in her room, Dors said, "Why *do* you have to see him, Hari? Is interviewing a heatsinker important to psychohistory too?"

Seldon thought he detected a small edge of sarcasm in her voice and he said tartly, "I don't have to base everything on this huge project of mine, in which I have very little faith anyway. I am also a human being with human curiosities. We were down in the heatsinks for hours and you saw what the working people there were like. They were obviously uneducated. They were low-level individuals—no play on words intended—and yet here was one who recognized me. He must have seen me on holovision on the occasion of the Decennial Convention and he remembered the word 'psychohistory.' He strikes me as unusual—as out of place somehow—and I would like to talk to him."

"Because it pleases your vanity to have become known even to heatsinkers in Dahl?"

"Well . . . perhaps. But it also piques my curiosity."

"And how do you know he hasn't been briefed and intends to lead you into trouble as has happened before."

Seldon winced. "I won't let him run his fingers through my hair. In any case, we're more nearly prepared now, aren't we? And I'm sure you'll be with me. I mean, you let me go Upperside alone, you let me go with Raindrop Forty-Three to the microfarms alone, and you're not going to do that again, are you?"

"You can be absolutely sure I won't," said Dors.

"Well then, I'll talk to the young man and you can watch out for traps. I have every faith in you."

65.

Amaryl arrived a few minutes before 1400, looking warily about. His hair was neat and his thick mustache was combed and turned up slightly at the edges. His T-shirt was startlingly white. He *did* smell, but it was a fruity odor that undoubtedly came from the slightly overenthusiastic use of scent. He had a bag with him.

Seldon, who had been waiting outside for him, seized one elbow lightly, while Dors seized the other, and they moved rapidly into the elevator. Having reached the correct level, they passed through the apartment into Seldon's room.

Amaryl said in a low hangdog voice, "Nobody home, huh?"

"Everyone's busy," said Seldon neutrally. He indicated the only chair in the room, a pad directly on the floor.

"No," said Amaryl. "I don't need that. One of you two use it." He squatted on the floor with a graceful downward motion.

Dors imitated the movement, sitting on the edge of Seldon's floor-based mattress, but Seldon dropped down rather clumsily, having to make use of his hands and unable, quite, to find a comfortable position for his legs.

Seldon said, "Well, young man, why do you want to see me?"

"Because you're a mathematician. You're the first mathematician I ever saw—close up—so I could touch him, you know."

"Mathematicians feel like anyone else."

"Not to me, Dr. . . . Dr. . . . Seldon?"

"That's my name."

Amaryl looked pleased. "I finally remembered. —You see, I want to be a mathematician too."

"Very good. What's stopping you?"

Amaryl suddenly frowned. "Are you serious?"

"I presume *something* is stopping you. Yes, I'm serious."

"What's stopping me is I'm a Dahlite, a *heatsinker* on Dahl. I don't have the money to get an education and I can't get the credits to get an education. A *real* education, I mean. All they taught me was to read and cipher and use a computer and then I knew enough to be a heatsinker. But I wanted more. So I taught myself."

"In some ways, that's the best kind of teaching. How did you do that?"

"I knew a librarian. She was willing to help me. She was a very nice woman and she showed me how to use computers for learning mathematics. And she set up a software system that would connect me with other libraries. I'd come on my days off and on mornings after my shift. Sometimes she'd lock me in her private room so I wouldn't be bothered by people coming in or she would let me in when the library was closed. She didn't know mathematics herself, but she helped me all she could. She was oldish, a widow lady. Maybe she thought of me as a kind of son or something. She didn't have children of her own."

(Maybe, thought Seldon briefly, there was some other emotion involved too, but he put the thought away. None of his business.)

"I liked number theory," said Amaryl. "I worked some things out from what I learned from the computer and from the book-films it used to teach me mathematics. I came up with some new things that weren't in the book-films."

Seldon raised his eyebrows. "That's interesting. Like what?"

"I've brought some of them to you. I've never showed them to anyone. The people around me—" He shrugged. "They'd either laugh or be annoyed. *Once* I tried to tell a girl I knew, but she just said I was weird and wouldn't see me anymore. Is it all right for me to show them to you?"

"Quite all right. Believe me."

Seldon held out his hand and after a brief hesitation, Amaryl handed him the bag he was carrying.

For a long time, Seldon looked over Amaryl's papers. The work was naïve in the extreme, but he allowed no smile to cross his face. He followed the demonstrations, not one of which was new, of course—or even nearly new—or of any importance.

But that didn't matter.

Seldon looked up. "Did you do all of this yourself?"

Amaryl, looking more than half-frightened, nodded his head.

Seldon extracted several sheets. "What made you think of this?" His finger ran down a line of mathematical reasoning.

Amaryl looked it over, frowned, and thought about it. Then he explained his line of thinking.

Seldon listened and said, "Did you ever read a book by Anat Bigell?"

"On number theory?"

"The title was *Mathematical Deduction.* It wasn't about number theory, particularly."

Amaryl shook his head. "I never heard of him. I'm sorry."

"He worked out this theorem of yours three hundred years ago."

Amaryl looked stricken. "I didn't know that."

"I'm sure you didn't. You did it more cleverly, though. It's not rigorous, but—"

"What do you mean, 'rigorous'?"

"It doesn't matter." Seldon put the papers back together in a sheaf, restored it to the bag, and said, "Make several copies of all this. Take one copy, have it dated by an official computer, and place it under computerized seal. My friend here, Mistress Venabili, can get you into Streeling University without tuition on some sort of scholarship. You'll have to start at the beginning and take courses in other subjects than mathematics, but—"

By now Amaryl had caught his breath. "Into Streeling University? They won't take me."

"Why not? Dors, you can arrange it, can't you?"

"I'm sure I can."

"No, you can't," said Amaryl hotly. "They won't take me. I'm from Dahl."

"Well?"

"They won't take people from Dahl."

Seldon looked at Dors. "What's he talking about?"

Dors shook her head. "I really don't know."

Amaryl said, "You're an Outworlder, Mistress. How long have you been at Streeling?"

"A little over two years, Mr. Amaryl."

"Have you ever seen Dahlites there—short, curly black hair, big mustaches?"

"There are students with all kinds of appearances."

"But no Dahlites. Look again the next time you're there."

"Why not?" said Seldon.

"They don't like us. We look different. They don't like our mustaches."

"You can shave your—" but Seldon's voice died under the other's furious glance.

"Never. Why should I? My mustache is my manhood."

"You shave your beard. That's your manhood too."

"To my people it is the mustache."

Seldon looked at Dors again and murmured, "Bald heads, mustaches . . . madness."

"What?" said Amaryl angrily.

"Nothing. Tell me what else they don't like about Dahlites."

"They make up things not to like. They say we smell. They say we're dirty. They say we steal. They say we're violent. They say we're *dumb.*"

"Why do they say all this?"

"Because it's easy to say it and it makes *them* feel good. Sure, if we work in the heatsinks, we get dirty and smelly. If we're poor and held down, some of us steal and get violent. But that isn't the way it is with all of us. How about those tall yellow-hairs in the Imperial Sector who think they own the Galaxy—no, they *do* own the Galaxy. Don't *they* ever get violent? Don't *they* steal sometimes? If they did my job, they'd smell the way I do. If they had to live the way I have to, they'd get dirty too."

"Who denies that there are people of all kinds in all places?" said Seldon.

"No one argues the matter! They just take it for granted. Master Seldon, I've got to get away from Trantor. I have no chance on Trantor, no way of earning credits, no way of getting an education, no way of becoming a mathematician, no way of becoming anything but what they say I am . . . a worthless nothing." This last was said in frustration—and desperation.

Seldon tried to be reasonable. "The person I'm renting this room from is a Dahlite. He has a clean job. He's educated."

"Oh sure," said Amaryl passionately. "There are some. They let a few do it so that they can say it can be done. And those few can live nicely as long as they stay in Dahl. Let them go outside and they'll see how they're treated. And while they're in here they make themselves feel good by treating the rest of us like dirt. That makes them yellow-hairs in their own eyes. What did this nice person you're renting this room from say when you told him you were bringing in a heatsinker? What did he say I would be like? They're gone now . . . wouldn't be in the same place with me."

Seldon moistened his lips. "I won't forget you. I'll see to it that you'll get off Trantor and into my own University in Helicon—once I'm back there myself."

"Do you promise that? Your word of honor? Even though I'm a Dahlite?"

"The fact that you're a Dahlite is unimportant to me. The fact that you are already a mathematician is! But I still can't quite grasp what you're telling me. I find it impossible to believe that there would be such unreasoning feeling against harmless people."

Amaryl said bitterly, "That's because you've never had any occasion to interest yourself in such things. It can all pass right under your nose and you wouldn't smell a thing because it doesn't affect *you.*"

Dors said, "Mr. Amaryl, Dr. Seldon is a mathematician like you and his head can sometimes be in the clouds. You must understand that. I am a historian, however. I know that it isn't unusual to have one group of people look down upon another group. There are peculiar and almost ritualistic hatreds that have no rational justification and that can have their serious historical influence. It's too bad."

Amaryl said, "Saying something is 'too bad' is easy. You say you disapprove, which makes you a nice person, and then you can go about your own business and not be interested anymore. It's a lot worse than 'too bad.' It's against everything decent and natural. We're all of us the same, yellow-hairs and black-hairs, tall and short, Easterners, Westerners, Southerners, and Outworlders. We're all of us, you and I and even the Emperor, descended from the people of Earth, aren't we?"

"Descended from *what?*" asked Seldon. He turned to look at Dors, his eyes wide.

"From the people of Earth!" shouted Amaryl. "The one planet on which human beings originated."

"One planet? Just *one* planet?"

"The only planet. Sure. Earth."

"When you say Earth, you mean Aurora, don't you?"

"Aurora? What's that? —I mean Earth. Have you never heard of Earth?"

"No," said Seldon. "Actually not."

"It's a mythical world," began Dors, "that—"

"It's not mythical. It was a real planet."

Seldon sighed. "I've heard this all before. Well, let's go through it again. Is there a Dahlite book that tells of Earth?"

"What?"

"Some computer software, then?"

"I don't know what you're talking about."

"Young man, where did you hear about Earth?"

"My dad told me. Everyone knows about it."

"Is there anyone who knows about it especially? Did they teach you about it in school?"

"They never said a word about it there."

"Then how do people know about it?"

Amaryl shrugged his shoulders with an air of being uselessly badgered over nothing. "Everyone just does. If you want stories about it, there's Mother Rittah. I haven't heard that she's died yet."

"Your mother? Wouldn't you know—"

"She's not *my* mother. That's just what they call her. Mother Rittah. She's an old woman. She lives in Billibotton. Or used to."

"Where's that?"

"Down in that direction," said Amaryl, gesturing vaguely.

"How do I get there?"

"Get there? You don't want to get there. You'd never come back."

"Why not?"

"Believe me. You don't want to go there."

"But I'd like to see Mother Rittah."

Amaryl shook his head. "Can you use a knife?"

"For what purpose? What kind of knife?"

"A cutting knife. Like this." Amaryl reached down to the belt that held his pants tight about his waist. A section of it came away and from one end there flashed out a knife blade, thin, gleaming, and deadly.

Dors's hand immediately came down hard upon his right wrist.

Amaryl laughed. "I wasn't planning to use it. I was just showing it to you." He put the knife back in his belt. "You need one in self-defense and if you don't have one or if you have one but don't know how to use it, you'll never get out of Billibotton alive. Anyway"—he suddenly grew very grave and intent—"are you really serious, Master Seldon, about helping me get to Helicon?"

"Entirely serious. That's a promise. Write down your name and where you can be reached by hypercomputer. You have a code, I suppose."

"My shift in the heatsinks has one. Will that do?"

"Yes."

"Well then," said Amaryl, looking up earnestly at Seldon, "this means I have my whole future riding on you, Master Seldon, so *please* don't go to Billibotton. I can't afford to lose you now." He turned beseeching eyes on Dors and said softly, "Mistress Venabili, if he'll listen to you, don't let him go. *Please.*"

BILLIBOTTON

. . . . .

DAHL— . . . Oddly enough, the best-known aspect of this sector is Billibotton, a semilegendary place about which innumerable tales have grown up. In fact, a whole branch of literature now exists in which heroes and adventurers (and victims) must dare the dangers of passing through Billibotton. So stylized have these stories become that the one well-known and, presumably, authentic tale involving such a passage, that of Hari Seldon and Dors Venabili, has come to seem fantastic simply by association . . .

ENCYCLOPEDIA GALACTICA

66.

When Hari Seldon and Dors Venabili were alone, Dors asked thoughtfully, "Are you really planning to see this 'Mother' woman?"

"I'm thinking about it, Dors."

"You're an odd one, Hari. You seem to go steadily from bad to worse. You went Upperside, which seemed harmless enough, for a rational purpose when you were in Streeling. Then, in Mycogen, you broke into the Elders' aerie, a much more dangerous task, for a much more foolish purpose. And now in Dahl, you want to go to this place, which that young man seems to think is simple suicide, for something altogether nonsensical."

"I'm curious about this reference to Earth—and must know if there's anything to it."

Dors said, "It's a legend and not even an interesting one. It is routine. The names differ from planet to planet, but the content is the same. There is always the tale of an original world and a golden age. There is a longing for a supposedly simple and virtuous past that is almost universal among the people of a complex and vicious society. In one way or another, this is true of all societies, since everyone imagines his or her own society to be too complex and vicious, however simple it may be. Mark *that* down for your psychohistory."

"Just the same," said Seldon, "I have to consider the possibility that one world did once exist. Aurora . . . Earth . . . the name doesn't matter. In fact—"

He paused and finally Dors said, "Well?"

Seldon shook his head. "Do you remember the hand-on-thigh story you told me in Mycogen? It was right after I got the Book from Raindrop Forty-Three . . . Well, it popped into my head one evening recently when we were talking to the Tisalvers. I said something that reminded me, for an instant—"

"Reminded you of what?"

"I don't remember. It came into my head and went out again, but somehow every time I think of the single-world notion, it seems to me I have the tips of my fingers on something and then lose it."

Dors looked at Seldon in surprise. "I don't see what it could be. The hand-on-thigh story has nothing to do with Earth or Aurora."

"I know, but this . . . thing . . . that hovers just past the edge of my mind seems to be connected with this single world anyway and I have the feeling that I *must* find out more about it at any cost. That . . . and robots."

"Robots too? I thought the Elders' aerie put an end to that."

"Not at all. I've been thinking about them." He stared at Dors with a troubled look on his face for a long moment, then said, "But I'm not sure."

"Sure about what, Hari?"

But Seldon merely shook his head and said nothing more.

Dors frowned, then said, "Hari, let me tell you one thing. In sober history—and, believe me, I know what I'm talking about—there is no mention of one world of origin. It's a popular belief, I admit. I don't mean just among the unsophisticated followers of folklore, like the Mycogenians and the Dahlite heatsinkers, but there are biologists who insist that there must have been one world of origin for reasons that are well outside my area of expertise and there are the more mystical historians who tend to speculate about it. And among the leisure-class intellectuals, I understand such speculations are becoming fashionable. Still, scholarly history knows nothing about it."

Seldon said, "All the more reason, perhaps, to go beyond scholarly history. All I want is a device that will simplify psychohistory for me and I don't care what the device is, whether it is a mathematical trick or a historical trick or something totally imaginary. If the young man we've just talked to had had a little more formal training, I'd have set him on the problem. His thinking is marked by considerable ingenuity and originality—"

Dors said, "And you're really going to help him, then?"

"Absolutely. Just as soon as I'm in a position to."

"But ought you to make promises you're not sure you'll be able to keep?"

"I *want* to keep it. If you're that stiff about impossible promises, consider that Hummin told Sunmaster Fourteen that I'd use psychohistory to get the Mycogenians their world back. There's just about zero chance of that. Even if I work out psychohistory, who knows if it can be used for so narrow and specialized a purpose? There's a *real* case of promising what one can't deliver."

But Dors said with some heat, "Chetter Hummin was trying to save our lives, to keep us out of the hands of Demerzel and the Emperor. Don't forget that. And I think he really *would* like to help the Mycogenians."

"And I really *would* like to help Yugo Amaryl and I am far more likely to be able to help him than I am the Mycogenians, so if you justify the second, please don't criticize the first. What's more, Dors"—and his eyes flashed angrily—"I really *would* like to find Mother Rittah and I'm prepared to go alone."

"Never!" snapped Dors. "If you go, I go."

67.

Mistress Tisalver returned with her daughter in tow an hour after Amaryl had left on this way to his shift. She said nothing at all to either Seldon or Dors, but gave a curt nod of her head when they greeted her and gazed sharply about the room as though to verify that the heatsinker had left no trace. She then sniffed the air sharply and looked at Seldon accusingly before marching through the common room into the family bedroom.

Tisalver himself arrived home later and when Seldon and Dors came to the dinner table, Tisalver took advantage of the fact that his wife was still ordering some last-minute details in connection with the dinner to say in a low voice, "Has that person been here?"

"And gone," said Seldon solemnly. "Your wife was out at the time."

Tisalver nodded and said, "Will you have to do this again?"

"I don't think so," said Seldon.

"Good."

Dinner passed largely in silence, but afterward, when the daughter had gone to her room for the dubious pleasures of computer practice, Seldon leaned back and said, "Tell me about Billibotton."

Tisalver looked astonished and his mouth moved without any sound issuing. Casilia, however, was less easily rendered speechless.

She said, "Is that where your new friend lives? Are you going to return the visit?"

"So far," said Seldon quietly, "I have just asked about Billibotton."

Casilia said sharply, "It is a slum. The dregs live there. No one goes there, except the filth that make their homes there."

"I understand a Mother Rittah lives there."

"I never heard of her," said Casilia, her mouth closing with a snap. It was quite clear that she had no intention of knowing anyone by name who lived in Billibotton.

Tisalver, casting an uneasy look at his wife, said, "I've heard of her. She's a crazy old woman who is supposed to tell fortunes."

"And does she live in Billibotton?"

"I don't know, Master Seldon. I've never seen her. She's mentioned sometimes in the news holocasts when she makes her predictions."

"Do they come true?"

Tisalver snorted. "Do predictions ever come true? Hers don't even make sense."

"Does she ever talk about Earth?"

"I don't know. I wouldn't be surprised."

"The mention of Earth doesn't puzzle you. Do you know about Earth?"

Now Tisalver looked surprised. "Certainly, Master Seldon. It's the world all people came from . . . supposedly."

"Supposedly? Don't you believe it?"

"Me? I'm educated. But many ignorant people believe it."

"Are there book-films about Earth?"

"Children's stories sometimes mention Earth. I remember, when I was a young boy, my favorite story began, 'Once, long ago, on Earth, when Earth was the only planet—' Remember, Casilia? You liked it too."

Casilia shrugged, unwilling to bend as yet.

"I'd like to see it sometime," said Seldon, "but I mean *real* book-films . . . uh . . . learned ones . . . or films . . . or printouts."

"I never heard of any, but the library—"

"I'll try that. —Are there any taboos about speaking of Earth?"

"What are taboos?"

"I mean, is it a strong custom that people mustn't talk of Earth or that outsiders mustn't ask about it?"

Tisalver looked so honestly astonished that there seemed no point in waiting for an answer.

Dors put in, "Is there some rule about outsiders not going to Billibotton?"

Now Tisalver turned earnest. "No *rule,* but it's not a good idea for *anyone* to go there. *I* wouldn't."

Dors said, "Why not?"

"It's dangerous. Violent! Everyone is armed. —I mean, Dahl is an armed place anyway, but in Billibotton they *use* the weapons. Stay in this neighborhood. It's safe."

"So far," said Casilia darkly. "It would be better if we left altogether. Heatsinkers go anywhere these days." And there was another lowering look in Seldon's direction.

Seldon said, "What do you mean that Dahl is an armed place? There are strong Imperial regulations against weapons."

"I know that," said Tisalver, "and there are no stun guns here or percussives or Psychic Probes or anything like that. But there are knives." He looked embarrassed.

Dors said, "Do you carry a knife, Tisalver?"

"Me?" He looked genuinely horrified. "I am a man of peace and this is a safe neighborhood."

"We have a couple of them in the house," said Casilia, sniffing again. "We're not *that* certain this is a safe neighborhood."

"Does everyone carry knives?" asked Dors.

"Almost everyone, Mistress Venabili," said Tisalver. "It's customary. But that doesn't mean everyone uses them."

"But they use them in Billibotton, I suppose," said Dors.

"Sometimes. When they're excited, they have fights."

"And the government permits it? The Imperial government, I mean?"

"Sometimes they try to clean Billibotton up, but knives are too easy to hide and the custom is too strong. Besides, it's almost always Dahlites that get killed and I don't think the Imperial government gets too upset over that."

"What if it's an outsider who gets killed?"

"If it's reported, the Imperials could get excited. But what happens is that no one has seen anything and no one knows anything. The Imperials sometimes round up people on general principles, but they can never prove anything. I suppose they decide it's the outsiders' fault for being there. —So don't go to Billibotton, even if you have a knife."

Seldon shook his head rather pettishly. "I wouldn't carry a knife. I don't know how to use one. Not skillfully."

"Then it's simple, Master Seldon. Stay out." Tisalver shook his head portentously. "Just stay out."

"I may not be able to do that either," said Seldon.

Dors glared at him, clearly annoyed, and said to Tisalver, "Where does one buy a knife? Or may we have one of yours?"

Casilia said quickly, "No one takes someone else's knife. You must buy your own."

Tisalver said, "There are knife stores all over. There aren't supposed to be. Theoretically they're illegal, you know. Any appliance store sells them, however. If you see a washing machine on display, that's a sure sign."

"And how does one get to Billibotton?" asked Seldon.

"By Expressway." Tisalver looked dubious as he looked at Dors's frowning expression.

Seldon said, "And once I reach the Expressway?"

"Get on the eastbound side and watch for the signs. But if you must go, Master Seldon"—Tisalver hesitated, then said—"you mustn't take Mistress Venabili. Women sometimes are treated . . . worse."

"She won't go," said Seldon.

"I'm afraid she will," said Dors with quiet determination.

68.

The appliance store dealer's mustache was clearly as lush as it had been in his younger days, but it was grizzled now, even though the hair on his head was still black. He touched the mustache out of sheer habit as he gazed at Dors and brushed it back on each side.

He said, "You're not a Dahlite."

"Yes, but I still want a knife."

He said, "It's against the law to sell knives."

Dors said, "I'm not a policewoman or a government agent of any sort. I'm going to Billibotton."

He stared at her thoughtfully. "Alone?"

"With my friend." She jerked her thumb over her shoulder in the direction of Seldon, who was waiting outside sullenly.

"You're buying it for him?" He stared at Seldon and it didn't take him long to decide. "He's an outsider too. Let him come in and buy it for himself."

"He's not a government agent either. And I'm buying it for myself."

The dealer shook his head. "Outsiders are crazy. *But* if you want to spend some credits, I'll take them from you. He reached under the counter, brought out a stub, turned it with a slight and expert motion, and the knife blade emerged.

"Is that the largest you have?"

"Best woman's knife made."

"Show me a man's knife."

"You don't want one that's too heavy. Do you know how to use one of these things?"

"I'll learn and I'm not worried about heavy. Show me a man's knife."

The dealer smiled. "Well, if you want to see one—" He moved farther down the counter and brought up a much fatter stub. He gave it a twist and what appeared to be a butcher's knife emerged.

He handed it to her, handle first, still smiling.

She said, "Show me that twist of yours."

He showed her on a second knife, slowly twisting one way to make the blade appear, then the other way to make it disappear. "Twist *and* squeeze," he said.

"Do it again, sir."

The dealer obliged.

Dors said, "All right, close it and toss me the haft."

He did, in a slow upward loop.

She caught it, handed it back, and said, "Faster."

He raised his eyebrows and then, without warning, backhanded it to her left side. She made no attempt to bring over her right hand, but caught it with her left and the blade showed tumescently at once—then disappeared. The dealer's mouth fell open.

"And this is the largest you have?" she said.

"It is. If you try to use it, it will just tire you out."

"I'll breathe deeply. I'll take a second one too."

"For your friend?"

"No. For me."

"You plan on using *two* knives?"

"I've got two hands."

The dealer sighed. "Mistress, *please* stay out of Billibotton. You don't know what they do to women there."

"I can guess. How do I put these knives on my belt?"

"Not the one you've got on, Mistress. That's not a knife belt. I can sell you one, though."

"Will it hold two knives?"

"I might have a double belt somewhere. Not much call for them."

"I'm calling for them."

"I may not have it in your size."

"Then we'll cut it down or something."

"It will cost you a lot of credits."

"My credit tile will cover it."

When she emerged at last, Seldon said sourly, "You look ridiculous with that bulky belt."

"Really, Hari? Too ridiculous to go with you to Billibotton? Then let's both go back to the apartment."

"No. I'll go on by myself. I'll be safer by myself."

Dors said, "There is no use saying that, Hari. We both go back or we both go forward. Under no circumstances do we separate."

And somehow the firm look in her blue eyes, the set to her lips, and the manner in which her hands had dropped to the hafts at her belt, convinced Seldon she was serious.

"Very well," he said, "but if you survive and if I ever see Hummin again, my price for continuing to work on psychohistory—much as I have grown fond of you—will be your removal. Do you understand?"

And suddenly Dors smiled. "Forget it. Don't practice your chivalry on me. *Nothing* will remove me. Do *you* understand?"

69.

They got off the Expressway where the sign, flickering in the air, said: BILLIBOTTON. As perhaps an indication of what might be expected, the second I was smeared, a mere blob of fainter light.

They made their way out of the car and down to the walkway below. It was early afternoon and at first glance, Billibotton seemed much like the part of Dahl they had left.

The air, however, had a pungent aroma and the walkway was littered with trash. One could tell that auto-sweeps were not to be found in the neighborhood.

And, although the walkway looked ordinary enough, the atmosphere was uncomfortable and as tense as a too-tightly coiled spring.

Perhaps it was the people. There seemed the normal number of pedestrians, but they were not like pedestrians elsewhere, Seldon thought. Ordinarily, in the press of business, pedestrians were self-absorbed and in the endless crowds on the endless thoroughfares of Trantor, people could only survive—psychologically—by ignoring each other. Eyes slid away. Brains were closed off. There was an artificial privacy with each person enclosed in a velvet fog of his or her own making. Or there was the ritualistic friendliness of an evening promenade in those neighborhoods that indulged in such things.

But here in Billibotton, there was neither friendliness nor neutral withdrawal. At least not where outsiders were concerned. Every person who passed, moving in either direction, turned to stare at Seldon and Dors. Every pair of eyes, as though attached by invisible cords to the two outsiders, followed them with ill will.

The clothing of the Billibottoners tended to be smudged, old, and sometimes torn. There was a patina of ill-washed poverty over them and Seldon felt uneasy at the slickness of his own new clothes.

He said, "Where in Billibotton does Mother Rittah live, do you suppose?"

"I don't know," said Dors. "You brought us here, so you do the supposing. I intend to confine myself to the task of protection and I think I'm going to find it necessary to do just that."

Seldon said, "I assumed it would only be necessary to ask the way of any passerby, but somehow I'm not encouraged to do so."

"I don't blame you. I don't think you'll find anyone springing to your assistance."

"On the other hand, there are such things as youngsters." He indicated one with a brief gesture of one hand. A boy who looked to be about twelve—in any case young enough to lack the universal adult male mustache—had come to a full halt and was staring at them.

Dors said, "You're guessing that a boy that age has not yet developed the full Billibottonian dislike of outsiders."

"At any rate," said Seldon, "I'm guessing he is scarcely large enough to have developed the full Billibottonian penchant for violence. I suppose he might run away and shout insults from a distance if we approach him, but I doubt he'll attack us."

Seldon raised his voice. "Young man."

The boy took a step backward and continued to stare.

Seldon said, "Come here," and beckoned.

The boy said, "Wa' for, guy?"

"So I can ask you directions. Come closer, so I don't have to shout."

The boy approached two steps closer. His face was smudged, but his eyes were bright and sharp. His sandals were of different make and there was a large patch on one leg of his trousers. He said, "Wa' kind o' directions?"

"We're trying to find Mother Rittah."

The boy's eyes flickered. "Wa' for, guy?"

"I'm a scholar. Do you know what a scholar is?"

"Ya went to school?"

"Yes. Didn't you?"

The boy spat to one side in contempt. "Nah."

"I want advice from Mother Rittah—if you'll take me to her."

"Ya want your fortune? Ya come to Billibotton, guy, with your fancy clothes, so I can tell ya your fortune. All bad."

"What's your name, young man?"

"What's it to ya?"

"So we can speak in a more friendly fashion. And so you can take me to Mother Rittah's place. Do you know where she lives?"

"Maybe yes, maybe no. My name's Raych. What's in it for me if I take ya?"

"What would you like, Raych?"

The boy's eyes halted at Dors's belt. Raych said, "The lady got a couple o' knives. Gimme one and I'll take ya to Mother Rittah."

"Those are grown people's knives, Raych. You're too young."

"Then I guess I'm too young to know where Mother Rittah lives." And he looked up slyly through the shaggy hair that curtained his eyes.

Seldon grew uneasy. It was possible they might attract a crowd. Several men had stopped already, but had then moved on when nothing of interest seemed to be taking place. If, however, the boy grew angry and lashed out at them in word or deed, people would undoubtedly gather.

He smiled and said, "Can you read, Raych?"

Raych spat again. "Nah! Who wants ta read?"

"Can you use a computer?"

"A talking computer? Sure. Anyone can."

"I'll tell you what, then. You take me to the nearest computer store and I'll buy you a little computer all your own and software that will teach you to read. A few weeks and you'll be able to read."

It seemed to Seldon that the boy's eyes sparkled at the thought, but—if so—they hardened at once. "Nah. Knife or nothin'."

"That's the point, Raych. You learn to read and don't tell anyone and you can surprise people. After a while you can bet them you can read. Bet them five credits. You can win a few extra credits that way and you can buy a knife of your own."

The boy hesitated. "Nah! No one will bet me. No one got credits."

"If you can read, you can get a job in a knife store and you can save your wages and get a knife at a discount. How about that?"

"When ya gonna buy the talking computer?"

"Right now. I'll give it to you when I see Mother Rittah."

"You got credits?"

"I have a credit tile."

"Let's see ya buy the computer."

The transaction was carried through, but when the boy reached for it, Seldon shook his head and put it inside his pouch. "You've got to get me to Mother Rittah first, Raych. Are you sure you know where to find her?"

Raych allowed a look of contempt to cross his face. "Sure I do. I'll take ya there, only ya better hand over the computer when we get there or I'll get some guys I know after you and the lady, so ya better watch out."

"You don't have to threaten us," said Seldon. "We'll take care of our end of the deal."

Raych led them quickly along the walkway, past curious stares.

Seldon was silent during the walk and so was Dors. Dors was far less lost in her own thoughts, though, for she clearly remained conscious of the surrounding people at all times. She kept meeting, with a level glare, the eyes of those passersby that turned toward them. On occasion, when there were footsteps behind them, she turned to look grimly back.

And then Raych stopped and said, "In here. She ain't homeless, ya know."

They followed him into an apartment complex and Seldon, who had had the intention of following their route with a view to retracing his steps later, was quickly lost.

He said, "How do you know your way through these alleys, Raych?"

The boy shrugged. "I been loafin' through them since I was a kid," he said. "Besides, the apartments are numbered—where they ain't broken off—and there's arrows and things. You can't get lost if you know the tricks."

Raych knew the tricks, apparently, and they wandered deeper into the complex. Hanging over it all was an air of total decay: disregarded debris, inhabitants slinking past in clear resentment of the outsiders' invasion. Unruly youngsters ran along the alleys in pursuit of some game or other. Some of them yelled, "Hey, get out o' the way!" when their levitating ball narrowly missed Dors.

And finally, Raych stopped before a dark scarred door on which the number 2782 glowed feebly.

"This is it," he said and held out his hand.

"First let's see who's inside," said Seldon softly. He pushed the signal button and nothing happened.

"It don't work," said Raych. "Ya gotta bang. Loud. She don't hear too good."

Seldon pounded his fist on the door and was rewarded with the sound of movement inside. A shrill voice called out, "Who wants Mother Rittah?"

Seldon shouted, "Two scholars!"

He tossed the small computer, with its small package of software attached, to Raych, who snatched it, grinned, and took off at a rapid run. Seldon then turned to face the opening door and Mother Rittah.

70.

Mother Rittah was well into her seventies, perhaps, but had the kind of face that, at first sight, seemed to belie that. Plump cheeks, a little mouth, a small round chin slightly doubled. She was very short—not quite 1.5 meters tall—and had a thick body.

But there were fine wrinkles about her eyes and when she smiled, as she smiled at the sight of them, others broke out over her face. And she moved with difficulty.

"Come in, come in," she said in a soft high-pitched voice and peered at them as though her eyesight was beginning to fail. "Outsiders . . . Outworlders even. Am I right? You don't seem to have the Trantor smell about you."

Seldon wished she hadn't mentioned smell. The apartment, overcrowded and littered with small possessions that seemed dim and dusty, reeked with food odors that were on the edge of rancidity. The air was so thick and clinging that he was sure his clothes would smell strongly of it when they left.

He said, "You are right, Mother Rittah. I am Hari Seldon of Helicon. My friend is Dors Venabili of Cinna."

"So," she said, looking about for an unoccupied spot on the floor where she could invite them to sit, but finding none suitable.

Dors said, "We are willing to stand, Mother."

"What?" she looked up at Dors. "You must speak briskly, my child. My hearing is not what it was when I was your age."

"Why don't you get a hearing device?" said Seldon, raising his voice.

"It wouldn't help, Master Seldon. Something seems to be wrong with the nerve and I have no money for nerve rebuilding. —You have come to learn the future from old Mother Rittah?"

"Not quite," said Seldon. "I have come to learn the past."

"Excellent. It is such a strain to decide what people want to hear."

"It must be quite an art," said Dors, smiling.

"It seems easy, but one has to be properly convincing. I earn my fees."

"If you have a credit outlet," said Seldon. "We will pay any reasonable fees if you tell us about Earth—without cleverly designing what you tell us to suit what we want to hear. We wish to hear the truth."

The old woman, who had been shuffling about the room, making adjustments here and there, as though to make it all prettier and more suitable for important visitors, stopped short. "What do you want to know about Earth?"

"What is it, to begin with?"

The old woman turned and seemed to gaze off into space. When she spoke, her voice was low and steady.

"It is a world, a very old planet. It is forgotten and lost."

Dors said, "It is not part of history. We know that much."

"It comes before history, child," said Mother Rittah solemnly. "It existed in the dawn of the Galaxy and before the dawn. It was the only world with humanity." She nodded firmly.

Seldon said, "Was another name for Earth . . . Aurora?"

And now Mother Rittah's face twisted into a frown. "Where did you hear that?"

"In my wanderings. I have heard of an old forgotten world named Aurora on which humanity lived in primordial peace."

"It's a *lie.*" She wiped her mouth as though to get the taste of what she had just heard out of it. "That name you mention must *never* be mentioned except as the place of Evil. It was the beginning of Evil. Earth was alone till Evil came, along with its sister worlds. Evil nearly destroyed Earth, but Earth rallied and destroyed Evil—with the help of heroes."

"Earth was *before* this Evil. Are you sure of that?"

"Long before. Earth was alone in the Galaxy for thousands of years— *millions* of years."

"Millions of years? Humanity existed on it for millions of years with no other people on any other world?"

"That's true. That's true. That's *true.*"

"But how do you know all this? Is it all in a computer program? Or a printout? Do you have anything I can read?"

Mother Rittah shook her head. "I heard the old stories from my mother, who heard it from hers, and so on far back. I have no children, so I tell the stories to others, but it may come to an end. This is a time of disbelief."

Dors said, "Not really, Mother. There are people who speculate about prehistoric times and who study some of the tales of lost worlds."

Mother Rittah made a motion of her arm as though to wipe it away. "They look at it with cold eyes. Scholarly. They try to fit it in with their notions. I could tell you stories for a year of the great hero Ba-Lee, but you would have no time to listen and I have lost the strength to tell."

Seldon said, "Have you ever heard of robots?"

The old woman shuddered and her voice was almost a scream. *"Why do you ask such things?* Those were artificial human beings, evil in themselves and the work of the Evil worlds. They were destroyed and should never be mentioned."

"There was one special robot, wasn't there, that the Evil worlds hated?"

Mother Rittah tottered toward Seldon and peered into his eyes. He could feel her hot breath on his face. "Have you come to mock me? You know of these things and yet you ask? Why do you ask?"

"Because I wish to know."

"There was an artificial human being who helped Earth. He was Da-Nee, friend of Ba-Lee. He never died and lives somewhere, waiting for his time to return. None knows when that time will be, but someday he will come and restore the great old days and remove all cruelty, injustice, and misery. That is the promise." At this, she closed her eyes and smiled, as if remembering . . .

Seldon waited a while in silence, then sighed and said, "Thank you, Mother Rittah. You have been very helpful. What is your fee?"

"So pleasant to meet Outworlders," the old woman replied. "Ten credits. May I offer you some refreshment?"

"No, thank you," said Seldon earnestly. "Please take twenty. You need only tell us how to get back to the Expressway from here. —And, Mother Rittah, if you can arrange to have some of your tales of Earth put into a computer disc, I will pay you well."

"I would need so much strength. How well?"

"It would depend on how long the story is and how well it is told. I might pay a thousand credits."

Mother Rittah licked her lips. "A thousand credits? But how will I find you when the story is told?"

"I will give you the computer code number at which I can be reached."

After Seldon gave Mother Rittah the code number, he and Dors left, thankful for the comparatively clean odor of the alley outside. They walked briskly in the direction indicated by the old woman.

71.

Dors said, "That wasn't a very long interview, Hari."

"I know. The surroundings were terribly unpleasant and I felt I had learned enough. Amazing how these folktales tend to magnify."

"What do you mean, 'magnify'?"

"Well, the Mycogenians fill their Aurora with human beings who lived for centuries and the Dahlites fill their Earth with a humanity that lived for millions of years. And both talk of a robot that lives forever. Still, it makes one think."

"As far as millions of years go, there's room for— Where are we going?"

"Mother Rittah said we go in this direction till we reach a rest area, then follow the sign for CENTRAL WALKWAY, bearing left, and keep on following the sign. Did we pass a rest area on the way in?"

"We may be leaving by a route different from the one we came in. I don't remember a rest area, but I wasn't watching the route. I was keeping my eye on the people we passed and—"

Her voice died away. Up ahead the alley swelled outward on both sides.

Seldon remembered. They *had* passed that way. There had been a couple of ratty couch pads resting on the walkway floor on either side.

There was, however, no need for Dors to watch passersby going out as she had coming in. There were no passersby. But up ahead in the rest area they spotted a group of men, rather large-sized for Dahlites, mustaches bristling, bare upper arms muscular and glistening under the yellowish indoor light of the walkway.

Clearly, they were waiting for the Outworlders and, almost automatically, Seldon and Dors came to a halt. For a moment or two, the tableau held. Then Seldon looked behind him hastily. Two or three additional men had stepped into view.

Seldon said between his teeth, "We're trapped. I should not have let you come, Dors."

"On the contrary. This is why I'm here, but was it worth your seeing Mother Rittah?"

"If we get out of this, it was."

Seldon then said in a loud and firm voice, "May we pass?"

One of the men ahead stepped forward. He was fully Seldon's height of 1.73 meters, but broader in the shoulders and much more muscular. A bit flabby at the waist, though, Seldon noted.

"I'm Marron," he said with self-satisfied significance, as though the name ought to have meaning, "and I'm here to tell you we don't like Outworlders in our district. You want to come in, all right—but if you want to leave, you'll have to pay."

"Very well. How much?"

"All you've got. You rich Outworlders have credit tiles, right? Just hand them over."

"No."

"No point saying no. We'll just take them."

"You can't take them without killing me or hurting me and they won't work without my voiceprint. My *normal* voiceprint."

"That's not so, Master—see, I'm being polite—we can take them away from you without hurting you *very* much."

"How many of you big strong men will it take? Nine? No." Seldon counted rapidly. "Ten."

"Just one. Me."

"With no help?"

"Just me."

"If the rest of you will clear away and give us room, I would like to see you try it, Marron."

"You don't have a knife, Master. You want one?"

"No, use yours to make the fight even. I'll fight without one."

Marron looked about at the others and said, "Hey, this puny guy is a sport. He don't even sound scared. That's sort of nice. It would be a shame to hurt him. —I tell you what, Master. I'll take the girl. If you want me to stop, hand over your credit tile and her tile and use your right voices to activate them. If you say no, then after I'm through with the girl . . . and that'll take some time"—he laughed—"I'll just have to hurt you."

"No," said Seldon. "Let the woman go. I've challenged you to a fight —one to one, you with a knife, me without. If you want bigger odds, I'll fight two of you, but let the woman go."

"Stop, Hari!" cried out Dors. "If he wants me, let him come and get me. You stay right where you are, Hari, and don't move."

"You hear that?" said Marron, grinning broadly. " 'You stay right where you are, Hari, and don't move.' I think the little lady wants me. You two, keep him still."

Each of Seldon's arms were caught in an iron grip and he felt the sharp point of a knife in his back.

"Don't move," said a harsh whisper in his ear, "and you can watch. The lady will probably like it. Marron's pretty good at this."

Dors called out again. "Don't move, Hari!" She turned to face Marron watchfully, her half-closed hands poised near her belt.

He closed in on her purposefully and she waited till he had come within arm's length, when suddenly her own arms flashed and Marron found himself facing two large knives.

For a moment, he leaned backward and then he laughed. "The little lady has two knives—knives like the big boys have. And I've only got one. But that's fair enough." His knife was swiftly out. "I hate to have to cut you, little lady, because it will be more fun for both of us if I don't. Maybe I can just knock them out of your hands, huh?"

Dors said, "I don't want to kill you. I'll do all I can to avoid doing so. Just the same, I call on all to witness, that if I do kill you, it is to protect my friend, as I am honor-bound to do."

Marron pretended to be terrified. "Oh, please don't kill me, little lady." Then he burst into laughter and was joined by the other Dahlites present.

Marron lunged with his knife, quite wide of the mark. He tried it again, then a third time, but Dors never budged. She made no attempt to fend off any motion that was not truly aimed at her.

Marron's expression darkened. He was trying to make her respond with panic, but he was only making himself seem ineffectual. The next lunge was directly at her and Dors's left-hand blade moved flashingly and caught his with a force that pushed his arm aside. Her right-hand blade flashed inward and made a diagonal slit in his T-shirt. A thin bloody line smeared the dark-haired skin beneath.

Marron looked down at himself in shock as the onlookers gasped in surprise. Seldon felt the grip on him weaken slightly as the two who held him were distracted by a duel not going quite as they had expected. He tensed himself.

Now Marron lunged again and this time his left hand shot outward to enclose Dors's right wrist. Again Dors's left-hand blade caught his knife and held it motionless, while her right hand twisted agilely and drew downward, even as Marron's left hand closed upon it. It closed on nothing but the blade and when he opened his hand there was a bloody line down the palm.

Dors sprang back and Marron, aware of the blood on his chest and hand, roared out chokingly, "Someone toss me another knife!"

There was hesitation and then one of the onlookers tossed his own knife underhanded. Marron reached for it, but Dors was quicker. Her right-hand blade struck the thrown knife and sent it flying backward, whirling as it went.

Seldon felt the grips on his arms weaken further. He lifted them suddenly, pushing up and forward, and was free. His two captors turned toward him with a sudden shout, but he quickly kneed one in the groin and elbowed the other in the solar plexus and both went down.

He knelt to draw the knives of each and rose as double-armed as Dors. Unlike Dors, Seldon did not know how to handle the blades, but he knew the Dahlites would scarcely be aware of that.

Dor said, "Just keep them off, Hari. Don't attack yet. —Marron, my next stroke will not be a scratch."

Marron, totally enraged, roared incoherently and charged blindly, attempting by sheer kinetic energy to overwhelm his opponent. Dors, dipping and sidestepping, ducked under his right arm, kicked her foot against his right ankle, and down he crashed, his knife flying.

She then knelt, placed one blade against the back of his neck and the other against his throat, and said, "Yield!"

With another yell, Marron struck out against her with one arm, pushed her to one side, then scrambled to his feet.

He had not yet stood up completely when she was upon him, one knife slashing downward and hacking away a section of his mustache. This time he yowled like a large animal in agony, clapping his hand to his face. When he drew it away, it was dripping blood.

Dors shouted, "It won't grow again, Marron. Some of the lip went with it. Attack once more and you're dead meat."

She waited, but Marron had had enough. He stumbled away, moaning, leaving a trail of blood.

Dors turned toward the others. The two that Seldon had knocked down were still lying there, unarmed and not anxious to get up. She bent down, cut their belts with one of her knives and then slit their trousers.

"This way, you'll have to hold your pants up when you walk," she said.

She stared at the seven men still on their feet, who were watching her with awestruck fascination. "And which of *you* threw the knife?"

There was silence.

She said, "It doesn't matter to me. Come one at a time or all together, but each time I slash, someone dies."

And with one accord, the seven turned and scurried away.

Dors lifted her eyebrows and said to Seldon, "This time, at least, Hummin can't complain that I failed to protect you."

Seldon said, "I still can't believe what I saw. I didn't know you could do anything like that—or talk like that either."

Dors merely smiled. "You have your talents too. We make a good pair. Here, retract your knife blades and put them into your pouch. I think the news will spread with enormous speed and we can get out of Billibotton without fear of being stopped."

She was quite right.

UNDERCOVER

· · · · ·

DAVAN— . . . In the unsettled times marking the final centuries of the First Galactic Empire, the typical sources of unrest arose from the fact that political and military leaders jockeyed for "supreme" power (a supremacy that grew more worthless with each decade). Only rarely was there anything that could be called a popular movement prior to the advent of psychohistory. In this connection, one intriguing example involves Davan, of whom little is actually known, but who may have met with Hari Seldon at one time when . . .

ENCYCLOPEDIA GALACTICA

72.

Both Hari Seldon and Dors Venabili had taken rather lingering baths, making use of the somewhat primitive facilities available to them in the Tisalver household. They had changed their clothing and were in Seldon's room when Jirad Tisalver returned in the evening. His signal at the door was (or seemed) rather timid. The buzz did not last long.

Seldon opened the door and said pleasantly, "Good evening, Master Tisalver. And Mistress."

She was standing right behind her husband, forehead puckered into a puzzled frown.

Tisalver said tentatively, as though he was unsure of the situation, "Are you and Mistress Venabili both well?" He nodded his head as though trying to elicit an affirmative by body language.

"Quite well. In and out of Billibotton without trouble and we're all washed and changed. There's no smell left." Seldon lifted his chin as he said it, smiling, tossing the sentence over Tisalver's shoulder to his wife.

She sniffed loudly, as though testing the matter.

Still tentatively, Tisalver said, "I understand there was a knife fight."

Seldon raised his eyebrows. "Is that the story?"

"You and the Mistress against a hundred thugs, we were told, and you killed them all. Is that so?" There was the reluctant sound of deep respect in his voice.

"Absolutely not," Dors put in with sudden annoyance. "That's ridiculous. What do you think we are? Mass murderers? And do you think a hundred thugs would remain in place, waiting the considerable time it would take me—us—to kill them all? I mean, *think* about it."

"That's what they're saying," said Casilia Tisalver with shrill firmness. "We can't have that sort of thing in this house."

"In the first place," said Seldon, "it wasn't in this house. In the second, it wasn't a hundred men, it was ten. In the third, no one was killed. There was some altercation back and forth, after which they left and made way for us."

"They just made way. Do you expect me to believe that, Outworlders?" demanded Mistress Tisalver belligerently.

Seldon sighed. At the slightest stress, human beings seemed to divide themselves into antagonistic groups. He said, "Well, I grant you one of them was cut a little. Not seriously."

"And you weren't hurt at all?" said Tisalver. The admiration in his voice was more marked.

"Not a scratch," said Seldon. "Mistress Venabili handles two knives excellently well."

"I dare say," said Mistress Tisalver, her eyes dropping to Dors's belt, "and that's not what I want to have going on here."

Dors said sternly, "As long as no one attacks us here, that's what you *won't* have here."

"But on account of you," said Mistress Tisalver, "we have trash from the street standing at the doorway."

"My love," said Tisalver soothingly, "let us not anger—"

"Why?" spat his wife with contempt. "Are you afraid of her knives? I would like to see her use them here."

"I have no intention of using them here," said Dors with a sniff as loud as any that Mistress Tisalver had produced. "What is this trash from the street you're talking about?"

Tisalver said, "What my wife means is that an urchin from Billibotton —at least, judging by his appearance—wishes to see you and we are not accustomed to that sort of thing in this neighborhood. It undermines our standing." He sounded apologetic.

Seldon said, "Well, Master Tisalver, we'll go outside, find out what it's all about, and send him on his business as quickly—"

"No. Wait," said Dors, annoyed. "These are *our rooms*. We pay for them. *We* decide who visits us and who does not. If there is a young man outside from Billibotton, he is nonetheless a Dahlite. More important, he's a Trantorian. Still more important, he's a citizen of the Empire and a human being. Most important, by asking to see us, he becomes our guest. Therefore, we invite him in to see us."

Mistress Tisalver didn't move. Tisalver himself seemed uncertain.

Dors said, "Since you say I killed a hundred bullies in Billibotton, you surely do not think I am afraid of a boy or, for that matter, of you two." Her right hand dropped casually to her belt.

Tisalver said with sudden energy, "Mistress Venabili, we do not intend to offend you. Of course these rooms are yours and you can entertain whomever you wish here." He stepped back, pulling his indignant wife with him, undergoing a burst of resolution for which he might conceivably have to pay afterward.

Dors looked after them sternly.

Seldon smiled dryly. "How unlike you, Dors. I thought I was the one who quixotically got into trouble and that you were the calm and practical one whose only aim was to prevent trouble."

Dors shook her head. "I can't bear to hear a human being spoken of with contempt just because of his group identification—even by other human beings. It's these respectable people here who create those hooligans out there."

"And other respectable people," said Seldon, "who create these respectable people. These mutual animosities are as much a part of humanity—"

"Then you'll have to deal with it in your psychohistory, won't you?"

"Most certainly—if there is ever a psychohistory with which to deal with anything at all. —Ah, here comes the urchin under discussion. And it's Raych, which somehow doesn't surprise me."

73.

Raych entered, looking about, clearly intimidated. The forefinger of his right hand reached for his upper lip as though wondering when he would begin to feel the first downy hairs there.

He turned to the clearly outraged Mistress Tisalver and bowed clumsily. "Thank ya, Missus. Ya got a lovely place."

Then, as the door slammed behind him, he turned to Seldon and Dors with an air of easy connoisseurship. "Nice place, guys."

"I'm glad you like it," said Seldon solemnly. "How did you know we were here?"

"Followed ya. How'd ya think? Hey, lady"—he turned to Dors—"you don't fight like no dame."

"Have you watched many dames fight?" asked Dors, amused.

Raych rubbed his nose, "No, never seen none whatever. They don't carry knives, except little ones to scare kids with. Never scared me."

"I'm sure they didn't. What do you do to make dames draw their knives?"

"Nothin'. You just kid around a little. You holler, 'Hey, lady, lemme—' "

He thought about it for a moment and said, "Nothin'."

Dors said, "Well, don't try that on me."

"Ya kiddin'? After what ya did to Marron? Hey, lady, where'd you learn to fight that way?"

"On my own world."

"Could ya teach me?"

"Is that what you came here to see me about?"

"Akchaly, no. I came to bring ya a kind of message."

"From someone who wants to fight me?"

"No one wants to fight ya, lady. Listen, lady, ya got a reputation now. Everybody knows ya. You just walk down anywhere in old Billibotton and all the guys will step aside and let ya pass and grin and make sure they don't look cross-eyed at ya. Oh, lady, ya got it made. That's why *he* wants to see ya."

Seldon said, "Raych, just exactly *who* wants to see us?"

"Guy called Davan."

"And who is he?"

"Just a guy. He lives in Billibotton and don't carry no knife."

"And he stays alive, Raych?"

"He reads a lot and he helps the guys there when they get in trouble with the gov'ment. They kinda leave him alone. He don't need no knife."

"Why didn't he come himself, then?" said Dors. "Why did he send you?"

"He don't like this place. He says it makes him sick. He says all the people here, they lick the gov'ment's—" He paused, looked dubiously at the two Outworlders, and said, "Anyway, he won't come here. He said they'd let me in cause I was only a kid." He grinned. "They almost didn't, did they? I mean that lady there who looked like she was smellin' somethin'?"

He stopped suddenly, abashed, and looked down at himself. "Ya don't get much chance to wash where I come from."

"It's all right," said Dors, smiling. "Where are we supposed to meet, then, if he won't come here? After all—if you don't mind—we don't feel like going to Billibotton."

"I told ya," said Raych indignantly. "Ya get free run of Billibotton, I swear. Besides, where he lives no one will bother ya."

"Where is it?" asked Seldon.

"I can take ya there. It ain't far."

"And why does he want to see us?" asked Dors.

"Dunno. But he says like this—" Raych half-closed his eyes in an effort to remember. " 'Tell them I wanna see the man who talked to a Dahlite heatsinker like he was a human being and the woman who beat Marron with knives and didn't kill him when she mighta done so.' I think I got it right."

Seldon smiled. "I think you did. Is he ready for us now?"

"He's waiting."

"Then we'll come with you." He looked at Dors with a trace of doubt in his eyes.

She said, "All right. I'm willing. Perhaps it won't be a trap of some sort. Hope springs eternal—"

74.

There was a pleasant glow to the evening light when they emerged, a faint violet touch and a pinkish edge to the simulated sunset clouds that were scudding along. Dahl might have complaints of their treatment by the Imperial rulers of Trantor, but surely there was nothing wrong with the weather the computers spun out for them.

Dors said in a low voice, "We seem to be celebrities. No mistake about that."

Seldon brought his eyes down from the supposed sky and was immediately aware of a fair-sized crowd around the apartment house in which the Tisalvers lived.

Everyone in the crowd stared at them intently. When it was clear that the two Outworlders had become aware of the attention, a low murmur ran through the crowd, which seemed to be on the point of breaking out into applause.

Dors said, "Now I can see where Mistress Tisalver would find this annoying. I should have been a little more sympathetic."

The crowd was, for the most part, poorly dressed and it was not hard to guess that many of the people were from Billibotton.

On impulse, Seldon smiled and raised one hand in a mild greeting that was met with applause. One voice, lost in the safe anonymity of the crowd called out, "Can the lady show us some knife tricks?"

When Dors called back, "No, I only draw in anger," there was instant laughter.

One man stepped forward. He was clearly not from Billibotton and bore no obvious mark of being a Dahlite. He had only a small mustache, for one thing, and it was brown, not black. He said, "Marlo Tanto of the 'Trantorian HV News.' Can we have you in focus for a bit for our nightly holocast?"

"No," said Dors shortly. "No interviews."

The newsman did not budge. "I understand you were in a fight with a great many men in Billibotton—and won." He smiled. "That's news, that is."

"No," said Dors. "We met some men in Billibotton, talked to them, and then moved on. That's all there is to it and that's all you're going to get."

"What's your name? You don't sound like a Trantorian."

"I have no name."

"And your friend's name?"

"He has no name."

The newsman looked annoyed, "Look, lady. You're news and I'm just trying to do my job."

Raych pulled at Dors's sleeve. She leaned down and listened to his earnest whisper.

She nodded and straightened up again. "I don't think you're a newsman, Mr. Tanto. What I think you are is an Imperial agent trying to make trouble for Dahl. There was no fight and you're trying to manufacture news concerning one as a way of justifying an Imperial expedition into Billibotton. I wouldn't stay here if I were you. I don't think you're very popular with these people."

The crowd had begun to mutter at Dors's first words. They grew louder now and began to drift, slowly and in a menacing way, in the direction of Tanto. He looked nervously around and began to move away.

Dors raised her voice. "Let him go. Don't anyone touch him. Don't give him any excuse to report violence."

And they parted before him.

Raych said, "Aw, lady, you shoulda let them rough him up."

"Bloodthirsty boy," said Dors, "take us to this friend of yours."

75.

They met the man who called himself Davan in a room behind a dilapidated diner. Far behind.

Raych led the way, once more showing himself as much at home in the burrows of Billibotton as a mole would be in tunnels underground in Helicon.

It was Dors Venabili whose caution first manifested itself. She stopped and said, "Come back, Raych. Exactly where are we going?"

"To Davan," said Raych, looking exasperated. "I told ya."

"But this is a deserted area. There's no one living here." Dors looked about with obvious distaste. The surroundings were lifeless and what light panels were there were did not glow—or did so only dimly.

"It's the way Davan likes it," said Raych. "He's always changing around, staying here, staying there. Ya know . . . changing around."

"Why?" demanded Dors.

"It's safer, lady."

"From whom?"

"From the gov'ment."

"Why would the government want Davan?"

"I dunno, lady. Tell ya what. I'll tell ya where he is and tell ya how to go and ya go on alone—if ya don't want me to take ya."

Seldon said, "No, Raych, I'm pretty sure we'll get lost without you. In fact, you had better wait till we're through so you can lead us back."

Raych said at once, "What's in it f'me? Ya expect me to hang around when I get hungry?"

"You hang around and get hungry, Raych, and I'll buy you a big dinner. Anything you like."

"Ya say that *now,* Mister. How do I know?"

Dors's hand flashed and it was holding a knife, blade exposed, "You're not calling us liars, are you, Raych?"

Raych's eyes opened wide. He did not seem frightened by the threat. He said, "Hey, I didn't see that. Do it again."

"I'll do it afterward—if you're still here. Otherwise"—Dors glared at him—"we'll track you down."

"Aw, lady, come on," said Raych. "Ya ain't gonna track me down. Ya ain't that kind. But I'll be here." He struck a pose. "Ya got my word."

And he led them onward in silence, though the sound of their shoes was hollow in the empty corridors.

Davan looked up when they entered, a wild look that softened when he saw Raych. He gestured quickly toward the two others—questioningly.

Raych said, "These are the guys." And, grinning, he left.

Seldon said, "I am Hari Seldon. The young lady is Dors Venabili."

He regarded Davan curiously. Davan was swarthy and had the thick black mustache of the Dahlite male, but in addition he had a stubble of beard. He was the first Dahlite whom Seldon had seen who had not been meticulously shaven. Even the bullies of Billibotton had been smooth of cheek and chin.

Seldon said, "What is your name, sir?"

"Davan. Raych must have told you."

3 1 4

"Your second name."

"I am only Davan. Were you followed here, Master Seldon?"

"No, I'm sure we weren't. If we had, then by sound or sight, I expect Raych would have known. And if he had not, Mistress Venabili would have."

Dors smiled slightly. "You have faith in me, Hari."

"More all the time," he said thoughtfully.

Davan stirred uneasily. "Yet you've already been found."

"Found?"

"Yes, I have heard of this supposed newsman."

"Already?" Seldon looked faintly surprised. "But I suspect he really was a newsman . . . and harmless. We called him an Imperial agent at Raych's suggestion, which was a good idea. The surrounding crowd grew threatening and we got rid of him."

"No," said Davan, "he was what you called him. My people know the man and he *does* work for the Empire. —But then you do not do as I do. You do not use a false name and change your place of abode. You go under your own names, making no effort to remain undercover. You are Hari Seldon, the mathematician."

"Yes, I am," said Seldon. "Why should I invent a false name?"

"The Empire wants you, does it not?"

Seldon shrugged. "I stay in places where the Empire cannot reach out to take me."

"Not openly, but the Empire doesn't have to work openly. I would urge you to disappear . . . really disappear."

"Like you . . . as you say," said Seldon, looking about with an edge of distaste. The room was as dead as the corridors he had walked through. It was musty through and through and it was overwhelmingly depressing.

"Yes," said Davan. "You could be useful to us."

"In what way?"

"You talked to a young man named Yugo Amaryl."

"Yes, I did."

"Amaryl tells me that you can predict the future."

Seldon sighed heavily. He was tired of standing in this empty room. Davan was sitting on a cushion and there were other cushions available, but they did not look clean. Nor did he wish to lean against the mildew-streaked wall.

He said, "Either you misunderstood Amaryl or Amaryl misunderstood me. What I have done is to prove that it is possible to choose starting conditions from which historical forecasting does not descend into chaotic conditions, but can become predictable within limits. However, what those starting conditions might be I do not know, nor am I sure that those conditions can be found by any one person—or by any number of people—in a finite length of time. Do you understand me?"

"No."

Seldon sighed again. "Then let me try once more. It is possible to predict the future, but it may be impossible to find out how to take advantage of that possibility. Do you understand?"

Davan looked at Seldon darkly, then at Dors. "Then you *can't* predict the future."

"Now you have the point, Master Davan."

"Just call me Davan. But you may be able to learn to predict the future someday."

"That is conceivable."

"Then that's why the Empire wants you."

"No," Seldon raised his finger didactically. "It's my idea that that is why the Empire is *not* making an overwhelming effort to get me. They might like to have me if I can be picked up without trouble, but they know that *right now* I know nothing and that it is therefore not worth upsetting the delicate peace of Trantor by interfering with the local rights of this sector or that. That's the reason I can move about under my own name with reasonable security."

For a moment, Davan buried his head in his hands and muttered, "This is madness." Then he looked up wearily and said to Dors, "Are you Master Seldon's wife?"

Dors said calmly, "I am his friend and protector."

"How well do you know him?"

"We have been together for some months."

"No more?"

"No more."

"Would it be your opinion he is speaking the truth?"

"I know he is, but what reason would you have to trust me if you do not trust him? If Hari is, for some reason, lying to you, might I not be lying to you equally in order to support him?"

Davan looked from one to the other helplessly. Then he said, "Would you, in any case, help us?"

"Who are 'us' and in what way do you need help?"

Davan said, "You see the situation here in Dahl. We are oppressed. You must know that and, from your treatment of Yugo Amaryl, I cannot believe you lack sympathy for us."

"We are fully sympathetic."

"And you must know the source of the oppression."

"You are going to tell me that it's the Imperial government, I suppose, and I dare say it plays its part. On the other hand, I notice that there is a middle class in Dahl that despises the heatsinkers and a criminal class that terrorizes the rest of the sector."

Davan's lips tightened, but he remained unmoved. "Quite true. Quite true. But the Empire encourages it as a matter of principle. Dahl has the potential for making serious trouble. If the heatsinkers should go on strike, Trantor would experience a severe energy shortage almost at once . . . with all that that implies. However, Dahl's own upper classes will spend money to hire the hoodlums of Billibotton—and of other places— to fight the heatsinkers and break the strike. It has happened before. The Empire allows some Dahlites to prosper—comparatively—in order to convert them into Imperialist lackeys, while it refuses to enforce the arms-control laws effectively enough to weaken the criminal element.

"The Imperial government does this everywhere—and not in Dahl alone. They can't exert force to impose their will, as in the old days when they ruled with brutal directness. Nowadays, Trantor has grown so complex and so easily disturbed that the Imperial forces must keep their hands off—"

"A form of degeneration," said Seldon, remembering Hummin's complaints.

"What?" said Davan.

"Nothing," said Seldon. "Go on."

"The Imperial forces must keep their hands off, but they find that they can do much even so. Each sector is encouraged to be suspicious of its neighbors. Within each sector, economic and social classes are encouraged to wage a kind of war with each other. The result is that all over Trantor it is impossible for the people to take united action. Everywhere, the people would rather fight each other than make a common stand against the central tyranny and the Empire rules without having to exert force."

"And what," said Dors, "do you think can be done about it?"

"I've been trying for years to build a feeling of solidarity among the peoples of Trantor."

"I can only suppose," said Seldon dryly, "that you are finding this an impossibly difficult and largely thankless task."

"You suppose correctly," said Davan, "but the party is growing stronger. Many of our knifers are coming to the realization that knives are best when they are not used on each other. Those who attacked you in the corridors of Billibotton are examples of the unconverted. However, those who support you now, who are ready to defend you against the agent you thought was a newsman, are my people. I live here among them. It is not an attractive way of life, but I am safe here. We have adherents in neighboring sectors and we spread daily."

"But where do we come in?" asked Dors.

"For one thing," said Davan, "both of you are Outworlders, scholars. We need people like you among our leaders. Our greatest strength is drawn from the poor and the uneducated because they suffer the most, but they can lead the least. A person like one of you two is worth a hundred of them."

"That's an odd estimate from someone who wishes to rescue the oppressed," said Seldon.

"I don't mean as people," said Davan hastily. "I mean as far as leadership is concerned. The party must have among its leaders men and women of intellectual power."

"People like us, you mean, are needed to give your party a veneer of respectability."

Davan said, "You can always put something noble in a sneering fashion if you try. But you, Master Seldon, are more than respectable, more than intellectual. Even if you won't admit to being able to penetrate the mists of the future—"

"Please, Davan," said Seldon, "don't be poetic and don't use the conditional. It's not a matter of admitting. I *can't* foresee the future. Those are not mists that block the view but chrome steel barriers."

"Let me finish. Even if you can't actually predict with—what do you call it?—psychohistorical accuracy, you've studied history and you may have a certain intuitive feeling for consequences. Now, isn't that so?"

Seldon shook his head. "I may have a certain intuitive understanding for mathematical likelihood, but how far I can translate that into anything of historical significance is quite uncertain. Actually, I have *not* studied history. I wish I had. I feel the loss keenly."

Dors said evenly, "I am the historian, Davan, and I can say a few things if you wish."

"Please do," said Davan, making it half a courtesy, half a challenge.

"For one thing, there have been many revolutions in Galactic history that have overthrown tyrannies, sometimes on individual planets, sometimes in groups of them, occasionally in the Empire itself or in the pre-Imperial regional governments. Often, this has only meant a change in tyranny. In other words, one ruling class is replaced by another—sometimes by one that is more efficient and therefore still more capable of maintaining itself—while the poor and downtrodden remain poor and downtrodden or become even worse off."

Davan, listening intently, said, "I'm aware of that. We all are. Perhaps we can learn from the past and know better what to avoid. Besides, the tyranny that now exists is *actual.* That which may exist in the future is merely potential. If we are always to draw back from change with the thought that the change may be for the worse, then there is no hope at all of ever escaping injustice."

Dors said, "A second point you must remember is that even if you have right on your side, even if justice thunders condemnation, it is usually the tyranny in existence that has the balance of force on its side. There is nothing your knife handlers can do in the way of rioting and demonstrating that will have any permanent effect as long as, in the extremity, there is an army equipped with kinetic, chemical, and neurological weapons that is willing to use them against your people. You can get all the downtrodden and even all the respectables on your side, but you must somehow win over the security forces and the Imperial army or at least seriously weaken their loyalty to the rulers."

Davan said, "Trantor is a multigovernmental world. Each sector has its own rulers and some of them are themselves anti-Imperial. If we can have a strong sector on our side, that would change the situation, would it not? We would then not be merely ragamuffins fighting with knives and stones."

"Does that mean you *do* have a strong sector on your side or merely that it is your ambition to have one?"

Davan was silent.

Dors said, "I shall assume that you are thinking of the Mayor of Wye. If the Mayor is in the mood to make use of popular discontent as a way of improving the chance of toppling the Emperor, doesn't it strike you that the end the Mayor would have in view would be that of succeeding to the Imperial throne? Why should the Mayor risk his present not-inconsiderable position for anything less? Merely for the blessings of justice and the decent treatment of people, concerning whom he can have little interest?"

"You mean," said Davan, "that any powerful leader who is willing to help us may then betray us."

"It is a situation that is all too common in Galactic history."

"If we are ready for that, might *we* not betray *him?*"

"You mean, make use of him and then, at some crucial moment, subvert the leader of his forces—or a leader, at any rate—and have him assassinated?"

"Not perhaps exactly like that, but some way of getting rid of him might exist if that should prove necessary."

"Then we have a revolutionary movement in which the principal players must be ready to betray each other, with each simply waiting for the opportunity. It sounds like a recipe for chaos."

"You will not help us, then?" said Davan.

Seldon, who had been listening to the exchange between Davan and Dors with a puzzled frown on his face, said, "We can't put it that simply. We would like to help you. We are on your side. It seems to me that no sane man wants to uphold an Imperial system that maintains itself by fostering mutual hatred and suspicions. Even when it seems to work, it can only be described as metastable; that is, as too apt to fall into instability in one direction or another. But the question is: *How* can we help? If I had psychohistory, if I could tell what is most likely to happen, or if I could tell what action of a number of alternative possibilities is most likely to bring on an apparently happy consequence, then I would put my abilities at your disposal. —But I don't have it. I can help you best by trying to develop psychohistory."

"And how long will that take?"

Seldon shrugged. "I cannot say."

"How can you ask us to wait indefinitely?"

"What alternative do I have, since I am useless to you as I am? But I will say this: I have until very recently been quite convinced that the development of psychohistory was absolutely impossible. Now I am not so certain of that."

"You mean you have a solution in mind?"

"No, merely an intuitive feeling that a solution might be possible. I have not been able to pin down what has occurred to make me have that feeling. It may be an illusion, but I am trying. Let me continue to try. —Perhaps we will meet again."

"Or perhaps," said Davan, "if you return to where you are now staying, you will eventually find yourself in an Imperial trap. You may think that the Empire will leave you alone while you struggle with psychohistory, but I am certain the Emperor and his toady Demerzel are in no mood to wait forever, any more than I am."

"It will do them no good to hasten," said Seldon calmly, "since I am not on their side, as I am on yours. —Come, Dors."

They turned and left Davan, sitting alone in his squalid room, and found Raych waiting for them outside.

76.

Raych was eating, licking his fingers, and crumpling the bag in which the food—whatever it was—had been. A strong smell of onions pervaded the air—different somehow, yeast-based perhaps.

Dors, retreating a little from the odor, said, "Where did you get the food from, Raych?"

"Davan's guys. They brought it to me. Davan's okay."

"Then we don't have to buy you dinner, do we?" said Seldon, conscious of his own empty stomach.

"Ya owe me *somethin'* " said Raych, looking greedily in Dors's direction. "How about the lady's knife? One of 'em."

"No knife," said Dors. "You get us back safely and I'll give you five credits."

"Can't get no knife for five credits," grumbled Raych.

"You're not getting anything but five credits," said Dors.

"You're a lousy dame, lady," said Raych.

"I'm a lousy dame with a quick knife, Raych, so get moving."

"All right. Don't get all perspired." Raych waved his hand. "This way."

It was back through the empty corridors, but this time Dors, looking this way and that, stopped. "Hold on, Raych. We're being followed."

Raych looked exasperated. "Ya ain't supposed to hear 'em."

Seldon said, bending his head to one side, "I don't hear anything."

"I do," said Dors. "Now, Raych, I don't want any fooling around. You tell me right now what's going on or I'll rap your head so that you won't see straight for a week. I mean it."

Raych held up one arm defensively. "You try it, you lousy dame. You try it. —It's Davan's guys. They're just taking care of us, in case any knifers come along."

"Davan's guys?"

"Yeah. They're goin' along the service corridors."

Dors's right hand shot out and seized Raych by the scruff of his upper garment. She lifted and he dangled, shouting, "Hey, lady. Hey!"

Seldon said, "Dors! Don't be hard on him."

"I'll be harder still if I think he's lying. You're my charge, Hari, not he."

"I'm not lyin'," said Raych, struggling. "I'm not."

"I'm sure he isn't," said Seldon.

"Well, we'll see. Raych, tell them to come out where we can see them." She let him drop and dusted her hands.

"You're some kind of nut, lady," said Raych aggrievedly. Then he raised his voice. "Yay, Davan! Come out here, some of ya guys!"

There was a wait and then, from an unlit opening along the corridor, two dark-mustached men came out, one with a scar running the length of his cheek. Each held the sheath of a knife in his hand, blade withdrawn.

"How many more of you are there?" asked Dors harshly.

"A few," said one of the newcomers. "Orders. We're guarding you. Davan wants you safe."

"Thank you. Try to be even quieter. Raych, keep on moving."

Raych said sulkily, "Ya roughed me up when I was telling the truth."

"You're right," said Dors. "At least, I think you're right . . . and I apologize."

"I'm not sure I should accept," said Raych, trying to stand tall. "But awright, just this once." He moved on.

When they reached the walkway, the unseen corps of guards vanished.

At least, even Dors's keen ears could hear them no more. By now, though, they were moving into the respectable part of the sector.

Dors said thoughtfully, "I don't think we have clothes that would fit you, Raych."

Raych said, "Why do ya want clothes to fit me, Missus?" (Respectability seemed to invade Raych once they were out of the corridors.) "I got clothes."

"I thought you'd like to come into our place and take a bath."

Raych said, "What for? I'll wash one o' these days. And I'll put on my other shirt." He looked up at Dors shrewdly. "You're sorry ya roughed me up. Right? Ya tryin' to make up?"

Dors smiled. "Yes. Sort of."

Raych waved a hand in lordly fashion. "That's all right. Ya didn't hurt. Listen. You're strong for a lady. Ya lifted me up like I was nothin'."

"I was annoyed, Raych. I have to be concerned about Master Seldon."

"Ya sort of his bodyguard?" Raych looked at Seldon inquiringly. "Ya got a lady for a bodyguard?"

"I can't help it," said Seldon, smiling wryly. "She insists. And she certainly knows her job."

Dors said, "Think again, Raych. Are you sure you won't have a bath? A nice warm bath."

Raych said, "I got no chance. Ya think that lady is gonna let me in the house again?"

Dors looked up and saw Casilia Tisalver outside the front door of the apartment complex, staring first at the Outworld woman and then at the slum-bred boy. It would have been impossible to tell in which case her expression was angrier.

Raych said, "Well, so long, Mister and Missus. I don't know if she'll let either of ya in the house." He placed his hands in his pocket and swaggered off in a fine affectation of carefree indifference.

Seldon said, "Good evening, Mistress Tisalver. It's rather late, isn't it?"

"It's very late," she replied. "There was a near riot today outside this very complex because of that newsman you pushed the street vermin at."

"We didn't push anyone on anyone," said Dors.

"I was there," said Mistress Tisalver intransigently. "I saw it." She stepped aside to let them enter, but delayed long enough to make her reluctance quite plain.

"She acts as though that was the last straw," said Dors as she and Seldon made their way up to their rooms.

"So? What can she do about it?" asked Seldon.

"I wonder," said Dors.

OFFICERS

. . . . .

RAYCH— . . . According to Hari Seldon, the original
meeting with Raych was entirely accidental. He was simply
a gutter urchin from whom Seldon had asked directions.
But his life, from that moment on, continued to be inter-
twined with that of the great mathematician until . . .
                    ENCYCLOPEDIA BRITANNICA

77.

The next morning, dressed from the waist down, having washed and
shaved, Seldon knocked on the door that led to Dors's adjoining room
and said in a moderate voice, "Open the door, Dors."

She did. The short reddish-gold curls of her hair were still wet and she
too was dressed only from the waist down.

Seldon stepped back in embarrassed alarm. Dors looked down at the
swell of her breasts indifferently and wrapped a towel around her head.
"What is it?" she asked.

Seldon said, looking off to his right, "I was going to ask you about
Wye."

Dors said very naturally, "About why in connection with what? And
for goodness sake, don't make me talk to your ear. Surely, you're not a
virgin."

Seldon said in a hurt tone, "I was merely trying to be polite. If *you*
don't mind, *I* certainly don't. And it's not why about what. I'm asking
about the Wye Sector."

"Why do you want to know? Or, if you prefer: Why Wye?"

"Look, Dors, I'm serious. Every once in a while, the Wye Sector is
mentioned—the Mayor of Wye, actually. Hummin mentioned him, you
did, Davan did. I don't know anything about either the sector or the
Mayor."

"I'm not a native Trantorian either, Hari. I know very little, but you're welcome to what I do know. Wye is near the south pole—quite large, very populous—"

"Very populous at the south pole?"

"We're not on Helicon, Hari. Or on Cinna either. This is Trantor. Everything is underground and underground at the poles or underground at the equator is pretty much the same. Of course, I imagine they keep their day-night arrangements rather extreme—long days in their summer, long nights in their winter—almost as it would be on the surface. The extremes are just affectation; they're proud of being polar."

"But Upperside they must be cold, indeed."

"Oh yes. The Wye Upperside is snow and ice, but it doesn't lie as thickly there as you might think. If it did, it might crush the dome, but it doesn't and that is the basic reason for Wye's power."

She turned to her mirror, removed the towel from her head, and threw the dry-net over her hair, which, in a matter of five seconds, gave it a pleasant sheen. She said, "You have no idea how glad I am not to be wearing a skincap," as she put on the upper portion of her clothing.

"What has the ice layer to do with Wye's power?"

"Think about it. Forty billion people use a great deal of power and every calorie of it eventually degenerates into heat and has to be gotten rid of. It's piped to the poles, particularly to the south pole, which is the more developed of the two, and is discharged into space. It melts most of the ice in the process and I'm sure that accounts for Trantor's clouds and rains, no matter how much the meteorology boggins insist that things are more complicated than that."

"Does Wye make use of the power before discharging it?"

"They may, for all I know. I haven't the slightest idea, by the way, as to the technology involved in discharging the heat, but I'm talking about political power. If Dahl were to stop producing usable energy, that would certainly inconvenience Trantor, but there are other sectors that produce energy and can up their production and, of course, there is stored energy in one form or another. Eventually, Dahl would have to be dealt with, but there would be time. Wye, on the other hand—"

"Yes?"

"Well, Wye gets rid of at least 90 percent of all the heat developed on Trantor and there is no substitute. If Wye were to shut down its heat emission, the temperature would start going up all over Trantor."

"In Wye too."

"Ah, but since Wye is at the south pole, it can arrange an influx of cold air. It wouldn't do *much* good, but Wye would last longer than the rest of Trantor. The point is, then, that Wye is a very touchy problem for the Emperor and the Mayor of Wye is—or at least can be—extremely powerful."

"And what kind of a person is the present Mayor of Wye?"

"That I don't know. What I've occasionally heard would make it seem that he is very old and pretty much a recluse, but hard as a hypership hull and still cleverly maneuvering for power."

"Why, I wonder? If he's that old, he couldn't hold the power for long."

"Who knows, Hari? A lifelong obsession, I suppose. Or else it's the game . . . the *maneuvering* for power, without any real longing for the power itself. Probably if he had the power and took over Demerzel's place or even the Imperial throne itself, he would feel disappointed because the game would be over. Of course he might, if he was still alive, begin the subsequent game of *keeping* power, which might be just as difficult and just as satisfying."

Seldon shook his head. "It strikes me that no one could possibly want to be Emperor."

"No sane person would, I agree, but the 'Imperial wish,' as it is frequently called, is like a disease that, when caught, drives out sanity. And the closer you get to high office, the more likely you are to catch the disease. With each ensuing promotion—"

"The disease grows still more acute. Yes, I can see that. But it also seems to me that Trantor is so huge a world, so interlocking in its needs and so conflicting in its ambitions, that it makes up the major part of the inability of the Emperor to rule. Why doesn't he just leave Trantor and establish himself on some simpler world?"

Dors laughed. "You wouldn't ask that if you knew your history. Trantor *is* the Empire through thousands of years of custom. An Emperor who is not at the Imperial Palace is not the Emperor. He is a place, even more than a person."

Seldon sank into silence, his face rigid, and after a while Dors asked, "What's the matter, Hari?"

"I'm thinking," he said in a muffled voice. "Ever since you told me that hand-on-thigh story, I've had fugitive thoughts that— Now your remark about the Emperor being a place rather than a person seems to have struck a chord.''

''What kind of chord?''

Seldon shook his head. ''I'm still thinking. I may be all wrong.'' His glance at Dors sharpened, his eyes coming into focus. ''In any case, we ought to go down and have breakfast. We're late and I don't think Mistress Tisalver is in a good enough humor to have it brought in for us.''

''You optimist,'' said Dors. ''My own feeling is that she's not in a good enough humor to want us to stay—breakfast or not. She wants us out of here.''

''That may be, but we're paying her.''

''Yes, but I suspect she hates us enough by now to scorn our credits.''

''Perhaps her husband will feel a bit more affectionate concerning the rent.''

''If he has a single word to say, Hari, the only person who would be more surprised than me to hear it would be Mistress Tisalver. —Very well, I'm ready.''

And they moved down the stairs to the Tisalver portion of the apartment to find the lady in question waiting for them with less than breakfast —and with considerably more too.

78.

Casilia Tisalver stood ramrod straight with a tight smile on her round face and her dark eyes glinting. Her husband was leaning moodily against the wall. In the center of the room were two men who were standing stiffly upright, as though they had noticed the cushions on the floor but scorned them.

Both had the dark crisp hair and the thick black mustache to be expected of Dahlites. Both were thin and both were dressed in dark clothes so nearly alike that they were surely uniforms. There was thin white piping up and over the shoulders and down the sides of the tubular trouser legs. Each had, on the right side of his chest, a rather dim Spaceship-and-Sun, the symbol of the Galactic Empire on every inhabited world of the Galaxy, with, in this case, a dark ''D'' in the center of the sun.

Seldon realized immediately that these were two members of the Dahlite security forces.

"What's all this?" said Seldon sternly.

One of the men stepped forward. "I am Sector Officer Lanel Russ. This is my partner, Gebore Astinwald."

Both presented glittering identification holo-tabs. Seldon didn't bother looking at them. "What it is you want?"

Russ said calmly, "Are you Hari Seldon of Helicon?"

"I am."

"And are you Dors Venabili of Cinna, Mistress?"

"I am," said Dors.

"I'm here to investigate a complaint that one Hari Seldon instigated a riot yesterday."

"I did no such thing," said Seldon.

"Our information is," said Russ, looking at the screen of a small computer pad, "that you accused a newsman of being an Imperial agent, thus instigating a riot against him."

Dors said, "It was I who said he was an Imperial agent, Officer. I had reason to think he was. It is surely no crime to express one's opinion. The Empire has freedom of speech."

"That does not cover an opinion deliberately advanced in order to instigate a riot."

"How can you say it was, Officer?"

At this point, Mistress Tisalver interposed in a shrill voice, "*I* can say it, Officer. She saw there was a crowd present, a crowd of gutter people who were just *looking* for trouble. She deliberately said he was an Imperial agent when she knew nothing of the sort and she shouted it to the crowd to stir them up. It was plain that she knew what she was doing."

"Casilia," said her husband pleadingly, but she cast one look at him and he said no more.

Russ turned to Mistress Tisalver. "Did you lodge the complaint, Mistress?"

"Yes. These two have been living here for a few days and they've done nothing but make trouble. They've invited people of low reputation into *my* apartment, damaging my standing with my neighbors."

"Is it against the law, Officer," asked Seldon, "to invite clean, quiet citizens of Dahl into one's room? The two rooms upstairs are our rooms.

We have rented them and they are paid for. Is it a crime to speak to Dahlites in Dahl, Officer?''

"No, it is not," said Russ. "That is not part of the complaint. What gave you reason, Mistress Venabili, to suppose the person you so accused was, in fact, an Imperial agent?"

Dors said, "He had a small brown mustache, from which I concluded he was not a Dahlite. I surmised he was an Imperial agent."

"You surmised? Your associate, Master Seldon, has no mustache at all. Do you surmise *he* is an Imperial agent?"

"In any case," said Seldon hastily, "there was no riot. We asked the crowd to take no action against the supposed newsman and I'm sure they didn't."

"You're sure, Master Seldon?" said Russ. "Our information is that you left immediately after making your accusation. How could you witness what happened after you left?"

"I couldn't," said Seldon, "but let me ask you— Is the man dead? Is the man hurt?"

"The man has been interviewed. He denies he is an Imperial agent and we have no information that he is. He also claims he was handled roughly."

"He may well be lying in both respects," said Seldon. "I would suggest a Psychic Probe."

"That cannot be done on the victim of a crime," said Russ. "The sector government is very firm on that. It might do if you two, as the *criminals* in this case, each underwent a Psychic Probe. Would you like us to do that?"

Seldon and Dors exchanged glances for a moment, then Seldon said, "No, of course not."

"Of *course* not," repeated Russ with just a tinge of sarcasm in his voice, "but you're ready enough to suggest it for someone else."

The other officer, Astinwald, who had so far not said a word, smiled at this.

Russ said, "We also have information that two days ago you engaged in a knife fight in Billibotton and badly hurt a Dahlite citizen named"—he struck a button on his computer pad and studied the new page on the screen—"Elgin Marron."

Dors said, "Does your information tell you how the fight started?"

"That is irrelevant at the moment, Mistress. Do you deny that the fight took place?"

"Of course we don't deny the fight took place," said Seldon hotly, "but we deny that we in any way instigated *that*. We were *attacked*. Mistress Venabili was seized by this Marron and it was clear he was attempting to rape her. What happened afterward was pure self-defense. Or does Dahl condone rape?"

Russ said with very little intonation in his voice, "You say you were attacked? By how many?"

"Ten men."

"And you alone—with a woman—defended yourself against ten men?"

"Mistress Venabili and I defended ourselves. Yes."

"How is it, then, that neither of you shows any damage whatever? Are either of you cut or bruised where it doesn't show right now?"

"No, Officer."

"How is it, then, that in the fight of one—plus a woman—against ten, you are in no way hurt, but that the complainant, Elgin Marron, has been hospitalized with wounds and will require a skin transplant on his upper lip?"

"We fought well," said Seldon grimly.

"Unbelievably well. What would you say if I told you that three men have testified that you and your friend attacked Marron, unprovoked?"

"I would say that it belies belief that we should. I'm sure that Marron has a record as a brawler and knifeman. I tell you that there were ten there. Obviously, six refused to swear to a lie. Do the other three explain why they did not come to the help of their friend if they witnessed him under unprovoked attack and in danger of his life? It must be clear to you that they are lying."

"Do you suggest a Psychic Probe for them?"

"Yes. And before you ask, I still refuse to consider one for us."

Russ said, "We have also received information that yesterday, after leaving the scene of the riot, you consulted with one Davan, a known subversive who is wanted by the security police. Is that true?"

"You'll have to prove that without help from us," said Seldon. "We're not answering any further questions."

Russ put away his pad. "I'm afraid I must ask you to come with us to headquarters for further interrogation."

"I don't think that's necessary, Officer," said Seldon. "We are Out-worlders who have done nothing criminal. We have tried to avoid a newsman who was annoying us unduly, we tried to protect ourselves against rape and possible murder in a part of the sector known for crimi-nal behavior, and we've spoken to various Dahlites. We see nothing there to warrant our further questioning. It would come under the head-ing of harassment."

"We make these decisions," said Russ. "Not you. Will you please come with us?"

"No, we will not," said Dors.

"Watch out!" cried out Mistress Tisalver. "She's got two knives."

Officer Russ sighed and said, "Thank you, Mistress, but I know she does." He turned to Dors. "Do you know it's a serious crime to carry a knife without a permit in this sector? Do you have a permit?"

"No, Officer, I don't."

"It was clearly with an illegal knife, then, that you assaulted Marron? Do you realize that that greatly increases the seriousness of the crime?"

"It was no crime, Officer," said Dors. "Understand that. Marron had a knife as well and no permit, I am certain."

"We have no evidence to that effect and while Marron has knife wounds, neither of you have any."

"Of course he had a knife, Officer. If you don't know that every man in Billibotton and most men elsewhere in Dahl carry knives for which they probably don't have permits, then you're the only man in Dahl who doesn't know. There are shops here wherever you turn that sell knives openly. Don't you know that?"

Russ said, "It doesn't matter what I know or don't know in this re-spect. Nor does it matter whether other people are breaking the law or how many of them do. All that matters at this moment is that Mistress Venabili is breaking the anti-knife law. I must ask you to give up those knives to me right now, Mistress, and the two of you must then accom-pany me to headquarters."

Dors said, "In that case, take my knives away from me."

Russ sighed. "You must not think, Mistress, that knives are all the weapons there are in Dahl or that I need engage you in a knife fight. Both my partner and I have blasters that will destroy you in a moment, before you can drop your hands to your knife hilt—however fast you are. We won't use a blaster, of course, because we are not here to kill you.

However, each of us also has a neuronic whip, which we can use on you freely. I hope you won't ask for a demonstration. It won't kill you, do you permanent harm of any kind, or leave any marks—but the pain is excruciating. My partner is holding a neuronic whip on you right now. And here is mine. —Now, let us have your knives, Mistress Venabili."

There was a moment's pause and then Seldon said, "It's no use, Dors. Give him your knives."

And at that moment, a frantic pounding sounded at the door and they all heard a voice raised in high-pitched expostulation.

79.

Raych had not entirely left the neighborhood after he had walked them back to their apartment house.

He had eaten well while waiting for the interview with Davan to be done and later had slept a bit after finding a bathroom that more or less worked. He really had no place to go now that all that was done. He had a home of sorts and a mother who was not likely to be perturbed if he stayed away for a while. She never was.

He did not know who his father was and wondered sometimes if he really had one. He had been told he had to have one and the reasons for that had been explained to him crudely enough. Sometimes he wondered if he ought to believe so peculiar a story, but he did find the details titillating.

He thought of that in connection with the lady. She was an old lady, of course, but she was pretty and she could fight like a man—better than a man. It filled him with vague notions.

And she had offered to let him take a bath. He could swim in the Billibotton pool sometimes when he had some credits he didn't need for anything else or when he could sneak in. Those were the only times he got wet all over, but it was chilly and he had to wait to get dry.

Taking a bath was different. There would be hot water, soap, towels, and warm air. He wasn't sure what it would feel like, except that it would be nice if *she* was there.

He was walkway-wise enough to know of places where he could park himself in an alley off a walkway that would be near a bathroom and still be near enough to where she was, yet where he probably wouldn't be found and made to run away.

He spent the night thinking strange thoughts. What if he did learn to read and write? Could he do something with that? He wasn't sure what, but maybe *she* could tell him. He had vague ideas of being paid money to do things he didn't know how to do now, but he didn't know what those things might be. He would have to be told, but how do you get told?

If he stayed with the man and the lady, they might help. But why should they want him to stay with them?

He drowsed off, coming to later, not because the light was brightening, but because his sharp ears caught the heightening and deepening of sounds from the walkway as the activities of the day began.

He had learned to identify almost every variety of sound, because in the underground maze of Billibotton, if you wanted to survive with even a minimum of comfort, you had to be aware of things before you saw them. And there was something about the sound of a ground-car motor that he now heard that signaled danger to him. It had an official sound, a hostile sound—

He shook himself awake and stole quietly toward the walkway. He scarcely needed to see the Spaceship-and-Sun on the ground-car. Its lines were enough. He knew they had to be coming for the man and the lady because they had seen Davan. He did not pause to question his thoughts or to analyze them. He was off on a run, beating his way through the gathering life of the day.

He was back in less than fifteen minutes. The ground-car was still there and there were curious and cautious onlookers gazing at it from all sides and from a respectful distance. There would soon be more. He pounded his way up the stairs, trying to remember which door he should bang on. No time for the elevator.

He found the door—at least he thought he did—and he banged, shouting in a squeak, "Lady! Lady!"

He was too excited to remember her name, but he remembered part of the man's. "Hari!" he shouted. "Let me in."

The door opened and he rushed in—*tried* to rush in. The rough hand of an officer seized his arm. "Hold it, kid. Where do you think you're going?"

"Leggo! I ain't done nothin'." He looked about. "Hey, lady, what're they doin'?"

"Arresting us," said Dors grimly.

"What for?" said Raych, panting and struggling. "Hey, leggo, you Sunbadger. Don't go with him, lady. You don't have to go with him."

"You get out," said Russ, shaking the boy vehemently.

"No, I ain't. You ain't either, Sunbadger. My whole gang is coming. You ain't gettin' out, less'n you let these guys go."

"What whole gang?" said Russ, frowning.

"They're right outside now. Prob'ly takin' your ground-car apart. And they'll take *you* apart."

Russ turned toward his partner, "Call headquarters. Have them send out a couple of trucks with Macros."

"No!" shrieked Raych, breaking loose and rushing at Astinwald. "Don't call!"

Russ leveled his neuronic whip and fired.

Raych shrieked, grasped at his right shoulder, and fell down, wriggling madly.

Russ had not yet turned back to Seldon, when the latter, seizing him by the wrist, pushed the neuronic whip up in the air and then around and behind, while stamping on his foot to keep him relatively motionless. Hari could feel the shoulder dislocate, even while Russ emitted a hoarse, agonized yell.

Astinwald raised his blaster quickly, but Dors's left arm was around his shoulder and the knife in her right hand was at his throat.

"Don't move!" she said. "Move a millimeter, any part of you, and I cut you through your neck to the spine. —Drop the blaster. Drop it! And the neuronic whip."

Seldon picked up Raych, still moaning, and held him tightly. He turned to Tisalver and said, "There are people out there. Angry people. I'll have them in here and they'll break up everything you've got. They'll smash the walls. If you don't want that to happen, pick up those weapons and throw them into the next room. Take the weapons from the security officer on the floor and do the same. Quickly! Get your wife to help. She'll think twice next time before sending in complaints against innocent people. —Dors, this one on the floor won't do anything for a while. Put the other one out of action, but don't kill him."

"Right," said Dors. Reversing her knife, she struck him hard on the skull with the haft. He went to his knees.

She made a face. "I *hate* doing that."

337

"They fired at Raych," said Seldon, trying to mask his own sick feeling at what had happened.

They left the apartment hurriedly and, once out on the walkway, found it choked with people, almost all men, who raised a shout when they saw them emerge. They pushed in close and the smell of poorly washed humanity was overpowering.

Someone shouted, "Where are the Sunbadgers?"

"Inside," called out Dors piercingly. "Leave them alone. They'll be helpless for a while, but they'll get reinforcements, so get out of here fast."

"What about you?" came from a dozen throats.

"We're getting out too. We won't be back."

"I'll take care of them," shrilled Raych, struggling out of Seldon's arms and standing on his feet. He was rubbing his right shoulder madly. "I can walk. Lemme past."

The crowd opened for him and he said, "Mister, lady, come with me. —Fast!"

They were accompanied down the walkway by several dozen men and then Raych suddenly gestured at an opening and muttered, "In here, folks. I'll take ya to a place no one will ever find ya. Even Davan prob'ly don't know it. Only thing is, we got to go through the sewer levels. No one will see us there, but it's sort of stinky . . . know what I mean?"

"I imagine we'll survive," muttered Seldon.

And down they went along a narrow spiraling ramp and up rose the mephitic odors to greet them.

80.

Raych found them a hiding place. It had meant climbing up the metal rungs of a ladder and it had led them to a large loftlike room, the use of which Seldon could not imagine. It was filled with equipment, bulky and silent, the function of which also remained a mystery. The room was reasonably clean and free of dust and a steady draft of air wafted through that prevented the dust from settling and—more important—seemed to lessen the odor.

Raych seemed pleased. "Ain't this nice?" he demanded. He still rubbed his shoulder now and then and winced when he rubbed too hard.

"It could be worse," said Seldon. "Do you know what this place is used for, Raych?"

Raych shrugged or began to do so and winced. "I dunno," he said. Then he added with a touch of swagger, "Who cares?"

Dors, who had sat down on the floor after brushing it with her hand and then looking suspiciously at her palm, said, "If you want a guess, I think this is part of a complex that is involved in the detoxification and recycling of wastes. The stuff must surely end up as fertilizer."

"Then," said Seldon gloomily, "those who run the complex will be down here periodically and may come at any moment, for all we know."

"I been here before," said Raych. "I never saw no one here."

"I suppose Trantor is heavily automated wherever possible and if anything calls for automation it would be this treatment of wastes," said Dors. "We may be safe . . . for a while."

"Not for long. We'll get hungry and thirsty, Dors."

"I can get food and water for us," said Raych. "Ya got to know how to make out if you're an alley kid."

"Thank you, Raych," said Seldon absently, "but right now I'm not hungry." He sniffed. "I may never be hungry again."

"You will be," said Dors, "and even if you lose your appetite for a while, you'll get thirsty. At least elimination is no problem. We're practically living over what is clearly an open sewer."

There was silence for a while. The light was dim and Seldon wondered why the Trantorians didn't keep it dark altogether. But then it occurred to him that he had never encountered true darkness in any public area. It was probably a habit in an energy-rich society. Strange that a world of forty billion should be energy-rich, but with the internal heat of the planet to draw upon, to say nothing of solar energy and nuclear fusion plants in space, it was. In fact, come to think of it, there was no energy-poor planet in the Empire. Was there a time when technology had been so primitive that energy poverty was possible?

He leaned against a system of pipes through which—for all he knew—sewage ran. He drew away from the pipes as the thought occurred to him and he sat down next to Dors.

He said, "Is there any way we can get in touch with Chetter Hummin?"

Dors said, "As a matter of fact, I did send a message, though I hated to."

"You hated to?"

"My orders are to protect you. Each time I have to get in touch with him, it means I've failed."

Seldon regarded her out of narrowed eyes. "Do you have to be so compulsive, Dors? You can't protect me against the security officers of an entire sector."

"I suppose not. We can disable a few—"

"I know. We did. But they'll send out reinforcements . . . armored ground-cars . . . neuronic cannon . . . sleeping mist. I'm not sure what they have, but they're going to throw in their entire armory. I'm sure of it."

"You're probably right," said Dors, her mouth tightening.

"They won't find ya, lady," said Raych suddenly. His sharp eyes had moved from one to the other as they talked. "They never find Davan."

Dors smiled without joy and ruffled the boy's hair, then looked at the palm of her hand with a little dismay. She said, "I'm not sure if you ought to stay with us, Raych. I don't want them finding *you*."

"They won't find me and if I leave ya, who'll get ya food and water and who'll find ya new hidin' places, so the Sunbadgers'll never know where to look?"

"No, Raych, they'll find us. They don't really look too hard for Davan. He annoys them, but I suspect they don't take him seriously. Do you know what I mean?"

"You mean he's just a pain in the . . . the neck and they figure he ain't worth chasing all over the lot."

"Yes, that's what I mean. But you see, we hurt two of the officers very badly and they're not going to let us get away with *that*. If it takes their whole force—if they have to sweep through every hidden or unused corridor in the sector—they'll get us."

Raych said, "That makes me feel like . . . like *nothin'*. If I didn't run in there and get zapped, ya wouldn't have taken out them officers and ya wouldn't be in such trouble."

"No, sooner or later, we'd have—uh—taken them out. Who knows? We may have to take out a few more."

"Well, ya did it beautiful," said Raych. "If I hadn't been aching all over, I could've watched more and enjoyed it."

Seldon said, "It wouldn't do us any good to try to fight the entire

340

security system. The question is: What will they do to us once they have us? A prison sentence, surely."

"Oh no. If necessary, we'll have to appeal to the Emperor," put in Dors.

"The Emperor?" said Raych, wide-eyed. "You know the Emperor?"

Seldon waved at the boy. "Any Galactic citizen can appeal to the Emperor. —That strikes me as the wrong thing to do, Dors. Ever since Hummin and I left the Imperial Sector, we've been *evading* the Emperor."

"Not to the extent of being thrown into a Dahlite prison. The Imperial appeal will serve as a delay—in any case, a diversion—and perhaps in the course of that delay, we can think of something else."

"There's Hummin."

"Yes, there is," said Dors uneasily, "but we can't consider him the do-it-all. For one thing, even if my message reached him and even if he was able to rush to Dahl, how would he find us here? And, even if he did, what could he do against the entire Dahlite security force?"

"In that case," said Seldon. "We're going to have to think of something we can do before they find us."

Raych said, "If ya follow me, I can keep ya ahead of them. I know every place there is around here."

"You can keep us ahead of one person, but there'll be a great many, moving down any number of corridors. We'll escape one group and bump into another."

They sat in uncomfortable silence for a good while, each confronting what seemed to be a hopeless situation. Then Dors Venabili stirred and said in a tense, low whisper, "They're here. I hear them."

For a while, they strained, listening, then Raych sprang to his feet and hissed, "They comin' that way. We gotta go this way."

Seldon, confused, heard nothing at all, but would have been content to trust the others' superior hearing, but even as Raych began moving hastily and quietly away from the direction of the approaching tread, a voice rang out echoing against the sewer walls. "Don't move. Don't move."

And Raych said, "That's Davan. How'd *he* know we were here?"

"Davan?" said Seldon. "Are you sure?"

"Sure I'm sure. He'll help."

81.

Davan asked, "What happened?"

Seldon felt minimally relieved. Surely, the addition of Davan could scarcely count against the full force of the Dahl Sector, but, then again, he commanded a number of people who might create enough confusion—

He said, "You should know, Davan. I suspect that many of the crowd who were at Tisalver's place this morning were your people."

"Yes, a number were. The story is that you were being arrested and that you manhandled a squadron of Sunbadgers. But *why* were you being arrested?"

"Two," said Seldon, lifting two fingers. "Two Sunbadgers. And that's bad enough. Part of the reason we were being arrested was that we had gone to see you."

"That's not enough. The Sunbadgers don't bother with me much as a general thing." He added bitterly, "They underestimate me."

"Maybe," said Seldon, "but the woman from whom we rent our rooms reported us for having started a riot . . . over the newsman we ran into on our way to you. You know about that. With your people on the scene yesterday and again this morning and with two officers badly hurt, they may well decide to clean out these corridors—and that means *you* will suffer. I really am sorry. I had no intention or expectation of being the cause of any of this."

But Davan shook his head. "No, you don't know the Sunbadgers. That's not enough either. They don't want to clean us up. The sector would have to do something about us if they did. They're only too happy to let us rot in Billibotton and the other slums. No, they're after you— *you*. What have you done?"

Dors said impatiently, "We've done nothing and, in any case, what does it matter? If they're not after you and they *are* after us, they're going to come down here to flush us out. If you get in the way, you'll be in deep trouble."

"No, not me. I have friends—powerful friends," said Davan. "I told you that last night. And they can help you as well as me. When you refused to help us openly, I got in touch with them. They know who you are, Dr. Seldon. You're a famous man. They're in a position to talk to the

Mayor of Dahl and see to it that you are left alone, whatever you have done. But you'll have to be taken away—out of Dahl."

Seldon smiled. Relief flooded over him. He said, "You know someone powerful, do you, Davan? Someone who responds at once, who has the ability to talk the Dahl government out of taking drastic steps, and who can take us away? Good. I'm not surprised." He turned to Dors, smiling. "It's Mycogen all over again. How does Hummin do it?"

But Dors shook her head. "Too quick. —I don't understand."

Seldon said, "I believe he can do anything."

"I know him better than you do—and longer—and I *don't* believe that."

Seldon smiled, "Don't underestimate him." And then, as though anxious not to linger longer on that subject, he turned to Davan. "But how did you find us? Raych said you knew nothing about this place."

"He don't," shrilled Raych indignantly. "This place is all mine. I found it."

"I've never been here before," said Davan, looking about. "It's an interesting place. Raych is a corridor creature, perfectly at home in this maze."

"Yes, Davan, we gathered as much ourselves. But how did *you* find it?"

"A heat-seeker. I have a device that detects infra-red radiation, the particular thermal pattern that is given off at thirty-seven degrees Celsius. It will react to the presence of human beings and not to other heat sources. It reacted to you three."

Dors was frowning. "What good is that on Trantor, where there are human beings everywhere? They have them on other worlds, but—"

Davan said, "But not on Trantor. I know. Except that they are useful in the slums, in the forgotten, decaying corridors and alleyways."

"And where did you get it?" asked Seldon.

Davan said, "It's enough that I have it. —But we've got to get you away, Master Seldon. Too many people want you and I want my powerful friend to have you."

"Where is he, this powerful friend of yours?"

"He's approaching. At least a new thirty-seven-degree source is registering and I don't see that it can be anyone else."

Through the door strode a newcomer, but Seldon's glad exclamation died on his lips. It was not Chetter Hummin.

WYE

. . . . .

WYE— . . . A sector of the world-city of Trantor . . .
In the latter centuries of the Galactic Empire, Wye was the
strongest and stablest portion of the world-city. Its rulers
had long aspired to the Imperial throne, justifying that by
their descent from early Emperors. Under Mannix IV, Wye
was militarized and (Imperial authorities later claimed) was
planning a planet-wide coup . . .
ENCYCLOPEDIA GALACTICA

82.

The man who entered was tall and muscular. He had a long blond mustache that curled up at the tips and a fringe of hair that went down the sides of his face and under his chin, leaving the point of his chin and his lower lip smoothly bare and seeming a little moist. His head was so closely cropped and his hair was so light that, for one unpleasant moment, Seldon was reminded of Mycogen.

The newcomer wore what was unmistakably a uniform. It was red and white and about his waist was a wide belt decorated with silver studs.

His voice, when he spoke, was a rolling bass and its accent was not like any that Seldon had heard before. Most unfamiliar accents sounded uncouth in Seldon's experience, but this one seemed almost musical, perhaps because of the richness of the low tones.

"I am Sergeant Emmer Thalus," he rumbled in a slow succession of syllables. "I have come seeking Dr. Hari Seldon."

Seldon said, "I am he." In an aside to Dors, he muttered, "If Hummin couldn't come himself, he certainly sent a magnificent side of beef to represent him."

The sergeant favored Seldon with a stolid and slightly prolonged look. Then he said, "Yes. You have been described to me. Please come with me, Dr. Seldon."

Seldon said, "Lead the way."

The sergeant stepped backward. Seldon and Dors Venabili stepped forward.

The sergeant stopped and raised a large hand, palm toward Dors. "I have been instructed to take Dr. Hari Seldon with me. I have not been instructed to take anyone else."

For a moment, Seldon looked at him uncomprehendingly. Then his look of surprise gave way to anger. "It's quite impossible that you have been told that, Sergeant. Dr. Dors Venabili is my associate and my companion. She *must* come with me."

"That is not in accordance with my instructions, Doctor."

"I don't care about your instructions in any way, Sergeant Thalus. I do not budge without her."

"What's more," said Dors with clear irritation, *"my* instructions are to protect Dr. Seldon at all times. I cannot do that unless I am with him. Therefore, where he goes, I go."

The sergeant looked puzzled. "My instructions are strict that I see to it that no harm comes to you, Dr. Seldon. If you will not come voluntarily, I must carry you to my vehicle. I will try to do so gently."

He extended his two arms as though to seize Seldon by the waist and carry him off bodily.

Seldon skittered backward and out of reach. As he did so, the side of his right palm came down on the sergeant's right upper arm where the muscles were thinnest, so that he struck the bone.

The sergeant drew a sudden deep breath and seemed to shake himself a bit, but turned, face expressionless, and advanced again. Davan, watching, remained where he was, motionless, but Raych moved behind the sergeant.

Seldon repeated his palm stroke a second time, then a third, but now Sergeant Thalus, anticipating the blow, lowered his shoulder to catch it on hard muscle.

Dors had drawn her knives.

"Sergeant," she said forcefully. "Turn in this direction. I want you to understand I may be forced to hurt you severely if you persist in attempting to carry Dr. Seldon off against his will."

The sergeant paused, seemed to take in the slowly waving knives solemnly, then said, "It is not in my instructions to refrain from harming anyone but Dr. Seldon."

His right hand moved with surprising speed toward the neuronic whip in the holster at his hip. Dors moved as quickly forward, knives flashing.

Neither completed the movement.

Dashing forward, Raych had pushed at the sergeant's back with his left hand and withdrew the sergeant's weapon from its holster with his right. He moved away quickly, holding the neuronic whip in both hands now and shouting, "Hands up, Sergeant, or you're gonna get it!"

The sergeant whirled and a nervous look crossed his reddening face. It was the only moment that its stolidity had weakened. "Put that down, sonny," he growled. "You don't know how it works."

Raych howled, "I know about the safety. It's off and this thing can fire. And it will if you try to rush me."

The sergeant froze. He clearly knew how dangerous it was to have an excited twelve-year-old handling a powerful weapon.

Nor did Seldon feel much better. He said, "Careful, Raych. Don't shoot. Keep your finger off the contact."

"I ain't gonna let him rush me."

"He won't. —Sergeant, please don't move. Let's get something straight. You were told to take me away from here. Is that right?"

"That's right," said the sergeant, eyes somewhat protruding and firmly fixed on Raych (whose eyes were as firmly fixed on the sergeant).

"But you were not told to take anyone else. Is that right?"

"No, I was not, Doctor," said the sergeant firmly. Not even the threat of a neuronic whip was going to make him weasel. One could see that.

"Very well, but listen to me, Sergeant. Were you told *not* to take anyone else?"

"I just said—"

"No no. Listen, Sergeant. There's a difference. Were your instructions simply 'Take Dr. Seldon!'? Was that the entire order, with no mention of anyone else, or were the orders more specific? Were your orders as follows: 'Take Dr. Seldon and don't take anyone else'?"

The sergeant turned that over in his head, then he said, "I was told to take you, Dr. Seldon."

"Then there was no mention of anyone else, one way or the other, was there?"

Pause. "No."

"You were not told to take Dr. Venabili, but you were not told *not* to take Dr. Venabili either. Is that right?"

Pause. "Yes."

"So you can either take her or not take her, whichever you please?"

Long pause. "I suppose so."

"Now then, here's Raych, the young fellow who's got a neuronic whip pointing at you—*your* neuronic whip, remember—and he is anxious to use it."

"Yay!" shouted Raych.

"Not yet, Raych," said Seldon. "And here is Dr. Venabili with two knives that she can use very expertly and there's myself, who can, if I get the chance, break your Adam's apple with one hand so that you'll never speak above a whisper again. Now then, do you want to take Dr. Venabili or don't you want to? Your orders allow you to do either."

And finally the sergeant said in a beaten voice, "I will take the woman."

"And the boy, Raych."

"And the boy."

"Good. Have I your word of honor—your word of honor as a soldier —that you will do as you have just said . . . honestly?"

"You have my word of honor as a soldier," said the sergeant.

"Good. Raych, give back the whip. —Now. —Don't make me wait."

Raych, his face twisted into an unhappy grimace, looked at Dors, who hesitated and then slowly nodded her head. Her face was as unhappy as Raych's.

Raych held out the neuronic whip to the sergeant and said, "They're *makin'* me, ya big—" His last words were unintelligible.

Seldon said, "Put away your knives, Dors."

Dors shook her head, but put them away.

"Now, Sergeant?" said Seldon.

The sergeant looked at the neuronic whip, then at Seldon. He said, "You are an honorable man, Dr. Seldon, and my word of honor holds." With a military snap, he placed his neuronic whip in his holster.

Seldon turned to Davan and said, "Davan, please forget what you have seen here. We three are going voluntarily with Sergeant Thalus. You tell Yugo Amaryl when you see him that I will not forget him and that, once this is over and I am free to act, I will see that he gets into a University. And if there's anything reasonable I can ever do for your cause, Davan, I will. —Now, Sergeant, let's go."

83.

"Have you ever been in an air-jet before, Raych?" asked Hari Seldon.

Raych shook his head speechlessly. He was looking down at Upperside rushing beneath them with a mixture of fright and awe.

It struck Seldon again how much Trantor was a world of Expressways and tunnels. Even long trips were made underground by the general population. Air travel, however common it might be on the Outworlds, was a luxury on Trantor and an air-jet like this—

How had Hummin managed it? Seldon wondered.

He looked out the window at the rise and fall of the domes, at the general green in this area of the planet, the occasional patches of what were little less than jungles, the arms of the sea they occasionally passed over, with its leaden waters taking on a sudden all-too-brief sparkle when the sun peeped out momentarily from the heavy cloud layer.

An hour or so into the flight, Dors, who was viewing a new historical novel without much in the way of apparent enjoyment, clicked it off and said, "I wish I knew where we were going."

"If you can't tell," said Seldon, "then I certainly can't. You've been on Trantor longer than I have."

"Yes, but only on the inside," said Dors. "Out here, with only Upperside below me, I'm as lost as an unborn infant would be."

"Oh well. —Presumably, Hummin knows what he's doing."

"I'm sure he does," replied Dors rather tartly, "but that may have nothing to do with the present situation. Why do you continue to assume any of this represents his initiative?"

Seldon's eyebrows lifted. "Now that you ask, I don't know. I just assumed it. Why shouldn't this be his?"

"Because whoever arranged it didn't specify that I be taken along with you. I simply don't see Hummin forgetting my existence. And because he didn't come himself, as he did at Streeling and at Mycogen."

"You can't always expect him to, Dors. He might well be occupied. The astonishing thing is not that he didn't come on this occasion but that he did come on the previous ones."

"Assuming he didn't come himself, would he send a conspicuous and lavish flying palace like this?" She gestured around her at the large luxurious jet.

"It might simply have been available. And he might have reasoned that no one would expect something as noticeable as this to be carrying fugitives who were desperately trying to avoid detection. The well-known double-double-cross."

"Too well-known, in my opinion. And would he send an idiot like Sergeant Thalus in his place?"

"The sergeant is no idiot. He's simply been trained to complete obedience. With proper instructions, he could be utterly reliable."

"There you are, Hari. We come back to that. Why didn't he get proper instructions? It's inconceivable to me that Chetter Hummin would tell him to carry you out of Dahl and not say a word about me. Inconceivable."

And to that Seldon had no answer and his spirits sank.

Another hour passed and Dors said, "It looks as if it's getting colder outside. The green of Upperside is turning brown and I believe the heaters have turned on."

"What does that signify?"

"Dahl is in the tropic zone so obviously we're going either north or south—and a considerable distance too. If I had some notion in which direction the nightline was I could tell which."

Eventually, they passed over a section of shoreline where there was a rim of ice hugging the domes where they were rimmed by the sea.

And then, quite unexpectedly, the air-jet angled downward.

Raych screamed, "We're goin' to hit! We're goin' to smash up!"

Seldon's abdominal muscles tightened and he clutched the arms of his seat.

Dors seemed unaffected. She said, "The pilots up front don't seem alarmed. We'll be tunneling."

And, as she said so, the jet's wings swept backward and under it and, like a bullet, the air-jet entered a tunnel. Blackness swept back over them in an instant and a moment later the lighting system in the tunnel turned on. The walls of the tunnel snaked past the jet on either side.

"I don't suppose I'll ever be sure they know the tunnel isn't already occupied," muttered Seldon.

"I'm sure they had reassurance of a clear tunnel some dozens of kilometers earlier," said Dors. "At any rate, I presume this is the last stage of the journey and soon we'll know where we are."

She paused and then added, "And I further presume we won't like the knowledge when we have it."

84.

The air-jet sped out of the tunnel and onto a long runway with a roof so high that it seemed closer to true daylight than anything Seldon had seen since he had left the Imperial Sector.

They came to a halt in a shorter time than Seldon would have expected, but at the price of an uncomfortable pressure forward. Raych, in particular, was crushed against the seat before him and was finding it difficult to breath till Dors's hand on his shoulder pulled him back slightly.

Sergeant Thalus, impressive and erect, left the jet and moved to the rear, where he opened the door of the passenger compartment and helped the three out, one by one.

Seldon was last. He half-turned as he passed the sergeant, saying, "It was a pleasant trip, Sergeant."

A slow smile spread over the sergeant's large face and lifted his mustachioed upper lip. He touched the visor of his cap in what was half a salute and said, "Thank you again, Doctor."

They were then ushered into the backseat of a ground-car of lavish design and the sergeant himself pushed into the front seat and drove the vehicle with a surprisingly light touch.

They passed through wide roadways, flanked by tall, well-designed buildings, all glistening in broad daylight. As elsewhere on Trantor, they heard the distant drone of an Expressway. The walkways were crowded with what were, for the most part, well-dressed people. The surroundings were remarkably—almost excessively—clean.

Seldon's sense of security sank further. Dors's misgivings concerning their destination now seemed justified after all. He leaned toward her and said, "Do you think we are back in the Imperial Sector?"

She said, "No, the buildings are more rococo in the Imperial Sector and there's less Imperial parkishness to this sector—if you know what I mean."

"Then where are we, Dors?"

"We'll have to ask, I'm afraid, Hari."

It was not a long trip and soon they rolled into a car-bay that flanked an imposing four-story structure. A frieze of imaginary animals ran along the top, decorated with strips of warm pink stone. It was an impressive façade with a rather pleasing design.

Seldon said, *"That* certainly looks rococo enough."

Dors shrugged uncertainly.

Raych whistled and said in a failing attempt to sound unimpressed, "Hey, look at that fancy place."

Sergeant Thalus gestured to Seldon, clearly indicating that he was to follow. Seldon hung back and, also relying on the universal language of gesture, held out both arms, clearly including Dors and Raych.

The sergeant hesitated in a slightly hangdog fashion at the impressive pink doorway. His mustache almost seemed to droop.

Then he said gruffly, "All three of you, then. My word of honor holds. —Still, others may not feel obligated by my own obligation, you know."

Seldon nodded. "I hold you responsible for your own deeds only, Sergeant."

The sergeant was clearly moved and, for a moment, his face lightened as though he was considering the possibility of shaking Seldon's hand or expressing heartfelt his approval in some other way. He decided against it, however, and stepped onto the bottom step of the flight that led to the door. The stairs immediately began a stately upward movement.

Seldon and Dors stepped after him at once and kept their balance without much trouble. Raych, who was momentarily staggered in surprise, jumped onto the moving stairs after a short run, shoved both hands into his pockets, and whistled carelessly.

The door opened and two women stepped out, one on either side in symmetrical fashion. They were young and attractive. Their dresses, belted tightly about the waist and reaching nearly to their ankles, fell in crisp pleats and rustled when they walked. Both had brown hair that was coiled in thick plaits on either side of their heads. (Seldon found it attractive, but wondered how long it took them each morning to arrange it just so. He had not been aware of so elaborate a coiffure on the women they had passed in the streets.)

The two women stared at the newcomers with obvious contempt. Seldon was not surprised. After the day's events, he and Dors looked almost as disreputable as Raych.

Yet the women managed to bow decorously and then made a half-turn and gestured inward in perfect unison and with symmetry carefully maintained. (Did they rehearse these things?) It was clear that the three were to enter.

They stepped through an elaborate room, cluttered with furniture and decorative items whose use Seldon did not readily understand. The floor was light-colored, springy, and glowed with luminescence. Seldon noted with some embarrassment that their footwear left dusty marks upon it.

And then an inner door was flung open and yet another woman emerged. She was distinctly older than the first two (who sank slowly as she came in, crossing their legs symmetrically as they did so in a way that made Seldon marvel that they could keep their balance; it undoubtedly took a deal of practice).

Seldon wondered if he too was expected to display some ritualized form of respect, but since he hadn't the faintest notion of what this might consist of, he merely bowed his head slightly. Dors remained standing erect and, it seemed to Seldon, did so with disdain. Raych was staring open-mouthed in all directions and looked as though he didn't even see the woman who had just entered.

She was plump—not fat, but comfortably padded. She wore her hair precisely as the young ladies did and her dress was in the same style, but much more richly ornamented—too much so to suit Seldon's aesthetic notions.

She was clearly middle-aged and there was a hint of gray in her hair, but the dimples in her cheeks gave her the appearance of having rather more than a dash of youth. Her light brown eyes were merry and on the whole she looked more motherly than old.

She said, "How are you? All of you." (She showed no surprise at the presence of Dors and Raych, but included them easily in her greeting.) "I've been waiting for you for some time and almost had you on Upperside at Streeling. You are Dr. Hari Seldon, whom I've been looking forward to meeting. You, I think, must be Dr. Dors Venabili, for you had been reported to be in his company. This young man I fear I do *not* know, but I am pleased to see him. But we must not spend our time talking, for I'm sure you would like to rest first."

"And bathe, Madam," said Dors rather forcefully, "Each of us could use a thorough shower."

"Yes, certainly," said the woman, "and a change in clothing. Especially the young man." She looked down at Raych without any of the look of contempt and disapproval that the two young women had shown.

She said, "What is your name, young man?"

"Raych," said Raych in a rather choked and embarrassed voice. He then added experimentally, "Missus."

"What an odd coincidence," said the woman, her eyes sparkling. "An omen, perhaps. My own name is Rashelle. Isn't that odd? —But come. We shall take care of you all. Then there will be plenty of time to have dinner and to talk."

"Wait, Madam," said Dors. "May I ask where we are?"

"Wye, dear. And please call me Rashelle, as you come to feel more friendly. I am always at ease with informality."

Dors stiffened. "Are you surprised that we ask? Isn't it natural that we should want to know where we are?"

Rashelle laughed in a pleasant, tinkling manner. "Really, Dr. Venabili, something must be done about the name of this place. I was not asking a question but making a statement. You asked where you were and I did not ask you why. I told you, 'Wye.' You are in the Wye Sector."

"In Wye?" said Seldon forcibly.

"Yes indeed, Dr. Seldon. We've wanted you from the day you addressed the Decennial Convention and we are so glad to have you now."

85.

Actually, it took a full day to rest and unstiffen, to wash and get clean, to obtain new clothes (satiny and rather loose, in the style of Wye), and to sleep a good deal.

It was during the second evening in Wye that there was the dinner that Madam Rashelle had promised.

The table was a large one—too large, considering that there were only four dining: Hari Seldon, Dors Venabili, Raych, and Rashelle. The walls and ceiling were softly illuminated and the colors changed at a rate that caught the eye but not so rapidly as in any way to discommode the mind. The very tablecloth, which was not cloth (Seldon had not made up his mind what it might be), seemed to sparkle.

The servers were many and silent and when the door opened it seemed to Seldon that he caught a glimpse of soldiers, armed and at the ready, outside. The room was a velvet glove, but the iron fist was not far distant.

Rashelle was gracious and friendly and had clearly taken a particular liking to Raych, who, she insisted, was to sit next to her.

Raych—scrubbed, polished, and shining, all but unrecognizable in his new clothes, with his hair clipped, cleaned, and brushed—scarcely dared to say a word. It was as though he felt his grammar no longer fit his appearance. He was pitifully ill at ease and he watched Dors carefully as she switched from utensil to utensil, trying to match her exactly in every respect.

The food was tasty but spicy—to the point where Seldon could not recognize the exact nature of the dishes.

Rashelle, her plump face made happy by her gentle smile and her fine teeth gleaming white, said, "You may think we have Mycogenian additives in the food, but we do not. It is all homegrown in Wye. There is no sector on the planet more self-sufficient than Wye. We labor hard to keep that so."

Seldon nodded gravely and said, "Everything you have given us is first-rate, Rashelle. We are much obliged to you."

And yet within himself he thought the food was not quite up to Mycogenian standards and he felt moreover, as he had earlier muttered to Dors, that he was celebrating his own defeat. Or Hummin's defeat, at any rate, and that seemed to him to be the same thing.

After all, he had been captured by Wye, the very possibility that had so concerned Hummin at the time of the incident Upperside.

Rashelle said, "Perhaps, in my role as hostess, I may be forgiven if I ask personal questions. Am I correct in assuming that you three do not represent a family; that you, Hari, and you, Dors, are not married and that Raych is not your son?"

"The three of us are not related in any way," said Seldon. "Raych was born on Trantor, I on Helicon, Dors on Cinna."

"And how did you all meet, then?"

Seldon explained briefly and with as little detail as he could manage. "There's nothing romantic or significant in the meetings," he added.

"Yet I am given to understand that you raised difficulties with my personal aide, Sergeant Thalus, when he wanted to take only you out of Dahl."

Seldon said gravely, "I had grown fond of Dors and Raych and did not wish to be separated from them."

Rashelle smiled and said, "You are a sentimental man, I see."

"Yes, I am. Sentimental. And puzzled too."

"Puzzled?"

"Why yes. And since you were so kind as to ask personal questions of us, may I ask one as well?"

"Of course, my dear Hari. Ask anything you please."

"When we first arrived, you said that Wye has wanted me from the day I addressed the Decennial Convention. For what reason might that be?"

"Surely, you are not so simple as not to know. We want you for your psychohistory."

"That much I do understand. But what makes you think that having me means you have psychohistory?"

"Surely, you have not been so careless as to lose it."

"Worse, Rashelle. I have never had it."

Rashelle's face dimpled. "But you said you had it in your talk. Not that I understood your talk. I am not a mathematician. I hate numbers. But I have in my employ mathematicians who have explained to me what it is you said."

"In that case, my dear Rashelle, you must listen more closely. I can well imagine they have told you that I have proven that psychohistorical predictions are conceivable, but surely they must also have told you that they are not practical."

"I can't believe that, Hari. The very next day, you were called into an audience with that pseudo-Emperor, Cleon."

"The *pseudo*-Emperor?" murmured Dors ironically.

"Why yes," said Rashelle as though she was answering a serious question. "Pseudo-Emperor. He has no true claim to the throne."

"Rashelle," said Seldon, brushing that aside a bit impatiently, "I told Cleon exactly what I have just told you and he let me go."

Now Rashelle did not smile. A small edge crept into her voice. "Yes, he let you go the way the cat in the fable lets a mouse go. He has been pursuing you ever since—in Streeling, in Mycogen, in Dahl. He would pursue you here if he dared. But come now—our serious talk is too serious. Let us enjoy ourselves. Let us have music."

And at her words, there suddenly sounded a soft but joyous instrumental melody. She leaned toward Raych and said softly, "My boy, if you are not at ease with the fork, use your spoon or your fingers. I won't mind."

Raych said, "Yes, mum," and swallowed hard, but Dors caught his eye and her lips silently mouthed: "Fork."

He remained with his fork.

Dors said, "The music is lovely, Madam"—she pointedly rejected the familiar form of address—"but it must not be allowed to distract us. There is the thought in my mind that the pursuer in all those places might have been in the employ of the Wye Sector. Surely, you would not be so well acquainted with events if Wye were not the prime mover."

Rashelle laughed aloud. "Wye has its eyes and ears everywhere, of course, but we were not the pursuers. Had we been, you would have been picked up without fail—as you were in Dahl finally when, indeed, we *were* the pursuers. When, however, there is a pursuit that fails, a grasping hand that misses, you may be sure that it is Demerzel."

"Do you think so little of Demerzel?" murmured Dors.

"Yes. Does that surprise you? We have beaten him."

"You? Or the Wye Sector?"

"The sector, of course, but insofar as Wye is the victor, then I am the victor."

"How strange," said Dors. "There seems to be a prevalent opinion throughout Trantor that the inhabitants of Wye have nothing to do with victory, with defeat, or with anything else. It is felt that there is but one will and one fist in Wye and that is that of the Mayor. Surely, you—or any other Wyan—weigh nothing in comparison."

Rashelle smiled broadly. She paused to look at Raych benevolently and to pinch his cheek, then said, "If you believe that our Mayor is an autocrat and that there is but one will that sways Wye, then perhaps you are right. But, even so, I can still use the personal pronoun, for my will is of account."

"Why yours?" said Seldon.

"Why not?" said Rashelle as the servers began clearing the table. "*I* am the Mayor of Wye."

86.

It was Raych who was the first to react to the statement. Quite forgetting the cloak of civility that sat upon him so uncomfortably, he laughed raucously and said, "Hey, lady, ya can't be Mayor. Mayors is guys."

Rashelle looked at him good-naturedly and said in a perfect imitation of his tone of voice, "Hey, kid, some Mayors is guys and some Mayors is dames. Put that under your lid and let it bubble."

Raych's eyes protruded and he seemed stunned. Finally he managed to say, "Hey, ya talk regular, lady."

"Sure thing. Regular as ya want," said Rashelle, still smiling.

Seldon cleared his throat and said, "That's quite an accent you have, Rashelle."

Rashelle tossed her head slightly. "I haven't had occasion to use it in many years, but one never forgets. I once had a friend, a good friend, who was a Dahlite—when I was very young." She sighed. "He didn't speak that way, of course—he was quite intelligent—but he could do so if he wished and he taught me. It was exciting to talk so with him. It created a world that excluded our surroundings. It was wonderful. It was also impossible. My father made that plain. And now along comes this young rascal, Raych, to remind me of those long-ago days. He has the accent, the eyes, the impudent cast of countenance, and in six years or so he will be a delight and terror to the young women. Won't you, Raych?"

Raych said, "I dunno, lady—uh, mum."

"I'm sure you will and you will come to look very much like my . . . old friend and it will be much more comfortable for me not to see you then. And now, dinner's over and it's time for you to go to your room, Raych. You can watch holovision for a while if you wish. I don't suppose you read."

Raych reddened. "I'm gonna read someday. Master Seldon says I'm gonna."

"Then I'm sure you will."

A young woman approached Raych, curtsying respectfully in Rashelle's direction. Seldon had not seen the signal that had summoned her.

Raych said, "Can't I stay with Master Seldon and Missus Venabili?"

"You'll see them later," said Rashelle gently, "but Master and Missus and I have to talk right now—so you must go."

Dors mouthed a firm "Go!" at Raych and with a grimace the boy slid out of his chair and followed the attendant.

Rashelle turned to Seldon and Dors once Raych was gone and said, "The boy will be safe, of course, and treated well. Please have no fears about that. And I will be safe too. As my woman approached just now, so will a dozen armed men—and much more rapidly—when summoned. I want you to understand that."

Seldon said evenly, "We are in no way thinking of attacking you, Rashelle—or must I now say, 'Madam Mayor'?"

"Still Rashelle. I am given to understand that you are a wrestler of sorts, Hari, and you, Dors, are very skillful with the knives we have removed from your room. I don't want you to rely uselessly on your skills, since I want Hari alive, unharmed, and friendly."

"It is quite well understood, Madam Mayor," said Dors, her lack of friendship uncompromised, "that the ruler of Wye, now and for the past forty years, is Mannix, Fourth of that Name, and that he is still alive and in full possession of his faculties. Who, then, are you really?"

"Exactly who I say I am, Dors. Mannix IV is my father. He is, as you say, still alive and in possession of his faculties. In the eyes of the Emperor and of all the Empire, he is Mayor of Wye, but he is weary of the strains of power and is willing, at last, to let them slip into my hands, which are just as willing to receive them. I am his only child and I was brought up all my life to rule. My father is therefore Mayor in law and name, but I am Mayor in fact. It is to me, now, that the armed forces of Wye have sworn allegiance and in Wye that is all that counts."

Seldon nodded. "Let it be as you say. But even so, whether it is Mayor Mannix IV or Mayor Rashelle I—it *is* the First, I suppose—there is no purpose in your holding me. I have told you that I don't have a workable psychohistory and I do not think that either I or anyone else will ever have one. I have told that to the Emperor. I am of no use either to you or to him."

Rashelle said, "How naïve you are. Do you know the history of the Empire?"

Seldon shook his head. "I have recently come to wish that I knew it much better."

Dors said dryly, "*I* know Imperial history quite well, though the pre-Imperial age is my specialty, Madam Mayor. But what does it matter whether we do or do not?"

"If you know your history, you know that the House of Wye is ancient and honorable and is descended from the Dacian dynasty."

Dors said, "The Dacians ruled five thousand years ago. The number of their descendants in the hundred and fifty generations that have lived and died since then may number half the population of the Galaxy—if all genealogical claims, however outrageous, are accepted."

"Our genealogical claims, Dr. Venabili"—Rashelle's tone of voice was, for the first time, cold and unfriendly and her eyes flashed like steel —"are not outrageous. They are fully documented. The House of Wye has maintained itself consistently in positions of power through all those generations and there have been occasions when *we* have held the Imperial throne and have ruled as Emperors."

"The history book-films," said Dors, "usually refer to the Wye rulers as 'anti-Emperors,' never recognized by the bulk of the Empire."

"It depends on who writes the history book-films. In the future, we will, for the throne which has been ours will be ours again."

"To accomplish that, you must bring about civil war."

"There won't be much risk of that," said Rashelle. She was smiling again. "That is what I must explain to you because I want Dr. Seldon's help in preventing such a catastrophe. My father, Mannix IV, has been a man of peace all his life. He has been loyal to whomever it might be that ruled in the Imperial Palace and he has kept Wye a prosperous and strong pillar of the Trantorian economy for the good of all the Empire."

"I don't know that the Emperor has ever trusted him any the more for all that," said Dors.

"I'm sure that is so," said Rashelle calmly, "for the Emperors that have occupied the Palace in my father's time have known themselves to be usurpers of a usurping line. Usurpers cannot afford to trust the true rulers. And yet my father has kept the peace. He has, of course, developed and trained a magnificent security force to maintain the peace, prosperity, and stability of the sector and the Imperial authorities have allowed this because they wanted Wye peaceful, prosperous, stable—and loyal."

"But is it loyal?" said Dors.

"To the true Emperor, of course," said Rashelle, "and we have now reached the stage where our strength is such that we can take over the government quickly—in a lightning stroke, in fact—and before one can say 'civil war' there will be a true Emperor—or Empress, if you prefer— and Trantor will be as peaceful as before."

Dors shook her head. "May I enlighten you? As a historian?"

"I am always willing to listen." And she inclined her head ever so slightly toward Dors.

"Whatever size your security force may be, however well-trained and well-equipped, they cannot possibly equal in size and strength the Imperial forces backed by twenty-five million worlds."

"Ah, but you have put your finger on the usurper's weakness, Dr. Venabili. There are twenty-five million worlds, with the Imperial forces scattered over them. Those forces are thinned out over incalculable space, under uncounted officers, none of them particularly ready for any action outside their own Provinces, many ready for action in their own interest rather than in the Empire's. Our forces, on the other hand, are all here, all on Trantor. We can act and conclude before the distant generals and admirals can get it through their heads that they are needed."

"But that response will come—and with irresistible force."

"Are you certain of that?" said Rashelle. "We will be in the Palace. Trantor will be ours and at peace. Why should the Imperial forces stir when, by minding their own business, each petty military leader can have his own world to rule, his own Province?"

"But is that what you want?" asked Seldon wonderingly. "Are you telling me that you look forward to ruling over an Empire that will break up into splinters?"

Rashelle said, "That is exactly right. I would rule over Trantor, over its outlying space settlements, over the few nearby planetary systems that are part of the Trantorian Province. I would much rather be Emperor of Trantor than Emperor of the Galaxy."

"You would be satisfied with Trantor only," said Dors in tones of the deepest disbelief.

"Why not?" said Rashelle, suddenly ablaze. She leaned forward eagerly, both hands pressed palms-down on the table. "That is what my father has been planning for forty years. He is only clinging to life now to witness its fulfillment. Why do we need millions of worlds, distant worlds that mean nothing to us, that weaken us, that draw our forces far away from us into meaningless cubic parsecs of space, that drown us in administrative chaos, that ruin us with their endless quarrels and problems when they are all distant nothings as far as we are concerned? Our own populous world—our own planetary city—is Galaxy enough for us. We have all we need to support ourselves. As for the rest of the Galaxy, let it splinter. Every petty militarist can have his own splinter. They needn't fight. There will be enough for all."

"But they *will* fight, just the same," said Dors. "Each will refuse to be satisfied with his Province. Each will fear that his neighbor is not satisfied with *his* Province. Each will feel insecure and will dream of Galactic rule as the only guarantee of safety. This is certain, Madam Empress of Nothing. There will be endless wars into which you and Trantor will be inevitably drawn—to the ruin of all."

Rashelle said with clear contempt, "So it might seem, if one could see no farther than you do, if one relied on the ordinary lessons of history."

"What is there to see farther?" retorted Dors. "What is one to rely on beyond the lessons of history?"

"What lies beyond?" said Rashelle. "Why, *he!*"

And her arm shot outward, her index finger jabbing toward Seldon.

"Me?" said Seldon. "I have already told you that psychohistory—"

Rashelle said, "Do not repeat what you have already said, my good Dr. Seldon. We gain nothing by that. —Do you think, Dr. Venabili, that my father was never aware of the danger of endless civil war? Do you think he did not bend his powerful mind to thinking of some way to prevent that? He has been prepared at any time these last ten years to take over the Empire in a day. It needed only the assurance of security beyond victory."

"Which you can't have," said Dors.

"Which we had the moment we heard of Dr. Seldon's paper at the Decennial Convention. I saw at once that that was what we needed. My father was too old to see the significance at once. When I explained it, however, he saw it too and it was then that he formally transferred his power to me. So it is to you, Hari, that I owe my position and to you I will owe my greater position in the future."

"I keep telling you that it cannot—" began Seldon with deep annoyance.

"It is not important what can or cannot be done. What is important is what people will or will not believe can be done. They will *believe* you, Hari, when you tell them the psychohistoric prediction is that Trantor can rule itself and that the Provinces can become Kingdoms that will live together in peace."

"I will make no such prediction," said Seldon, "in the absence of true psychohistory. I won't play the charlatan. If you want something like that, *you* say it."

"Now, Hari. They won't believe me. It's you they will believe. The great mathematician. Why not oblige them?"

"As it happens," said Seldon, "the Emperor also thought to use me as a source of self-serving prophecies. I refused to do it for him, so do you think I will agree to do it for you?"

3 6 4

Rashelle was silent for a while and when she spoke again her voice had lost its intense excitement and became almost coaxing.

"Hari," she said, "think a little of the difference between Cleon and myself. What Cleon undoubtedly wanted from you was propaganda to preserve his throne. It would be useless to give him that, for the throne can't be preserved. Don't you know that the Galactic Empire is in a state of decay, that it cannot endure for much longer? Trantor itself is slowly sliding into ruin because of the ever-increasing weight of administering twenty-five million worlds. What's ahead of us is breakup and civil war, no matter what you do for Cleon."

Seldon said, "I have heard something like this said. It may even be true, but what then?"

"Well then, help it break into fragments *without* any war. Help me take Trantor. Help me establish a firm government over a realm small enough to be ruled efficiently. Let me give freedom to the rest of the Galaxy, each portion to go its own way according to its own customs and cultures. The Galaxy will become a working whole again through the free agencies of trade, tourism, and communication and the fate of cracking into disaster under the present rule of force that barely holds it together will be averted. My ambition is moderate indeed; one world, not millions; peace, not war; freedom, not slavery. Think about it and help me."

Seldon said, "Why should the Galaxy believe me any more than they would believe you? They don't know me and which of our fleet commanders will be impressed by the mere word 'psychohistory'?"

"You won't be believed *now*, but I don't ask for action now. The House of Wye, having waited thousands of years, can wait thousands of days more. Cooperate with me and I will make your name famous. I will make the promise of psychohistory glow through all the worlds and at the proper time, when I judge the movement to be the chosen moment, you will pronounce your prediction and we will strike. Then, in a twinkling of history, the Galaxy will exist under a New Order that will render it stable and happy for eons. Come now, Hari, can you refuse me?"

OVERTHROW

. . . . .

THALUS, EMMER— . . . A sergeant in the armed security forces of the Wye Sector of ancient Trantor . . .
. . . Aside from these totally unremarkable vital statistics, nothing is known of the man except that on one occasion he held the fate of the Galaxy in his fist.

ENCYCLOPEDIA GALACTICA

87.

Breakfast the next morning was served in an alcove near the rooms of the captured three and it was luxurious indeed. There certainly was a considerable variety to the food and more than enough of everything.

Seldon sat at the breakfast table with a mound of spicy sausages before him, totally ignoring Dors Venabili's gloomy predictions concerning stomachs and colic.

Raych said, "The dame . . . the Madam Mayor said when she came to see me last night—"

"She came to see you?" said Seldon.

"Yeah. She said she wanted to make sure I was comfortable. She said when she had a chance she would take me to a zoo."

"A zoo?" Seldon looked at Dors. "What kind of zoo can they have on Trantor? Cats and dogs?"

"There are some aboriginal animals," said Dors, "and I imagine they import some aboriginals from other worlds and there are also the shared animals that all the worlds have—other worlds having more than Trantor, of course. As a matter of fact, Wye has a famous zoo, probably the best on the planet after the Imperial Zoo itself."

Raych said, "She's a nice old lady."

"Not *that* old," said Dors, "but she's certainly feeding us well."

"There's that," admitted Seldon.

When breakfast was over, Raych left to go exploring.

Once they had retired to Dors's room, Seldon said with marked discontent, "I don't know how long we'll be left to ourselves. She's obviously plotted ways of preoccupying our time."

Dors said, "Actually, we have little to complain of at the moment. We're much more comfortable here than we were either in Mycogen or Dahl."

Seldon said, "Dors, you're not being won over by that woman, are you?"

"Me? By Rashelle? Of course not. How can you possibly think so?"

"Well, you're comfortable. You're well-fed. It would be natural to relax and accept what fortune brings."

"Yes, very natural. And why not do that?"

"Look, you were telling me last night about what's going to happen if she wins out. I may not be much of a historian myself, but I am willing to take your word for it and, actually, it makes sense—even to a nonhistorian. The Empire will shatter and its shards will be fighting each other for . . . for . . . indefinitely. She must be stopped."

"I agree," said Dors. "She must be. What I fail to see is how we can manage to do that little thing right at this moment." She looked at Seldon narrowly. "Hari, you didn't sleep last night, did you?"

"Did *you?*" It was apparent *he* had not.

Dors stared at him, a troubled look clouding her face. "Have you lain awake thinking of Galactic destruction because of what I said?"

"That and some other things. Is it possible to reach Chetter Hummin?" This last was said in a whisper.

Dors said, "I tried to reach him when we first had to flee arrest in Dahl. He didn't come. I'm sure he received the message, but he didn't come. It may be that, for any of a number of reasons, he just couldn't come to us, but when he can he will."

"Do you suppose something has happened to him?"

"No," said Dors patiently. "I don't think so."

"How can you know?"

"The word would somehow get to me. I'm sure of it. And the word hasn't gotten to me."

Seldon frowned and said, "I'm not as confident as you are about all this. In fact, I'm not confident at all. Even if Hummin came, what can he do in this case? He can't fight all of Wye. If they have, as Rashelle claims, the best-organized army on Trantor, what will he be able to do against it?"

"There's no point in discussing that. Do you suppose you can convince Rashelle—bang it into her head somehow—that you don't have psychohistory?"

"I'm sure she's aware that I don't have it and that I'm not going to get it for many years—if at all. But she'll *say* I have psychohistory and if she does that skillfully enough, people will believe her and eventually they will act on what she says my predictions and pronouncements are—even if I don't say a word."

"Surely, that will take time. She won't build you up overnight. Or in a week. To do it properly, it might take her a year."

Seldon was pacing the length of the room, turning sharply on his heel and striding back. "That might be so, but I don't know. There would be pressure on her to do things quickly. She doesn't strike me as the kind of woman who has cultivated the habit of patience. And her old father, Mannix IV, would be even more impatient. He must feel the nearness of death and if he's worked for this all his life, he would much prefer to see it done a week before his death rather than a week after. Besides—" Here he paused and looked around the empty room.

"Besides what?"

"Well, we *must* have our freedom. You see, I've solved the psychohistory problem."

Dors's eyes widened. "You have it! You've worked it out."

"Not worked it out in the full sense. That might take decades . . . centuries, for all I know. But I now know it's practical, not just theoretical. I know it can be done so I must have the time, the peace, the facilities to work at it. The Empire must be held together till I—or possibly my successors—will learn how best to keep it so or how to minimize the disaster if it does split up despite us. It was the thought of having a beginning to my task and of not being able to work at it, that kept me up last night."

88.

It was their fifth day in Wye and in the morning Dors was helping Raych into a formal costume that neither was quite familiar with.

Raych looked at himself dubiously in the holomirror and saw a reflected image that faced him with precision, imitating all his motions but without any inversion of left and right. Raych had never used a holomirror before and had been unable to keep from trying to feel it, then laughing, almost with embarrassment, when his hand passed through it while the image's hand poked ineffectually at his real body.

He said at last, "I look funny."

He studied his tunic, which was made of a very pliant material, with a thin filigreed belt, then passed his hands up a stiff collar that rose like a cup past his ears on either side.

"My head looks like a ball inside a bowl."

Dors said, "But this is the sort of thing rich children wear in Wye. Everyone who sees you will admire you and envy you."

"With my hair all stuck down?"

"Certainly. You'll wear this round little hat."

"It'll make my head more like a ball."

"Then don't let anyone kick it. Now, remember what I told you. Keep your wits about you and don't act like a kid."

"But I *am* a kid," he said, looking up at her with a wide-eyed innocent expression.

"I'm surprised to hear you say that," said Dors. "I'm sure you think of yourself as a twelve-year-old adult."

Raych grinned. "Okay. I'll be a good spy."

"That's not what I'm telling you to be. Don't take chances. Don't sneak behind doors to listen. If you get caught at it, you're no good to anyone—especially not to yourself."

"Aw, c'mon, Missus, what do ya think I am? A kid or somethin'?"

"You just said you were, didn't you, Raych? You just listen to everything that's said without seeming to. And remember what you hear. And tell us. That's simple enough."

"Simple enough for you to say, Missus Venabili," said Raych with a grin, "and simple enough for me to do."

"And be careful."

Raych winked. "You bet."

A flunky (as coolly impolite as only an arrogant flunky can be) came to take Raych to where Rashelle was awaiting him.

Seldon looked after them and said thoughtfully, "He probably won't see the zoo, he'll be listening so carefully. I'm not sure it's right to thrust a boy into danger like that."

"Danger? I doubt it. Raych was brought up in the slums of Billibotton, remember. I suspect he has more alley smarts than you and I put together. Besides, Rashelle is fond of him and will interpret everything he does in his favor. —Poor woman."

"Are you actually *sorry* for her, Dors?"

"Do you mean that she's not worth sympathy because she's a Mayor's daughter and considers herself a Mayor in her own right—and because she's intent on destroying the Empire? Perhaps you're right, but even so there are some aspects of her for which one might show some sympathy. For instance, she's had an unhappy love affair. That's pretty evident. Undoubtedly, her heart was broken—for a time, at least."

Seldon said, "Have you ever had an unhappy love affair, Dors?"

Dor considered for a moment or two, then said, "Not really. I'm too involved with my work to get a broken heart."

"I thought as much."

"Then why did you ask?"

"I might have been wrong."

"How about you?"

Seldon seemed uneasy. "As a matter of fact, yes. I have spared the time for a broken heart. Badly cracked, anyway."

"I thought as much."

"Then why did *you* ask?"

"Not because I thought I might be wrong, I promise you. I just wanted to see if you would lie. You didn't and I'm glad."

There was a pause and then Seldon said, "Five days have passed and nothing has happened."

"Except that we are being treated well, Hari."

"If animals could think, they'd think they were being treated well when they were only being fattened for the slaughter."

"I admit she's fattening the Empire for the slaughter."

"But when?"

"I presume when she's ready."

"She boasted she could complete the coup in a day and the impression I got was that she could do that on *any* day."

"Even if she could, she would want to make sure that she could cripple the Imperial reaction and that might take time."

"How much time? She plans to cripple the reaction by using me, but she is making no effort to do so. There is no sign that she's trying to build up my importance. Wherever I go in Wye I'm unrecognized. There are no Wyan crowds gathering to cheer me. There's nothing on the news holocasts."

Dors smiled. "One would almost suppose that your feelings are hurt at not being made famous. You're naïve, Hari. Or not a historian, which is the same thing. I think you had better be more pleased that the study of psychohistory will be bound to make a historian of you than that it may save the Empire. If all human beings understood history, they might cease making the same stupid mistakes over and over."

"In what way am I naïve?" asked Seldon, lifting his head and staring down his nose at her.

"Don't be offended, Hari. I think it's one of your attractive features, actually."

"I know. It arouses your maternal instincts and you *have* been asked to take care of me. But in what way am I naïve?"

"In thinking that Rashelle would try to propagandize the population of the Empire, generally, into accepting you as seer. She would accomplish nothing in that way. Quadrillions of people are hard to move quickly. There is social and psychological inertia, as well as physical inertia. And, by coming out into the open, she would simply alert Demerzel."

"Then what is she doing?"

"My guess is that the information about you—suitably exaggerated and glorified—is going out to a crucial few. It is going to those Viceroys of sectors, those admirals of fleets, those people of influence she feels look kindly upon her—or grimly upon the Emperor. A hundred or so of those who might rally to her side will manage to confuse the Loyalists just long enough to allow Rashelle the First to set up her New Order firmly enough to beat off whatever resistance might develop. At least, I imagine that is how she reasons."

"And yet we haven't heard from Hummin."

"I'm sure he must be doing something just the same. This is too important to ignore."

"Has it occurred to you that he might be dead?"

"That's a possibility, but I don't think so. If he was, the news would reach me."

"Here?"

"Even here."

Seldon raised his eyebrows, but said nothing.

Raych came back in the late afternoon, happy and excited, with descriptions of monkeys and of Bakarian demoires and he dominated the conversation during dinner.

It was not until after dinner when they were in their own quarters that Dors said, "Now, tell me what happened with Madam Mayor, Raych. Tell me anything she did or said that you think we ought to know."

"One thing," said Raych, his face lighting up. "That's why she didn't show at dinner, I bet."

"What was it?"

"The zoo was closed except for us, you know. There were lots of us—Rashelle and me and all sorts of guys in uniforms and dames in fancy clothes and like that. Then this guy in a uniform—a different guy, who wasn't there to begin with—came in toward the end and he said something in a low voice and Rashelle turned to all the people and made with her hand like they shouldn't move and they didn't. And she went a little ways away with this new guy, so she could talk to him and no one could hear her. Except I kept paying no attention and kept looking at the different cages and sort of moved near to Rashelle so I could hear her.

"She said, 'How dare they?' like she was real mad. And the guy in the uniform, he looked nervous—I just got quick looks because I was trying to make out like I was watching the animals—so mostly I just heard the words. He said somebody—I don't remember the name, but he was a general or somethin'. He said this general said the officers had sworn religious to Rashelle's old man—"

"Sworn allegiance," said Dors.

"Somethin' like that and they was nervous about havin' to do what a dame says. He said they wanted the old man or else, if he was kind of sick, he should pick some guy to be Mayor, not a dame."

"*Not* a dame? Are you sure?"

"That's what he said. He like whispered it. He was so nervous and Rashelle was so mad she could hardly speak. She said, 'I'll have his head. They will all swear allegiance to me tomorrow and whoever refuses will have cause to regret it before an hour has passed.' That's *exactly* what she said. She broke up the whole party and we all came back and she didn't say one word to me all the time. Just sat there, looking kinda mean and angry."

Dors said, "Good. Don't you mention this to anyone, Raych."

"Course not. Is it what you wanted?"

"Very much what I wanted. You did well, Raych. Now, go to your room and forget the whole thing. Don't even think about it."

Once he was gone, Dors turned to Seldon and said, "This is very interesting. Daughters have succeeded fathers—or mothers, for that matter—and held Mayoralties or other high offices on any number of occasions. There have even been reigning Empresses, as you undoubtedly know, and I can't recall that there was ever in Imperial history any serious question of serving under one. It makes one wonder why such a thing should now arise in Wye."

Seldon said, "Why not? We've only recently been in Mycogen, where women are held in a total lack of esteem and couldn't possibly hold positions of power, however minor."

"Yes, of course, but that's an exception. There are other places where women dominate. For the most part, though, government and power have been more or less equisexual. If more men tend to hold high positions, it is usually because women tend to be more bound—biologically—to children."

"But what is the situation in Wye?"

"Equisexual, as far as I know. Rashelle didn't hesitate to assume Mayoral power and I imagine old Mannix didn't hesitate to grant it to her. And she was surprised and furious at encountering male dissent. She can't have expected it."

Seldon said, "You're clearly pleased at this. Why?"

"Simply because it's so unnatural that it must be contrived and I imagine Hummin is doing the contriving."

Seldon said thoughtfully, "You think so?"

"I do," said Dors.

"You know," said Seldon, "so do I."

89.

It was their tenth day in Wye and in the morning Hari Seldon's door signal sounded and Raych's high-pitched voice outside was crying out, "Mister! Mister Seldon! It's war!"

Seldon took a moment to snap from sleep to wakefulness and scrambled out of bed. He was shivering slightly (the Wyans liked their domiciles on the chilly side, he had discovered quite early in his stay there) when he threw the door open.

Raych bounced in, excited and wide-eyed. "Mister Seldon, they have Mannix, the old Mayor! They have—"

"*Who* have, Raych?"

"The Imperials. Their jets came in last night all over. The news holocasts are telling all about it. It's on in Missus's room. She said to let ya sleep, but I figured ya would wanna know."

"And you were quite right." Seldon, pausing only long enough to throw on a bathrobe, burst into Dors's room. She was fully dressed and was watching the holo-set in the alcove.

Behind the clear, small image of a desk sat a man, with the Spaceship-and-Sun sharply defined on the left-front of his tunic. On either side, two soldiers, also wearing the Spaceship-and-Sun, stood armed. The officer at the desk was saying, "—is under the peaceful control of his Imperial Majesty. Mayor Mannix is safe and well and is in full possession of his Mayoral powers under the guidance of friendly Imperial troops. He will be before you soon to urge calm on all Wyans and to ask any Wyan soldiers still in arms to lay them down."

There were other news holocasts by various newsmen with unemotional voices, all wearing Imperial armbands. The news was all the same: surrender by this or that unit of the Wyan security forces after firing a few shots for the record—and sometimes after no resistance at all. This town center and that town center were occupied—and there were repeated views of Wyan crowds somberly watching Imperial forces marching down the streets.

Dors said, "It was perfectly executed, Hari. Surprise was complete. There was no chance of resistance and none of consequence was offered."

Then Mayor Mannix IV appeared, as had been promised. He was standing upright and, perhaps for the sake of appearances, there were no

Imperials in sight, though Seldon was reasonably certain that an adequate number were present just out of camera range.

Mannix was old, but his strength, though worn, was still apparent. His eyes did not meet the holo-camera and his words were spoken as though forced upon him—but, as had been promised, they counseled Wyans to remain calm, to offer no resistance, to keep Wye from harm, and to cooperate with the Emperor who, it was hoped, would survive long on the throne.

"No mention of Rashelle," said Seldon. "It's as though his daughter doesn't exist."

"No one has mentioned her," said Dors, "and this place, which is, after all, her residence—or one of them—hasn't been attacked. Even if she manages to slip away and take refuge in some neighboring sector, I doubt she will be safe anywhere on Trantor for long."

"Perhaps not," came a voice, "but I'll be safe here for a little while."

Rashelle entered. She was properly dressed, properly calm. She was even smiling, but it was no smile of joy; it was, rather, a cold baring of teeth.

The three stared at her in surprise for a moment and Seldon wondered if she had any of her servants with her or if they had promptly deserted her at the first sign of adversity.

Dors said a little coldly, "I see, Madam Mayor, that your hopes for a coup can not be maintained. Apparently, you have been forestalled."

"I have not been forestalled. I have been betrayed. My officers have been tampered with and—against all history and rationality—they have refused to fight for a woman but only for their old master. And, traitors that they are, they then let their old master be seized so that he cannot lead them in resistance."

She looked about for a chair and sat down. "And now the Empire must continue to decay and die when I was prepared to offer it new life."

"I think," said Dors, "the Empire has avoided an indefinite period of useless fighting and destruction. Console yourself with that, Madam Mayor."

It was as though Rashelle did not hear her. "So many years of preparation destroyed in a night." She sat there beaten, defeated, and seemed to have aged twenty years.

Dors said, "It could scarcely have been done in a night. The suborning of your officers—if that took place—must have taken time."

"At that, Demerzel is a master and quite obviously I underestimated him. How he did it, I don't know—threats, bribes, smooth and specious argument. He is a master at the art of stealth and betrayal—I should have known."

She went on after a pause. "If this was outright force on his part, I would have had no trouble destroying anything he sent against us. Who would think that Wye would be betrayed, that an oath of allegiance would be so lightly thrown aside?"

Seldon said with automatic rationality, "But I imagine the oath was made not to you, but to your father."

"Nonsense," said Rashelle vigorously. "When my father gave me the Mayoral office, as he was legally entitled to do, he automatically passed on to me any oaths of allegiance made to him. There is ample precedence for this. It is customary to have the oath repeated to the new ruler, but that is a ceremony only and not a legal requirement. My officers know that, though they choose to forget. They use my womanhood as an excuse because they quake in fear of Imperial vengeance that would never have come had they been staunch or tremble with greed for promised rewards they will surely never get—if I know Demerzel."

She turned sharply toward Seldon. "He wants you, you know. Demerzel struck at us for you."

Seldon started. "Why me?"

"Don't be a fool. For the same reason I wanted you . . . to use you as a tool, of course." She sighed. "At least I am not utterly betrayed. There are still loyal soldiers to be found. —Sergeant!"

Sergeant Emmer Thalus entered with a soft cautious step that seemed incongruous, considering his size. His uniform was spruce, his long blond mustache fiercely curled.

"Madam Mayor," he said, drawing himself to attention with a snap.

He was still, in appearance, the side of beef that Hari had named him —a man still following orders blindly, totally oblivious to the new and changed state of affairs.

Rashelle smiled sadly at Raych. "And how are you, little Raych? I had meant to make something of you. It seems now I won't be able to."

"Hello, Missus . . . Madam," said Raych awkwardly.

"And to have made something of you too, Dr. Seldon," said Rashelle, "and there also I must crave pardon. I cannot."

"For me, Madam, you need have no regrets."

"But I do. I cannot very well let Demerzel have you. That would be one victory too many for him and at least I can stop that."

"I would not work for him, Madam, I assure you, any more than I would have worked for you."

"It is not a matter of work. It is a matter of being used. Farewell, Dr. Seldon. —Sergeant, blast him."

The sergeant drew his blaster at once and Dors, with a loud cry, lunged forward—but Seldon reached out for her and caught her by the elbow. He hung on desperately.

"Stay back, Dors," he shouted, "or he'll kill you. He won't kill me. You too, Raych. Stand back. Don't move."

Seldon faced the sergeant. "You hesitate, Sergeant, because you know you cannot shoot. I might have killed you ten days ago, but I did not. And you gave me your word of honor at that time that you would protect me."

"What are you waiting for?" snapped Rashelle. "I said shoot him down, Sergeant."

Seldon said nothing more. He stood there while the sergeant, eyes bulging, held his blaster steady and pointed at Seldon's head.

"You have your order!" shrieked Rashelle.

"I have your word," said Seldon quietly.

And Sergeant Thalus said in a choked tone, "Dishonored either way." His hand fell and his blaster clanged to the floor.

Rashelle cried out, "Then you too betray me!"

Before Seldon could move or Dors free herself from his grip, Rashelle seized the blaster, turned it on the sergeant, and closed contact.

Seldon had never seen anyone blasted before. Somehow, from the name of the weapon perhaps, he had expected a loud noise, an explosion of flesh and blood. This Wyan blaster, at least, did nothing of the sort. What mangling it did to the organs inside the sergeant's chest Seldon could not tell but, without a change in expression, without a wince of pain, the sergeant crumbled and fell, dead beyond any doubt or any hope.

And Rashelle turned the blaster on Seldon with a firmness that put to rest any hope for his own life beyond the next second.

It was Raych, however, who jumped into action the moment the sergeant fell. Racing between Seldon and Rashelle, he waved his hands wildly.

"Missus, Missus," he called. "Don't shoot."

For a moment, Rashelle looked confused. "Out of the way, Raych. I don't want to hurt you."

That moment of hesitation was all Dors needed. Breaking loose violently, she plunged toward Rashelle with a long low dive. Rashelle went down with a cry and the blaster hit the ground a second time.

Raych retrieved it.

Seldon, with a deep and shuddering breath, said, "Raych, give that to me."

But Raych backed away. "Ya ain't gonna kill her, are ya, Mister Seldon? She was nice to me."

"I won't kill anyone, Raych," said Seldon. "She killed the sergeant and would have killed me, but she didn't shoot rather than hurt you and we'll let her live for that."

It was Seldon, who now sat down, the blaster held loosely in his hand, while Dors removed the neuronic whip from the dead sergeant's other holster.

A new voice rang out. "I'll take care of her now, Seldon."

Seldon looked up and in sudden joy said, "Hummin! Finally!"

"I'm sorry it took so long, Seldon. I had a lot to do. How are you, Dr. Venabili? I take it this is Mannix's daughter, Rashelle. But who is the boy?"

"Raych is a young Dahlite friend of ours," said Seldon.

Soldiers were entering and, at a small gesture from Hummin, they lifted Rashelle respectfully.

Dors, able to suspend her intent surveillance of the other woman, brushed at her clothes with her hands and smoothed her blouse. Seldon suddenly realized that he was still in his bathrobe.

Rashelle, shaking herself loose from the soldiers with contempt, pointed to Hummin and said to Seldon, "Who is this?"

Seldon said, "It is Chetter Hummin, a friend of mine and my protector on this planet."

"Your *protector?*" Rashelle laughed madly. "You fool! You idiot! That man is Demerzel and if you look at your Venabili woman, you will see from her face that she is perfectly aware of that. You have been trapped all along, far worse than ever you were with me!"

90.

Hummin and Seldon sat at lunch that day, quite alone, a pall of quiet between them for the most part.

It was toward the end of the meal that Seldon stirred and said in a lively voice, "Well, sir, how do I address you? I think of you as 'Chetter Hummin' still, but even if I accept you in your other persona, I surely cannot address you as 'Eto Demerzel.' In that capacity, you have a title and I don't know the proper usage. Instruct me."

The other said gravely, "Call me 'Hummin'—if you don't mind. Or 'Chetter.' Yes, I am Eto Demerzel, but with respect to you I am Hummin. As a matter of fact, the two are not distinct. I told you that the Empire is decaying and failing. I believe that to be true in both my capacities. I told you that I wanted psychohistory as a way of preventing that decay and failure or of bringing about a renewal and reinvigoration if the decay and failure must run its course. I believe *that* in both my capacities too."

"But you had me in your grip—I presume you were in the vicinity when I had my meeting with His Imperial Majesty."

"With Cleon. Yes, of course."

"And you might have spoken to me, then, exactly as you later did as Hummin."

"And accomplished what? As Demerzel, I have enormous tasks. I have to handle Cleon, a well-meaning but not very capable ruler, and prevent him, insofar as I can, from making mistakes. I have to do my bit in governing Trantor and the Empire too. And, as you see, I had to spend a great deal of time in preventing Wye from doing harm."

"Yes, I know," murmured Seldon.

"It wasn't easy and I nearly lost out. I have spent years sparring carefully with Mannix, learning to understand his thinking and planning a countermove to his every move. I did not think, at any time, that while he was still alive he would pass on his powers to his daughter. I had not studied her and I was not prepared for her utter lack of caution. Unlike her father, she has been brought up to take power for granted and had no clear idea of its limitations. So she got you and forced me to act before I was quite ready."

"You almost lost me as a result. I faced the muzzle of a blaster twice."

"I know," said Hummin, nodding. "And we might have lost you Up-perside too—another accident I could not foresee."

"But you haven't really answered my question. Why did you send me chasing all over the face of Trantor to escape from Demerzel when you yourself were Demerzel?"

"You told Cleon that psychohistory was a purely theoretical concept, a kind of mathematical game that made no practical sense. That might indeed have been so, but if I approached you officially, I was sure you would merely have maintained your belief. Yet I was attracted to the notion of psychohistory. I wondered whether it might not be, after all, just a game. You must understand that I didn't want merely to use you, I wanted a real and practical psychohistory.

"So I sent you, as you put it, chasing all over the face of Trantor with the dreaded Demerzel close on your heels at all times. That, I felt, would concentrate your mind powerfully. It would make psychohistory some-thing exciting and much more than a mathematical game. You would try to work it out for the sincere idealist Hummin, where you would not for the Imperial flunky Demerzel. Also, you would get a glimpse of various sides of Trantor and that too would be helpful—certainly more helpful than living in an ivory tower on a far-off planet, surrounded entirely by fellow mathematicians. Was I right? Have you made progress?"

Seldon said, "In psychohistory? Yes, I did, Hummin. I thought you knew."

"How should I know?"

"I told Dors."

"But you hadn't told me. Nevertheless, you tell me so now. That is good news."

"Not entirely," said Seldon. "I have made only the barest beginning. But it *is* a beginning."

"Is it the kind of beginning that can be explained to a nonmathematician?"

"I think so. You see, Hummin, from the start I have seen psychohis-tory as a science that depends on the interaction of twenty-five million worlds, each with an average population of four thousand million. It's too much. There's no way of handling something that complex. If I was to succeed at all, if there was to be any way of finding a useful psychohis-tory, I would first have to find a simpler system.

"So I thought I would go back in time and deal with a single world, a world that was the only one occupied by humanity in the dim age before the colonization of the Galaxy. In Mycogen they spoke of an original world of Aurora and in Dahl I heard word of an original world of Earth. I thought they might be the same world under different names, but they were sufficiently different in one key point, at least, to make that impossible. And it didn't matter. So little was known of either one, and that little so obscured by myth and legend, that there was no hope of making use of psychohistory in connection with them.''

He paused to sip at his cold juice, keeping his eyes firmly on Hummin's face.

Hummin said, ''Well? What then?''

''Meanwhile, Dors had told me something I call the hand-on-thigh story. It was of no innate significance, merely a humorous and entirely trivial tale. As a result, though, Dors mentioned the different sex mores on various worlds and in various sectors of Trantor. It occurred to me that she treated the different Trantorian sectors as though they were separate worlds. I thought, idly, that instead of twenty-five million different worlds, I had twenty-five million plus eight hundred to deal with. It seemed a trivial difference, so I forgot it and thought no more about it.

''But as I traveled from the Imperial Sector to Streeling to Mycogen to Dahl to Wye, I observed for myself how different each was. The thought of Trantor—not as a world but as a complex of worlds—grew stronger, but still I didn't see the crucial point.

''It was only when I listened to Rashelle—you see, it was good that I was finally captured by Wye and it was good that Rashelle's rashness drove her into the grandiose schemes that she imparted to me—When I listened to Rashelle, as I said, she told me that all she wanted was Trantor and some immediately adjacent worlds. It was an Empire in itself, she said, and dismissed the outer worlds as 'distant nothings.'

''It was then that, in a moment, I saw what I must have been harboring in my hidden thoughts for a considerable time. On the one hand, Trantor possessed an extraordinarily complex social system, being a populous world made up of eight hundred smaller worlds. It was in itself a system complex enough to make psychohistory meaningful and yet it was simple enough, compared to the Empire as a whole, to make psychohistory perhaps practical.

''And the Outer Worlds, the twenty-five million of them? They were 'distant nothings.' Of course, they affected Trantor and were affected by

Trantor, but these were second-order effects. If I could make psychohistory work as a first approximation for Trantor alone, then the minor effects of the Outer Worlds could be added as later modifications. Do you see what I mean? I was searching for a single world on which to establish a practical science of psychohistory and I was searching for it in the far past, when all the time the single world I wanted was under my feet *now.*"

Hummin said with obvious relief and pleasure, "Wonderful!"

"But it's all left to do, Hummin. I must study Trantor in sufficient detail. I must devise the necessary mathematics to deal with it. If I am lucky and live out a full lifetime, I may have the answers before I die. If not, my successors will have to follow me. Conceivably, the Empire may have fallen and splintered before psychohistory becomes a useful technique."

"I will do everything I can to help you."

"I know it," said Seldon.

"You trust me, then, despite the fact I am Demerzel?"

"Entirely. Absolutely. But I do so because you are *not* Demerzel."

"But I am," insisted Hummin.

"But you are not. Your persona as Demerzel is as far removed from the truth as is your persona as Hummin."

"What do you mean?" Hummin's eyes grew wide and he backed away slightly from Seldon.

"I mean that you probably chose the name 'Hummin' out of a wry sense of what was fitting. 'Hummin' is a mispronunciation of 'human,' isn't it?"

Hummin made no response. He continued to stare at Seldon.

And finally Seldon said, "Because you're not human, are you, 'Hummin/Demerzel'? You're a robot."

DORS

. . . . .

SELDON, HARI— . . . It is customary to think of Hari
Seldon only in connection with psychohistory, to see him
only as mathematics and social change personified. There is
no doubt that he himself encouraged this for at no time in
his formal writings did he give any hint as to how he came
to solve the various problems of psychohistory. His leaps of
thought might have all been plucked from air, for all he
tells us. Nor does he tell us of the blind alleys into which he
crept or the wrong turnings he may have made.
    . . . As for his private life, it is a blank. Concerning his
parents and siblings, we know a handful of factors, no
more. His only son, Raych Seldon, is known to have been
adopted, but how that came about is not known. Concerning his wife, we only know that she existed. Clearly, Seldon
wanted to be a cipher except where psychohistory was concerned. It is as though he felt—or wanted it to be felt—that
he did not live, he merely psychohistorified.

ENCYCLOPEDIA GALACTICA

91.

Hummin sat calmly, not a muscle twitching, still looking at Hari Seldon
and Seldon, for his part, waited. It was Hummin, he thought, who should
speak next.

Hummin did, but said merely, "A robot? Me? —By robot, I presume
you mean an artificial being such as the object you saw in the Sacratorium
in Mycogen."

"Not quite like that," said Seldon.

"Not metal? Not burnished? Not a lifeless simulacrum?" Hummin
said it without any evidence of amusement.

"No. To be of artificial life is not necessarily to be made of metal. I
speak of a robot indistinguishable from a human being in appearance."

"If indistinguishable, Hari, then how do you distinguish?"

"Not by *appearance.*"

"Explain."

"Hummin, in the course of my flight from yourself as Demerzel, I heard of two ancient worlds, as I told you—Aurora and Earth. Each seemed to be spoken of as a first world or an only world. In both cases, robots were spoken of, but with a difference."

Seldon was staring thoughtfully at the man across the table, wondering if, in any way, he would give some sign that he was less than a man—or more. He said, "Where Aurora was in question, one robot was spoken of as a renegade, a traitor, someone who deserted the cause. Where Earth was in question, one robot was spoken of as a hero, one who represented salvation. Was it too much to suppose that it was the same robot?"

"Was it?" murmured Hummin.

"This is what I thought, Hummin. I thought that Earth and Aurora were two separate worlds, co-existing in time. I don't know which one preceded the other. From the arrogance and the conscious sense of superiority of the Mycogenians, I might suppose that Aurora was the original world and that they despised the Earthmen who derived from them—or who degenerated from them.

"On the other hand, Mother Rittah, who spoke to me of Earth, was convinced that Earth was the original home of humanity and, certainly, the tiny and isolated position of the Mycogenians in a whole galaxy of quadrillions of people who lack the strange Mycogenian ethos might mean that Earth was indeed the original home and that Aurora was the aberrant offshoot. I cannot tell, but I pass on to you my thinking, so that you will understand my final conclusions."

Hummin nodded. "I see what you are doing. Please continue."

"The worlds were enemies. Mother Rittah certainly made it sound so. When I compare the Mycogenians, who seem to embody Aurora, and the Dahlites, who seem to embody Earth, I imagine that Aurora, whether first or second, was nevertheless the one that was more advanced, the one that could produce more elaborate robots, even ones indistinguishable from human beings in appearance. Such a robot was designed and devised in Aurora, then. But he was a renegade, so he deserted Aurora. To the Earthpeople he was a hero, so he must have joined Earth. Why he did this, what his motives were, I can't say."

Hummin said, "Surely, you mean why *it* did this, what *its* motives were."

"Perhaps, but with you sitting across from me," said Seldon, "I find it difficult to use the inanimate pronoun. Mother Rittah was convinced that the heroic robot—*her* heroic robot—still existed, that he would return when he was needed. It seemed to me that there was nothing impossible in the thought of an immortal robot or at least one who was immortal as long as the replacement of worn-out parts was not neglected."

"Even the brain?" asked Hummin.

"Even the brain. I don't really know anything about robots, but I imagine a new brain could be re-recorded from the old. —And Mother Rittah hinted of strange mental powers. —I thought: It must be so. I may, in some ways, be a romantic, but I am not so much a romantic as to think that one robot, by switching from one side to the other, can alter the course of history. A robot could not make Earth's victory sure, nor Aurora's defeat certain—unless there was something strange, something peculiar about the robot."

Hummin said, "Does it occur to you, Hari, that you are dealing with legends, legends that may have been distorted over the centuries and the millennia, even to the extent of building a veil of the supernatural over quite ordinary events? Can you make yourself believe in a robot that not only seems human, but that also lives forever and has mental powers? Are you not beginning to believe in the superhuman?"

"I know very well what legends are and I am not one to be taken in by them and made to believe in fairy tales. Still, when they are supported by certain odd events that I have seen—and even experienced—myself—"

"Such as?"

"Hummin, I met you and trusted you from the start. Yes, you helped me against those two hoodlums when you didn't need to and that predisposed me in your favor, since I didn't realize at the time that they were your hirelings, doing what you had instructed them to do. —But never mind that."

"No," said Hummin, a hint of amusement—finally—in his voice.

"I trusted you. I was easily convinced not to go home to Helicon and to make myself a wanderer over the face of Trantor. I believed everything you told me without question. I placed myself entirely in your hands. Looking back on it now, I see myself as *not* myself. I am not a person to be so easily led, yet I was. More than that, I did not even think it strange that I was behaving so far out of character."

"You know yourself best, Hari."

"It wasn't only me. How is it that Dors Venabili, a beautiful woman with a career of her own, should abandon that career in order to join me in my flight? How it it that she should risk her life to save mine, seeming to take on, as a kind of holy duty, the task of protecting me and becoming single-minded in the process? Was it simply because you asked her to?"

"I did ask her to, Hari."

"Yet she does not strike me as the kind of person to make such a radical changeover in her life merely because someone asks her to. Nor could I believe it was because she had fallen madly in love with me at first sight and could not help herself. I somehow wish she had, but she seems quite the mistress of her emotional self, more—I am now speaking to you frankly—than I myself am with respect to her."

"She is a wonderful woman," said Hummin. "I don't blame you."

Seldon went on. "How is it, moreover, that Sunmaster Fourteen, a monster of arrogance and one who leads a people who are themselves stiff-necked in their own conceit, should be willing to take in tribespeople like Dors and myself and to treat us as well as the Mycogenians could and did? When we broke every rule, committed every sacrilege, how is it that you could still talk him into letting us go?

"How could you talk the Tisalvers, with their petty prejudices, into taking us in? How can you be at home everywhere in the world, be friends with everyone, influence each person, regardless of their individual peculiarities? For that matter, how do you manage to manipulate Cleon too? And if he is viewed as malleable and easily molded, then how were you able to handle his father, who by all accounts was a rough and arbitrary tyrant? How could you do all this?

"Most of all, how is that Mannix IV of Wye could spend decades building an army without peer, one trained to be proficient in every detail, and yet have it fall apart when his daughter tries to make use of it? How could you persuade them to play the Renegade, all of them, as you have done?"

Hummin said, "Might this mean no more than that I am a tactful person used to dealing with people of different types, that I am in a position to have done favors for crucial people and am in a position to do additional favors in the future? Nothing I have done, it might seem, requires the supernatural."

"Nothing you have done? Not even the neutralization of the Wyan army?"

"They did not wish to serve a woman."

"They must have known for years that any time Mannix laid down his powers or any time he died, Rashelle would be their Mayor, yet they showed no signs of discontent—until you felt it necessary that they show it. Dors described you at one time as a very persuasive man. And so you are. More persuasive than any *man* could be. But you are not more persuasive than an immortal robot with strange mental powers might be. —Well, Hummin?"

Hummin said, "What is it you expect of me, Hari? Do you expect me to admit I'm a robot? That I only look like a human being? That I am immortal? That I am a mental marvel?!"

Seldon leaned toward Hummin as he sat there on the opposite side of the table. "Yes, Hummin, I do. I expect you to tell me the truth and I strongly suspect that what you have just outlined *is* the truth. You, Hummin, are the robot that Mother Rittah referred to as Da-Nee, friend of Ba-Lee. You must admit it. You have no choice."

92.

It was as though they were sitting in a tiny Universe of their own. There, in the middle of Wye, with the Wyan army being disarmed by Imperial force, they sat quietly. There, in the midst of events that all of Trantor—and perhaps all the Galaxy—was watching, there was this small bubble of utter isolation within which Seldon and Hummin were playing their game of attack and defense—Seldon trying hard to force a new reality, Hummin making no move to accept that new reality.

Seldon had no fear of interruption. He was certain that the bubble within which they sat had a boundary that could not be penetrated, that Hummin's—no, the *robot's*—powers would keep all at a distance till the game was over.

Hummin finally said, "You are an ingenious fellow, Hari, but I fail to see why I must admit that I am a robot and why I have no choice but to do so. Everything you say may be true as facts—your own behavior, Dors's behavior, Sunmaster's, Tisalver's, the Wyan generals'—all, all may have happened as you said, but that doesn't force your *interpretation* of the meaning of the events to be true. Surely, everything that happened can have a natural explanation. You trusted me because you accepted what I said; Dors felt your safety to be important because she felt psychohistory to be crucial, herself being a historian; Sunmaster and Tisalver were beholden to me for favors you know nothing of, the Wyan generals resented being ruled by a woman, no more. Why must we flee to the supernatural?"

Seldon said, "See here, Hummin, do you really believe the Empire to be falling and do you really consider it important that it not be allowed to do so with no move made to save it or, at the least, cushion its Fall?"

"I really do." Somehow Seldon knew this statement was sincere.

"And you really want me to work out the details of psychohistory and you feel that you yourself cannot do it?"

"I lack the capability."

"And you feel that only I can handle psychohistory—even if I sometimes doubt it myself?"

"Yes."

"And you must therefore feel that if you can possibly help me in any way, you must."

"I do."

"Personal feelings—selfish considerations—could play no part?"

A faint and brief smile passed over Hummin's grave face and for a moment Seldon sensed a vast and arid desert of weariness behind Hummin's quiet manner. "I have built a long career on paying no heed to personal feelings or to selfish considerations."

"Then I ask your help. I can work out psychohistory on the basis of Trantor alone, but I will run into difficulties. Those difficulties I may overcome, but how much easier it would be to do so if I knew certain key facts. For instance, was Earth or Aurora the first world of humanity or was it some other world altogether? What was the relationship between Earth and Aurora? Did either or both colonize the Galaxy? If one, why didn't the other? If both, how was the issue decided? Are there worlds descended from both or from only one? How did robots come to be abandoned? How did Trantor become the Imperial world, rather than another planet? What happened to Aurora and Earth in the meantime? There are a thousand questions I might ask right now and a hundred thousand that might arise as I go along. Would you allow me to remain ignorant, Hummin, and fail in my task when you could inform me and help me succeed?"

Hummin said, "If I were the robot, would I have room in my brain for all of twenty thousand years of history for millions of different worlds?"

"I don't know the capacity of robotic brains. I don't know the capacity of yours. But if you lack the capacity, then you must have that information which you cannot hold safely recorded in a place and in a way that would make it possible for you to call upon it. And if you have it and I need information, how can you deny and withhold it from me? And if you cannot withhold it from me, how can you deny that you are a robot —*that* robot—the Renegade?"

Seldon sat back and took a deep breath. "So I ask you again: Are you that robot? If you want psychohistory, then you must admit it. If you still deny you are a robot and if you convince me you are not, then my chances at psychohistory become much, much smaller. It is up to you, then. Are you a robot? Are you Da-Nee?"

And Hummin said, as imperturbable as ever. "Your arguments are irrefutable. I am R. Daneel Olivaw. The 'R' stands for 'robot.' "

93.

R. Daneel Olivaw still spoke quietly, but it seemed to Seldon that there was a subtle change in his voice, as though he spoke more easily now that he was no longer playing a part.

"In twenty thousand years," said Daneel, "no one has guessed I was a robot when it was not my intention to have him or her know. In part, that was because human beings abandoned robots so long ago that very few remember that they even existed at one time. And in part, it is because I do have the ability to detect and affect human emotion. The detection offers no trouble, but to affect emotion is difficult for me for reasons having to do with my robotic nature—although I can do it when I wish. I have the ability but must deal with my will not to use it. I try never to interfere except when I have no choice but to do so. And when I do interfere, it is rarely that I do more than strengthen, as little as I can, what is there. If I can achieve my purposes without doing even so much, I avoid it.

"It was not necessary to tamper with Sunmaster Fourteen in order to have him accept you—I call it 'tampering,' you notice, because it is not a pleasant thing to do. I did not have to tamper with him because he did owe me for favors rendered and he is an honorable man, despite the peculiarities you found in him. I did interfere the second time, when you had committed sacrilege in his eyes, but it took very little. He was not anxious to hand you over to the Imperial authorities, whom he does not like. I merely strengthened the dislike a trifle and he handed you over to my care, accepting the arguments I offered, which otherwise he might have considered specious.

"Nor did I tamper with you noticeably. You distrusted the Imperials too. Most human beings do these days, which is an important factor in the decay and deterioration of the Empire. What's more, you were proud of psychohistory as a concept, proud of having thought of it. You would not have minded having it prove to be a practical discipline. That would have further fed your pride."

Seldon frowned and said, "Pardon me, Master Robot, but I am not aware that I am quite such a monster of pride."

Daneel said mildly, "You are not a monster of pride at all. You are perfectly aware that is neither admirable nor useful to be driven by pride, so you try to subdue that drive, but you might as well disapprove of having yourself powered by your heartbeat. You cannot help either fact. Though you hide your pride from yourself for the sake of your own peace of mind, you cannot hide it from me. It is there, however carefully you mask it over. And I had but to strengthen it a touch and you were at once willing to take measures to hide from Demerzel, measures that a moment before you would have resisted. And you were eager to work at psychohistory with an intensity that a moment before you would have scorned.

"I saw no necessity to touch anything else and so you have reasoned out your robothood. Had I foreseen the possibility of that, I might have stopped it, but my foresight and my abilities are not infinite. Nor am I sorry now that I failed, for your arguments are good ones and it is important that you know who I am and that I use what I am to help you.

"Emotions, my dear Seldon, are a powerful engine of human action, far more powerful than human beings themselves realize, and you cannot know how much can be done with the merest touch and how reluctant I am to do it."

Seldon was breathing heavily, trying to see himself as a man driven by pride and not liking it. "Why reluctant?"

"Because it would be so easy to overdo. I had to stop Rashelle from converting the Empire into a feudal anarchy. I might have bent minds quickly and the result might well have been a bloody uprising. Men are men—and the Wyan generals are almost all men. It does not actually take much to rouse resentment and latent fear of women in any man. It may be a biological matter that I, as a robot, cannot fully understand.

"I had but to strengthen the feeling to produce a breakdown in her plans. If I had done it the merest millimeter too much, I would have lost what I wanted—a bloodless takeover. I wanted nothing more than to have them not resist when my soldiers arrived."

Daneel paused, as though trying to pick his words, then said, "I do not wish to go into the mathematics of my positronic brain. It is more than I can understand, though perhaps not more than you can if you give it enough thought. However, I am governed by the Three Laws of Robotics that are traditionally put into words—or once were, long ago. They are these:

" 'One. A robot may not injure a human being or, through inaction, allow a human being to come to harm.

" 'Two. A robot must obey the orders given it by human beings, except where such orders would conflict with the First Law.

" 'Three. A robot must protect its own existence, as long as such protection does not conflict with the First or Second Law.'

"But I had a . . . a friend twenty thousand years ago. Another robot. Not like myself. He could not be mistaken for a human being, but it was he who had the mental powers and it was through him that I gained mine.

"It seemed to him that there should be a still more general rule than any of the Three Laws. He called it the Zeroth Law, since zero comes before one. It is:

" 'Zero. A robot may not injure humanity or, through inaction, allow humanity to come to harm.'

"Then the First Law must read:

" 'One. A robot may not injure a human being or, through inaction, allow a human being to come to harm, except where that would conflict with the Zeroth Law.'

"And the other laws must be similarly modified. Do you understand?"

Daneel paused earnestly and Seldon said, "I understand."

Daneel went on. "The trouble is, Hari, that a human being is easy to identify. I can point to one. It is easy to see what will harm a human being and what won't—relatively easy, at least. But what is *humanity?* To what can we point when we speak of humanity? And how can we define harm to humanity? When will a course of action do more good than harm to humanity as a whole and how can one tell? The robot who first advanced the Zeroth Law died—became permanently inactive—because he was forced into an action that he felt would save humanity, yet which he could not be *sure* would save humanity. And as he became inactivated, he left the care of the Galaxy to me.

"Since then, I have tried. I have interfered as little as possible, relying on human beings themselves to judge what was for the good. They could gamble; I could not. They could miss their goals; I did not dare. They could do harm unwittingly; I would grow inactive if I did. The Zeroth Law makes no allowance for unwitting harm.

"But at times I am forced to take action. That I am still functioning shows that my actions have been moderate and discreet. However, as the Empire began to fail and to decline, I have had to interfere more frequently and for decades now I have had to play the role of Demerzel, trying to run the government in such a way as to stave off ruin—and yet I still function, you see.

"When you made your speech to the Decennial Convention, I realized at once that in psychohistory there was a tool that might make it possible to identify what was good and bad for humanity. With it, the decisions we would make would be less blind. I would even trust to human beings to make those decisions and again reserve myself only for the greatest emergencies. So I arranged quickly to have Cleon learn of your speech and call you in. Then, when I heard your denial of the worth of psychohistory, I was forced to think of some way to make you try anyway. Do you understand, Hari?"

More than a little daunted, Seldon said, "I understand, Hummin."

"To you, I must remain Hummin on those rare occasions when I will be able to see you. I will give you what information I have if it is something you need and in my persona as Demerzel I will protect you as much as I can. As Daneel, you must never speak of me."

"I wouldn't want to," said Seldon hurriedly. "Since I need your help, it would ruin matters to have your plans impeded."

"Yes, I know you wouldn't want to." Daneel smiled wearily. "After all, you are vain enough to want full credit for psychohistory. You would not want anyone to know—ever—that you needed the help of a robot."

Seldon flushed. "I am not—"

"But you are, even if you carefully hide it from yourself. And it is important, for I am strengthening that emotion within you minimally so that you will never be able to speak of me to others. It will not even occur to you that you might do so."

Seldon said, "I suspect Dors knows—"

"She knows of me. And she too cannot speak of me to others. Now that you both know of my nature, you can speak of me to each other freely, but not to anyone else."

Daneel rose. "Hari, I have my work to do now. Before long, you and Dors will be taken back to the Imperial Sector—"

"The boy Raych must come with me. I cannot abandon him. And there is a young Dahlite named Yugo Amaryl—"

"I understand. Raych will be taken too and you can do with any friend as you will. You will all be taken care of appropriately. And you will work on psychohistory. You will have a staff. You will have the necessary computers and reference material. I will interfere as little as possible and if there is resistance to your views that does not actually reach the point of endangering the mission, then you will have to deal with it yourself."

"Wait, Hummin," said Seldon urgently. "What if, despite all your help and all my endeavors, it turns out that psychohistory cannot be made into a practical device after all? What if I fail?"

Daneel rose. "In that case, I have a second plan in hand. One I have been working on a long time on a separate world in a separate way. It too is very difficult and in some ways even more radical than psychohistory. It may fail too, but there is a greater chance of success if two roads are open than if either one alone was.

"Take my advice, Hari! If the time comes when you are able to set up some device that may act to prevent the worst from happening, see if you can think of two devices, so that if one fails, the other will carry on. The Empire must be steadied or rebuilt on a new foundation. Let there be two such, rather than one, if that is possible."

He rose, "Now I must return to my ordinary work and you must turn to yours. You will be taken care of."

With one final nod, he rose and left.

Seldon looked after him and said softly, "First I must speak to Dors."

94.

Dors said, "The palace is cleared. Rashelle will not be physically harmed. And you'll return to the Imperial Sector, Hari."

"And you, Dors?" said Seldon in a low tight voice.

"I presume I will go back to the University," she said. "My work is being neglected, my classes abandoned."

"No, Dors, you have a greater task."

"What is that?"

"Psychohistory. I cannot tackle the project without you."

"Of course you can. I am a total illiterate in mathematics."

"And I in history—and we need both."

Dors laughed. "I suspect that, as a mathematician, you are one of a kind. I, as a historian, am merely adequate, certainly not outstanding. You will find any number of historians who will suit the needs of psychohistory better than I do."

"In that case, Dors, let me explain that psychohistory needs more than a mathematician and a historian. It also needs the will to tackle what will probably be a lifetime problem. Without you, Dors, I will not have that will."

"Of course you'll have it."

"Dors, if you're not with me, I don't intend to have it."

Dors looked at Seldon thoughtfully. "This is a fruitless discussion, Hari. Undoubtedly, Hummin will make the decision. If he sends me back to the University—"

"He won't."

"How can you be sure?"

"Because I'll put it to him plainly. If he sends you back to the University, I'll go back to Helicon and the Empire can go ahead and destroy itself."

"You can't mean it."

"But I certainly do."

"Don't you realize that Hummin can arrange to have your feelings change so that you *will* work on psychohistory—even without me?"

Seldon shook his head. "Hummin will not make such an arbitrary decision. I've spoken to him. He dares not do much to the human mind because he is bound by what he calls the Laws of Robotics. To change my mind to the point where I will not want you with me, Dors, would mean a change of the kind he can not risk. On the other hand, if he leaves me alone and if you join me in the project, he will have what he wants—a true chance at psychohistory. Why should he not settle for that?"

Dors shook her head. "He may not agree for reasons of his own."

"Why should he disagree? You were asked to protect me, Dors. Has Hummin canceled that request?"

"No."

"Then he wants you to continue your protection. And *I* want your protection."

"Against what? You now have Hummin's protection, both as Demerzel and as Daneel, and surely that is all you need."

"If I had the protection of every person and every force in the Galaxy, it would still be yours I would want."

"Then you don't want me for psychohistory. You want me for protection."

Seldon scowled. "No! Why are you twisting my words? Why are you forcing me to say what you must *know?* It is neither psychohistory nor protection I want you for. Those are excuses and I'll use any other I need. I want *you*—just you. And if you want the real reason, it is because you are *you*."

"You don't even know me."

"That doesn't matter. I don't care. —And yet I *do* know you in a way. Better than you think."

"Do you indeed?"

"Of course. You follow orders and you risk your life for me without hesitation and with no apparent care for the consequences. You learned how to play tennis so quickly. You learned how to use knives even more quickly and you handled yourself perfectly in the fight with Marron. *Inhumanly*—if I may say so. Your muscles are amazingly strong and your reaction time is amazingly fast. You can somehow tell when a room is being eavesdropped and you can be in touch with Hummin in some way that does not involve instrumentation."

Dors said, "And what do you think of all that?"

"It has occurred to me that Hummin, in his persona as R. Daneel Olivaw, has an impossible task. How can one robot try to guide the Empire? He must have helpers."

"That is obvious. Millions, I should imagine. I am a helper. You are a helper. Little Raych is a helper."

"You are a *different* kind of helper."

"In what way? Hari, *say* it. If you hear yourself say it, you will realize how crazy it is."

Seldon looked long at her and then said in a low voice, "I will *not* say it because . . . I don't *care.*"

"You really don't? You wish to take me as I am?"

"I will take you as I must. You are Dors and, whatever else you are, in all the world I want nothing else."

Dors said softly, "Hari, I want what is good for you because of what I am, but I feel that if I wasn't what I am, I would still want what is good for you. And I don't think I am good for you."

"Good for me or bad, I don't care." Here Hari looked down as he paced a few steps, weighing what he would say next. "Dors, have you ever been kissed?"

"Of course, Hari. It's a social part of life and I live socially."

"No no! I mean, have you ever *really* kissed a man? You know, passionately?"

"Well yes, Hari, I have."

"Did you enjoy it?"

Dors hesitated. She said, "When I've kissed in that way, I enjoyed it more than I would have enjoyed disappointing a young man I liked, someone whose friendship meant something to me." At this point, Dors blushed and she turned her face away. "Please, Hari, this is difficult for me to explain."

But Hari, more determined now than ever, pressed further. "So you kissed for the wrong reasons, then, to avoid hurt feelings."

"Perhaps everyone does, in a sense."

Seldon mulled this over, then said suddenly, "Did *you* ever ask to be kissed?"

Dors paused, as though looking back on her life. "No."

"Or wish to be kissed again, once you had?"

"No."

"Have you ever slept with a man?" he asked softly, desperately.

"Of course. I told you. These things are a part of life."

Hari gripped her shoulders as if he was going to shake her. "But have you ever felt the desire, a need for that kind of closeness with just one special person? Dors, have you ever felt *love?*"

Dors looked up slowly, almost sadly, and locked eyes with Seldon. "I'm sorry, Hari, but no."

Seldon released her, letting his arms fall dejectedly to his sides.

Then Dors placed her hand gently on his arm and said, "So you see, Hari. I'm not really what you want."

Seldon's head drooped and he stared at the floor. He weighed the matter and tried to think rationally. Then he gave up. He wanted what he wanted and he wanted it beyond thought and beyond rationality.

He looked up. "Dors, dear, even so, *I don't care.*"

Seldon put his arms around her and brought his head close to hers slowly, as though waiting for her to pull away, all the while drawing her nearer.

Dors made no move and he kissed her—slowly, lingeringly, and then passionately—and her arms suddenly tightened around him.

When he stopped at last, she looked at him with eyes that mirrored her smile and she said:

"Kiss me again, Hari. —Please."